Praise for the *InCryptid* novels:

"The only thing more fun than an October Daye book is an InCryptid book. Swift narrative, charm, great world-building . . . all the McGuire trademarks."
—Charlaine Harris, #1 *New York Times*-bestselling author

"[*Half-Off Ragnarok* is] slightly over-the-top fun; a genuinely entertaining good time, [and] an urban fantasy that, despite the title, isn't about the imminent end of the world."
—Tor.com

"Seanan McGuire's *Discount Armageddon* is an urban fantasy triple threat—smart and sexy and funny. The Aeslin mice alone are worth the price of the book, so consider a cast of truly original characters, a plot where weird never overwhelms logic, and some serious kickass world-building as a bonus."
—Tanya Huff, bestselling author of *The Future Falls*

"McGuire's InCryptid series is an ever-evolving, fast-paced, and wonderfully witty series, but this fifth installment may very well be the most entertaining yet. McGuire has an uncanny talent for voices, and the narrative in this story is snarky, sweet and instantly engrossing. . . . New readers will have very little trouble jumping into this adventure, but there are added benefits for readers who have followed the adventures of the Price family throughout the series."
—*RT Book Reviews*

"Exciting . . . McGuire creates a sense of wonder and playfulness with her love for mythology and folklore, weaving together numerous manifestations of a single theme. Her enthusiastic and fast-paced style makes this an entertaining page-turner."
—*Publishers Weekly*

"McGuire has created a rich, tongue-in-cheek, and wholly unique urban fantasy world."
—[...]s' Picks

"*Discou[...]* [...]ed look at what [...]sely our urban f[...]ne. The pacing [...]u're left wanting [...]"
—C. E. Murphy, author of *Raven Calls*

**DAW Books presents the finest in urban fantasy
from Seanan McGuire:**

InCryptid Novels

DISCOUNT ARMAGEDDON

MIDNIGHT BLUE-LIGHT SPECIAL

HALF-OFF RAGNAROK

POCKET APOCALYPSE

CHAOS CHOREOGRAPHY

MAGIC FOR NOTHING

TRICKS FOR FREE *

SPARROW HILL ROAD

October Daye Novels

ROSEMARY AND RUE

A LOCAL HABITATION

AN ARTIFICIAL NIGHT

LATE ECLIPSES

ONE SALT SEA

ASHES OF HONOR

CHIMES AT MIDNIGHT

THE WINTER LONG

A RED ROSE CHAIN

ONCE BROKEN FAITH

THE BRIGHTEST FELL *

Coming soon from DAW Books

MAGIC FOR NOTHING

An *InCryptid* Novel

SEANAN McGUIRE

DAW BOOKS, INC.

DONALD A. WOLLHEIM, FOUNDER

375 Hudson Street, New York, NY 10014

ELIZABETH R. WOLLHEIM
SHEILA E. GILBERT
PUBLISHERS

www.dawbooks.com

Published by DAW Books, Inc.
375 Hudson Street, New York, NY 10014.

First Printing, March 2017

1 2 3 4 5 6 7 8 9

For Shawn, because he wouldn't let me get him an axolotl.

Love and amphibians, you nerd.

Price Family Tree

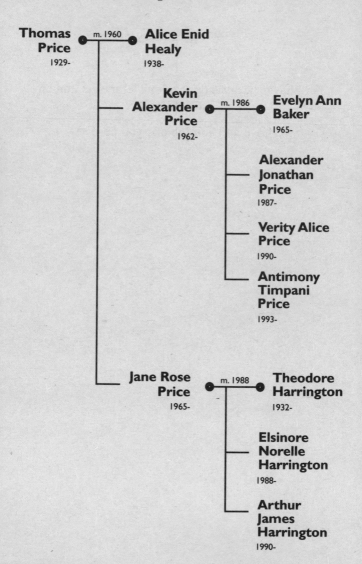

Thomas Price 1929-
m. 1960
Alice Enid Healy 1938-

Kevin Alexander Price 1962-
m. 1986
Evelyn Ann Baker 1965-

Alexander Jonathan Price 1987-

Verity Alice Price 1990-

Antimony Timpani Price 1993-

Jane Rose Price 1965-
m. 1988
Theodore Harrington 1932-

Elsinore Norelle Harrington 1988-

Arthur James Harrington 1990-

Baker Family Tree

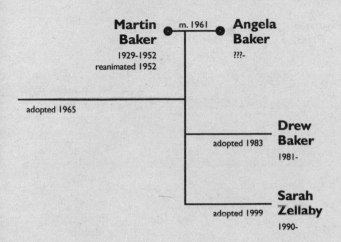

Martin Baker
1929-1952
reanimated 1952

m. 1961

Angela Baker
???-

adopted 1965

Drew Baker
adopted 1983
1981-

Sarah Zellaby
adopted 1999
1990-

Impossible, adjective:

1. Not possible; unable to happen.

Improbable, adjective:

1. Not very likely to happen; not probable.

2. Probably not a very good idea anyway.

3. See also "bad plan."

Prologue

"Every time I think my family has plumbed
the depths of stupidity, somebody goes and
finds a goddamn shovel."
—Jane Harrington-Price

*The upstairs bedroom of a small survivalist
compound about an hour's drive east of Portland,
Oregon*

Three months ago

ANTIMONY SAT CROSS-LEGGED in the middle of the
room, one hand pressed hard against her thigh and
the other held open in front of her, palm up and fingers
spread. She stared at the air above her hand like it had
personally done her wrong and needed to be punished
for its sins.

"Just breathe," said the room's other occupant. Mary
Dunlavy—family babysitter and family ghost, even
though she hadn't been a part of the family until long
after she died—sat with her knees drawn to her chest,
watching Antimony concentrate. "We both know you
can do this. You've done it over and over again without
meaning to. You just need to find the focus that turns it
voluntary."

"Because look how well 'involuntary' worked for
Carrie," said Antimony, still glaring at the air.

Mary raised her eyebrows, looking bemused.

Antimony swallowed a sigh. Getting exasperated with
the one person even semi-equipped to help her was a

bad plan. Sure, it was a plan she was familiar with and really good at executing, but ... still a bad plan. "Fictional character," she said. "Stephen King book. She moved things with her mind. Burned down half the town where she lived before dying horribly."

"Huh," said Mary. "I'll have to check it out."

She wouldn't. Mary knew it, and Antimony knew it, and so neither of them needed to say anything about it. Mary existed in a ghost story—they couldn't call it living, not when she'd been dead so much longer than she'd ever been alive—and she didn't need horror novels if she wanted to be spooked by the things that went "bump" in the night. They were all around her, even when she was alone, because she was one of them.

Mary was also the only person who was both reliably available and had actually known Grandpa Thomas before he disappeared. (Grandma Alice, who probably knew him better than anyone else in the world, wasn't around enough, and Antimony wasn't sure asking a woman who thought bear traps were appropriate gifts for children to help her get her powers under control would be a *good* plan.) Mary had seen Grandpa Thomas do magic. Real, practical magic, the sort that ran in families and meant that sometimes having a nightmare meant waking up because the sheets were on fire.

Antimony was tired of taking the batteries out of her smoke detector and telling her parents she'd burned her hand on the hotplate during roller derby practice. She wanted this under control, and she wanted it under her own terms. She knew she wasn't supposed to ask Mary for favors, but she was allowed to ask about family history, and Grandpa was family history. Grandpa was a loophole. Hence the closed door and a moment of privacy stolen while the rest of her family was downstairs watching her older sister Verity dance on live television. Because *that* was a good idea.

"Focus," said Mary. "If you can do it while you're asleep, you can do it while you're awake."

"I can *fly* when I'm asleep," muttered Antimony. She narrowed her eyes, still staring at the air above her hand.

It was all molecules. Little air molecules, moving faster and faster, until—

There was a spark, like someone had tried to strike a lighter and failed. It flared and was gone in an instant, leaving the smell of heat hanging in the air. Antimony yelped and dropped her hand. Mary smiled.

"I remember when your grandfather showed me that trick," she said. "He was so proud of himself. 'Look at this thing I can do,' he said, to the girl who can walk through walls and won't ever age. But it was just the tip of the iceberg. Magic is so much more."

"Holy crap," said Antimony.

Someone flung the bedroom door open so hard that it slammed against the opposite wall. Antimony and Mary whipped around. Kevin Price—normally the calmest and most level-headed member of the family—was standing in the doorway, wild-eyed behind his wire-framed glasses and panting slightly, with either exertion or distress.

"Annie, we need you," he said.

Antimony pushed herself off the floor as she said, "You're supposed to knock before you barge into my room." The words sounded like whining even to her own ears.

Kevin shook his head. "It's an emergency," he said, before turning and running back down the hall. The sound of feet pounding on the stairs followed. Mary and Antimony exchanged a look. Mary disappeared, presumably reappearing in the living room. Antimony bolted for the door.

The word "emergency" wasn't used casually in the Price home. It could mean a lot of things. It could mean a death, or a kidnapping, or a Covenant purge starting in one of the cities under their protection. It could mean a cryptid sighting they couldn't explain away, something that would bring the Covenant down on their heads once and for all. It could mean genuine, inescapable disaster.

By the time she reached the bottom of the stairs, Antimony was moving so fast that she had to grab the banister to stop herself from slamming into the wall. She used her remaining momentum to whip around and into the living room, where the rest of her family—Mom, Dad, her older brother Alex and his fiancée, Shelby, both visiting from Ohio—were fixated on the television. Mary was in front of the screen, but that wasn't a problem, since she was half-transparent with shock: Antimony could see through her to the image of her big sister, Verity, missing her wig and covered in blood, launching herself at the giant snake that had broken through the dance floor.

"Is this going out live?" she asked. Her voice was very loud.

"Yes," said her father, and his voice was very soft.

They watched in mute horror as the battle played out, ending with an explosion and the great snake crumpling to the stage. Verity stood, battered but unbroken, and turned to the camera. She looked exhausted. She looked infuriated. It was a common combination for her. "My name is Verity Price," she said. "This is my continent. Stay out." Then she shot the camera. The picture died, replaced by a "technical difficulties" sign.

The living room was silent for a long moment before Alex breathed, "Holy *shit*."

That about summed it up, really. Antimony looked to her father. "What's going to happen now?" she asked. She hated how *young* she sounded, like a little girl asking her parents to make everything better—but in that moment that was how she felt.

"I don't know," said Kevin. "I really don't."

"Everything is about to change," said Evelyn, and she put her face in her hands and cried.

One

"It's better to act than it is to react. Acting gets you in trouble. Reacting all too frequently gets you dead."

—Alice Healy

A deserted house on the outskirts of Salem, Oregon

Now

DON'T GET ME WRONG. Poltergeists have a place in a healthy spectral ecosystem. They wouldn't exist if they didn't. Everything evolves for a reason, even the different sorts of ghost people become after they die. Nothing in this or any other dimension is inherently evil.

And none of that was really a comfort with the ghost of an eleven-year-old boy doing his level best to drop an entire house on my head.

"Tyler! I'm here to *help* you!" I shouted, ducking around the nearest corner. A waterlogged dresser flew past overhead, shattering when it hit an exposed support beam. Either it had been full of beetles—eww—or Tyler was somehow creating them. When the dresser gave way, the bugs came flowing out, so plentiful that it seemed impossible they could have fit inside there. I squeaked and plastered myself against the wall, trying not to hyperventilate. I don't have a specific problem with bugs, but there's a big difference between seeing a single beetle and having a wave of them flowing toward your feet.

Mary sighed, stepping in front of me and drawing an arc across the floor with her toe. The beetles parted as they ran up against it, running in either direction, never crossing the line. After they had gone about three feet, they popped, becoming clouds of green mist that rose into the air and dissipated.

"Okay, this is officially the grossest ghostbusting job I have ever been on," I said, as calmly as I could. It wasn't all that calm. "Where the hell is Artie?"

"I can check, but it means leaving you alone with Tyler," cautioned Mary. A splintering sound from the other side of the wall confirmed that Tyler's tantrum was still in full force. "Are you sure you're down for that?"

"If it means finding out where my so-called backup is, *yes*," I said.

Mary vanished. A microwave flew through the doorway and slammed into the wall next to the dresser. Unlike the dresser, it didn't burst into spectral cockroaches or break into a pile of splinters. Also, it could have crushed my skull, which I am fond of leaving uncrushed. I swallowed a yelp and moved farther down the hall, trying to keep my exits in view. With the way this had been going so far, I was going to need to run again before much longer.

The trouble with going up against ghosts is that most of them aren't bad, just confused. They don't get why I'm alive and they're not. Sometimes that's a fair question, like with Tyler, who died when he was eleven. He'd been riding his bike, following all the rules of the road—even wearing a helmet—when a drunk driver blasted around a corner and slammed into him, not giving him a chance to swerve. If there was any mercy in the situation, it was that Tyler had died instantly.

But maybe that wasn't actually merciful. Because he'd died instantly, he hadn't had any time to process what was happening. One moment he was there. The next moment he was gone. The moment after *that*, he was back, spectral, confused, and coming home to haunt his family. They'd only lasted six months before they moved away; who could live in a house that shook and groaned and sometimes cried in the voice of your dead son in the middle of the night?

That all happened four years ago. Tyler had been alone ever since, growing stronger, angrier, and more confused. It was a terrible situation for a kid to be in, alive or dead.

I would have had a lot more sympathy if he hadn't insisted on throwing things at my head, but hey. Nobody's perfect.

"Tyler, dammit, could you calm *down*?" I stayed pressed against the wall, hoping that by shouting at the kid without giving him an immediate target, I could get him to chill out—or at least to stop throwing things. "We're not here to hurt you!"

The air in front of me shimmered, and a spectral preteen boy appeared. He looked more like a ghost than either of our family phantoms: Rose and Mary both tended to manifest as fairly normal-looking teenage girls. Sure, Mary had white hair and terrifying babysitter eyes that could make me confess to damn near anything, but fashion hair dyes and cosplay contacts exist. You know what *doesn't* exist? Makeup that can make a living person transparent and faintly blue, that's what. Tyler looked like a really good CGI effect, the sort of thing I had exactly zero interest in getting up close and personal with.

"*Liar*," he hissed. "Exorcist. *Liar*."

"If I were an exorcist, would I have a ghost with me?" It seemed like a reasonable question.

Apparently not. Tyler scowled. "You're trying to *trick* me," he accused. Behind him—well, technically, through him—I saw the busted remains of the dresser start to pull themselves together. He was getting ready for another volley.

Swell. That was just what I needed. "I am not trying to trick you, Tyler," I said firmly. "If I were trying to trick you, I'd have brought . . . shit, I don't even know. I have no idea how to trick a kid your age. I don't even like kids. I never have."

He blinked. I had apparently gone far enough off-script to confuse him. "You were a kid once."

"And when I was a kid, I was not my own biggest fan,"

I said. "Kids are sticky by default, and annoying almost all the damn time. I am not the person you choose to trick a kid. Look, I'm running out of novel ways to say this, but I'm here because I want to help you. That starts with you helping me. You help me by not throwing that damn dresser at my head again. I am mortal, I am breakable, I do not want to be broken."

Tyler scowled. "If you want to help me, where are my parents?"

"They're gone. You died and they moved away, because they couldn't handle the pain of living here and knowing you weren't ever going to grow up, or come back, or be their little boy again." They'd also moved away because he'd scared the pants off them when he started haunting the place, but saying that seemed a little impolitic. Tyler had just been doing what his new instincts told him to do. It wasn't his fault that those instincts sort of sucked.

"You're *lying*!" he howled, face distorting until it was less that of a preteen boy and more that of an unspeakable nightmare. I prepared to brace for impact.

Artie burst in through the front door and thrust a rectangular object at Tyler.

"Hey," he said, panting slightly. "You wanna play RoboRally?"

The nightmare bled back out of Tyler's face, replaced by an expression of deep, profound confusion. I could sort of understand where he was coming from. This wasn't exactly normal procedure.

I put a hand over my face and groaned. "I asked for backup, not a comedy routine, Artie."

"This *is* backup," he said, sounding stung. "I was an eleven-year-old boy and you weren't, and I'm telling you, this is backup. C'mon, Tyler. When's the last time you sat down and played a game?"

My cousin is an enormous nerd—and when I'm the one saying that, it means something. After all, I'm the girl who shares her room with a floor-to-ceiling bookshelf full of X-Men trades, and who once stayed up for three days straight to organize an attack plan for the

Comic-Con hotel lottery. Somehow, despite all that, Artie out-nerds me.

But he's got good instincts. I lowered my hand. Tyler was looking thoughtfully at the box in Artie's hands.

"Is this a trick?" he asked. "When you open the lid, will it be a Ouija board or something?"

Artie looked hurt. "I don't screw around with the spirit world," he said. "Aunt Mary would hit me in the head."

"Damn right," said Mary, appearing next to him. "And you shouldn't believe all the press about Ouija boards. They can't be used in an exorcism. Trivial Pursuit can, but that's another story. Come on, kid. What can it hurt?"

Tyler looked at Mary, frowning. Finally, he heaved a heavy sigh and said, "I guess. But I get firsts."

"No problem," I said.

The four of us sat on the floor around the board, which Artie had laid out with the utmost care, as fussy as if he were getting set up in a clean, well-lit game store, and not in a decrepit house that would probably be condemned as soon as it stopped being haunted. (Most construction firms are sensibly hands-off about really haunted houses, even if they don't like to admit that ghosts are real. There's making a profit and then there's getting possessed. Only one of them is good for business.) I was going to need a six-hour shower when we got out of here, after all the things I'd touched without meaning to.

On the plus side, the game seemed to be helping. Tyler was still blue and faintly transparent, but at least he looked like a kid again, and not the sort of thing that had been designed to give me nightmares for the rest of my life.

Our little robots were making good progress through their robotic death factory, even if Tyler never touched the cards or pieces. He just looked at them and they moved. There was a good chance he was cheating, since he could presumably control which card he pulled from the deck, but it didn't seem worth pointing out, especially since we were supposed to be calming him down, not getting into a weird family game night fight. Besides, it wasn't like he was hurting anyone.

Unlike Tyler, Mary used her hands when it was her turn to move, pulling her cards with relish, leaning across anyone who got in her way in order to reach her avatar. Like Tyler, she had allowed herself to grow less and less solid, until she'd become transparent enough for me to see right through her. It seemed to be helping him calm down. He kept stealing little glances in her direction, like he couldn't believe another ghost would take this sort of interest in him. Or that *anyone* would take this sort of interest in him. Like most poltergeists, he'd been confined to the house he was haunting since his death. And he was lonely.

The more relaxed Tyler got, the more he talked, going on and on about shows he liked to watch and movies he was looking forward to seeing. He didn't seem to realize that it was all four years out of date. Most of his shows had been canceled; most of those movies had not only been released, they had come out on DVD and been consigned to the bargain shelf. He was a boy without a country in more ways than one.

Artie caught my eye and grimaced. I wrinkled my nose in apology. Artie and his sister Elsie are only half-human. Their father, my Uncle Ted, is an incubus. Artie inherited his father's empathic abilities, which would be a neat superpower to have if we lived in a world where wearing spandex out of the house was not only socially acceptable but magically automatically flattering. Instead, poor Artie gets to pick up the emotional state of every living person around him, whether he wants to or not. Since Mary and Tyler weren't alive, they weren't putting off emotions he could read. But I was. And I was feeling so much pity for Tyler that it must have been like swimming through treacle.

"Sorry," I mouthed.

"'S okay," he mouthed back.

"What are you whispering about?" asked Tyler suspiciously.

We hadn't been whispering—we hadn't been making a sound—but it was a good opening. "Whose turn it is to do the dishes. It's Artie's. He always tries to get out of it."

"So do you," said Artie.

I stuck my tongue out at him. Tyler giggled.

He was starting to sound like a real kid again. "What did you want to be when you grew up, Tyler?" I asked, trying to make my tone light.

He glanced at me through the translucent fringe of his hair. "A football player. Or maybe a fireman. I was trying to make up my mind when I got hit." His lips drew downward. "I guess it doesn't matter now."

"Maybe, maybe not," said Mary. "I know some ghost kids who still like to play football. Best part? You can't get hurt when you're dead. So they can just tackle and shove and do whatever they want, forever. And it's never time to go in for dinner, and there's never homework to make them stop playing."

"Yeah?" asked Tyler. "What if I wanted to be a fireman?"

"You're a poltergeist, right?" asked Artie. "I mean, if you figured out how to control what you can do, and you decided what you really wanted to do with your time was fight fires, I bet you could. You could get the water and the foam deeper into the building, you could move smoke away from kids who are trapped . . ."

"You wouldn't be the first," said Mary. "There are lots of constructive ways to haunt."

"Yeah?" asked Tyler again. He seemed more solid, and almost hopeful. Then he flickered, becoming a cellophane boy. "What about my parents?"

"Not everyone becomes a ghost," said Mary. "Mostly only people who feel like they're leaving something behind. Because you died so young, they're likely to hurry on to whatever comes after this world, looking for you. I'm sorry. You probably won't see them until you decide to move past haunting. But maybe you will. Sticking around to see can't hurt anything, and it might make you feel less like you got cheated out of everything you should have had."

"But I *did* get cheated," said Tyler. That horror movie mask was starting to ooze around the edges of his face again, darkening the whole room. "That man shouldn't have been driving. I was being good. I was following the rules. I just wanted to go *home*."

The game board began to shake. Artie looked alarmed. Right. If there's one thing I've learned from being the youngest of three, it's how to throw a good tantrum—and how to defuse one.

"You got screwed," I said amiably. Tyler's face stopped shifting toward the horrific and snapped back into little boy innocence as he turned to gape at me. I shrugged. "It's true. You got screwed over. That asshole stole every year you should have had. Your high school, dating, college, kids if that's what you wanted, everything, he took it, because he couldn't take a taxi home after slamming back a few beers. God, that sucks. I'd be mad, too. I don't know if I'd be 'haunt the house I lived in, throwing the furniture at people' mad, but who knows? It didn't happen to me. Even if you brought the roof down on my head right now—"

"Uh, maybe don't give him ideas?" said Artie, with a nervous glance at the ceiling.

"—I would still have lived longer and done more than you ever got to, and I am sorry, and that is fucked up, but throwing shit at us is not going to make it better, and it's not going to make you alive again." I gestured to Mary. "She wants to take you someplace where you can meet other kids who got screwed like you did. You can make friends. You can do stuff. And, yeah, you can wait to see if your parents come to join you. You're a ghost. You've got time. Maybe this isn't what you would have chosen, but it's what you've got, so make the best of it."

Tyler gaped at me for several seconds before he turned to Mary and asked, "You can really take me someplace better?"

She nodded. "I can. It's why I'm here."

"And I can wait to see if my parents come?"

"You can. I can't promise they will, but Annie's right: you can at least have a good time while you're waiting. You've been alone for too long. You don't have to be alone anymore."

Tyler bit his lip and nodded. I realized he was trying not to cry, screwing his eyes tight the way my brother always used to when he was upset but didn't want to show it.

"Hey." I leaned over, putting my hand on the air where his shoulder seemed to be. It was a little chilly there, but there was nothing for me to rest against. Ghosts are not always concrete companions. "It's okay to cry. Like I said, you got screwed."

Tyler sniffled, tears starting to roll down his cheeks, and turned to offer Mary his hand. "Can you take me?" he asked.

"I can," said Mary, and took his hand, and they were both gone. There was no flash or displacement of air: one moment they were there; the next they weren't.

I looked at Artie. Artie looked at me.

"Wasn't she our ride home?" asked Artie.

"Yeah," I said, and leaned forward, starting to reset the board. "Guess we're going to play another round."

"I want to be the yellow one."

Mary came back just before dawn. As usual, she didn't want to talk about where she'd been. Despite being with my family for three generations, she's managed to do a remarkable job of not spilling secret ghost business. My Aunt Rose isn't as good at keeping her mouth shut, but she's a different sort of ghost, so maybe she doesn't have secrets that are quite as important.

(Aunt Rose is a hitchhiker, the ghost of someone who died on the road and is still trying, in her own idiosyncratic fashion, to find her way home. She's harmless, as the dead go. Aunt Mary, on the other hand, is a crossroads ghost. She serves something greater than most of the dead, and none of her gifts comes without a price. We can love her. We can offer her a place at the table and a profile on the family Netflix account. We can be her family forever. But we can't ask her for favors, because that's when the crossroads come into play. If we ask, if her little internal counter deems the request to be big and important enough, she might have to call her bosses. No Price has gone down to the crossroads since Grandpa Thomas, and we're all pretty determined to keep the streak going.)

"You two ready?" Mary asked, prodding me with the toe of her foot. I opened my eyes and smiled sleepily up at her. I had fallen asleep with my head on Artie's leg; he was using the RoboRally box as a pillow, which was as adorable as it was impractical. Sometimes family is awesome.

"Do you feel like making a stop for donuts?" I asked.

She laughed.

This is my life.

I wouldn't trade it for the world.

Two

"It's important to have things you care about outside of the family. Insularity is always a risk, and it's the first step toward total isolation. Be an island, but build bridges, not walls."

—Evelyn Baker

A nondescript warehouse in Northeast Portland, Oregon, three days later

THE SLASHER CHICKS circled the track like sharks, and, like sharks, we were constantly in motion. To stop moving was to die, or at least to learn the hard way what it feels like when you get hip-checked to the floor by one of your own teammates. We were all wearing our practice uniforms, "bloodstained" tank tops and green running shorts with "CAMP SLASH-A-LOT" blazoned across the butt. It made for a fascinating dash of uniformity in a group that was otherwise intentionally *un*-uniform. Derby girls are not cast from a single mold, unless tattoos and hair dye are somehow genetic. (For some species of cryptid, they are.)

The other three teams in my home roller derby league—the Concussion Stand, the Block Busters, and the Stunt Troubles—lounged on the bleachers or stretched the kinks out of their legs as they waited for their metaphorical turn at bat. I didn't spare them much thought. This was a practice run, but even during a practice run, paying attention to the track is key: take your eyes off the prize and you're eating floor. It didn't help that the other jammer currently skating was my team captain, the lovely and sarcastic Elmira Street, who knows exactly what I'm capable of when I apply myself.

Of the two of us, I'm more nimble, more innovative, and better at turning momentum into crowd-pleasing tricks—an artifact of my high school cheerleading days. Elmira has an edge on me when it comes to raw speed; the only person on the team who can reliably beat her in a race is Fern, better known as "Meggie Itwasthewind," and Fern doesn't jam. She's a blocker and she's content to stay that way, despite Elmira's repeated attempts to get her to change positions.

(Fern is fast and Fern is good and Fern is *never* going to be a jammer, because a large percentage of Fern's speed comes from the fact that she's not human. She's a Sylph, a humanoid cryptid capable of modifying her own body density, which makes her ultra-fast when she's ultra-light, and an incredible blocker when she's ultra-heavy, since people slam into this skinny little slip of a girl, expecting to knock her out of the way, only to discover that they've actually run into an immovable object. It's comedy gold every time. But if someone hit her like that when she was moving at full speed, she'd literally go flying, and that's the sort of thing we want to avoid if possible.)

"Look alive, Thompson!" shouted Elmira as she lapped me. I wrinkled my nose at her and kept moving. I couldn't shout back, thanks to my mouth guard: it was one of the heavy-duty ones, intended to keep me from racking up the kind of dental bills that would make my parents weep. Elmira's mouth guard was equally impressive, when she bothered to use it; as our captain, she has a tendency to take it out during practice, and trust the rest of us not to bounce her head off the track more than strictly necessary.

It's nice that she has that sort of faith in us. Misplaced and a little stupid, but nice.

Before I became a derby girl, I spent four years as a cheerleader at Lewis and Clark High School. People make a lot of assumptions about cheerleaders, like that we're all plastic airheads who just want to jump high and look pretty. But it's sort of like the whole Ginger Rogers thing, where she did everything Fred Astaire did, only backward and in high heels. A good competitive cheerleader does everything a gymnast does while wearing a pleated skirt and never letting themselves stop smiling. Cheerleading is the leading—no pun intended—cause of injuries among high school and collegiate athletes, and the fact that no one takes it seriously is part of why people keep getting hurt. When you say cheerleading deserves the safety standards and funding of football, you're likely to be laughed right off the team.

But cheerleaders have their tricks. I crouched to lower my center of gravity as I approached the inside curve of the track. My team has skated with me long enough to know my go-to moves, and a few blockers tried to get into position to stop me, but they were too slow. I sped up, tensing for what I was about to do.

In flat track roller derby, when a skater touches space outside the lines defining the track itself—whether they skate into the center or get hip-checked into the bleachers—they're considered "out of bounds," which is a penalty and annoying and disruptive and can mean losing valuable time. But that's only if you touch the ground. An apex jump carries a skater over a portion of the inside of the track. As long as no wheels touch the forbidden ground, it's still clean and there's no penalty. I jumped, and suddenly I was ahead of the pack, leaving all eight of my own team's blockers behind me and skating for the fences.

"Cheater!" shouted Elmira amiably.

I held my hands out behind me like a little kid playing bird, and showed her my middle fingers, just in case she missed the point. Her laughter was better than Red Bull when it came to giving me wings, and I skated onward, for freedom, for glory, and for bragging rights. Sometimes those are the only things that matter.

Every roller derby league has a theme of some kind, even if it's just "we robbed a Hot Topic and this is what we came up with." The league I belong to, the Silver Screams, has a cinema theme. Consequently, there's usually a movie playing during practice, for the teams that have finished their time on the track to enjoy and snark at. It's a nice social thing. It would be an *awesome* social thing if there were, say, showers anywhere in the building. Since there aren't, the enjoyment of the movie must be measured against the agony of sitting that close to a bunch of sweat-drenched derby girls.

Today's film was *Night of the Creeps*. A classic, but one I'd seen before. I settled for sitting at a safe distance and unpacking my lunch. We'd be doing league speed trials after the Concussion Stand and Block Busters finished their track passes, and I needed to keep my strength up. Also, I had cookies.

"Hi, Annie," said a sweet, wispy voice as soon as I had my mouth full.

I grunted a greeting, turning to offer Fern a nod. I didn't chew any faster. Fern's my friend, but my mom's cookies are *amazing*.

Like the rest of us, she was still in her practice gear: there was no point in changing when she'd have to put her nasty, sweaty shorts back on in an hour. She'd removed her helmet and mouth guard, at least, revealing a face just as angelic as her voice.

"You skated real good today," she said, glancing around. Apparently satisfied that we were alone, she lowered her voice, and asked, "Has there been any movement from the you-know-who?"

I swallowed. "No, Fern," I said. "Just like there wasn't any movement last week, or the week before. I promised I'd call you as soon as something changed, and I will. Right now, nothing's changing. Thank God."

She crinkled her nose in a way that would have been adorable, if not for the obvious concern in her eyes. "Is that good? Maybe it's taking so long because they're going to do something really big and awful and we're all going to die."

"Don't get yourself too worked up, please." I put down my second cookie and leaned over to touch her elbow. For me, that was a big deal. I am not the most physically demonstrative person in the world. "You know Elmira will notice, and then we'll have to explain why you're upset, and I'm getting tired of lying to her."

Elmira knows not all the girls in the league are strictly human. She calls them "skaters with diffabilities," and tries not to ask too many questions. Amusingly, I'm pretty sure she thinks I'm one of them, since I'm right in the middle of things every time something goes wrong. She's sort of right. Most people can't light a match by thinking about it really hard. She's also sort of wrong, because I'm not a cryptid. I'm a cryptozoologist.

Just like my stupid sister, Verity, who had the incredible bad judgment to go on national TV—*live* national TV—and declare war on the Covenant of St. George, aka, "that global organization of zealous monster hunters." When we were younger, she liked to say that cheerleading would rot my brain. Guess she was projecting. The most cheer ever caused me to do was spend a lot of money on spirit ribbons. She, on the other hand, took up ballroom dance, and it caused her to fight a snake god on the air. Yeah. I'm *definitely* the one with the brain rot.

Fern kept looking at me anxiously. "I'm scared, Annie," she said. "What if they come here? What if they come here and hurt me?"

"That isn't going to happen, okay?" I offered her my hands. After a moment's hesitation, she took them. Her fingers were squishy; she was so nervous she was dialing back her density. I squeezed, and they firmed up as she remembered what the human norm felt like. "I am not going to let that happen. You're my friend. Everyone here is my friend."

"Even Carlotta?"

"Maybe not Carlotta." Carlotta is the captain of the Concussion Stand. She's also my cousin Elsie's ex-girlfriend, and a definite security risk. She's not a member of the Covenant. She *is* aware of the identity of half the cryptids in the league, and that worried me. If someone came around promising to get rid of the "monsters" . . .

We'd cross that bridge when we came to it. For the time being, I focused on Fern, trying to look as encouraging as possible.

"Verity did what she did because she didn't have a choice," I said. That was the official family line, and maybe it was true. Once you've battled a titanic snake live on television, it's pretty hard to maintain anything resembling a cover. The fact that she didn't have to go on TV in the first place seemed to have missed everyone but me. Verity's selfish. She always has been, she always will be, and she should never have been on that show. Still, I kept smiling. Fern didn't need to know about my personal problems. "Maybe she scared the Covenant away. I mean, they *did* see her take down a snake god almost single handedly. So maybe they're not coming. If they are coming, maybe they're not going to come here. The show was filmed in Los Angeles. The cryptids down there are very good at hiding. I don't think you have anything to be worried about."

"Thompson!"

That's not my name, but I've been answering to it for long enough that I turned automatically. Elmira was standing by the track, hands on hips, frowning. I let go of Fern.

"I think that's my cue," I said, keeping my voice as light and unconcerned as I could. "You want the rest of my cookies? Cookies always make you feel better."

"Okay," said Fern, with a quick, almost shy smile.

I left her sitting on the bleachers and munching her way through the last of my mother's cookies. Bribery is sometimes the solution to all the world's problems.

Elmira lowered her hands when I was close enough to talk to without shouting, and said, "Your cousin's here."

"What, Elsie?" I looked around, but didn't see her. Technically, I have three cousins, but Artie almost never leaves his house, and Sarah has been in Ohio for the last two years. If she was well enough to travel, someone would have told me. "Where?"

"Outside," she said. "She didn't want to come in, since Carlotta's here." Elmira grimaced. "This is why you shouldn't shit where you eat, or date where you skate. It makes everything awkward."

"At least Elsie's not a skater."

"No, but she used to be one of our best volunteers and cheering sections, and now we only see her when she's coming to pick you up or drop you off. She's had breakups in the league before. I don't get why this one is so different. She even went to Cherry's wedding."

"Look, Carlotta's your friend and Elsie's my family, so I don't think there's any way for us to have this conversation without someone coming off as a biased asshole," I said. "Did you tell her practice wasn't over?"

"I did," said Elmira. "She said to tell you it's not an emergency, but there's a family meeting about your grandfather, and your parents want you there. You're free to go as far as I'm concerned; it's sort of refreshing to hear that the two of you aren't the Boxcar Children or something."

"Points for the retro reference," I said, mouth running on autopilot as my brain raced to process this information. The league knows Elsie is my cousin mostly because she's the one who convinced me to go out for the team: by the time I'd realized I might want a better cover story, it was already too late. That was *all* they knew about my family, and since Elsie and I don't look a damn thing alike, it was possible they thought one or both of us had been adopted, which was fine by me. Keeping people from figuring out more about my family than they need to know is part of my job. "It's really okay if I leave early?"

"It's fine," said Elmira. She smirked a little. "But I'm going to need you to help me work on my apex jumps."

"It's a deal," I said, and skated for the locker room.

Here's the 4-1-1—which is another retro reference that's probably going to be incomprehensible before too much longer, thank you march of technology. "Here's the top Google result" might be a better opening. Anyway:

My name is Antimony Price. My friends call me "Annie," my siblings call me "Timmy," the people I do roller derby with call me either "Annie Thompson" or "Final Girl," and if I had a therapist, they'd probably call me on the brink of a serious identity disorder, given all the names I have to juggle on a daily basis. I'm not James Bond or Black Widow. I didn't go to spy school. I went to something much worse. I went to the Price Family Academy of Hiding in Plain Sight Because Assholes Want to Kill You.

As you can probably guess, our graduation ceremonies are a *lot* of fun.

See, either two or four generations ago, depending on which branch of the family you start counting from, we were part of an organization of asshole monster hunters called, wait for it, the Covenant of St. George. Yes, the same assholes my sister declared war on while she was live on the air. The Covenant felt, and presumably still feels, that anything they considered "unnatural" should be wiped from the face of the planet, preferably with extreme prejudice. (A lot of their rationale is based on the idea that if something wasn't on the Ark—as in Noah's—then it's evil and bad and doesn't deserve to exist. Which sort of begs the question of how they got a manifest for *that* particular voyage.) My great-great-grandparents decided they were done being professional assholes, and walked. Two generations later, my grandmother convinced a Covenant operative named Thomas Price that *he* was done being a professional asshole, and married him.

Professional assholes do not take kindly to people walking out on them, especially when those people not only walk out, but use all their training and institutional knowledge to set themselves up as the competition. Where the Covenant kills, we protect. We nurture, we teach, and we try to find the delicate balance between the needs of the human community and the needs of the cryptid community. And because we're not really excited by the idea of being assassinated for our beliefs, we do it all while keeping ourselves hidden from the world. Hence my having a different name when I'm skating. Hence my sister wearing a wig when she dances, and my brother going to the middle of nowhere and Clark Kenting his way through a herpetology degree.

All of which Verity fucked seven kinds of up when she declared war. (Mom says I shouldn't blame her, since it's not like *she* decided to summon the giant interdimensional snake on live television. I say we still suffer from the Healy family luck we inherited from Grandma Alice. If Verity hadn't been there, the snake wouldn't have been there either.) See, up until that moment, we had mostly managed to convince the professional assholes that we were all dead—or, more accurately, that most of us had never been born, on account of Grandma Alice and both her children having been killed when the Covenant came after them in Michigan. It may have been the biggest hoax any member of our family ever successfully pulled, and it was all undone in an instant because Cryptozoologist Barbie just wanted to *dance*.

For the last three months, my entire extended family has been on high alert, waiting to see whether or not the Covenant of St. George had access to either basic cable or the Internet, and more importantly, what they were going to do about Verity's little stunt. Our code for Covenant action getting started?

"It's about your grandfather."

In other words, we were screwed.

Elsie was waiting outside the warehouse, her little Honda snuggled up to the curb like the two of them were planning an elopement. As usual, her windows were down, but no bubblegum pop blasted from the stereo; the car was eerily silent. I approached cautiously.

"Elsie?"

"Get in," she said, not taking her hands off the wheel, not turning her head. Her breakup with Carlotta had been ugly enough to have me and Artie quietly plotting about filling the other woman's apartment with spiders until Elsie caught on and asked us to leave her ex alone. Since then, Elsie had stayed in the car when she came to pick me up, and never risked catching a glimpse of the woman who broke her heart.

"Right." I slung my gym bag into the backseat, where the stink would hopefully be a little less offensive, and slung myself into the front, taking slightly more care about where I landed. I used fumbling with my seatbelt as an opportunity to take a good look at my cousin, trying to get a read on the situation from her.

Elsinore Harrington—"Elsie"—inherited what most of us think of as the Healy "look." She's short, curvy without being aggressively stacked, blonde, and adorable. Drop her in 1940s Hollywood and she'd be running the place inside of the week. She'd probably mourn the limited range of available hair dye shades, but then she'd lead the fashion color revolution a few decades early, and make it possible for the humanoid cryptids with naturally blue-and-green hair to come out in public much sooner. Today, the bottom two inches of her hair were dyed a shockingly bright aquamarine, subtly blending up into a soft blue-green before melding into her natural blonde. She was wearing a Slasher Chicks booster T-shirt and well-worn jeans, and she looked more somber than I'd ever seen her.

"How bad is it?" I asked.

"Oh, you know." She put the car in gear, pulling away from the curb and hitting the button to roll up the windows in the same motion. Once we were moving, and she was reasonably confident we couldn't be overheard, she said, "Verity called to check in."

Verity was in New York, helping to marshal the cryptids who lived there in anticipation of a Covenant attack, and making sure the local Nest of dragons—which included the last known living male of their species—was locked down. I don't like my sister much, if at all, but I have a lot of respect for the way she does her job. If you want to prepare the cryptids in an urban area for disaster, she's the girl to call.

It doesn't hurt that her husband, Dominic, is ex-Covenant, and knows all the tricks his former fellows might use to invade the city. (Although it does raise the question of whether the Covenant still thinks he's dead. My cousin Sarah, the telepathic super-wasp, once used her powers to make a Covenant field team think Verity was an imposter Dominic had trained because ... reasons, and that they were both deceased. Well, now they knew Verity was the real thing, and also alive. Did they know the same about him? Were they going to be *looking* for him?)

"And?" I asked tightly.

"And the Freakshow burned down last night."

I clapped a hand over my mouth, fighting the urge to gasp. The Freakshow was a bogeyman-owned burlesque club. Verity worked there for a while during her first stint in New York, and she'd talked a lot about the other employees when she came home. There were more than forty people working there, only a few of them human.

"No one was killed, although there were injuries," said Elsie. "Istas—the waheela—smelled gasoline, and the owner was able to evacuate the patrons out the front and the employees through the basement. None of them were seen leaving the club, which will hopefully slow the Covenant when it comes to figuring out who survived."

"We're sure it was the Covenant?"

"Dominic said the burn pattern and flash marks matched the methods he was trained to use if he ever had to burn out a monster den. Then he apologized about eleven times for using the word 'monster,' which would have been adorable, but ..."

"But you were trying to find out what was going on," I said grimly. "So the Covenant's in New York. Any idea how they got there without someone seeing them coming?"

"Manhattan isn't the only port in the country, assuming they even landed in America—flying into Canada might be safer if they're coming from Europe. Touch down in Toronto, switch identities, and head down to New York. There are so many routes. We were fools to think we could cover them all."

Elsie sounded so resigned that I couldn't say anything. I touched her shoulder lightly, trying to lend her my support. She smiled, sad and wry, and kept driving.

I settled in my seat, trying not to let my nervousness—or my anger—show. Mom kept saying a confrontation with the Covenant had been unavoidable all along: once they'd started taking interest in North America again, there was no way we'd be able to keep flying below their radar. And that was all well and good, but Verity didn't need to out herself on video. She didn't need to remind the Covenant that not only did a family descended from some of their greatest traitors still exist, but was likely to be actively working against them. Because as much as the human part of our family had to lose, the cryptid parts were in even greater danger.

As far as the Covenant is concerned, none of my cousins are people. They're monsters, horrific abominations of nature, put on this planet solely to be exterminated by the human race. I've read all Grandpa Thomas' books on the Covenant, and I've read Great-Great-Grandpa Alexander's diaries, and there's not much leeway where things that look human but technically aren't human are concerned. They go back and forth on the topic of magic-users, shifting them from "human" to "monster" as needed, but Sarah, who bleeds clear, or Elsie, who can talk almost anyone into almost anything thanks to a dose of persuasive telepathy, would always be the enemy. There's no room for them in the Covenant's view of the natural world.

"They're not going to come here," I said.

"You think they don't know how to get on a *plane*?" Her voice was bitter. Unsurprising, but still painful to hear. "We're fucked. We're well and truly fucked."

"Maybe not."

"Why, because you've got some genius idea to make everything better?" Elsie shook her head. "This is the real world. Verity screwed up, and now we get to pay for her mistakes."

Normally, I would have been happy to start up a healthy session of complaining about my sister. Under the circumstances, silence seemed like a better reply, and we sat quietly as we made the hour-long drive out of the city, into the woods, and through them to the house.

Three

"Sometimes a change of scene means more
than just going someplace new. Sometimes
it means becoming somebody new at the
same time. That's not necessarily a bad
thing. It's not necessarily a good one, either."

—Frances Brown

A small survivalist compound about an hour's drive east of Portland, Oregon

THE DRIVEWAY WAS PACKED when Elsie pulled through
the gate and up to the house. Mom and Dad were
both home. Aunt Jane's station wagon was parked at an
angle, the bumper dangerously close to Mom's herb garden. Elsie pulled in between the station wagon and
Dad's truck, killing the engine before letting her head
fall forward against the wheel.

"I don't want to go in there," she said mournfully.

"Your brother's probably already in there," I said. "Is
it really fair to leave Artie alone to deal with this shit-
show?"

"He stole one of my Barbies when he was like, six,
and I've been holding it against him ever since," she said.
"I'll text and tell him all is forgiven if you don't make me
go in there."

"Tempting, but no," I said. "This is a family meeting.
You're part of the family, and that means you're part of
the family even when things are rotten. And it's really

not fair to leave Artie in there by himself, so let's short-cut the part where I talk you into this and go inside."

"I hate you," said Elsie.

"I know," I agreed amiably and got out of the car, pausing to retrieve my gym bag from the backseat. Elsie was being a brat, but that didn't mean she deserved the sort of punishment that comes from leaving used derby gear in a hot car.

When my parents moved to Oregon, it was with an eye toward establishing a permanent home for our family—one that wouldn't have the bad memories associated with our previous family home in Buckley, Michigan. One big enough to support us all, if necessary. They'd started by buying an oversized house originally built by a would-be lumber baron who'd decided he didn't like living in the middle of a big creepy forest that environmental regulations kept him from cutting down. The house was positioned in the middle of a large patch of already-cleared land, and they'd been able to get the whole thing, if not for a song, then for a cover album of Journey's greatest hits.

Their first move had been building a wall around the whole thing. Their second move had been building a large guesthouse in the back, and a smaller gatehouse in the front, and then to really start digging in. By this point, it's been almost thirty years of constant innovation and improvement, and we could house thirty people for up to a month without anyone getting stabbed. It'll be a few more generations before we have that many family members, but my parents think ahead.

Of course, if the Covenant came for us tomorrow, all the thinking ahead in the world wouldn't save us. Uncle Ted and Artie are noncombatants. Elsie can hold her own in a bar fight, but not much more than that. Dad, Aunt Jane, Mom, and me would be the only ones prepared to fight. We couldn't stand against Covenant numbers. Calling Alex and Verity home, even with their respective significant others, wouldn't tip the balance in our favor. About the only thing that could help would be—

The front door opened. The heavily tattooed, short-haired woman in the doorway beamed at me, her frilled apron entirely at odds with her combat boots, cut-offs, and tattered khaki shirt.

"Grandma!" Elsie and I broke into a run at the same time, and we both slammed into my maternal grandmother. Alice laughed, putting her arms around us and squeezing us tight.

There's something about grandma hugs that puts the world into perspective. Alice held us for a count of ten, long enough that it qualified as a good, solid embrace, but short enough that we weren't blocking the doorway long enough to get yelled at. Then she let go, stepping back so we could come inside.

"Hello, my darling girls," she said, still beaming. "Oh, Annie, haven't you grown? Elsie, dearest, I love your hair."

"I'd have dyed the tips red if I'd known you were coming," said Elsie, almost shyly.

Alice beamed. "It looks lovely as it is. Now come on, both of you. We have cookies, cocoa, and battle planning to get to."

"Yes, Grandma," we chorused dutifully, and filed inside. I hung back, trying to get a good look at the tattoos on her arm and shoulder. They change every time I see her, and while some of the same designs show up over and over again, they're almost never in the same place. I'd been studying Grandpa Thomas' books as closely as I could, and I was starting to puzzle out the meanings behind some of the tattoos. They're not just art. They're pictographic representations of the spells and runes in his notes, inked on flesh and turned into something practical.

My grandmother being a living spellbook isn't nearly as weird as the fact that she looks roughly the same age as Elsie. She spends most of her time in parallel dimensions, searching for her husband. She ages—I saw her looking almost as old as Mom once—and then she somehow runs the clock backward, keeping herself young enough for the strain she puts her body under. The rest of the family is pretty sure Grandpa Thomas is long dead, although no one wants to say it to her face.

I'm still reserving judgment. After all, if she can survive out there, maybe so could he.

We stepped into the living room. The mice on the coffee table started cheering, causing the people who were already there to stop what they were doing and turn to look. And the kids I used to go to school with thought *their* families were weird.

"HAIL!" shouted the mice. "HAIL THE RETURN OF THE PRECISE AND POLYCHROMATIC PRIESTESSES!"

"Oh, goodie," said Elsie.

"HAIL THE GATHERING OF THE FIVE PRIESTESSES!" continued the mice.

"At least they can count?" I said.

"HAIL!" said the mice.

Elsie groaned.

Aeslin mice look basically like normal, nonintelligent, nonreligious rodents. They have a tendency to clothe themselves in scraps of paper, candy wrappers, fabric, and whatever else they can find, and their front paws are more like hands, but apart from that, if seen from a distance, there's really no way to tell the Aeslin mice from something the cat might drag in. Until they open their mouths. Aeslin mice are *highly* prone to religious mania, and like to share their worshipful joy at every possible turn. Our colony worships the family. So yeah, that's fun.

"Did Elsie fill you in?" asked my father. There was a large whiteboard in the center of the room. He was standing next to it, a marker in his hand. It looked like they were trying to work out what sort of resources we had available to us in case of an attack that didn't give us time to call in reinforcements. The little columns were dauntingly short.

"She said there'd been an attack." I walked over to the stairs, throwing my gym bag as far up the steps as it would go. "On a scale of one to 'we're all about to die,' is there any chance I can stop to take a shower?"

"Not just yet, dear," said my grandmother, appearing

at my elbow and guiding me toward the rest of the family. "We need to talk to you."

I blinked at her before turning to really *look* at the front room. Dad was next to the whiteboard; Artie was on the couch with Uncle Ted, looking like he was about to be physically ill. Mom and Aunt Jane had set up a folding card table, and were drawing on what looked like a map of North America. Their placement coincidentally put as much distance as possible between Grandma and Aunt Jane. They don't get along. It looked pretty normal for an impromptu family gathering . . . except for Artie. He never looked that upset unless Sarah was in danger, or he had to leave the house and interact with girls he wasn't related to.

"Okay," I said slowly. "What's going on?"

Mom and Dad exchanged a look. She shook her head. "Oh, no," she said. "This is *your* plan. This is *your* fault. You get to be the one who tries to sell it as a good idea, instead of a good way to get our baby killed."

"Uh, hello?" I said. "I'm standing right here."

Dad grimaced and said nothing.

"Annie, look at me," said my grandmother. I obligingly turned to look at her. "Who do I look like?"

"That's easy," I said. "Every other woman in the family." If there's a Healy mold, it was struck using my grandmother as the model. She's short, blonde, and curvy—just like her daughter, my sister, and my cousin. Even Mom and Shelby fit that general description, like Dad and Alex both went out and found girls who reminded them of dear old mom. It's a little creepy, if I think about it too hard: family resemblances are one thing, but I like to think a family should have slightly more genetic variation than your average hive of bees.

"That's right. Your grandfather always called it the 'Carew look'— said we took after my grandmother's side of the family. My mother was also short and blonde, so I suppose we started reinforcing it early." Alice reached out and cupped my chin in her hand. I would have pulled away from almost anyone else, including Mom, but something about the sadness in her eyes kept me from moving. "You, though ... you look just like your grandfather."

"Not seeing how that's any better when the Covenant comes calling," I said.

"Thomas was the last of his line. He thought the Price name would die with him." Alice's smile was bitter as she released me. "They probably have a picture of him in their files somewhere—those bastards never let go of anything—but there's no 'Price look,' not the way there's a 'Carew look.' You could walk past a strike team on the street and they wouldn't stop looking for the Price they'd heard was in the area."

I stared at her, slow horror uncurling in my chest as I realized what she was getting at.

It's true: I don't look like any of the other women in my family. They're all dainty, petite blondes, and I'm a tall brunette with the sort of ass that comes from spending years working on your lower body strength. Technically, I suppose my tits are proportional, but since I'm bigger, so are they. Even my face doesn't match up with theirs. They tend toward these sweet pixie bone structures, while my cheekbones could be used to slice bread. When I was little, I used to think I'd been adopted, or maybe rescued from a swarm of ghouls after they'd devoured my real parents.

I'd say I was an imaginative child, but when your family outings consist of "okay, kids, try to find your way out of these woods without being eaten by a bear," sometimes the thought of having a different, better, less murderous family gets really damn tempting.

"Thanks to Dominic, we know the location of three Covenant recruiting facilities in the United Kingdom," said Aunt Jane, looking up from her map. "None of them will take you without a strong background and a referral, but those are easy enough to arrange. The referral doesn't even have to come from a standing member. They're so wedded to their 'knights errant' self-image that if you show up and say an old man told you to go there to fulfill your destiny, they'll take it."

I gaped at her before turning to gape at the rest of my

family. Gaping seemed like the only real answer. If they were going to have to identify my body by my dental records, I was going to make sure they all got a good look at my teeth.

Mom looked apologetic but unwavering. Artie just looked miserable. Being in this room had to be causing him physical pain. Dad wouldn't meet my eyes.

I started getting angry.

"So wait, you got your heir and your spare, and they're both doing a dandy job of lining up the next generation, since Verity's married and Alex is about to be, so I'm extraneous to needs? Is that what's going on here?"

"Antimony," said my father sharply.

"No, Dad, don't you 'Antimony' me! Unless I'm reading the situation completely wrong, your response to Verity fucking up on national television is going to be sending me—your *other* daughter—to the Covenant of St. George to get killed by the professional assholes we ran away from a hundred fucking years ago. Well, you can—"

"*Antimony.*"

It was rare enough for him to take that sort of tone with me that I stopped, giving him a wide-eyed, wounded look.

Dad shook his head. "You're not wrong, Annie. We're asking if you'll help us infiltrate the Covenant of St. George. And sadly, you're our only option. Elsie looks too much like a Carew, and Arthur is still trying to get his abilities under control. We'd talked about sending Sarah—"

Artie's head snapped up, eyes narrowing as he suddenly engaged with the conversation in a whole new way. Whenever the discussion of sending Sarah had taken place, Artie had *not* been a part of it.

"—but she isn't strong enough yet, and she's not as equipped to take care of herself as you are. We know you can get in and get out with the lowest odds of getting hurt. You always say we don't take you seriously enough, that we treat you like a child. Well, Annie, this is us taking you seriously. This is us treating you like an adult.

You are the only one who stands a chance of finding out what we need to know to keep this family safe—to keep this *continent* safe." My father looked at me solemnly. "We need to know what they know. We need to know what they're planning. That means we need someone on the inside, someone they won't spot on sight."

"Someone who isn't one blood test away from being revealed as nonhuman and hence suitable for extermination," said Elsie.

She'd known. When she came to pick me up from the warehouse, she'd already known what they wanted me to do. It was oddly difficult not to see that as a betrayal. She was my cousin and my friend. She was supposed to be on *my* side.

"You could've asked before you started making plans that involved sending me to my doom," I muttered.

"We're asking now," said my mother. She moved to stand next to Dad. "Annie, will you do this? For the sake of our family, for the sake of our community, will you do this?"

The only person who hadn't said anything was my Uncle Ted. I turned to him. "What do you think I should do?"

He shrugged. "Annie, I'm the only person in this room with no human blood at all. These people have been treating my kind like vermin for centuries. I've lost relatives to their European field teams. I want to see them dead. All of them. I don't say that when your sister's home, because I know she loves her husband, and I'm sorry, Mrs. Price-Healy, but it's how I feel."

"No offense taken," said Alice.

"They're monsters. They call us monsters, but that's because they've never looked in a mirror. Do I want to leave you alone with them? No. But do I need, all the way down to my bones, to know what's going on? Whether I should be grabbing my family and running as far as I possibly can? Yeah. So I'm sorry, baby girl, but I'm on board with this idea. We need a miracle. Maybe it's you."

I looked at him silently for a long moment before

turning to my parents and saying, in a subdued voice, "Yeah. I'll do it. I'll go to the Covenant for you."

Silence fell over the room. The mice didn't cheer. Some things, apparently, were too serious even for that.

Swell.

The conversation continued for more than two hours, my parents updating their map and whiteboard while Aunt Jane took notes and Grandma Alice contributed everything she'd ever been able to glean about the Covenant of St. George. Most of it was corroborated by the information we had from Dominic. The Covenant is made of traditionalists, which is another way of saying that they're set in their ways. If something isn't broken, they don't go out of their way to fix it.

Fascinatingly, being traditionalists working off of a centuries-old model doesn't make them sexists. The Covenant of St. George has been recruiting women since the Middle Ages, apparently recognizing that sometimes the most effective warriors are the ones no one would see coming. My gender wasn't going to be an impediment. My background, on the other hand, was.

"They don't get many North American recruits, because they've never been able to establish a strong presence here," said my grandmother. "They mostly operate by sending strike teams, purging whatever cryptid presence they find, and retreating back to Europe to lick their wounds. This continent has never offered them fertile soil on which to plant their specific flavor of hate."

"Which is amazing, because it's not like America has been quick to reject all the *other* kinds of racism people have tried to encourage here," said Artie in a low voice. His mother shot him a sharp look. I tried not to snicker. I failed.

"Most of the North American recruits they *do* get are people who've been harmed by cryptid activity in some way," said Mom. I looked back to her. "We have a cover story for you. Remember the Black Family Carnival?"

"Apraxis wasps, right?" I asked. "They took out the whole company."

"As of right now, they took out all but one," she said. "We're setting you up as a daughter of two of their acrobats, who was in New York taking your SATs when the wasps hit the carnival. You finished college, but you never stopped thinking about what happened to your family. You want revenge. You heard a rumor about a group that could help you get it."

"Carnie brat," I said. "Okay. That's something I can do." Before roller derby, I was a cheerleader, and before I was a cheerleader, I was a tumbler, spending my summers training with the Campbell Family Carnival, otherwise known as "Great-Grandma Fran's side of the family." I'd loved it there. It had been clear almost from the start that I wasn't going to have the right build for competitive gymnastics, so we'd moved me into circus classes, teaching me trampoline and trapeze routines, all performed with a dizzying array of safety precautions standing by to keep me from breaking anything I might need later.

(My sister has a tendency to throw herself off buildings for fun. Apparently, she thinks gravity doesn't apply to pretty people. I don't mind falling—it can be pretty cool under the right circumstances—but falling without a net is *not* my idea of a good time.)

"The fact that you supposedly went to college for four years will explain why you're a little rusty, and your core skills should still be good enough that you can fake anything you don't feel totally up for. Artie's going to set up a new ID for you, and run it through Uncle Al for any bells or whistles that you need."

"Nobody does a fake ID like Big Al," I said.

"That's right," said Mom, missing the humor entirely. "It should be ready by the end of the week. We'll fly you to Toronto, have you take the train to New York, and fly you from there to London. That way, there's no clear connection between your new identity and the West Coast, much less Portland."

"You've thought of everything," I said. We had no

idea what kind of monitoring capacity the Covenant had. We as a family and an extended network don't have the ability to put a trace on a passport—we can watch the airports, we can monitor known crossings, but we can't tell exactly when someone entered or left the country. We had to assume the Covenant could. We had to avoid drawing obvious lines.

"Yes. Everything." My mother closed the distance between us with remarkable speed. My father was right behind her. They engulfed me in their arms, giving me no time to dodge or backpedal.

"*Everything*," she whispered, and I realized two things. One, that she was crying, and two, that they had really tried to find another option. They had *searched*. Because there was every chance they were sending me to my death for the sake of the rest of my family, and for them to be willing to do that, they had to be absolutely sure there wasn't any other way. What the hell was I getting myself into?

"I'm going to go pack," I muttered, and ducked out of their embrace, fleeing up the stairs.

As I should probably have expected, Mary was sitting on my bed when I got to my room. "We need to talk," she said, without preamble.

"Nope," I said, heading for the dresser. "I need to pack. You can help, if you want. But no talking."

"Annie . . ."

"You're still talking."

"Annie, I can't come to England with you."

I stopped in the act of opening the top drawer, trying not to show how much that simple statement rattled. Then I shrugged, and said, "So? Neither is anyone else. Is the Covenant a good place for granny panties, do you think?"

"Annie, *look* at me."

I turned to look at her. "What? I have to go. You know I have to go."

"I know you're still setting things on fire. I know you can't control your pyrokinesis. I know it took your great-grandfather *years* to get his magic to do what he told it. You're going to get caught, and you're going to get hurt."

"I can handle myself." I rolled my shoulders in a shrug. "Trust me, okay? I know what I'm doing."

"I don't think you do. Annie—"

"You can't tell them!" I paused, surprised by the vehemence in my own voice. Then I sighed. "Please. You can't tell them. They need me to do this. They never need me to do anything. I'm the backup kid. If I'm ever going to prove myself . . . please. Don't blow my cover." I didn't want to go. I didn't want anyone else to go in my place.

Brains are complicated sometimes.

Mary looked at me gravely. Finally, she echoed my sigh with one of her own and stood, walking over to offer me her hands. I took them.

"I've been this family's babysitter for more than fifty years," she said. "You're the youngest of your generation, and no one's been making me new kids to watch lately. I'm going to be a little over-attentive."

"I know," I said. "But you have to let me grow up sometime."

"Just promise me you'll run if you have to."

I nodded. "I will. I don't want to join you in the ghost world yet."

Mary smiled. "You couldn't handle the ghost world."

"Damn straight," I said, and she hugged me, and if she noticed that I was shaking, she didn't say a word.

Four

"You can't go home again. Especially not if
you've already burned it to the ground."
—Enid Healy

*A nameless café somewhere in Manhattan, nine days, a
cross-continental flight, a really long train ride, two
taxis, a confusing subway trip, and a cup of coffee later*

THE CAFÉ PROBABLY WASN'T NAMELESS, but as the owners hadn't bothered to put a sign outside and the
counter was staffed entirely by unsmiling, bored-looking
hipsters with lip piercings and multiple tattoos, I wasn't
going to push my luck by asking what it was called. I was
already pushing my luck by being there, comparatively
uncool as I am. Why, I didn't have a single tattoo! The
only things I have pierced are my ears, and I was only
able to get away with that because it's so socially standard that unpierced ears are almost more visible.

My parents raised us to be nonconformists who always look like we just ran away from church camp.
Thanks, Mom and Dad. Thanks *loads*.

New Yorkers like to say they have the best public
transit system in the world. I think this is because they're
all high off whatever weird subterranean fumes are
blowing around in those damn tunnels. I'd departed
Grand Central Station with a series of careful directions
written on an index card, and had promptly gotten totally turned around in a maze of complicated train routes
that bore no resemblance whatsoever to anything my
poor little Portland brain had ever encountered.

(Yes, yes, I'm sure they make *perfect sense* to the people who navigate them on a daily basis, but for me? The most complex public transit system I'd ever dealt with was the bus. Which does not run underground, or according to a system of "uptown" and "downtown" that assumes a degree of local knowledge I would need to live locally for months, if not years, to acquire. People who say *they* live in the only place on Earth with a public transit system that makes sense are *assholes*.)

Eventually, I'd managed to get myself un-turned-around and had found the café from my notes, where I was now holed up in the very back, my luggage forming a barrier between me and the rest of the room, nursing a cup of black coffee and thinking longingly of my bed at home. It was a good bed. Just the right size, with a mattress new enough to have some bounce, and pillows I had beaten to that perfect stage of worn-in—

"You Melody?"

I looked up. One of the bored baristas (say that five times fast) was standing in front of me, a piece of paper in her hand. I haven't been Melody in a long, long time. That ID got retired when I graduated high school.

"Yes," I said, without hesitation.

"Great. I'm not your message service." She thrust the paper at me and went stomping back to the bar.

I unfolded the note. CALL YOUR MOM, it read.

Since my mother knew—well, not *exactly* where I was, but essentially where I was, this was my signal to grab my things, throw a dollar on the table for whoever had to clean up after me, and slip out the front door. The sidewalk was empty. I'd expected that. I walked to the corner, turned left, and kept going, looking for an alley. When in doubt, always look for an alley.

When I found one, it was narrower than I'd expected, almost claustrophobic, lined with trash cans and rickety-looking fire escapes. I started walking down it anyway, and was halfway to the next street when someone whistled.

I stopped. I looked up.

Verity and Dominic were standing on a fire escape.

Verity bounced onto her toes and started waving violently when she saw me, which was almost enough to make me reconsider my decision never to ride the subway again. Call me weird, but an overly enthusiastic sister is not something I want to deal with after a trip involving planes, trains, *and* automobiles.

Dominic, unsmiling as usual, held up a can of Red Bull. I decided against heading back to the café. Instead, I gripped the handle of my suitcase a little tighter and stayed where I was, waiting for them to make their descent. Dominic came down the sensible way, using the ladder to reach the nearest line of trashcans, then hopping down, first onto their lids, finally to ground level.

Verity just jumped, like she was auditioning for a whitewashed live-action production of *Sailor Moon* and thought she was going to be a Soldier for Love and Justice. She hit the ground the same time Dominic did, and didn't look like the fall had bothered her in the slightest. God, I hate her sometimes.

"Ta-da," I said flatly. "Should we really risk being seen together?"

"The last Covenant field team left Manhattan after the Freakshow burned," said Verity. "We have people watching for them to come back, but so far, there's been no sign they plan to turn around. Sarah's patch on the last field team really convinced them that there wasn't much to deal with here. We probably shouldn't go for a fun shopping spree through Midtown, but we're okay for now."

"I'll trade you for your bag," said Dominic, offering me the Red Bull.

I gave him my suitcase and had the tab popped on my energy drink before he finished adjusting his grip. Verity began to walk without another word. The bounce in her steps spoke of a nervousness she wasn't admitting, and her eyes, as always, were turned high, scanning the rooftops and fire escapes for signs of movement.

Dominic was more grounded. He kept his eyes forward, and was more discreet in his surveillance. Verity lives and dies by the idea that the flashier something was, the less attention people would pay to the details . . .

although not, I realized, today. She was wearing blue jeans and a gray hoodie with "I ♥ New York" blazoned across the front. It was the uniform of the tourist, and no one would look at her twice in this neighborhood, especially not with her uncombed hair and neutral makeup. She looked like an extra, rather than a star. Not normal for my stage-hungry sister. Not normal at all.

Dominic's transformation was more subtle but almost as striking once I started looking for it. Instead of his cheesy leather duster, he was wearing a denim jacket over a button-up white shirt and had his hair slicked back with so much pomade that I could smell it three feet away. He looked like he was preparing to be an extra on *Law & Order*, and that, too, was a uniform of a sort. Neither of them was going to stand out in a crowd.

I wasn't either. My hair was tied in a thick, frizzy braid, and I was wearing the Toronto version of Verity's outfit: fuzzy boots, blue jeans, and a "Canada Proud" sweatshirt I'd purchased at the Vancouver airport with a credit card issued under the name "Marigold Price." I'd cut the card up and dumped the pieces in five different trashcans before catching a bus back to Seattle and taking a plane from there to Toronto. Elsie would be calling to report the card stolen in three days, and the beat would go on. The beat always went on.

There was a cab waiting on the corner. More uncharacteristic behavior for Verity: she hates being cooped up, and she hates being cooped up with strangers even more. I was about to ask if she was feeling okay when the cab window rolled down to reveal a gorgeous, sour-faced blonde woman.

"Are you getting in?" she demanded. "I can't take *real* fares when I'm stuck chauffeuring you around."

"We paid your Nest-mother for your time," said Verity wearily. Apparently, this was a conversation that had been going on for a while.

"She'll give me less than half. I get to keep more than half of my usual fares. Get in."

"I can pay," I said, before Verity could object. "I have a travel budget."

Verity gave me a sharp look. "She's already been paid," she said. "Get in the cab."

I rolled my eyes but didn't argue. The last thing I wanted to do was have a sister-fight on the sidewalk, especially when I only had eight hours in New York to shed this identity before I flew to London. I was going to arrive jet lagged and exhausted in a foreign country, which was just going to make this mission even more fun than it had looked on paper.

My suitcase went in the trunk; my backpack went on my lap. Dominic wound up in the front seat with our dragon driver, leaving me and Verity in the back. She waited until we'd pulled away from the curb to pull a glass-and-tourmaline charm from her pocket. She passed it up to the driver.

"Get us out of here," she said.

The driver nodded and slipped the charm onto the rearview mirror. Then she hit the gas, accelerating faster than was strictly a good idea, given the traffic. The other drivers let us know they didn't appreciate this approach by honking their horns and flashing their lights and, in several cases, sticking their hands out their windows and flipping us off with enough vigor to give themselves carpal tunnel. Our driver flipped them off right back and kept on driving.

"So, how was your flight?" asked Verity blithely, apparently unbothered by the fact that we were hurtling through traffic at unsafe speeds.

"The flight was fine. Long and cramped, but fine. The train was better. The subway was horrifying." I tried to keep my eyes on the window without being too blatant about it. Streets and landmarks I'd only ever seen on television flashed by outside, temptingly close, impossibly far away. Even if I'd been here to play tourist, there wouldn't have been time, and it wouldn't have been safe.

Speaking of safety . . . I turned to Verity, frowning. "I thought somebody from the Freakshow was going to pick me up."

"They're a little preoccupied right now," she said. "Arson tends to distract people."

"As we said before, the Covenant currently has no presence in Manhattan," said Dominic, in what was probably meant to be a soothing tone, but mostly made him sound like a condescending asshole. I considered telling him that. I decided it wouldn't do much to help maintain the already tenuous current peace.

See? I can have self-control. I *can*.

"As long as the Covenant doesn't have a field team on the ground, we can move around freely," said Verity. "We've been sweeping the airports and major transit hubs for cameras and listening devices daily. Even if they had the sort of tech they could hide from us, they wouldn't be able to hide it from the bogeymen or the mice. New York is as safe as it gets, for the moment. Besides, this way you can dump your old ID and change into your new one someplace private, where no one's going to walk in on you."

"It *will* be nice to henna my hair in a bathroom I don't have to share," I admitted.

"And I wanted to apologize."

Okay. On a scale of one to "*that's* never going to happen," I'd been putting the chances of those words somewhere around "none." I stared at her.

Verity grimaced and shrugged at the same time. "This is my fault. Well, technically, it's the snake cult's fault, but if I hadn't been on that show, I wouldn't have blown my cover, and we wouldn't be in this mess. I'm sorry. I'd take your place if I could."

"Well, you can't," I said. "You look too much like Grandma."

"I know. That doesn't mean you should have to be the one who pays for what I did. Look, Annie, I know we're not the best of friends, but we're still sisters, and I'm really, really sorry that this is landing on your shoulders. It shouldn't be."

Part of me—the part that's been fighting with her since I was a little girl—wanted to snap and say that she was just jealous that I was going to have a big adventure and she wasn't, for a change. The rest of me knew better. Verity looked like she meant every word she was saying,

like my believing and forgiving her was the most important thing in the world.

And I felt like a jerk, but I couldn't do it. There's too
much bad blood between us to fix with a "sorry" and a
smile. "Yeah, well, it is," I said. "I'll be fine. I got the same
training you did. If you can go undercover on that silly
dance show, I can handle going undercover with the
scary para-military organization of murderers."

"They're not para-military," said Dominic. "They *are*
military. Do not make the mistake of thinking of them as
anything short of an army. They'll destroy you if they
catch you. More importantly, they'll *unmake* you, and
take whatever they learn from you to use as a weapon
against your family."

"They can try," I said flatly.

"And what will you do when they ask you to kill for
them? Because they will. They train soldiers. They train
assassins. Neither is useful if it can't finish the job."

"I'll run," I said.

"You can try," he said, and his voice was as flat as
mine had been, and his eyes were so very, very cold.

I shivered, turning to Verity. "He always this cheery?"
I asked.

Verity shook her head. "Sometimes he's downright
dour."

Dominic grumbled wordlessly.

He was wrong. I wouldn't become a killer for them. I
would lie. I would cheat, and steal, and pretend to be
someone I wasn't. But they were *not* going to change me.
I could kill, if I had to, if the danger was great enough.
That didn't make me a killer.

It made me a survivor.

Our driver pulled up in front of a convenience store
that looked like it was two steps away from either being
shut down for health code violations or "accidentally"
bursting into flame for the insurance money. I couldn't
imagine anyone shopping there if they had any other
option—and since I could see two more healthier-
looking convenience stores and a big chain pharmacy on
the same block, there were definitely other options.

"Here we are," said Verity cheerfully. "Hey, thanks, Pris."

Our driver flipped her off, and didn't help us get my stuff out of the trunk. The second the doors were shut she was gone, hitting the gas and peeling out so fast that Dominic jumped to avoid getting his foot run over. Rather than rushing to her husband's side, Verity shook her head and said fondly, "Dragons. They never really change, and that's amazing. Come on, this way."

Then, to my disgust and dismay—but not surprise— she turned and walked into the convenience store.

The inside was as bad as the outside. I've shopped in some pretty sketchy establishments (usually because the cruddy hole-in-the-wall comic book stores are the ones where you're most likely to find the buried treasures), but this one made me want to take a shower. And then maybe another shower. And then maybe a third shower, just to be safe.

A beautiful blonde woman sat behind the counter, face buried in a trashy romance novel. She didn't look up when the door opened, or when it swung closed behind us.

"Afternoon, Miri," said Verity.

Miri grunted, and continued her unbroken streak of not looking up.

"This way," said Verity, beckoning for me to follow her to a door marked EMPLOYEES ONLY. The sign was Sharpie on what looked like the top of a pizza box. Definitely some high-tech security.

Only maybe there was, because Verity had to undo three locks to get the door open, and only one of them had been visible. "The dragons closed this bodega for a while, when they first moved in with William," she explained, opening the door and holding it for me and Dominic to pass by. "They still owned the property, though, and when the Freakshow burned down, Kitty convinced them to reopen it as part of the temporary rental agreement between them and the bogeymen. They provide a guard, Kitty promises not to make any noises about getting her security deposit back when time comes for the locals to move on."

"Some guard," I said.

"Oh, she is," said Verity. "She has a panic button linked to the main room, and we always have at least one therianthrope waiting for signs of trouble. She pushes that button, there's an angry tanuki in the bodega five minutes later. I just wish the dragons would let us clean the place. It used to be spotless, difficult as that may be to believe, and it was a lot more feasible that people would actually shop there. Now, they want it to look abandoned when they move back out, so we're not even allowed to mop."

"Ew," I said.

"Precisely my thought," said Dominic.

The employee door connected to a short hallway. It ended at another door, this one unlocked. Verity pushed it open. On the other side was a boxy little space with no exits to the street. The walls were brick; it looked like maybe it was an alley in the beginning, until too many buildings got jammed up against it and cut it off from its original purpose.

Someone had chalked a hopscotch grid on the pavement. Verity stepped carefully around the lines. Dominic, to my surprise, hopped on one foot through half the grid before turning to wink at me. I grinned. He smiled back.

"This was the original home of the dragons of Manhattan, until they found out about William," explained Verity, heading for a nearby door. "They're not selling the property for a lot of reasons. Using it as a rental space for cryptids in crisis is one of them. They're also thinking it might be nice to have an aboveground place where their kids can play in a few years, once they figure out how to deal with the little boys. They have wings, and can fly until they're about ten years old. So there's definitely something to be said for giving them the chance to see the sky before they're grounded."

"Right," I said, trying to figure out where she was going with this.

Verity opened the door, flashed me a smile, and stepped through. I moved to follow. Dominic put a hand on my shoulder, stopping me. I looked up at him, warily.

"Try not to be too hard on her, if you could," he said. His voice was soft, sympathetic; he understood why I'd be hard on her, even if he didn't agree with it. "Your sister genuinely regrets what happened. The people who died on that stage were her friends, and she couldn't save them. That, alone, should buy her a measure of sympathy. To have her failure compounded by the loss of the Freakshow, and now you being sent to my former fellows to learn how much they know . . . this is killing her inside. She never meant for this to be the outcome of her dancing."

"But it is," I said. "She was selfish. She was *always* selfish. She knew she was putting the rest of us at risk when she went onstage, and she did it anyway, over and over, because she wanted to. Because she thought having a gift meant she got to decide whether the rest of us get put in danger. Because she thought Alex and I didn't count as much as she did. This is her fault. She has to own that."

"She's trying," he said, casting a quick glance in the direction Verity had gone. "Every day, she's trying. So please, for my sake, if you could try as well, that would be . . . well, that would be an enormous favor."

"I'm only here for a few hours; I can try for a few hours," I said. "But I'm not going to stop being mad at her, and you don't get to ask me to do that."

"That's fine," said Dominic, looking relieved. "A few hours is all I can in good conscience ask of you. Thank you, Annie."

"You're welcome," I said, and pushed past him through the door.

The room on the other side looked more like the sort of place I usually hung out than the sort of place where I expected to find Verity: it was huge, with a polished wooden floor and a catwalk around the edges of the second floor. The roof was easily twenty feet overhead. I looked at it, eyes wide, and wished desperately that I had time to strap on my skates and find out how fast I could go from one side of the space to the other. The people would have made for an interesting obstacle course, which just made it more tempting. They were scattered around, mostly sitting on camp chairs at card tables, like they were roughing it in the great indoors.

There was no furniture that couldn't be moved quickly, and there were some dubious-looking chains hanging from the ceiling. I eyed them before turning to Dominic. "Slaughterhouse?"

"A very long time ago," he said. "Prior to our current occupation, this was the Nest of the local dragons."

"So you've said." Verity was heading toward us, a short, plump, apparently Inuit woman wearing an explosion of lace and black fishnet following close behind her. The woman was carrying a parasol, despite the fact that there was no sun to block. I gave the pair a dubious look. "Um."

"Ta-da!" Verity stopped in front of me, gesturing to her companion. "Istas, meet my baby sister, Antimony. Antimony, meet Istas. She's going to help you with your hair."

"Nice to meet you," I said automatically, before following it up with, "Wait, what? I'm sorry. There seems to have been some confusion. I can handle my own hair. I've been doing it for years."

"That may be so, but it will be a faster, cleaner process if you have help," said Istas. She spun her parasol. "Henna is more pleasant with an extra set of hands."

"It's really not necessary," I said.

"It will be easier," said Istas. Her tone remained neutral the whole time, like this was a discussion about how much she was willing to pay for coffee. "Trust me. I was the stylist for the Freakshow, before the building was burned by cowards. I am very skilled."

"Istas is the best," said Verity.

The name finally clicked home with something Verity had said in her letters home. "You're waheela, right?" I asked.

Istas nodded. "I am," she agreed.

"Okay, cool." I'd never spent much time with a waheela. I really do prefer to do my own hair, but the chance to hang out with a new type of therianthrope was too much to resist. "There's just one thing we have to do first."

"What is that?" asked Istas.

"This," I said, took a deep breath, and said, more loudly, "Professor Xavier is a jerk!"

One of the outside pockets of my backpack stirred before the zipper eased open a few inches and a mouse popped out. She looked cautiously from side to side. Then she ran up the backpack and jumped into my waiting hand. I raised it to chest height, giving her a clear view of the room around us.

"Istas, may I present the current junior priest of my line, and my companion on this voyage. I can't pronounce her name, since I'm not an Aeslin mouse, but she and I have agreed that 'Mindy' is an acceptable thing for me to call her. Mindy, this is Istas. She's a waheela. She will not eat you."

"Hello, carnivore," said Mindy, forcing her whiskers forward in the wide fan that served the Aeslin as a gesture of greeting. She was only trembling a little. I was very proud of her.

Verity looked impressed. "Okay, how in the hell did you convince an Aeslin mouse to be quiet for that long?"

"I am on a Spy Mission," said Mindy proudly. She pulled herself to her full, if diminutive, height, and squeaked, "Hail to the Arboreal Priestess, who did not know I was here!"

"Hail," agreed Verity, sounding faintly amused. "My colony's in the wall, if you wanted to say hello."

Mindy looked to me for permission. I nodded.

"Go say hello," I said. "I'll call for you when it's time for us to go."

"Thank you, Priestess," squeaked Mindy. She jumped back down to the backpack, ran from there down to the floor, and scampered away. Some of the people in the room turned to watch her go, but none of them moved to stop her or interfere. They really had been living with Verity for a while.

Speaking of Verity . . . I turned back to her, and said,

"Mindy's going with me to serve as a black box, in case I don't come back."

Her face fell, amusement transforming into guilt. "Annie, I'm so—"

"I know, and this isn't the time to get into it, okay? She's the only mouse going with me, because there's no way I can hide a colony *and* keep the Covenant from realizing something's up. She has safe words to tell her when she can come out—hence the thing about Professor Xavier—and signals to tell her when she needs to hide and stay hidden until I give her the all-clear. She takes her mission very seriously."

"Aeslin always do," said Verity, still looking guilty. "I really am sorry."

"And I really do mean it when I say this isn't the time. It would be fun to yell at you and know that you'd just take it, but if Istas and I are going to fix my hair and get me ready, we need to get started." I turned to Istas. "You know the layout. Lead the way."

She sniffed the air twice, in an almost canine gesture, and wrinkled her nose. "A shower first, I think. After that, we will begin."

When the terrifying shapeshifting carnivore says it's time to shower, it's time to shower. I grabbed my backpack in one hand, the handle of my suitcase in the other, and followed Istas across the slaughterhouse to something less complicated than my family.

I sat wrapped in a towel while Istas applied the henna to my hair, humming in a not-unpleasant voice while she worked. Occasionally, she'd ask me to move my head to one side or the other, but for the most part, she seemed content to treat me like a living prop, and I was happy to let her. Again: less complicated than my family.

Being a natural brunette in a family of blondes, it took me a while to learn to love my hair. Henna helped a lot. From the first box I bought at the Hot Topic in the mall to the better-quality stuff I started having delivered to the family post office box when I turned eighteen, henna has never let me down. It doesn't damage my hair like box color and bleach, and it doesn't require hours sitting at the salon. Best of all, even "brightening" henna will never turn me into a blonde. I don't have to feel like I'm trying to make myself look like someone I'm not. I'm just turning myself into a brighter version of, well, *myself*, and that's okay. That doesn't speak to a bad self-image. That doesn't mean trying to find a therapist.

(When your family works with things that officially don't exist, therapy is an interesting proposition. Pretty much anyone you talk to *has* to be a part of the community, since otherwise "this morning I helped a harpy lay her eggs" is the sort of sentence that can lead to medication or involuntary committal. I could probably use some therapy. I think the same is true of most of my relatives. But that doesn't make it easy.)

Mindy was off with Verity's mice, swapping newly-developed rituals and reinforcing the strength of their respective oral histories. Aeslin mice never forget anything they see or hear, and there doesn't seem to be an upper limit to their memories—at this point, our family colony contains the memory of dozens of generations of mice, chronicling the lives of seven generations of Prices, Healys, Harringtons, and Carews. Mindy probably doesn't know the intricate details of the worship of my mother, since she has never been a part of that priesthood, but she can provide the rough shapes of every major life event Mom has experienced since meeting my father. Where she shines, as a member of my priesthood, is at remembering *my* life. Everything that has ever happened to me is preserved in the memories of the mice.

What happened to me in Europe would be preserved, too. That was why Mindy wore a very small tracking device built by my cousin Artie on a beaded string around her neck. It was inert and untraceable unless activated. She was incredibly proud of the responsibility, which marked her as chosen above all others in my priesthood. And if something happened to me—if the Covenant caught on, if I wasn't going to be coming home—that tracking device would give the rest of my family something to look for. Because even when something was as far as possible from the desired outcome, it was important to plan for it.

"This is a good color for your skin tone," said Istas, beginning to wrap my head. "Once it is set, I would like you to permit me to trim your split ends and shape the hair around your face."

"It doesn't need—"

"It is clear that you prefer a hairstyle with a minimum of fuss. I can provide that, and you will lose very little length. But doing this will change the way your cheekbones appear to the casual onlooker, and may complicate facial recognition from photographs. Not enough, should you say something you should not, but sufficient to reduce your resemblance to yourself." Istas continued wrapping. "I will not even attempt to talk to you about makeup."

"Thanks."

"You should not thank me. You have an excellent complexion. You would make a beautiful canvas."

"I know *how* to do makeup. I just generally don't, unless there's a good reason." Being a high school cheerleader was like going to cosmetology school, only without the degree at the end. If there's a trick to blending foundation or enhancing eye color, I know it. I even remember most of it, thanks to the parts that are also applicable to roller derby. (We don't wear nearly as much makeup, and what we do wear trends toward the waterproof and aggressively Gothic, but there's only one way to hold the average mascara brush.)

"May I suggest deciding this is a good reason?" Istas finished wrapping and stripped her gloves off, dropping them into the waiting basin. "Makeup is excellent armor against some of the things the world will throw in your direction. This would not be a poor time to go armored."

"I'll think about it," I said. I'd been thinking about it. Most of the carnie kids I knew didn't wander around fully made-up at all times, but there's reality, and then there's expectation. The Covenant might think that someone who came from an American carnival would always look like a Kardashian sister. If that was the case, there was going to be a lot of lip liner in my future.

"Excellent," said Istas. "Please sit still until I return. The henna needs to set." She turned and left the room, stylish kitten heels clacking against the floor, and I was alone.

I closed my eyes, settling deeper into the seat as I took a deep breath and considered the merits of freaking out. This was it: this was the last time I was going to be Antimony Price for I didn't even know how long. Unlike Verity, who's been running from her family and her identity since as far back as I could remember, I'd never wanted to be anyone but me. I *liked* being me. I wasn't perfect, but no one was, and at least I was familiar with my imperfections.

Footsteps approached me. I didn't open my eyes.

"Annie?"

The voice was Verity's. I didn't open my eyes even harder.

She sighed. "Look, I know you're mad, and I know Dominic asked you to take it easy on me, and I know we're not like, great friends or anything, but this isn't me coming to try apologizing again. This is me coming with an update on your mission."

"Okay." I opened my eyes. "What's the sitch?"

"I have your paperwork." She handed me a large manila envelope with a Las Vegas postmark. "Passport, credit card, ATM card, New York driver's license, student ID card, New York library card, birth certificate on specially aged paper, and a medallion of St. Julian the Hospitaller. He's—"

"The patron saint of carnival workers," I said, and kicked my backpack with the toe of one foot. "Good detail. Can you open the front pocket and pass me my wallet?"

"Sure." She looked slightly deflated. She'd probably been hoping I'd be impressed by the medallion, or give her a sisterly high-five or something. Sadly, that was not on the docket for the day. She probably hadn't even been the one who asked for it. Big Al was notorious for including little extras like that to make a new ID more believable.

My wallet is a battered old leather thing I purchased at a flea market when I was fifteen, thinking it looked cool and would probably take a lot of abuse, given that it was already at least twenty years old. I was right on both counts. Better yet, it's traveled so far and passed through so many pairs of hands that even the route-witches can't read its owner anymore. If I ever lose it, I'm not getting it back; some trucker or bus driver will pick it up and keep it as a lucky charm without ever asking themselves why they felt the urge to do so.

I'd already emptied it of everything that could be used to tie me to Oregon or Antimony Price. My real ID had been abandoned in my bedroom, left on the dresser to gather dust until I either came home for it or the mice claimed it as a religious artifact, to be preserved with the rest of the reminders of my too-short life. The trouble was the distance between here and there, the receipts, the ticket stubs, the proofs of purchase. The small detritus of a life can seem exactly that—small—but it's all too often the thing that trips people up. Someone who claims to have never been outside of Florida has a receipt for a Washington coffee shop. Someone who's supposedly never left the West Coast has a photo strip showing themselves at the Statue of Liberty.

The devil's in the details, and so is the hook. Good deceit begins at the molecular level, and works its way up from there.

"Got any receipts I can have?"

Verity nodded. "There's a bunch in the envelope. All cash, so no one can use them to track us down, all either things that make sense for a carnival girl attending college to buy before going back to her family, or things she would have bought after learning they were dead."

And the dates and locations would be good, too: I knew that much. Verity might be self-centered and a little shortsighted at times, but she was smart, and she knew her shit. She wouldn't give me something that could blow my cover, and I wouldn't insult her by checking each individual receipt in front of her. I'd check them later, at the airport; maybe even discard a few, creating a trail of breadcrumbs for anyone who wanted to use psychometry to verify that I'd really flown out of New York. "ATM code the usual?"

"Yeah. There's about eight hundred dollars in the account. Try to avoid using it unless you have to, since we're not in a position to refill it right now. Save it for emergencies."

"Do my best." I began swapping my new self into the wallet, sliding IDs into place, shoving receipts in willy-nilly. "Social?"

"In the envelope."

I looked. It was there, along with a stack of bills. Mixed dollars and pounds; good. I put them in the wallet with everything else. "How am I getting to the airport? You can't drive me."

"We're going to drive you across town and drop you off. You can hail a cab from there."

That way my starting point wouldn't be the slaughterhouse or the decrepit bodega. It was good thinking. I nodded. "Artie was supposed to be arranging my tech?"

"New phone and laptop are preloaded with your files and ready to go," she said. "The phone has a lot of local numbers, and a bunch of entries for people who died at the Black Family Carnival. We even put in some 'local friends,' in case they try to do a background check by calling random people from your phonebook. They're all cryptids we know, and they'll answer any calls from your new number by addressing you by name and asking if you're enjoying your London vacation."

They seemed to be thinking of everything. I nodded again. I was starting to feel like a bobble head toy. "Did he remember to send me a new iPod?"

"He did. Preloaded, through the new laptop, so it won't have any relict data that could give you away."

"Cool. I think we're good."

"I hope we're good." Verity looked at me gravely.

"You're the only sister I've got, Annie. I don't want anything to happen to you. Be safe over there, okay?"

"I'll do my best." On an impulse, I offered her my free hand. Looking confused and pleased, she took it. "Keep things going over here, all right? I don't want to come home to a smoking wasteland."

Verity laughed unsteadily. I realized, with dull surprise, that she was probably trying not to cry. "I'll do my best, too."

There didn't seem to be anything to say after that. We sat in silence, waiting for Istas to come and wash the henna out of my hair; waiting for the next step of my voyage to begin.

Five

"No matter how fast you run, you can't change who you are."

—Jane Harrington-Price

London, England, walking down Charing Cross Road, approaching Cecil Court, one transatlantic flight later

I WAS DONE.

No. That wasn't quite right. I was a hundred miles past done, cresting into the Fjords of Nope, heading for Fuck-That-Ville. The sidewalk was uneven, traffic was moving in the wrong direction, pedestrians kept looking at me like I was an accident about to happen—which, let's be honest, I probably was—and I was ready to lie down in the street and sleep for a month. Which was exactly why I had to keep going.

Antimony Price, cryptozoologist, derby girl, and sensible person, would have gone straight to a hotel upon arriving in the United Kingdom, where she would have slept and showered and done all those other wonderful things that make the world a less unrelentingly awful place. Antimony Price would never have done this to herself. But I wasn't Antimony Price anymore. No, I was Timpani Brown, last survivor of the Black Family Carnival, and I wasn't here to have fun or take care of my physical needs. I was here for revenge. And revenge did not need a nap.

(That was another advantage to doing this while sleep-deprived: as long as my story didn't slip, the screwed-up chemicals rampaging through my brain would make it harder for a lie detector, magical or mundane, to tell that I wasn't telling the complete truth. Staggering through their door exhausted and miserable made me more credible, not less.)

Dominic's intel said there I'd find a Covenant recruiting office hidden in an antiquarian bookstore on Cecil Court, off Charing Cross Road. Which was all well and good, except for the part where the entire damn neighborhood was made of antiquarian bookstores. I'd never seen so many old, dusty, potentially creepy books shoved into window displays like it was no big deal. If I'd been more awake, they would have been incredibly tempting. As it was, I wished there were a few less of them, just to make this easier. Making things even more fun, England does not believe in American-style street signs. I wound up standing and scowling at a dead end, trying to figure out what to do next. Going back to the airport was sadly not an option.

A hand tapped my shoulder. I suppressed my first impulse, which involved breaking fingers. I suppressed my second impulse, which involved stabbing. Jet lag does terrible things to my nerves. In the end, lacking any other nonviolent options, I turned around.

The man behind me was tall, thin, and dressed like a clerk, which hopefully meant he worked in the area. His wire-framed glasses somehow looked more "scholar" and less "hipster," maybe because his bow tie was accessorized with a camel-hair jacket and a cross-body book bag.

"You look lost," he said. Oh, *definitely* a local: his accent would have gotten him a dozen dates and a marriage proposal at a Harry Potter convention. "Tourist, yeah?"

"First time in London," I admitted. I flapped my free hand helplessly at the buildings around us. "I'm looking for Cecil Court, but I can't figure out what any of these streets are called. I only know I'm on Charing Cross because the man at the ticket booth told me so."

"There's no housing on Cecil Court," said the man,

visibly perplexed. "You know that, right? If you're looking for a hotel, or a hostel, you're going to have to look elsewhere."

"I know. This is an ... errand, before I go and get some sleep. I'm Annie, by the way."

"Leonard, although most people call me Leo," he said, still looking bewildered. "Well, far be it from me to leave a beautiful young woman in distress. I was heading for Cecil Court anyway. Follow me, and we'll get you to your destination."

"You work there?" I asked, falling into step next to him as he started up the street—back in the direction I'd come from, naturally. Sometimes my sense of direction is unforgivable.

"Family business," he said. "I put in a few days a month, to keep my hand in. What brings you to London?"

"Family business," I said. I tried to grimace and yawn at the same time. The resulting expression probably looked like an animation error.

Leo chuckled. "Let's get you where you're going before you pass out on your feet."

"Thanks," I said gratefully, and kept following him. He could have been leading me into a trap and I would have gone willingly, just to know where I was. In a way, I suppose that's exactly what he was doing. He was leading me to the Covenant.

We crossed the street and entered what I had assumed was an alley when I'd passed it before. Silly me. Leo stopped at a storefront. Ornate gold letters on a window display packed with antique hardcovers proclaimed CUNNINGHAM & SONS, EST. 1751.

"This is where I get off," he said. "I hope you find what you're looking for."

"I just did," I said.

He frowned. "Excuse me?"

"Cunningham and Sons," I said, indicating the door behind him. "This is where I'm supposed to go."

His eyes widened, surprise radiating through his features. Then his face smoothed out, turning neutral. "Oh," he said. "I see."

"Yeah," I said.

"I'll just—"

"Yeah."

He held the door for me. That was a nice touch. He closed and locked it once I was inside. That was less nice, more "this is how the horror movie begins." I would have been concerned, but honestly, I was too tired for concern, and this was only the beginning. If I couldn't survive my initial encounter with the Covenant, I might as well not have come. Mindy could find her way home. She knew where the airport was, and mice make amazingly good stowaways when you couple their small size with human intelligence. She'd be okay.

If I'd been aware that exhaustion would make me this calm in the face of death, I would have stopped sleeping years ago.

"Are you not open?" I asked, turning to watch as he pulled the shade over the door. "Because I can come back later, if you need me to. I saw a coffee shop up the street."

"You saw a few dozen, I'm sure," said Leo. He pushed past me, heading for a door behind the counter. "Please stay where you are, and touch nothing. I'm going to get my grandfather."

"Sure," I said, and yawned again, smothering it with my hand.

Leo vanished, leaving me alone with the door—which, while locked, I could easily have opened. This was a test. I wasn't sure whether it was the sort of test where they hunted me down and killed me for letting myself out, or the sort of test where they were giving me one last chance to change my mind. It honestly didn't matter, because I wasn't going anywhere. I stayed where I was, yawning occasionally, and waited.

Seconds ticked by, becoming minutes. I began considering going somewhere after all: to sleep on their floor. They could wake me when they wanted me to talk.

The door behind the counter opened. Leo reappeared, followed by a man who looked a lot like an older version of him. Much older: unlike my grandparents, his had the good grace to show their actual age. He was still in good shape, with a trim figure and surprisingly regal bearing. He was just wrinkled and gray-haired at the same time. Leo's grandfather was well-groomed, what my mother would have called a "natty dresser" in his suit and tie, and leaning on a polished wooden cane that probably contained a sword, or at least had a poisoned tip. I stood a little straighter, smothering another yawn. You only get one chance to make a first impression. I wanted to survive this one.

They walked toward me, taking their time. I didn't say anything, giving them the space to look me over. Leo's grandfather seemed to be looking harder than Leo himself; Leo, in fact, looked slightly sick, like he hadn't been planning on spending his day hiding a body. The urge to say something pithy and reassuring was almost overwhelming. I swallowed it and kept waiting.

Finally, the older man spoke. "My name is Reginald Cunningham," he said. "This is my establishment. Please state your business in a succinct and coherent fashion."

"My name is Timpani Brown," I said. Technically, that was the truth: "Timpani" is my middle name, and "Brown" was my great-grandmother's maiden name, which means it's mine to claim if I want it. The Covenant only ever knew her as Frances Healy, and she'd been a foundling: the name had been a gift to her by the people who did the finding, and she'd given it to the rest of the family, a get-out-of-jail free card in its own way. If the Covenant had a routewitch to sic on my name, they'd find nothing about it that wasn't true. "I'm looking for . . . I mean, I was told that if I came here, I could find . . ." I stopped, letting my fear and uncertainty shine through.

The best lies are built on a sturdy foundation of truth. The more honesty you can put into a con, the more chance you'll have to run it all the way to the end.

"Looking for what?" asked the older Mr. Cunningham. There was still no gentleness in his voice, but he sounded a little less cold: my routine was working. "A first edition? A folio? This is a rare bookstore."

"But that's not . . . all it is, is it?" I looked between

them, trying to project anxiety. "I didn't fly to London for a bookstore."

"What *did* you fly here for?"

Here it was: the big moment. If I couldn't convince them to buy what I was selling, I might as well pack it up and go home — and there was a good chance I wouldn't be able to do that, because I would be dead. I took a deep breath, and said, "I'm looking for the Covenant of St. George. I was told this was a recruitment center, and I want to sign up. Um. Please."

They exchanged a look. Leo gave the strong impression that he was pleading silently with his grandfather. Reginald shook his head before focusing his attention back on me. He took a step forward, suddenly menacing. The cane in his hand looked very much like a weapon.

"Who told you those words, little girl?" he demanded, voice low. "Who spoke those things to you?"

They were definitely choosing "menace" from their menu of options. That was fine. I know how to deal with menace. I swallowed, and said, "I met a man in a bar in New York City. I was . . . my family, my whole family died. Monsters killed them. I guess I got sort of drunk. I was trying to tell people monsters were real, that the government was lying to us and hiding them, and this man, he bought me a coffee, and he sat with me until I sobered up, and he told me about the Covenant. He said St. George was a dragon slayer who founded an order dedicated to keeping humanity safe. He said they were heroes."

I was laying it on a little thick, but my audience seemed to be lapping it up. At least Reginald Cunningham hadn't shown me what was inside his cane, and under the circumstances that was good enough for me. I sniffled, letting myself break eye contact and look down at my feet. There are people who think too much eye contact is just as sure a sign of a liar as not enough.

"He said no one would believe what happened to my family, and he was right, because I've tried to tell a lot of people, and no one's been willing to listen. And he said if I came to London, if I found this bookstore, I'd find the Covenant. I could offer my services. Maybe I could get some peace, or at least a whole lot of revenge." I looked up. "I just want to make sure no one else has to go through what I've gone through."

"Monsters, you say," said Reginald. "What kind of monsters?"

"Wasps. Wasps the size of kittens. They killed everyone, and when I came home to bury my parents, they talked to me from the trees." I shuddered. "They had my mother's voice. They called me by name. They wanted me to go with them. God help me, I wanted to go. I wanted to let them take me into the trees and make the hurting stop. I guess I would have, if one of them hadn't flown too close to the light."

"Apraxis wasps," said Leo.

"Quiet," said Reginald.

"But, Grandfather—"

"I said *quiet*, Leonard," snapped Reginald. His eyes never left me. "Where did this happen?"

"Vancouver. My family owned a small traveling carnival. Um. The Black Family Carnival? I was away taking my SATs when they stopped for repairs and the wasps came. I didn't . . . I wasn't there with them. I lived because I wasn't with them. I don't know whether to be happy I survived or guilty, because maybe if I'd been there, we would have been able to keep the wasps at bay."

Reginald raised his hand. I forced myself not to flinch as he reached out and set it gently on my shoulder. His skin was cool and papery where it touched mine.

"There was nothing you could have done, child," he said. "Apraxis wasps come out of the dark like a wave, and they flow over everything in their path. Your family wouldn't have had any time to flee before the oncoming devastation."

"I should have been there," I said.

"You're here now," he said. His expression hardened. "I don't trust you yet. You'll be questioned, and you'll be tested. But you have come this far, and never let it be said that an order founded in St. George's name turned any earnest supplicant away."

Well, score.

He turned to Leo. "If you would do the honors?"

"Yes, Grandfather," said Leo apologetically. He reached into his coat pocket and pulled out a white rag.

"Whoa, hold on," I said, putting up a hand. "Is this where you ask me whether that smells like chloroform? Is there *any* other way? I'm here because I want to be, but I'm really not in the mood for a three-day headache and depressed breathing, if that's okay."

They both stared at me. Belatedly, I remembered that while Antimony Price was intimately acquainted with the effects of chloroform, Timpani Brown probably wasn't. Exhaustion also had its downsides.

"We had lions for a while," I fibbed. Hopefully the carnival records would support that, or at least not contradict it. "Their trainer preferred to control them with chloroform. All of us had to learn what the risks were, for safety reasons. I *really* don't like chloroform."

"That is a fascinating story, Miss Brown," said Reginald slowly. "Regardless, you cannot be awake when we remove you from this shop. What would you suggest?"

I grimaced. "My jet lag is so bad you could wait fifteen minutes and I'd probably start snoring?"

He raised an eyebrow. I sighed.

"Okay. Chloroform it is. Just try to keep it brief? I'd rather have a clear head when you tell me what I'm trying to sign up for." I yawned. I couldn't help myself. Jet lag really *was* a terrifying mixed blessing: I was about to let myself be knocked unconscious by two members of the Covenant of St. George, who might not be buying my cover story the way I was trying to sell it, and I couldn't work up a decent panic over the idea. I was reaching "mild annoyance," and that's where I ran out of steam. At least if they knocked me out, I'd be able to get a nap before I needed to talk to anyone else.

(And I did need to let them knock me out for real. I can feign unconsciousness pretty well on the other end, but no one has the muscle control to fool a pro into thinking they've been successfully drugged.)

Leo clapped the chloroform-soaked rag over my mouth and nose. The characteristic paint-thinner and rotten fruit taste of chloroform overwhelmed my senses, and the world went gracefully away, taking me with it into the dark.

I was alone. Well, that, or I was in the company of someone who was so good at being quiet that they should probably sign up for the Creepy Lurker Olympics. I didn't open my eyes, instead focusing on my arms and legs, trying to determine whether I was tied down. There's this thing people always do in the movies, where they wake up, try to move, and dramatically discover their chains. Amateurs. There's no way to do that without making noise and attracting attention. I didn't want either of those things.

But there were no manacles around my wrists, and no cuffs around my ankles; unless the Covenant had managed to devise weightless restraints, I was free to move. I opened my eyes.

The room I was in was dim but not dark, like the people who'd put me here wanted to be sure I got the sleep I needed. There was a wall to my left, and a bedside table to my right, complete with lamp, in case I needed more light. I touched my thigh, and found my jeans. They hadn't undressed me or changed my clothes. They might have searched me—*I* would have searched me—but if they had, all my ID matched the identity I was claiming as my own, and I had my St. Julian pendant around my neck, which was a form of ID in and of itself.

The hardest thing about packing to fly to London had been leaving my weapons behind. I'd felt naked getting on the plane, and would probably have been paralyzed with fear walking into the bookstore, if not for the miracle of jet lag. I was starting to think that all dangerous activities should come directly after a transatlantic flight. Regardless, a Covenant search wouldn't have turned up anything more dangerous than the Swiss Army knife in my suitcase, which was there mostly so I'd seem more believable as a world traveler.

I wanted to check on Mindy. I didn't know if the room

was bugged. I rolled into a sitting position, waking the chloroform headache that had been lurking patiently in my skull, and let out a pained moan that tapered upward into a squeak. I *hate* chloroform. People think it's a game, but nothing that knocks a person out is actually funny. The hangover is never worth it.

Once the room stopped spinning, I lifted my head and got a better look at it. It was ... well, it was a room. A proper room. I was sitting on a proper bed, the sort of thing you'd find in a cheap hotel or a college dormitory. There was a dresser against the wall in front of me, next to a glass-fronted bookshelf filled with actual books. My suitcase was next to a chair, with my backpack propped against it; on the chair was a folded towel, two wash-cloths, and a bar of soap.

"Hello?" I said. I didn't have to work to make my voice sound querulous. The headache, and a slowly-waking, bone-deep hunger did that for me. Chloroform and jet lag. The perfect pair.

No one answered. Either the room wasn't bugged, or the people doing the bugging didn't feel like tipping their hand yet. That was fine. I could do some tipping of my own.

"Hello?" I said again, pushing myself to my feet. A wave of nausea swept over me. Pain and hunger are not awesome when taken together. Swallowing the urge to vomit, I took a shaky step toward the door. "Is anyone there? Can I have some toast? Or maybe a bucket?"

No answer. I glanced at my backpack. The urge to check on Mindy was so strong it hurt, and I couldn't. It was too much of a risk. She'd understand. She knew what she was doing when she signed up for this journey. It still ached to turn my back on her and reach for the door.

The doorknob turned easily. All this, and they hadn't even locked me in. I opened the door.

Leo was right outside, looking at his watch. "Ten hours, seventeen minutes," he said, looking up. "Good evening."

It took a moment to realize what he was talking about. I blinked. "You're kidding me."

"I am not."

"You're *fucking* kidding me."

He cracked a smile. "Again, I am not, and also, language, Miss Brown. You've been asleep for over ten hours. Jet lag alone will do that to a person, if it's bad enough, and when it's jet lag plus chloroform, well ... honestly, I wouldn't have blamed you if you'd been out for another three hours."

"What time is it?"

"Half-seven in the evening. We're about to sit down to dinner, if you'd like to join us."

"'We' being ... ?" I was starting to feel like I'd fallen into a really weird BBC production, probably scripted by Neil Gaiman, possibly featuring half the cast of *Downton Abbey*. If someone walked by in a bonnet, there was a strong chance I was going to scream.

"My family and I. Come on. Some food would do you good."

He was right about that. Eating is one of the only things that really minimizes a chloroform hangover. I still hesitated, giving him a careful sidelong look. "Does that mean you've decided to trust me?"

"On a provisional basis, yes," said Leo easily. "We went through your things—you knew that was going to happen, I won't insult you by pretending otherwise—and didn't find anything to set off any alarm bells. You seem to be legitimate. It'll be a while before there's a final verdict, of course, so I wouldn't get too comfortable, if I were you."

"Understood," I said, trying not to let my face show how relieved I felt. If they hadn't found anything suspicious, they hadn't found *Mindy*. Really, that was the important thing. All the rest was just details. "I'd love food. Am I okay to come down as I am, or should I change my clothes first?"

"If you'd woken an hour ago, I'd be suggesting a shower," said Leo. "As it stands, run a brush through your hair and put on a different jumper, and my mother will at least see that you've put in an effort, yeah?"

"Yeah," I agreed. "Um, I'm going to ..." I gestured over my shoulder.

Leo nodded. "I'll be here."

"Cool," I said, and shut the door in his face. Not quite striking a blow against the Covenant that would echo through the ages, but it was still pretty satisfying, especially since I was going to have to make nice with these people.

Very, *very* nice. I wasn't stupid enough to think that infiltrating an organization of monster hunters that had managed to stay under the radar for centuries would be as easy as walking in and saying "what's up, I wanna join." There were going to be tests. There were going to be trials. There was every chance in the world that they were going to ask me to do things that went against my moral code.

But first, there was going to be dinner. I still didn't know whether the room was bugged—I was leaning toward "yes," given how quickly Leo had shown up after I woke—so I didn't call for Mindy, just turned on the light, hoisted my suitcase onto the bed, and got to work making myself halfway presentable.

My hair was still relaxed and well-behaved from the henna. I brushed it as smooth as I could before pulling off my shirt and pulling on a clean sweater. It was demure enough to wear around people I was trying to make nice with, but had a deep enough V-front to show my St. Julian medallion to good advantage. Every little bit helps.

Makeup would probably have helped also, but there was only so far I was willing to go for these people when I was planning to fall right back into bed after dinner. I didn't have a mirror. I looked down, determined that I wasn't showing too much boob, and called it good.

Leo was still waiting in the hall. He raised his eyebrows at the sight of me, and said, "Well, then, you did that faster than I'd expected. Come on. Everyone's dying to meet you."

"I'm excited to meet them, too," I said.

He offered me his arm. I took it. In for a dime, in for a dollar, as the sages say.

My temporary accommodations were at the end of a

long hall, one wall of which was lined in doors, while the other wall was lined in portraits—real, painted portraits. Leo saw me looking as we walked, and grimaced.

"My illustrious ancestors," he said. "The Cunningham line is ancient, distinguished, and all too fond of leaving our elders on the walls to look down their noses at the new generations, which must, after all, be doing *something* wrong."

"Kids these days," I said, deadpan. He couldn't see the part of my mind that was racing, wondering whether I was about to play Dorian Grey. If there was a painted Price somewhere in this building . . .

Leo laughed. "Exactly so. We're always getting into trouble, with our rock music and our flashy trousers."

"I like me some rock and roll," I allowed.

"You seem like a rock and roll kind of girl," he said.

I couldn't tell if he was flirting or not. I sort of hoped for "not." If he was flirting, I'd have to figure out how to deal with it, and no one with a hall full of painted ancestors to remind him of how spiffy keen the Covenant was would do what Dominic had done and run away with a scrappy American cryptozoologist. Even if I wanted him to which, thus far, was not so much. He was nice and he was helpful and he was the enemy. I'd forget that at my peril.

Please don't be flirting, I thought, and kept walking.

The hall ended at a narrow staircase. Leo let go of my arm, taking the lead. Halfway down, I could hear voices. All the way down, they were joined by the faint rustling sounds that accompany any large group sitting down to dinner but not eating yet. They were waiting for us. Way to make a good first impression. I don't like *anyone* who gets between me and my food.

"Chin up," murmured Leo. "We haven't decided to kill you yet."

I forced a smile, trying to look like I thought he was kidding. Timpani would have thought he was kidding. Antimony, though, Antimony *knew* he wasn't kidding.

The stairs ended in a nicely appointed parlor that looked basically like I'd always assumed a London parlor would look, which meant either this place hadn't been redecorated since before World War I, or they maintained the house for the benefit of unexpected Americans. I was inclined toward the first, given the way the wallpaper had weathered. The Covenant had always operated on a "if it's not broken, don't fix it" basis according to Dominic, and that ideology was reflected in their home décor.

Leo led me to a pair of swinging, slatted doors and pushed them open, revealing a dining room easily the size of the living room at home. There was a chandelier. An actual *chandelier*, like that was a reasonable thing to have in a private home. There were also eight people, all of them already seated, who turned to look at us the way cats look at mice.

I did not pull away from Leo and run for the hills. I am still very proud of myself. "Um," I said, to the largest gathering of Covenant members that anyone in my family (not counting Dominic) had seen in decades. "Hi."

"Hello," said a woman, whose sandy brown hair and pointed chin marked her as Leo's mother. She offered a warm smile that would have looked sincere, if it had touched her eyes at all. "You must be Timpani."

"Annie's fine, ma'am," I said. "My folks were carnival people, and they got a little creative with the names."

"I see that," she said. "My name is Joanne Cunningham; you may call me what you like."

Ah: so this was a guessing game, and I could tell that if I guessed wrong, I was going to regret it. "You have a lovely home, Mrs. Cunningham," I said.

She thawed fractionally. "Thank you," she said. "Leo and my father-in-law, you've already met. This is my husband, William Cunningham," she indicated the man next to her, who nodded, "my mother-in-law, Louise, and my other children, Chloe and Nathaniel."

That left two people at the table unnamed. Unlike the Cunninghams, who all seemed to have been hired from the same Central Casting office, they were dark-skinned and black-haired. The man was in a nice button-up shirt and slacks; the woman was wearing a bright orange sari over a white sheath dress.

"Our guests, Hasin and Kumari Pillai," said Joanne. Either she was the family spokesperson, or the rest of them had decided it was better to let her handle this sort of situation. "They were very interested to hear of your arrival, and wanted to meet you for themselves, since there's a chance you won't be staying around long enough for a more general introduction."

Translation: at least one of them was probably with whatever served as the Covenant's security wing, and if I slipped up tonight, I was going to disappear. But no pressure.

Leo led me to a seat, blessedly next to his, which meant I could watch to see which spoons he reached for over the course of the meal. Hopefully, any slips in my table manners would be chalked up to a combination of "jet lag" and "American heathen," and not taken as a sign that I was nervous and needed to be interrogated to find out why.

Once we were seated, Chloe and Nathaniel rose and vanished through a door at the back of the room, returning with large serving trays that would have seemed more ordinary in a restaurant. Leo stood to help them set out the food: roast leg of lamb, rosemary potatoes, green peas, and three cheese plates, one for each third of the table, each with an assortment of cheeses and jams. The trays went against the wall, and the Cunningham children retook their seats.

(It was odd to think of them as "children": Nathaniel looked to be the youngest, and he was at least my age. But the attitude of the older people at the table made it clear that the kids were supposed to bring out the food. I wouldn't be surprised if they were also supposed to clean up and do the dishes. Oh, family.)

"We eat from communal trays, so no one thinks it's poisoned," said Chloe, while Nathaniel drew a finger across his throat in a slicing gesture. "Of course, we could have taken the antitoxin first. Eat up!"

"Chloe," said Joanne sharply. "Do not taunt our guest."

"Is she a guest now, Mum? I thought she was still a prisoner. Possible spy. Or did the blood test results come back already?" She smiled in my direction. "In case that didn't make sense, while you were asleep my dear brother stuck a needle in your arm, and took a bit of your blood for analysis. Have to make sure you're a human being, and not some unspeakable terror trying to infiltrate and devour our delicious flesh. What do you think of that?"

"I think I wish they'd waited until I was awake and could give permission, but I understand why it had to be done," I said. Blood analysis is still the best way to detect certain types of human-seeming cryptid, like dragon or wadjet females. Fortunately for me, my blood didn't have any secrets to betray. "It explains why I'm so hungry, though. Can someone please pass the lamb?"

Chloe looked nonplussed. Apparently, I wasn't rising to the bait the way I was supposed to. That's me, always ruining everyone's fun.

"Reginald tells us you belonged to the Black Family Carnival," said Hasin. He sounded Scottish rather than English, with a more pronounced accent, especially on his consonants. "Terrible what happened to them."

He didn't say "what happened to your family." I took note of that, even as I cast my eyes toward my plate and said, "I wasn't there. I should have been there. I know there probably wouldn't have been anything I could have done, but maybe . . . maybe one more person would have made the carnival seem like a big enough target not to be worth taking. Maybe . . ."

"It wouldn't have made a bit of difference," said an older female voice. I glanced up to find Louise Cunningham looking at me sympathetically. No matter what else happened, I could apparently snow grandma. "Apraxis wasps have been known to destroy entire towns, when they were desperate enough for new minds to absorb. You would have been taken with the rest if you'd been there."

"You can't know that for sure," I said, barely above a whisper.

"No, I can't, and neither can you. But I can be confident enough to tell you that what happened to your family wasn't your fault." She shook her head a little. "You mustn't blame yourself for things you didn't do and couldn't have prevented. That way lies madness."

"It's interesting that your response to what happened wasn't to tell yourself that monsters aren't real and try to find another explanation," said Chloe. "Most people refuse to believe the truth, even when it's staring them right in the face. What's so special about you?"

Wow: dinner *and* an inquisition. I took a deep breath. "I know this is going to sound a little unbelievable, but when I was a kid, I saw a Bigfoot . . ." I began.

Somewhere in the middle of my story, even Chloe started to nod. Maybe I didn't have them yet, but I was getting there.

Maybe this was going to work out after all.

Six

"When your back's to the wall, just remember: you're allowed to take those bastards with you."

— Alice Healy

Handcuffed to the frame of an unmarked black van, being driven through the English countryside

"YOU REALIZE THIS ISN'T NECESSARY," I said, keeping my voice as level as possible. My wrists ached from all the bouncing around. I'd be lucky to get out of this without at least a couple of bone-deep bruises. My things were strapped next to me, and I had to fight not to look at them. I hadn't seen Mindy in three days, not since I'd arrived in London and started the slow, delicate process of convincing the Covenant that I was as clueless and eager as I appeared.

She was a smart mouse. She knew what'd she signed up for, and she'd made her peace with the colony before we'd left Portland. There was plenty of food in the bottom of the bag, along with a bottle of water she had the manual dexterity to open. She was fine. She had to be fine. If she wasn't fine . . .

My brother had taken six mice to Australia with him, and he came back with five. The Aeslin don't blame him—the Aeslin never blame their gods for anything—but he blames himself. He probably always will. There's a flip side to being worshipped by something as innocent and earnest as an Aeslin mouse, and it's knowing that when something bad happens to them, you were supposed to be able to prevent it. You were supposed to be able to protect them. Failure hurts more than anything.

Leo made an apologetic face. I swallowed the urge to slap it off. It wasn't like I could, anyway. Stupid handcuffs. "I'm sorry," he said. "This is standard protocol."

"I put up with the chloroform and the weird questions and being woken up in the middle of the night so you could see if sleep deprivation made my story change." Although if jet lag hadn't changed it, I doubted a little drowsiness was going to; they hadn't thought that one through. "I don't understand what's going on."

"What's going on is your story has checked out enough that we're taking you to the recruitment center," he said. "The bookshop is a family business, Annie. We're not equipped to train new people, and even if we were, Mum would never let us keep you there. It's unseemly."

"I don't think I've ever heard that word used in an actual sentence before," I said.

Leo laughed. "I'll miss having you around. I'm at the recruitment center with reasonable frequency, so I'll still see you, but it won't be the same as sharing a bathroom."

I eyed him dubiously. I still couldn't get a good read on him, and if I didn't know better, I'd assume he was trying to flirt. But he couldn't be trying to flirt, because no human being with the brains to dress themselves in the morning would think flirting with a girl they had chained to a van's internal frame was a good idea. "I wouldn't say we were sharing a bathroom, since your house has five of them," I said. "I grew up in a carnival. Mobile home chemical toilets are about what I'm used to. Your house was the lap of luxury."

"We've had it for a long time," he said, as if the family home wouldn't fetch several million pounds on the current London real estate market. "It's going to be fine. The recruitment center is set up for intake and education. They'll be able to help you avenge your family."

"And I'm handcuffed because . . . ?"

"Because you have to look at things from our perspective for a moment, all right? You came out of nowhere. You went straight for the only safe house we have in central London. Your story checks out, and Lord knows you talk like a carnie, but we have to take precautions in case you're working for the enemy."

"I'm not a wasp," I said, yanking on my handcuffs as if in punctuation.

Leo sighed. "There's a lot more out there than just wasps. Assuming the elders agree that you are who you say you are, you're going to learn that the world is a much darker and more dangerous place than you ever thought it was. I'm almost sorry you've been able to get this far, because you can't go back. You're never going to look at the shadows the same way. You're lost. Just like the rest of us, you're lost."

There was something sad in his voice at the end, like he wished something better for me, something other than this unmarked van ploughing through the British countryside. It was impossible not to feel bad for him. Anger followed close on the heels of my sympathy. He was a member of the *Covenant*. Even if he'd never done fieldwork, even if he was just a secretary sitting in his safe little bookstore, he was still supporting an organization that killed sapient beings for no good reason beyond "we don't like them."

Dominic had been willing to quit for Verity. Dominic had also been disillusioned, in love, and an orphan: he had no family ties to keep him with the Covenant. Leo was different. Leo had a family. He wasn't going to walk away, even if I'd been in a position to ask him to—which I was not. My situation was nothing like my sister's, because I couldn't start making Leo see things from my point of view, and I wasn't here to seduce us another turncoat. That's the sort of battle of attrition we can't win. I had to pretend to see things the way he did, and pray it didn't get me killed.

"My whole family's dead because of the things that came out of the woods, and nobody believes me when I try to say what happened," I said. I didn't have to fake the quaver in my voice. It was born of fear and frustration, not sorrow, but those things can sound suspiciously alike. "I'm already lost. I'm hoping that maybe this is where I can be found."

The van shuddered to a stop. Leo smiled.

"I suppose we're going to find out." He stood, the motion exposing the stun gun strapped to his hip—in case I somehow ripped my cuffs free of the van's frame and went for him, which seemed ludicrous, but was probably standard procedure—and walked, slightly hunched, to the back doors. He hit them with the side of his fist three times. Someone outside knocked back twice. He replied with another three knocks, a pause, and a fourth knock. Code. Lovely.

The doors opened. Light flooded the van. I squinted, only turning my face partially away; I wanted to *see*, no matter how much it hurt.

What I saw was green, the rolling green hills of the English countryside, stretching out toward what seemed like forever. What I saw was a hedgerow of blackberries and brambles and little yellow flowers I didn't recognize. There was a man standing to one side, ordinary looking, the sort of man I wouldn't have given a second glance if I'd passed him working in his garden or walking his dog. He looked like he was in his mid-to-late thirties, with sandy blond hair that was going gray at the temples and wire-framed glasses that somehow hid the color of his eyes. They were probably tinted for some reason, maybe to treat a vision problem, maybe because he spent a lot of time seeking out gorgons and making their lives a short, painful experience.

He looked at me with the slow gaze of the career serial killer, and it took everything I had to keep from shying away. It didn't feel like he was undressing me with his eyes: that would actually have been better, or at least more familiar. It was like he was checking me for weapons without taking a step toward me. Somehow, I had no doubt this man would be able to spot the knives I usually carried and considered so well-concealed, or the various other tricks of my trade that I'd been forced to leave behind when I flew to London.

I have never been so glad to be unarmed. There was no question in my mind that this man would have been happy to make me disappear if I'd been carrying so much as a garrote.

"What's this, then?" he asked, eyes still on me.

"Her name is Timpani, and she's here for assessment," said Leo. He produced a set of keys and unlocked the cuffs holding me in place. I immediately sat farther back on my bench, rubbing my wrists. I made no effort to hide my discomfort. Anyone would have been uncomfortable in this situation, infiltrator or not.

Anyone.

"Where'd you find her?" asked the man.

"She found us. Her family was killed by a swarm of Apraxis wasps, and someone pointed her at the bookstore." Leo was talking like I wasn't there, but his body was angled to partially block me from the stranger's view, giving me time to adjust to both the light and my new freedom. He was trying, in his own small way, to protect me. "She checks out as human, carrying no charms or contraband, and I've been cleared to bring her for further assessment."

"We're taking in strays now?"

"Strays with useful skills, yes. Having an American passport and the specific knowledge set for carnival infiltration are useful skills."

The stranger was silent for a count of five. Then he turned to me, and said, "Come out of there. I want a better look at you, and it's not as if you can hide from me forever. Not if you're planning to train with us."

"Sorry," I said, and scooted down the bench toward the door before standing and hopping out of the van. Leo touched my shoulder as I passed him—a light, reassuring moment of contact. I didn't look at him. My attention was reserved for the stranger, who was continuing to watch me like he hadn't yet decided whether I should live or die.

He cocked his head once I had my feet on the ground. "What's your name?"

"Timpani Brown," I said.

"Funny name."

"Funny parents. Most people call me 'Annie.'"

"What, not 'Tim'?" He smirked. It wasn't attractive. "I'm Robert Bullard. Security in this place funnels through me. I don't like your attitude—or I don't like your face—and they never find your body. How do you feel about that?"

"I'm here because there's no one left to miss me," I said. "Those things took everything when they killed my family. So you can threaten if you want to. I guess you're going to anyway. But if staying here means I can learn how to keep what happened to me from happening to anyone else, I'm going to stay, and you can learn to live with it."

"She's got you there, Robby," said Leo. "Annie, Rob's in charge of security, so when he says something like 'don't climb under that fence' or 'the third floor is off-limits,' you have to listen. But apart from that, he's not going to be in charge of your training, and he's not going to handle your day-to-day. All right?"

"All right," I said, as timidly as I could. "Can I get my things?"

"Please."

My luggage had been assembled to bolster my cover story without overwhelming me in things I'd have to carry. The only piece that was even slightly out of place were the roller skates at the bottom of my suitcase, which were there for my sanity as much as anything else. If they asked me to show them what I could do, skating was on the list, and was a believable carnival skill. Also, I'd lose my mind if I had to play the good little Covenant girl *and* couldn't stay in decent shape.

No one helped me wrestle the suitcase out of the van. Leo looked like he wanted to, but he kept his distance. Probably more tradition, something about the new recruits coming to the Covenant under their own power and without aid. Sometimes the urge to punch tradition solidly in the nose is the only thing that keeps me going.

"All right," I said, finally getting my suitcase into a position where I could drag it if necessary. I looked at the rolling hills, trying to ignore the sensation that the hills were looking back. "Where are we going?"

Robert threw his head back and roared with laughter. Even Leo smiled, although there was less meanness in his expression than there was in Robert's laugh.

"Look behind you," he said.

The van was behind me, but I took his meaning. Hoisting my suitcase, I moved three feet to my right and looked.

We were parked on a graveled hilltop, with a small path winding down from our location to the gates of a stately manner home whose green manicured lawn somehow managed to be even brighter than the hills behind me. Topiary dotted the grounds, and I could see the corner of what I assumed was a hedge maze. There were actual standing stones in the field around the path, and the manor house itself looked like, well . . .

"Shades of Pemberley," I breathed.

Leo laughed. "I suppose it would look like that, to an American," he said. "Welcome to Penton Hall."

"Uh-huh."

"Follow me," he said, and started down the path. I followed him, and Robert followed *me*, so close that I thought I could feel his breath on the back of my neck.

I had good reason for my paranoia. I'd known his name was familiar, and as we walked, I realized where I'd seen it before: in Verity's report on what happened in New York. Robert Bullard was one of the two Covenant agents who'd been whammied by Sarah, when she wiped the memory of Verity from their minds. We don't know much about how Sarah's powers work, especially when she's using them to actively rewrite someone's ideas about the world. When Robert had seen the footage of Verity on TV, had he thought he was seeing her for the first time? Or had Sarah's careful lie come tumbling down?

Maybe more importantly—or at least, more frighteningly—if he was here, did that mean he'd been demoted from fieldwork after his failure in Manhattan? He hadn't been working alone. Was Margaret Healy here, too? The fact that she was a distant relative shouldn't make it harder for me to maintain my cover around her, and yet . . . If there was *anything* about my physical appearance that could give me away, she'd see it, even if no one else would.

The closer we got to the house, the larger it loomed. It was like something out of a Jane Austen novel, as re-interpreted by Stephen King.

"One of the topiaries moves, I am out of here," I said.

Leo cast me a blithe smile. "It's all right, I promise. We do not have killer hedges. The worst we've produced is a few prize-winning carrots at harvest time, and those won't kill you, although they may make you wish for a more varied diet."

The gates were locked. They were also, judging by their size and the lack of cars visible on the grounds, at least partially ornamental. Leo led us a few feet down the fence, where there was a smaller, wooden door, deeply inset to keep it from offending anyone's sensibilities.

"Most of the house rules will be explained once you've been assigned to a room and a training schedule," he said. "The main thing to remember is that, at least for right now, you're considered a guest. That means you need to be on your best behavior, but that also, people will treat you fairly and be willing to answer your questions."

"This is all really complicated," I said. "I thought it would be more like the movies. I'd show up, and say 'monsters are bad,' and you'd hand me a crossbow or something."

"Joss Whedon has so very much to answer for," said Leo, and opened the door.

Curtains twitched in the windows of the big house as we walked along a decorative pathway to the front steps. By the time we got there, the main doors were open, revealing a palatial hallway. Leo kept going, and so I followed, feeling increasingly like I was walking into a museum. A curator was probably going to appear and offer to give me a walking tour. I would have enjoyed that. It would have been less stressful.

"All right: answer any questions you're asked politely and succinctly, consider very carefully before refusing any tests that people want to perform, and remember, I'll be here for the rest of the day," said Leo.

"This is not encouraging me," I said.

"It's not meant to," said a new voice, and Reginald Cunningham stepped into the hall. He was dressed much more formally than he'd been back at the house, with a buttoned-up suit jacket over his white shirt, and shoes polished until they gleamed.

"Sir," said Leo, placing a hand flat across the base of his throat.

"Sir," said Robert, with the same gesture.

Shit.

Reginald's private office was almost as large as the kitchen back home. The walls were lined in bookcases, the shelves groaning under the weight of leather-bound volumes. Portraits hung above them—not of Cunninghams this time, but of elegantly-dressed, stiffly-posed people from at least eight different families, their hairstyles and clothing spanning centuries.

Reginald saw me looking, and said, "With an organization as large and complex as ours, hierarchy is key. We cannot allow our great work to fall to anarchy. These brave men and women have led us as we fought to bring humanity closer to safety, closer to protection. Their names echo through the generations, unsung heroes of the human race. Penton, Fairborn, Carew, McNeil—and yes, Cunningham. I am the second member of our line to hold the august position of minister. You're very fortunate, you know."

"How so?" I asked meekly. Carew. He'd said Carew. One of these people was my ancestor, however many years and generations back. This was where my family came from. No wonder so many of the cryptids we tried to help still referred to us as "that Covenant family." To an organization like this, a few generations was nothing.

Some of the longer-lived cryptids might still be waiting for us to change our minds and go back where we began.

"You stumbled into my home, and not into one of our other more public strongholds. There are those, Miss Brown, who oppose our sacred work: those who feel the human race should willingly share this beautiful world that we've been given with monsters. We must be always on guard for them, and your arrival was . . . ill-timed, in some ways."

I blinked. "Why?"

"Because one of those traitors recently declared war upon us. Do you watch much television, Miss Brown?"

"Some," I said, struggling not to let my discomfort show. "I've been a little busy recently, trying to track you down. Was there something I should have seen?"

"A woman, in an indecent mockery of dress, fighting a giant snake."

"Oh! The *Dance or Die* thing. That was special effects, wasn't it?" I allowed my face to fall. "Wasn't it?"

"I'm afraid not. The giant snake was very real, as was the threat she offered to the Covenant of St. George at the end of her performance. A rogue branch of this organization has been protecting the monsters of North America for decades, complicating our attempts to keep its people safe. The deaths of your family members could have been avoided, had we been allowed to serve the New World as we have served the Old."

I ducked my chin toward my chest, not saying anything. Let him take my silence for shock and anger, not for the fury that it was. How dare he? How dare this stuffed shirt of a man tell Timpani—whose background would have left her a little sheltered, a little credulous—that it was my family's fault that hers was dead? That was a lie.

But it was a lie being told to a lie, and it couldn't be the thing that revealed me.

"Since you've been with us, your blood has been tested repeatedly; your identity has been verified by our researchers; your intentions have not wavered. I am thus inclined to believe that you are who you seem to be, one more pilgrim in an unkind world, looking for the chance to avenge what you have lost. We'll train you, if you truly want that chance. We'll teach you what's in the darkness, and how to defend yourself against it. In return, we'll ask for your loyalty. We'll ask for your obedience. We'll ask for your willingness to accept that we have been fighting this fight in the name of St. George for centuries, and we have reasons for the things we do. I know unthinking submission to the law is not something that comes easily for your generation, but it is necessary, Timpani. Trust in the sword. Trust in the shield. Trust in the hand that holds them."

He'd been moving around the office as he spoke, lingering for a moment in front of each of the portraits. As he finished, he stopped in front of the largest painting, one which showed a man I presumed was meant to be St. George himself, standing atop the body of a slain dragon. It was a heartbreaking portrait of the death of a sapient being, and I was supposed to see it as triumphant and inspiring. Humans are the worst.

"If you stay with us, you'll be asked to swear to the shield regardless of your training, to keep our secrets and to protect the interests of the Covenant. Depending on where your strengths lie, you may be sworn to the secret and the sword, to go into the world and protect an ignorant humanity from the dangers that lurk in the shadows, unseen and unsuspected. Or you may be sworn to the pen and the page, to stay safely home and research ways of making this a safer place for all of us to live. The choice will not be yours. If all you seek is vengeance— immediate, unfulfilling vengeance—this is not the place for you. But if you would change the world for the better, if you would change yourself for the better, we can help you along that road. We can make you better. We can make you more prepared."

The opening narration from *The Six Million Dollar Man* was clawing at my brain, demanding to be recited. I looked gravely at Reginald Cunningham and said, "I would like that."

"Your training begins in the morning, Miss Brown. I

do hope you won't disappoint me." He turned to the door, opening it to reveal Leo. "She's agreed. You may take her to her room now. Don't dilly-dally."

"No, sir," said Leo, stepping nimbly around his grandfather to pick up my suitcase. "Come on, Annie, I'll show you where you'll be bunking until we either break or promote you."

"Thanks, I think," I said. I still had my backpack. I swung it on, offered Reginald a quick, respectful nod, and followed Leo out of the room before either of them could change their minds.

Being slightly smarter than the average bear, I waited until we had gone up a broad, lushly-carpeted staircase and were halfway down the hallway at the top before I asked, "Was there a point to all that?"

"Yes and no," he said. "I'm not going to say we're hurting for recruits, because we're not, but it's a bit hard to get new blood when the official party line is 'none of these things exist, we don't exist, if you think you saw something, you're wrong.' Have you seen that film, *Men in Black*?"

"Classic," I said.

"Well, it's a bit like that. We get a decent number of recruits from the families who've been with the Covenant for generations, and sometimes one of them will marry out and bring in their in-laws, but for the most part, we're a bit of a pyramid scheme gone wrong when it comes to getting new blood. As soon as we were sure you were human and who you said you were, you were going to wind up here, and he was going to give you that speech."

"So that's the 'no' side, then," I said carefully.

Leo nodded. "There was a time when even getting this far would have meant three days of trials, riddles, and sword fighting and all that Camelot crap. But that was long ago. People were more willing to believe in dragons when they'd seen them with their own eyes. The danger hasn't passed; it's just become more clever and more secretive."

"So why keep this a secret at all?" I asked. "Why not

tell everyone, right from the start, 'Hey, PS, there are monsters, and we fight them, and if you send your kids over here, we'll teach them to fight monsters, too.'"

"We did in the beginning, when 'here be monsters' was a warning, and not something clever to put on a T-shirt. I mean 'we' in the academic sense here, not in an 'I was there' sense." Leo chuckled. "If I were as old as the Covenant, I'd be something in need of hunting."

"I suppose that's true," I agreed. If this hall wasn't the length of the house, it was close; we were still walking, and the far wall didn't seem to be any closer.

"But there were always noblemen who didn't want us scaring people with our talk of monsters, and clergy who didn't want us associated with the church—we've been an officially secular organization since the fifteenth century, when the archbishop declared that all monsters had perished in the Flood, and called us zealots and fools for thinking otherwise. Really, the church just didn't like that women were allowed to do as they liked within the Covenant, because we couldn't afford to turn anyone away. We didn't have land or power or much to offer beyond a sword and a chance to make the world a better place."

"Huh," I said, as noncommittally as I could.

Leo didn't appear to notice my lack of enthusiasm. "As to why that little speech *was* important . . . this is dangerous work, Annie. Important, but dangerous. Three of the people I went through my training with are dead, victims of powers beyond our ken. The things we hunt, they're not like lions or tigers or bears. They're not animals. They're monsters, capable of turning a man to stone or melting you from the inside out. They can kill with a breath, a glance, the slightest touch. You needed to understand that before you formally decided to join us."

"Was that also why you drove me here in the back of a van? To make me see how serious this was?"

"That, and it was fun to watch you trying not to yell at me."

I narrowed my eyes. "Watch it. I'm not handcuffed now."

"Ah, but now you're a Covenant trainee, which makes

me your superior. Yelling at me would be a breach of protocol." Leo stopped at an unmarked door, rapping his knuckles against it and waiting for a moment before he pushed it open. "Here we are, then."

"Here we are," I agreed, and followed him into what could have been any college dorm in the world. There was a bed on either side of the room; two nightstands; two bookcases. One side of the room was clearly occupied. There was a colorful duvet on the bed, there were books in the case, and most importantly, there was a large crossbow hanging on the wall next to the window. The other side was featureless and plain, waiting for an occupant.

"This is where you'll be sleeping, for now," he said. "Your roommate should be along at some point. She'll get you acclimatized to the way we do things. Meals are served in the dining room, and the kitchen is open between times, but only for those in active training. Have you got clothes that you can move in?"

"You've been through all my stuff. You know I do."

"Ah, but you see, I'm allowing you the polite fiction of my *not* knowing what your underthings look like. I'll wait in the hall while you get changed. Choose sensible shoes."

I blinked at him. "Why? What are we doing?"

His smile was quick and sharp. "Skills assessment, of course. Hurry now, no time to waste." He stepped out of the room, leaving me to stare in blank confusion at the door.

Skills assessment. I should probably have been expecting that.

With a heavy sigh, I hoisted my suitcase onto the bed intended for my use. Fortunately for me, my cover identity wasn't one to travel without workout clothes. There were yoga pants at the bottom of the case, and a tank top from the first episode of *The Devil's Carnival*, which seemed to be in both character and poor taste. I stripped quickly, changed even faster, and pulled my hair into a ponytail before unzipping my backpack and sticking my head inside.

"I don't know if it's safe, so be careful," I whispered. "But Professor Xavier is a jerk, so please, can you let me know that you're alive?"

A squeak answered from the bottom of the bag. Mindy was still with me. Relief washed over me, stronger than I would have thought possible. I hadn't failed her before I even got started. I could do this. I was Antimony Price, youngest daughter of the greatest family of traitors these people had ever known, and I could *do* this.

I straightened my shoulders and walked to the door. Leo was standing on the other side, patiently waiting for me. He grinned a little at my shirt.

"Did you see episode two?" he asked.

"Oh, yeah," I said. "I liked the soundtrack for episode one better, but they both held together well. We going to do this?"

"We are," he said, and offered me his arm.

I took it.

Seven

"There is no skill so specialized that it cannot be adapted to the business of survival. When all else fails, look to yourself for answers."

—Evelyn Bakcr

In the training room at Penton Hall, trying not to freak out

MY FIRST IMPRESSION OF the training room at Penton Hall was simple: I was back in high school, and this time there was no chance I was going to be able to get a pass to let me skip P.E. All the requisite athletic gear was there, the balance beams, the tumbling mats, the horse; the open area currently playing host to a vicious game of dodgeball, with the players hurling the red rubber sphere at each other like they were hoping for a fatality; the basketball hoops, the climbing ropes, and—slightly less standard—the competition-size trampoline next to the indoor rock wall. It was the sort of place you'd use to train for the next season of *American Ninja Warrior*, and it was swarming with Covenant operatives.

Well. Maybe not swarming. There were maybe thirty people in the space, which was big enough to qualify as "Olympic sized," and half of them were playing dodgeball. But this was still more Covenant operatives than I'd ever seen, and most of them looked cheerfully equipped to kill me if they thought they needed to. Chloe Cunningham was on the climbing ropes, having reached the top before locking her legs around her specific rope and flipping over backward. She hung there, content as a roosting bat, arms dangling and her fingers pointed toward the floor.

"Okay, this is a lot," I said, watching one of the trainees hit another in the face with the dodgeball. "I feel like I should go have a nap before I try doing anything in this room."

"It's all right, Annie," said Leo soothingly. "We just need to get a basic idea of what you can do, and then we can start your training. You grew up in the carnival. What can you do?"

"Um. I'm pretty good on a trapeze, I can do trampoline, I'm *really* good at falling without freaking out about it . . . I don't have the center of gravity for tightrope, but I'm a decent tumbler." I was lowballing myself. A lot. I'm a *great* tumbler, and if I'd had my sister's itty bitty build and willingness to risk exposure, I could have been a medalist. Sadly, I'm too big for the competition circuit, and too ethical to do that to my family.

Being the good daughter that everyone thinks of as the bad daughter sucks.

"Trampoline, okay. We can start there." Leo started across the room, picking his way between the various pieces of equipment with practiced skill. "I don't suppose you know how to use any weapons, do you?"

"Um, knives."

"Knives?"

"Throwing knives, you know." I mimed a flinging motion. "I started practicing when I was a kid. Sometimes the townies could get a little aggressive with the carnie kids, and my mom wanted me to be able to take care of myself if something, um. Happened."

Leo's face softened. "I'm sorry. This has to be bringing up a lot of painful memories."

"Yeah, but it's going to equip me to avenge them. That matters more."

"Good way of thinking about it," said Leo. He looked up and shouted, "Hey! Chloe! Get your worthless butt down here! I need a spotter!"

"Fuck off," replied Chloe genially, before flipping

around and sliding down the rope. She landed primly on the balls of her feet, looking me over before asking her brother, "What, Granddad actually approved her membership application? We'll take any old riffraff these days. What do you want me to do with her?"

"I need to find some throwing knives while she gets warmed up on the trampoline. Can you make sure she doesn't split her skull open?"

Chloe rolled her eyes. "Not my job to babysit your recruits."

"And yet you're going to do it anyway, because you don't want to explain to Granddad how we just got this one and she's somehow already dead."

I didn't say anything. This was the sort of conversation I recognized from dealing with my own siblings, and I wanted no part of it. It would probably end in tears, or at least in someone getting punched.

Chloe rolled her eyes again, harder this time. "Fine. *Fine.* But if she breaks a leg or something, it's not my fault."

"It never is," said Leo. He looked to me. "You okay to get started with Chloe as your spotter?"

"Not if she has a tire iron," I said. "Yeah, we're fine. No one's getting killed today. Go on."

"Going," he said, and trotted off.

Chloe looked at me. "You're a scruffy little American thing that my brother dragged home for no good reason, and I'm not going to go easy on you. All right?"

"Fine," I said. "Let's get started, so we can get this over with. I'm exhausted." That, and I didn't actually want to have a conversation with Chloe. She was clearly the younger sister, resentful of being told what to do, even more resentful when she had to do it. I knew the type. Hell, I *am* the type. Nothing good would come of my trying to talk to her when she was already annoyed.

"Fine," she said, and started toward the trampoline.

Either it wasn't a popular piece of equipment, or everyone else was on some sort of schedule and I'd been lucky enough to choose their off day. Regardless, no one was on the trampoline or the nearby climbing wall. I removed my shoes, dusted my hands and feet with chalk dust from a nearby trough, and climbed the ladder to the bounce mat. It was six feet off the ground, high enough that I could hit it without worrying about breaking an ankle. Also high enough that if I misjudged a landing, I could do myself some serious damage.

"What in the world possessed you to learn the trampoline?" asked Chloe.

She sounded genuinely curious: I decided she deserved an answer. "I was already learning trapeze, and the two complement each other. You can do a lot of tricks moving between them. So I asked some of the clowns to teach me." All true, in a modified sense. Timpani was who I could have been in another life. That made it easier to stick to her story, because it was so close to my own.

"It's still odd."

"Odd but fun." I gave an experimental bounce. The trampoline was top of the line, firm without being unyielding, springy without being squishy. Half the gyms I'd trained with would have killed for this trampoline. The Campbell Family Carnival would have committed acts of mass mayhem, and I would have helped them. I bounced again, higher this time, letting my legs get used to the idea that this was what we were doing now.

The majority of amateur trampoline accidents involve bouncing off the trampoline and slamming into some hard surface that doesn't feel the need to help you out. It's a lot like jumping on a really big bed that way. The majority of professional trampoline accidents—and yes, there are professional trampoline accidents—involve muscle strain and dislocated joints, from getting started before the body is ready.

I bounced again. Chloe was starting to look disgusted. I didn't care enough about her opinion of me to hurt myself. I sat down on the bounce mat with my legs spread in a wide V, bending forward to press my forehead against the rubber as I reached for my feet.

"What are you doing?" she asked.

"Stretching," I said. She knew that—she *had* to know that—and was being a snot for the sake of being a snot.

Again, an impulse I understood, and sometimes even shared, but not one I could indulge right now.

For all that I was basically going through my paces for the Covenant of St. George, I was excited by the opportunity to move. Endorphins are as addictive as anything else, and I'd never gone this long without a decent workout. If being potentially useful as a field agent meant I got access to this room while I was doing my recon, I'd take it. Letting myself get out of shape for the sake of maintaining my cover would just make it harder to escape when the time came.

"You are very dull," said Chloe.

"Safety first," I replied. My muscles felt sufficiently loose for some starting tricks, and so I climbed to my feet, beginning to bounce with greater enthusiasm. I kept my upper body straight while allowing my knees to bend on each impact, absorbing the shock and distributing it throughout my body. Once I had sufficient height built up, I bounced and flipped, doing a three-sixty in the air before landing on my feet once again.

Chloe scoffed. I smiled sweetly in her direction as I continued bouncing, building more and more momentum.

"Seriously, did no one teach you about safety? You must have at least the basics, since Leo asked you to play spotter. Some of the things you can do on a trampoline will leave you dead or paralyzed if you don't go about them the right way." I did another flip, landed on my butt, and bounced back up to my feet. All very flashy, if you didn't do trampoline work. All pretty basic, if you did.

Sometimes the simplest things are the showiest because they don't have hidden difficulties. They're exactly as hard as they look. As if in answer to that thought, my fingertips started heating up. Pyrokinesis is the easiest, showiest trick in the magic-user's arsenal, hence why it tends to be the first to manifest. Lucky me. If I started a fire here, I'd see a lot more fire in short order, when the Covenant strapped me to a stake and lit me up. I shook my hands frantically as I continued bouncing. Chloe gave me an odd look. I stopped shaking my hands and started flapping my arms. She rolled her eyes and turned away.

Still hot still hot still—*damn*. I stuck the fingers of my left hand in my mouth just as they caught fire. Leo was walking back in our direction, a bundle in his arms. He wasn't close enough to have seen the spark. I kept bouncing and flapping, willing my right hand to cool down.

Dammit, Mary, I thought. She was the one who'd been teaching me to deal with this crap, and where was she now? Back in America, haunting her familiar ground, and staying well clear of this nest of dangerous people with terrible ideas. I would have switched places with her in a second, if only to keep them from catching on.

My fingertips were cooling down. I pulled my hand out of my mouth and stuck my arm out by my side, jumping in a T-shape for a moment before executing a series of flips, timing it so I was hitting the trampoline feet first and bouncing up again. A badly timed landing could result in a concussion (best case) or a broken neck (worse, more common case), but I was pretty confident about things like this, and more, I was showing off.

I knew Leo had reached the trampoline when I heard him say, in a distinctly impressed tone, "Damn, Annie, I didn't know you could get that kind of height out of this old thing!"

"If this is what you think of as 'old,' I volunteer to test all your new equipment," I said, and stopped flipping, beginning to bleed momentum back into the mat. After I'd dropped enough to feel like it was safe, I stopped bouncing, landing on my knees and turning the last of my kinetic energy into a slide to the side of the trampoline. Leo was standing there, face turned upward to watch me work. He *looked* impressed.

My cheeks reddened. I didn't want Leo looking at me that way, like he was a person and I was a person and we were just two people who happened to be in the same place somehow. This wasn't a coincidental meeting at a coffee shop or a comic book store. This was a Covenant training facility, and his grandfather was in charge of the whole damn thing.

"Here," he said, offering me his bundle.

It unrolled to reveal a stack of blunt throwing knives. They looked cold-forged, the sort of thing you'd find at a Renaissance Faire "try your luck" stall. I raised my head and eyebrows at the same time, giving him a curious look.

"What do you want me to do with these?"

"Well, that's a bit up to you," said Leo. "I'm trying to assess you. Impress me."

Statements like that have always awakened the part of me that has more competitive urge than sense. I looked around the room, finally focusing on the banners hanging near the ceiling. "Are you using those for anything?"

"Hmm?" Leo looked up. "Those? No, they're leftover decorations from the last ball we hosted. Why?"

I wanted to say something about the . . . the arrogance, and *cruelty* of an organization that hunted intelligent beings having balls so casually, but I didn't. It wouldn't have fit my cover story. So instead, I filled my hands with knives, and said, "Watch this."

It took a few minutes of bouncing to build the kind of height I needed. I was going more slowly this time, both to avoid showing off, and because there's a word for people who bounce full-speed with their hands full of knives. The word is "skewered." Besides, nothing was attacking me or rushing to break my concentration; for once, I had the luxury of going as fast or as slow as I desired. I bounced while Leo watched with anticipation and Chloe watched with exasperation. And once I had the kind of air I needed, I started throwing knives.

There's this character from the X-Men. Clarice Ferguson, better known as "Blink." She teleports and throws energy daggers at people, which means that a lot of the time, she's drawn flying through the air or falling as she impales things. I've done Blink cosplay for four different cons, and I have a pretty good grasp on her style of throwing shit. I jumped and I flung, and one by one, the banners fluttered to the floor, neatly cut away from the rope that held them.

When my hands were empty, I landed on the trampoline in a perfect Spider-Gwen crouch and waited for the reactions. I didn't have to wait long.

"Holy *fuck*," breathed Chloe, finally looking like she was taking an interest in the program. "How did you do that? Can you teach *me* to do that?"

"Annie," said Leo, wide-eyed and staring. "What in the world . . . ?"

"I'd do displays of marksmanship between acts some nights," I said, rolling into a seated position and trying to look shy. "They'd set up the trampoline and hang balloons around the ring, and I'd see how many of them I could break before I ran out of time. I got pretty good. Some nights, they'd fill the balloons with glitter, and the air would sparkle as it fell."

Details can make or break a story. In this case, the details were taken from real life, from acts I'd seen or participated in when visiting the Campbell Family Carnival. Most of the backstory for "Timpani" came from my friends and acquaintances with the show. The Campbells aren't technically family—not by blood—but they raised Dad and Aunt Jane, and they're always happy to see us. I wasn't the one who'd broken the balloons around their ring, at least not the first time I'd seen it. That image will still be with me for the rest of my life.

"How are you with a bow?" Leo asked, leaning forward, eyes suddenly sharp.

I fought the urge to lean away. He looked too interested, like I had suddenly transformed from a toy into something worth coveting. "Crossbow, good, anything else, not good. You can't safely draw a bow while you're bouncing up and down, and I pretty much stick to trapeze and trampoline. Things that keep me as high up as possible." That's the only thing I have in common with my sister. Neither of us has ever been happy with our feet on the ground—although for her, high heels will work in a pinch, and for me, it's always been roller skates.

"All right; we can work with that," said Leo, and offered his hand to help me down from the trampoline. After a moment's hesitation, I took it. This was part of the con. I was going to pull it off, or I was going to die trying.

He held on a trifle too long before letting me go, and he was still looking at me with those covetous eyes. Dying trying might still be on the table.

The next wrinkle in my plan came while I was unpacking my things and getting ready to ask where a girl was supposed to go for a shower in this joint. The door to my room opened. Chloe stepped inside. I stopped what I was doing and plastered a smile onto my face, in case she was here to haul me off for some new series of tests I didn't want to take and couldn't afford to fail. Instead, she glared, marched to the dead center of the room, and pointed at the floor.

"This," she said, in a tone that was distinctly shriller than it had been earlier, "is *my* side of the room. If your filthy things wind up on my side of the room, I'll have them burned."

I blinked. "You're my roommate?"

"No," she said. "*You* are going to be *my* roommate. Temporarily. And you're never to forget the hierarchy in this room. I was here first. You're a short-term do-it-yourself project, and I will not yield to you on matters of cleanliness, window positioning, or anything else."

"Wow." I blinked again. "You're super important, aren't you?"

Now it was Chloe's turn to blink. "I beg your pardon?"

"I mean, I wouldn't trust me, if I were you. I'm a stranger from America, with a story that isn't exactly easy to verify and some really weird skills that only make sense if you believe everything I've said. Which I wouldn't do. So if they're putting you in here to keep an eye on me while they verify my story, you must be super important."

Chloe stared at me for a moment before the corner of her mouth began to twitch. "You're fucking with me. Either I agree that I'm super important and stop questioning you, or I deny being super important and you don't have to listen to me. You have siblings, don't you?"

"I'm the youngest," I agreed, before remembering my cover story. I forced my face to fall, looking down at the open drawer in front of me. "Or I guess I *was* the youngest. I'm an only child now. Not the way I wanted it to happen."

"And since we don't know yet whether you're lying or not, I don't know whether to feel bad for reminding you, or annoyed that you're such a bald-faced liar." Chloe shook her head and sat on the edge of her bed. "You're good. I'll give you that much, no questions asked. You're very, very good."

"If you think I'm lying, why am I even here?" I finished shoving my stuff into the dresser—sans Mindy, who was off investigating the house—before sitting on my own bed and frowning at her, hoping I looked more perplexed than annoyed. "Wouldn't it have been easier to dispose of me in London?"

"It's harder than you'd think to hide a body in London, especially if you're planning to stay there," she said. "We have a private graveyard here at Penton Hall. Your body would never be found, not by the best investigators in the world. London is a city with a remarkable number of cameras."

"So?"

"So those cameras will show you leaving the bookshop shortly after you entered, in your rubbish hoodie, with that odious suitcase of yours, and catching the Tube all the way to Wimbledon. You walked into a residential neighborhood after that. No cameras there. No sign of what happened to you either."

She sounded almost unspeakably smug, and was roughly my height and build. I raised an eyebrow. "You did that?"

"While you were having a nap in the guest room, right after you'd arrived. Having you reappear won't raise alarm bells unless someone reports you missing—and if you're really an orphan, as you say, no one's going to do that."

"And they loaded me into the van through a back door. No cameras there either, huh?"

Chloe's smug silence was answer enough. I shook my head.

"Moments like this make me glad I'm telling you the truth," I said. "You'd just make me disappear."

"I think Leo would be sad about it. He's a little sweet on you, you know. He's also my brother, and your superior, so I'll thank you to keep a safe distance."

"Don't worry about it," I said. "Romance is the last thing on my mind. I'm here to avenge my family, not to start a new one." Leo wasn't hard on the eyes. But Leo wasn't my type, and more, he wasn't Dominic, ripe and ready to be swayed from the creed he'd lived by for his entire life. Leo was a believer. This was where he belonged; this was what he wanted to be doing. Nothing he'd shown me gave me any cause to think differently. And dating Darth Prepboy *really* wasn't why I was here.

Chloe looked at me thoughtfully for a moment. Then she smiled. "You know, I believe you," she said. "Not about everything, mind—that's still being looked into— but about my brother. You're not here to try picking up a husband."

"No, still not doing that," I said.

"Sorry. Leo's quite well-regarded among the Covenant girls, and he's not betrothed yet. Some of them are thinking he might be engaged one day instead, and they're keen for the job."

I frowned. "The difference being ... ?"

"Betrothed is when they do it for you, according to the bloodlines and what's hoped for. I'm to marry a Bullard, for example—Anthony, thank God, not Robert, who's too old and a dreadful bore—because our families haven't been combined in generations. Engaged is when you do it for yourself. Mum and Dad were engaged. He was meant to marry a Post girl, and she a Carew boy, when they fell in love and simply couldn't be talked out of it. It's part of why Grandfather's still in charge. Normally, he'd have stepped aside by now, but there are some members of his cabinet who don't feel my father has what it takes to lead the Covenant, because he broke tradition marrying as he did."

I stared at her like she was speaking a foreign language—which, to be fair, she sort of was. "Um, okay. See, back in America, everybody just sort of falls in love, gets married, maybe gets divorced, whatever. The normal way. No bloodlines involved."

"That's because you're heathens," said Chloe, and laughed, presumably at my expression. Then she shook her head, and said, "It's not like we can exactly go to the club and meet people. The Covenant is a secret society. We protect mankind. We have a sacred duty to keep doing that until all threats are eliminated, until humanity is able to walk in the night without fear. It's easier if our marriages are arranged for us. Avoids inbreeding, guarantees healthy children. Everything we do is for the sake of the next generation, which might be fortunate enough to be the first born without this fight."

She spoke like a rational person, like the things she was saying made perfect sense. Of course they'd have arranged marriages, because who else would understand? And of course they'd go along with it willingly, for the sake of the children as yet unborn, the ones who would inherit a better world built on bones. It was a perfectly reasonable way to look at things.

It was disturbingly close to the way *we'd* always looked at things. It bore a striking resemblance to my family's expectation that one day, you'd go on a job and come back with a fiancé, someone who'd seen how bad things could get, someone who would *understand*. And of course we'd raise our children with smiles on their faces and knives behind their backs, because the Covenant was out there, lurking, a faceless, amorphous monster in the night. We had to be prepared to defend what was ours. We had to be ready to die for a better world.

Whether we'd intended to or not, we'd created ourselves to mirror them, and it had never been more obvious than it was right now, with Chloe making cheerful, measured statements that sounded utterly insane to my unfamiliar ears.

"So what happens now?" I asked, just to break the silence.

Chloe sobered. "We get changed. We go to dinner. Leo and my father continue looking into your story. You train with us, while they do. And when they decide one way or another, whether you're a traitor or an ally, they come for you. They offer you a choice."

"What's the choice?" I asked.

Her smile was almost sympathetic. "I think you know, don't you? Now get something decent on, I won't let you make me late for food—and I meant what I said about touching my things. Don't do it. You'll be sorry."

I already was. "Got it," I said, and turned back to the dresser. It was time to keep playing make-believe, only this time, I wasn't playing for the hand of Prince Thrushbeard from the Butterfly Kingdom.

I was playing for my life.

Eight

"Trust the mice. They may lead you weird, and they may lead you stupid, but they'll never lead you wrong."

— Frances Brown

In a bedroom at Penton Hall, still trying not to freak out

CHLOE WAS ASLEEP: I was absolutely sure of that. The best actress in the world couldn't have snored that loudly, or that consistently, or continued doing it even after I'd started flicking balls of wadded-up paper at her face. The mystery of why there'd been an open bed in her room was answered. Anyone with any status whatsoever around here would demand a new roommate after their first night with her, for the sake of ever sleeping again.

I rolled out of bed and onto the floor, trusting the rug to cushion my fall. It did an admirable job: I landed with barely a thud. Chloe continued snoring without a hitch. As white noise generators went, I couldn't have asked for better. I already knew that there were no cameras on the room—that had been confirmed when Chloe stripped for bed without hesitation or making any effort to cover herself, something I couldn't imagine her doing if she knew there was a chance her grandfather might see the footage—and now I was confident that even if there *were* microphones, they wouldn't be particularly sensitive. They couldn't be.

When I got out of here, I was going to leave Chloe a

note suggesting she look into some sort of sleep study. There was clearly *something* wrong with her breathing.

Sticking my head under the edge of the bed, I whispered as loudly as I dared, "Professor Xavier is a jerk."

Mindy popped out from behind my suitcase and ran to sit primly in front of my face, curling her tail around her paws. Her ears were up and her whiskers were tilted forward; she looked smug, inasmuch as it was possible for a mouse to look smug.

She wasn't alone.

The mouse next to her was slightly larger, its brindled fur spotted with white. It had a downy black feather and a bone bead on a string around its neck, but was otherwise naked. That was unusual for an Aeslin mouse, or at least for the ones at home: most of them wore so much in the way of regalia that they could be mistaken for taxidermied toys. This mouse had his—definitely his; remember, naked—ears flat and his eyes cast down in a gesture of respect. Which meant he wasn't just a field mouse she'd slapped a necklace onto.

I blinked. Mindy preened, clearly waiting for me to be the first to speak.

"You . . . found a friend," I said finally. "Who's your friend?"

"Priestess, I present to you a representative of the Lost Catechisms," said Mindy, her whiskers pushing even farther forward. "His are the descendants of those who remained behind when the Patient Priestess and the God of Uncommon Sense were forced to leave the Obedient Priestess and the God of Bitter Honesty behind as they struck out across the Great Water. For did not the Patient Priestess say, 'Charles, I know you'll never forgive us, but please believe me when I say I love you. Ask the mice. They remember'?"

"Wait." I would have shaken my head, but that wasn't exactly easy, considering I was on the floor. "Wait just a second. Are you saying there are *Aeslin mice* here? Like, *here*-here? At the Covenant?"

"Yes, Priestess," said Mindy patiently.

"Whoa," I breathed.

It's a matter of family record that my great-great-grandparents had been forced to leave their two elder children behind when they left the Covenant: Charles and Ada Healy had been under the age of consent, and the Covenant hadn't been willing to let them go. The thought that a branch of the family colony might have chosen to stay, even knowing how much danger they were putting themselves in, had never crossed my mind. But of course they would have stayed. Of *course*. Where there were members of our family, there were Aeslin mice.

I focused on Mindy. "Did you—did the colony—know about this when they sent you with me? That there might be other Aeslin here?"

"We suspected, Priestess," she said, with a quick, almost human nod. They'd picked up the gesture from us, along with so much else about the way they lived. "Those who chose to stay and chronicle the lives of the Obedient Priestess and the God of Bitter Honesty knew they might never have a close relationship with their gods, for they were to be raised Outside the Family, by those who Did Not Understand. But still, we had a duty, and Duty Must Be Fulfilled."

The strange mouse glanced at me, head still bowed, like he was trying to assess my reaction.

I held very still, largely because my first response was the strong desire to leave the room, find any distant cousins I had in the building, and punch them until my knuckles hurt. Aeslin mice put their faith in us, in every sense of the phrase, and all they ask in return is protection, the occasional plate of cheese and cake, and the security of knowing their gods love them. The mice who'd chosen to stay with Charles and Ada—them and their descendants—had given up those things for the cold comfort of doing what they saw as their duty to the family. They had been *neglected*. They had been *ignored*. And it wasn't fair.

"What's your name?" I asked finally, in a soft voice.

The strange mouse made a chittering noise and twitched his tail in a complex pattern, accompanied by a half-swivel of one ear and a systematic bristling of his whiskers. It took about as much time to perform as my own name would take to say: Aeslin are nothing if not efficient.

"Okay," I said. "I don't have the anatomy to say that— I'm sorry—so I'm going to have to give you a nickname if I'm going to identify you. Is that acceptable?"

The mouse puffed up like I'd offered him a medal and a pony. "To be so named, to be so nicked, would be the greatest of honors." He hesitated before adding, shyly, "Priestess."

And there came the urge to punch the world again. I kept my voice gentle, and said, "Then I'm going to call you 'Mork.' Are you okay with that?"

He puffed up further. "It is an Honor, Priestess!" he squeaked loudly.

Too loudly. Chloe's snoring broke, becoming confused snuffling. I looked over my shoulder. She rolled over and went back to snoring. I returned my attention to the mice.

"You have to be quiet," I said. Mindy was glaring at Mork. I shook my head. "Go easy on him, he's just excited. Mindy, what's the goal here? I can't smuggle a whole colony home."

"We have Made Contact," she said, irritation forgotten now that I was speaking to her again. "Mork will travel with me across the Great Water, and he will speak to the Council of Lineages, and we will decide among ourselves what is to be done. Now that we know they were not Lost, merely Misplaced, we can begin planning properly."

She was such a small mouse, talking so earnestly about finding a way to reunite her people, even though they were continents apart. It would have been inspiring, if it hadn't been so damn terrifying.

It might also be useful. Aeslin mice saw everything, heard everything, and remembered everything they saw and heard. Depending on where the colony lived in the building, Mork could be an invaluable resource.

I'd worry about that later. "Apart from your lost colony, what have you found?" I asked.

"They do not suspect your origins, Priestess; they are

still confirming that you are as you claim to be, but they do not question the shape of your eyes or the color of your hair," said Mindy. "There is one here who is related to you— "

"The Impassioned Priestess," supplied Mork. "She dedicates herself to finding and destroying her colony's lost ones."

I could only think of one person who would fit that description. "Margaret Healy," I said grimly. "That's great. That's just awesome. What's she doing here?"

"Assisting in the education of the young," said Mindy. "You will need to mind yourself in her company."

"Got it," I said. "Anything else?"

"The kitchen stocks a wide assortment of cheeses," said Mindy.

I smiled. "I believe it. Mork, it was lovely to meet you."

"Likewise, Priestess," he said reverently.

"Mindy, keep looking. We need to know anything the Covenant is planning for North America, and *everything* they think they know about us. Nothing is too small, all right?"

"Yes, Priestess," she said. She bobbed her head once, then turned and ran into the shadows under the bed. Mork lingered, studying my face like it was the most impossible thing he'd ever seen. Then he ran after her, and I was alone with Chloe, and Chloe's snoring.

I climbed back into bed and stared at the ceiling. It took a long, long time for me to go to sleep.

The sound of the door slamming woke me. I sat up in the bed to find Chloe already gone, and a note on her pillow:

ARE ALL AMERICANS AS LAZY AS YOU? BREAKFAST DOESN'T WAIT FOR SLUG-ABEDS, YOU CLOD.

She hadn't signed it. To be fair, she hadn't needed to.

She obviously hadn't come anywhere near my bed while she was getting ready—that would have woken me immediately—and since she hadn't opened the door until she was leaving, there hadn't been anything else my brain would register as an automatic danger sound. Chloe was the only possible person who could have left that note. Chloe who snored all night, and then was shitty about me sleeping in.

Chloe, whose nose would probably make an *awesome* crunching sound if I got the opportunity to accidentally punch her in the face.

If the Covenant had a dress code—and let's face it, the Covenant probably had a dress code—no one had gotten around to sharing it with me yet. I dressed as fast as I could, yanking on jeans and a sweatshirt and running a brush through the tangled mess of my hair. I still felt naked without a weapon. I was still smart enough not to carry one. This was enemy territory, no matter how much it tried to look like a boarding school for weirdos; if I put so much as a knife in my pocket, I risked blowing everything.

My family knew they'd been asking a lot of me, asking me to do this. They had. But I don't think any of them really understood what it would be like for me, opening a door and stepping into a hallway with no way to defend myself, no knives or guns or cleverly concealed pit traps. My older siblings have been complaining about playing with me since I was a little kid and realized they would gang up unless I escalated things as fast as possible. What they'd never seemed to realize was that I was smaller than them, and already on the outside of the closed unit they formed. I'd been trying to protect myself. That's what I've been doing ever since.

Here, now, I couldn't protect myself, and I couldn't count on anyone else to protect me. All I could do was continue forward, and hope I could build up enough momentum to let me get away.

Thankfully, I've always had a good memory for directions. I followed the hall to a stairway, narrower and shabbier than the one at the front of the house, and descended it to the room where I'd eaten dinner the night before. Then I stopped, dumbstruck.

The room was massive, easily the size of the high school gymnasium where I'd learned to do a double-tuck back handspring. But the night before, dinner had been me, Leo, Chloe, and Reginald, sitting in an awkward foursome around the edge of one of the long dining tables, making awkward conversation over lamb stew and home-baked biscuits. Apparently, that was either because I'd been in some sort of social quarantine, or because everyone else had been hiding.

They weren't hiding now. The room was packed with people, ranging in age from a large group of teenagers that surged around two full tables—and each table could seat at least twenty people—all by themselves, to a cluster of decorous, much calmer senior citizens. There had to be a hundred and fifty Covenant members present. Most were seated, but some were still in line for what looked like a breakfast buffet, chatting among themselves as they waited for their turn.

I realized the people nearest where I'd frozen were looking at me, some curious, some wary, none of them especially unfriendly. There was no uniform: while the teenagers were all dressed in some variant of black and white, with skirts and slacks combined with plain polo shirts, everyone else seemed to have gone with the "whatever I want" school of fashion. A few men wore kilts. One of the women—Kumari, I presumed, although she was too far away for me to be sure—was wearing a sari. They looked like they'd dressed to be comfortable, not to impress.

My legs didn't want to start working again. I forced them, descending the last of the stairs before anyone could come over and ask if I needed help. A little cluelessness was all to the good, but I needed to avoid letting it look like I was scared of these people, even though I was. They'd been remarkably accepting so far, maybe because my cover story was solid and believable, and maybe because they were the honey badger of evil asshole organizations: they were big enough that they didn't need to give a fuck. If I tried to challenge them, they'd take me out, no fuss, no muss, and certainly no chance of my surviving the experience.

But Timpani wouldn't be afraid. Timpani would see these people as the key to avenging her family. I tried to keep that in mind as I walked across the room to the buffet line, ignoring the way people turned to watch me go. This was . . . this was *ridiculous*. There was no way all these people lived here. There had been a crowd in the gym, but it hadn't been anything like this. I should have seen more of them the day before, unless the Covenant had sent everyone on a holiday to London or something to keep them from being seen by the new girl. That didn't make any sense at all. This was their home. Why would I be allowed to turf them out?

Rescue appeared in a semi-expected form: Leo, stepping up next to me in the line, with a glass of grape juice in his hand. He was dressed similarly to the teenagers, which made me suspect that he was spending the day at Penton; Reginald would never have allowed him to go to work dressed like that.

He was still looking at me like I was a useful tool. That was good. That meant I would never make the mistake of relaxing in his presence. He was nice enough, but something about him still made my skin crawl.

"Bit of a culture shock, hmm?" he asked, sipping his juice. "There was a . . . project on yesterday. Had most of our people out in the field, and then Grandfather asked those who came home to keep to their quarters and to the areas you're not cleared to enter yet, to give you a bit of time to settle."

A project. That, coupled with Chloe's attitude the day before, could only mean one thing. "They were hunting?" I asked, trying to project curiosity, hoping it would cover my disapproval.

It must have worked, because Leo nodded, and said, "Yes. A bit of nasty cropped up over in Bristol. I can't tell you much about it—you're not even an initiate yet—but I can tell you the city is safe, and the mothers can sleep easy, knowing that nothing will come up through the sewers to steal their sleeping children away."

There were so many things it could have been, with the data point of "up through the sewers," and it wouldn't do me any good at all to dwell on them. I couldn't raise the dead. I could only try to make sure there would be fewer casualties in the future—and that started with me. I forced a smile.

"Good," I said. The line moved. I moved with it. "Is it usually so crowded around here?"

"No—like I said, there was a project yesterday. Some folks came in from their usual postings for that. Everyone loves a guaranteed win. Others are here to discuss, well, you. You're a special one, Annie. We don't get that many recruits seeking us out. Usually, we have to go and find them. Add the carnival background, and well. You could open a lot of doors for us, if we handle things correctly."

"Carnivals are important?" I asked.

"You probably don't realize, since your family's human, but a lot of monsters hide in traveling shows. It's easier to be a freak when there's a banner to convince people that you're faking it. If you can infiltrate those places, you can be an enormous asset."

"Whatever it takes to avenge my family," I said firmly.

Leo grinned. "That's the spirit."

The buffet was surprisingly varied, as long as what you liked for breakfast involved butter, frying, more butter, more frying, and possibly a soft-boiled egg. I stared in dismay until Leo took the plate from my hand.

"Let me," he said, and led me down the length of the serving table, dishing up portions of various things. He handed the plate back when it was full. I transferred my dismayed stare to its contents.

"Is this a joke?" I asked. Mushrooms have no place on a breakfast plate. Neither do baked beans, or fried tomato, or whatever that slice of squishy black stuff was. There was bacon, but it was outsized and soggy-looking, and there was a dismaying absence of potatoes.

"No, this is a celebratory breakfast for our brave warriors, and half of these things won't be here tomorrow, when we go back to eating normally, so you ought to tuck in now." Leo smiled encouragingly. "It's all right. I promise, nothing's poisoned. You're special, but you're not worth killing half the field agents in England to take down."

"You sure know how to flatter a girl," I said, and followed him obediently back to a table. Reginald wasn't there. Chloe was, and she looked mildly dismayed to see me. I offered her my sunniest smile. "Morning, Chloe. Thanks for letting me sleep in. Hey, did anybody ever tell you that you snore? You should maybe get that looked into."

Chloe's jaw dropped. "What?" she demanded. "How dare you—"

"Relax, Chloe; everyone knows you snore," said Leo, settling into a seat. "It's why there's always an open bed in your room, even when the rest of us are sleeping two to a bunk. Honestly, I'm surprised she's that nice about it. Or looks that well rested."

"Carnivals can be noisy," I said. "I just had to tell myself it was the noise from the road, and I was fine." That wasn't *quite* true—sleep had involved a lot more sticking my head under my pillow and praying—but it sounded good, and sounding good was key.

Chloe sulked. Actually sulked, sticking her lower lip out like a toddler and slouching in her chair. "It's not *fair*," she said. "Everyone else got to go chasing beasts through Bristol, and we had to sit here and babysit your little American girl. If she'd shown up just two days later, I'd have already been in the field."

"But she didn't, and I wouldn't have been in the field anyway," said Leo. He glanced to me, and explained, "I'm a researcher, sworn to the pen and the page. I prefer to keep my hands and my cuffs clean, and support the Covenant in other ways."

"He means he can't hit the broad side of a barracks," said a new voice, immediately followed by a woman with auburn hair sliding into one of the free spaces at our table. She had a plate of food, a cup of tea, and a face I could have picked out of any crowd in the world, because I'd grown up surrounded by variations on the same theme.

Margaret Healy looked at me, polite indifference writ across her features. For the first time, I was grateful to be the odd man out in my family's genetic party game, because judging by the total lack of recognition in her eyes, she didn't take me for a Healy. But give her a dye job, and she could have been my older sister.

"You must be the new American recruit," she said. "Have they started putting you through your paces yet?"

"I did, um, some assessment yesterday," I said. "I don't really know what comes next."

"Annie, this is Maggie Healy, one of our field specialists," said Leo. "She's on assignment to Penton right now, to help with the training process. She'll be working with you on your marksmanship and general fitness."

"Oh," I said. So that was the punishment for blowing a field assignment: demotion to P.E. teacher for the new kids. I couldn't decide whether that was unconscionably cruel, or just cruel enough.

Then I remembered Mork, and the way he'd looked at me, like he'd never been allowed in the presence of a Priestess before. Margaret's punishment was nowhere near cruel enough. It never could have been.

"I'm sure we'll get on fine," said Margaret, apparently taking my shortness for worry. "Just do everything I say without question or complaint, and I'll have you ready for the field in no time."

"What if I'm not suited for fieldwork?" I blurted the question before I had time to think about it, and it was all I could do not to wince. I forced a weak smile, and amended, "I mean, Leo did the training, and Chloe says he can't do it, and I just . . . I want to know that I'm doing some good. My family deserves that."

Chloe narrowed her eyes, like she didn't believe my hasty cover-up. Leo shook his head.

"After your display with the knives yesterday, I wouldn't worry about that. You've got the skills for this, and you've got the drive for it as well; honestly, the only thing that's going to keep you out of the field is the review of your background, and the need to get you properly trained." Leo's smile was encouraging. "You've got a very good shot at avenging your family."

"You're Batman now," said Margaret, leaning over the table and nabbing a sausage off my plate.

I wasn't sure which dismayed me more: the food theft, or the reminder that she was a person. All of them were *people*. They watched television. They read books. They existed in the same world I did, and they thought it was okay to kill innocent creatures for the crime of not being human. I'd never felt more isolated from my own species than I did in that moment, or farther from the chance of going home.

"Buck up, new girl," said Chloe. "Looks like you're going to get everything you want."

"Yay," I said, with as much enthusiasm as I could muster. I picked up my fork. I needed to keep my strength up if I was going to get through this without stabbing anyone.

Nine

"Sometimes doing the right thing is the hardest thing in the entire world. Sometimes it costs you everything you have."

—Enid Healy

Waiting outside the library in Penton Hall, six weeks and a lot of bruises later

THE CLOCK ABOVE THE doors had an irregularly loud tick. Sometimes it was silent, counting off the seconds without making a fuss, and then, with no warning, it would amp up to sounding like someone snapping their fingers next to my ear. That was probably one of the dangers of having a clock that was several centuries old and hadn't been repaired since the birth of the United States, but that didn't stop me wanting to "accidentally" break it. A lot. With a hammer.

I forced myself to keep breathing evenly and maintain a neutral expression. I'd survived six weeks of training with these people without breaking a single nose, limb, or piece of treasured property. I wasn't going to fuck up now, not when I was so close to the brass ring of acceptance into the Covenant of St. George. My fingertips were getting hot again. I balled my hands into fists, pressing them against my palms. Hopefully, the gesture would read as nervous to anyone watching me.

(And there was *always* someone watching, except when I was in bed. I guess they figured Chloe could keep an eye on me in the wee hours of the night, which would have been a great theory, if she hadn't been practicing so hard for the Sleep Olympics. Every night, she snored and I held quiet conclaves with the mice, making sure the record was up to date, making sure that when I slipped — and I was *going* to slip if I stayed here long enough — Mindy would be able to tell my family what I'd learned, and what I'd done, and how I'd died. Fatalism. It's what's for dinner.)

Six weeks of training under the watchful eye of Margaret Healy, with occasional assists from Leo, who came down from London on the weekends and was much more easy-going than she was. He took me running and counted off my push-ups and crunches. She taught me knife-throwing tricks I wasn't sure even the Incredible Cristopher knew, and he was the one who'd handled my initial training. She had a vicious eye for traps, and didn't hesitate to make them more lethal than they needed to be. A great teacher, in other words, but not the sort of woman I wanted for my enemy — and she *was* my enemy. She just didn't realize it yet. I didn't get to pick my own exercises, and I was going to be rusty when I got back on skates or back on the trapeze, but I was still working out enough to stay sane.

Six weeks of classes, some taught by Reginald Cunningham for a room packed with teenagers in black-and-white semi-uniforms who giggled at me behind their hands, viewing my placement in their ranks as some sort of punishment or remedial training. None of them seemed to know where I'd come from, and I was grateful for that. I'd managed to avoid most of the mean girls and asshole boys in high school by joining the cheerleading squad and never looking back. That didn't mean I wanted to Drew Barrymore myself back into the scene for a second try.

I'd learned a lot. I'd learned, honestly, more than I'd been counting on. No deep secrets, no inner workings — we knew enough about those from the various ex-Covenant members of our family who'd been kind enough to write things down before dying or being sucked into parallel dimensions — but when it came to "what we've killed recently," they were all too open. My classes had included lectures on how to kill most of the things we shared the planet with, sometimes accompanied by cheerful recitations of the last time those things were killed. Which was always, always much more recent than it should have been. And they talked about North America like it was the holy grail of monster hunting, the continent that resisted all attempts at a proper cleansing, no matter how many teams they sent to try, and die, upon its shores.

(Australia, amusingly, was never mentioned. They appeared to have decided that the right way to deal with the land down under was to pretend it didn't exist, since it wasn't like they could even get an agent onto Australian soil without the native cryptids, and cryptozoologists, bouncing them right back to Europe. North America was still viewed as somehow reclaimable, if they worked hard enough and never gave up. Australia was one big ol' nope.)

Lucky me, I'd also been given a crash course on the Covenant's enemies, with a starring role for—drumroll please—my family. The Price-Healys were the descendants of traitors to the Covenant, and had proven themselves to be traitors to the human race through their ongoing efforts to keep the Covenant out of North America and hence away from all those monsters that needed killing. They knew about Verity, which made sense, since she'd been on television. They also knew about Grandma Alice, who had also been there when Verity declared war. The rest of us were a mystery to them.

Good news: they thought there were substantially more of us than there really were. As in, they were assuming dozens. I wasn't sure how fast Covenant girls were expected to breed, but their projections for the size of our family made me want to cross my legs, like, *forever*. Better news: Margaret didn't remember seeing Verity before her television appearance. Sarah's makeshift mind wipe had been complete enough that it hadn't left any holes. The Covenant still thought Dominic was dead, and thank God and our local telepath for that.

Bad news: they were planning to quadruple their

presence in North America over the next three years and take us out, assuming they could find us. And they *would* find us. They talked about torturing cryptids for information like they were discussing what to have for dinner. To them, anything done to a nonhuman didn't really count and couldn't be considered "wrong." They would come up from South America or down from Canada, and they would find us, and they would kill us all. I needed to warn people. I needed to tell them our fears were justified.

I needed to keep standing in this hallway, waiting for Reginald to invite me into the library and tell me what the hell was going on.

Playing the good little Covenant recruit was sometimes easier than I wanted it to be. I've always tried to be a team player, and when we were doing sprints or practicing marksmanship, we were a team. It was like being back at cheer camp. Only this time, cheer camp was being run by an evil organization bent on stomping my family off the face of the planet, and every time I caught myself having fun, I felt like I was betraying everything I was supposed to stand for.

I needed to get out of here.

The library door swung open just as the clock gave another resounding "tick," and there was Reginald Cunningham, smiling an indulgent, grandfatherly smile. "Timpani," he said. "Thank you for waiting. You can come in now."

"Yes, sir," I said, and stepped over the threshold, stopping when I saw that he was not, as I'd previously assumed, alone. Margaret Healy and Robert Bullard were there, seated in the plush leather chairs and watching me. Leo was also there, but he wasn't sitting down; he was standing by the window, looking distinctly unhappy.

My fingertips flashed hot and my chest got tight. They knew. Somehow, they knew. They'd caught Mindy running through the kitchen, or Chloe was a better actress than she seemed, and had heard me talking to the mice. They were going to kill me. But they were going to torture me first, to find out what I knew about my—

"You've done excellently in your time with us, and I believe it's time we let you put your skills to a genuine test," said Reginald.

I snapped out of my panic spiral and stared at him. "Sir?" I managed.

"I must object," said Robert. He sounded bored. That was better than him sounding homicidal, I supposed. "She's too untried, and she's too *new*. New recruits shouldn't be sent into the field until we're certain they have the stomach for the work."

My stomach twisted. If they were talking about sending me into the field, then they were talking about me killing things. *Sapient* things, or at the least endangered things, things I'd spent my life up to this point protecting.

I could talk a good game, and I could pretend with the best of them, but I couldn't kill an innocent person. Not even for my family's sake.

"That's the beauty of this particular assignment," said Reginald. "She doesn't need the stomach for anything. She just needs eyes, and a quick mind, and the ability to blend in. She's already demonstrated all those things. Margaret will be accompanying her, and can handle any actual conflict. Annie merely needs to observe."

"Um," I said. "If I'm not going to be doing anything, why do I need to go . . . ? I mean, I want to prove myself, but this doesn't seem like proving myself. It seems like making Margaret babysit me."

"Ah," said Reginald. "Yes, I suppose we're getting ahead of ourselves. Timpani, when someone becomes a full member of the Covenant, regardless of whether they were born to it or trained, they customarily complete a trial suited to their particular skills. Now, we're not offering you full membership yet, but we are willing to remove your probationary status if you're willing to undertake a trial now. One that's particularly well-suited to your skills and background. I don't want to rush you into anything you don't feel prepared for, but this is something we didn't expect. An opportunity for all of us to gain ground in an area where we've traditionally been unable to break through."

"What's that?" I asked.

"There is a carnival."

I went cold. If he said the word "Campbell," I was going to have to run, and if I got caught, at least I could tell Mindy: at least I could send out a warning. "Where?" I asked.

"North America. Wisconsin at present, although carnivals move. Our sources say that *this* carnival harbors several inhuman creatures, concealing them among the performers. Not uncommon, we're afraid: we've found quite a few monsters hiding in plain sight."

I did my best to look shocked. "I never knew."

"Some shows are still human in origin. You were fortunate to belong to one of them. This particular corruption is so endemic that we haven't traditionally pursued it ... unless."

"Unless?" I asked warily.

"Unless there have been reports of disappearances in the vicinity of the carnival or circus. Three teenagers have been reported missing by their parents following this show's appearance in their area. We suspect foul play. That, my dear Timpani, is where you come in."

It took me a moment to find my voice. "You ... want to send me back to America so I can infiltrate a carnival for the Covenant?"

"Yes," said Reginald. "Exactly. You won't be unsupervised, of course: Margaret will be nearby at all times, and you'll be able to contact her if you feel you're in danger or find proof that the carnival is behind the disappearances."

"Why not just send in a field team?"

"Several reasons. We don't know if the children are still alive. You might be able to find them. We don't know whether the reports of monsters are accurate, or simply people seeing performers in costume and letting their imaginations run away with them. Most of all, you're already part of the carnival community. If you can make contact here, if you can *convince* them, we may be able to use you as the lever through which we pry open their pretty painted tents and let the light shine through. Show us you're loyal. Show us that you want this. And show us that you're worth our time."

I stared at him. Margaret and Robert continued to watch me calmly from their chairs, while Leo, by the window, looked miserable. I swallowed hard.

"Well," I said, in the lightest tone I could manage. "No pressure, huh?"

They were going to transfer me and Margaret to the London house for three days while our travel arrangements were made. We'd be flying separately to Madison, Wisconsin, where she'd take up residence in a furnished apartment rented off Airbnb, while I'd spend a night in a local Motel 6 before heading out to find the carnival. It was a good plan. It was a solid plan. It was a plan that hinged entirely on my actually being Timpani Brown, former carnival brat, and not Antimony Price, undercover cryptozoologist.

Boy, wasn't the Covenant going to be surprised.

In a way, this was a good thing: they were getting me back to North America. Once I was there, I'd be within shouting distance of dozens of allies, contacts, and honorary family members who could bail me out if necessary. But I was going to be accompanied by Margaret Healy, who hated my family more than anything in the world; and more, I was being sent to a carnival that was already on the Covenant's radar. If I walked in, announced myself, and ran, they'd all wind up slaughtered. No. That wasn't acceptable. I needed to do what I was being sent to Wisconsin to do, at least within reasonable limits. I needed to look for the missing kids and determine how much of the carnival was or was not human.

Once I knew whether they were innocent targets or killers, I could figure out how to tell them they'd attracted the attention of the Covenant—and whether I also needed to notify my parents. The peace between the humans and cryptids of North America can be a tenuous one. Humanity can't know that the cryptids are there, because our response is all too frequently "here there be monsters, kill them, kill them with fire." But that means that when something is actually dangerous, there's no way for the humans to know they need to be taking care of themselves. In our efforts to protect one community, we can inadvertently put the other in harm's way.

There was a knock behind me. I turned to see Leo standing there, collar unbuttoned and hands shoved into the pockets of his slacks, a frustrated expression on his face.

"Annie, I'm sorry," he said. "I tried to talk them out of sending you, but once my grandfather makes his mind up, he's not overly interested in changing it."

"It's okay." I turned back to my suitcase, picking up the next sweater to be folded. "It'll be nice to be back in the States. Halloween is next month, and you people don't even have candy corn. How can you exist in a world without candy corn? It's criminal, I tell you. So this will be good for me."

"I know you're not ready for this."

"Way to show faith in me."

"That's not what I meant and you know it. You've been here less than two months. Sending you to America half-trained, with only Margaret for backup, and into a situation that's going to remind you so much of your family—it's not fair. It's more than we have the right to ask of you."

"I promise I'm made of sterner stuff than that." I smiled at him. "I made it this far, didn't I? I tracked down the mythical Covenant of St. George and convinced you to let me in the doors. I can handle a carnival. It'll be like a vacation after dealing with Margaret's idea of 'light training.'"

Leo laughed. "She can be a bit aggressive, yeah. But you understand why, don't you?"

I shrugged. "I know she shares a last name with those traitors your grandfather was teaching me about. I figured she's probably related."

"She's more than related. She's close family. Her father's father was the son of Alexander and Enid Healy, who deserted the Covenant after being led astray by heathen teachings." Leo said this like it was perfectly reasonable, and not bizarro revisionist history. "They left their children behind when they went, they were in such a hurry to put an ocean between them and people who thought rightly about humanity's place in the world. Margaret should have been like my sister. She should have been born a princess within the Covenant. Good bloodline, centuries of service, grand knights in her family tree. Instead, she's been watched like a hawk her entire life, because some people think deceit runs in the blood. She's angry, and she has every right to be. Those people destroyed her life before she was even born, and there was never anything she could have done."

"That's . . . wow." I tried to look shocked, instead of furious. I wasn't sure it was working. "Why did they leave their kids behind? My parents would have *never* done that to me."

"They were traitors. Who knows how a traitor thinks?"

There was a flicker of motion near his foot. I glanced down and saw Mork running at Leo's ankle, whiskers flat, looking for all the world like he was about to attack the man for the sake of his gods.

Great-Great-Grandpa Alexander and Great-Great-Grandma Enid have been dead for a long time, and I didn't think they were going to be particularly upset by one Covenant member badmouthing them. Mork, on the other hand, wasn't dead, and had become my responsibility the moment he announced his intention to come back to America with me. Quick as I could, I stepped forward, grabbed Leo's hands in what I hoped would seem like an impulsive gesture, and pulled him toward me, away from the enraged Aeslin mouse.

"I don't know how a traitor thinks, but I know I want to thank you, truly, for being so kind to me," I said, staring into his eyes and praying my own hands wouldn't choose this moment to heat up. "I knew I was taking a risk when I came to England. This could have ended so incredibly badly. It didn't, and a lot of that is down to you being such a good friend. We're friends, right?"

Leo blinked, a flicker of surprise rolling across his face before he smiled. "Sure," he said. "Friends. You'll be back here soon enough, mission done, and then you can swear properly, and be a true member of the Covenant. We'll have to go out to celebrate. Just the two of us. Do you dance?"

The question came far enough out of left field that I answered honestly: "Does a mosh pit count?"

His smile could have lit up the room. "Oh, we are going to have a *lot* of fun when you get back, Annie. Keep yourself in one piece, all right? You have training to do, and we need to go dancing."

Mindy had grabbed Mork by the tail and was dragging him under the nearest dresser. Given the utter lack of self-preservation he was currently exhibiting, I had no idea how the Aeslin mice had been able to survive in this building for as long as they had.

Leo was still beaming at me. I smiled back, somewhat weakly. This wasn't part of my playbook. It never had been.

Is he going to kiss me? I thought. *If he kisses me, I'm going to have to let him. For the mice.*

He did not kiss me. Thank God. Instead, he let go of my hands and took a decorous step back before saying, "I think it's going to be lovely having you here. I'll even see about getting you moved to a different room, without Chloe to snore in your ear all night."

"That's okay, I don't—you know what, no. No one is that good of a liar. *Please* move me. She could wake the dead."

"She did, once. We'd been trying to track down this nasty little spirit that kept haunting its childhood home. Finally popped Chloe into the girl's room. The thing materialized to ask us to get my sister out of there."

"What did you do with her?"

"Woke her up and told her to sleep in her own bed."

"I meant the ghost."

"Oh, that. We stuffed the thing into a spirit jar. It's not going to bother anyone else." Leo's smile had a different edge on it this time. "Just think. Soon, that sort of story is going to be yours. Car leaves for London in an hour. See you then."

He turned and left the room, leaving me to stare after him. These people . . .

I had to get out of here. Luckily for me, that was exactly what I was doing.

Ten

"The trick is not learning to disappear. The
trick is learning to hide in plain sight, until
everyone around you swears you belong exactly where you are."

— Jane Harrington-Price

*The baggage claim area at the Minneapolis/St. Paul
International Airport, getting real sick of time zones*

FOR REASONS OF "they can't catch us both if we're never
in the same place at the same time," Margaret and I
flew in on different planes, under the auspices of different airlines. I didn't know what they arranged for her, but
I'd been on a London to Chicago American Airlines
flight, followed by a Southwest Air short-range hopper
to Minneapolis. My next trick was going to involve a
five-hour bus ride to Madison. By the time I got there, I
expected to be just this side of homicidal, possibly with
a side order of setting every damn thing in the world on
fire.

Margaret was going to beat me by at least six hours,
courtesy of *not* having been routed through Minnesota
for no good reason. Madison was only three hours from
Chicago, by bus. This was the Covenant's idea of misdi-
rection, and I *hated* it.

(On the plus side, there weren't many people taking
the middle-of-the-week flight from London to Chicago.
I'd been able to claim a row at the back of the plane as
my very own, allowing Mork and Mindy to crawl out of
my bag and spend most of the flight playing with the

seatback entertainment system while I dozed. It was the most normal thing I'd done in weeks.)

Other things I hated: the fact that I'd just bounced through Chicago, where my Uncle Mike and Aunt Lea lived, and where the Carmichael Hotel with its staff of friendly gorgons was located, and I hadn't been able to tell them I was there. Margaret was going to be watching me like a hawk—for all I knew, she already was. I was pretty sure there'd been no Covenant spies on the plane, because there's devotion to the mission and then there's doing that to yourself voluntarily, and besides, I'd been at the back of the plane, where I could see people coming, but as soon as my feet hit American soil, all bets were off. She could be following me, having lied about her travel plans. They could have sent someone else to make sure I went where I was supposed to go. There were too many variables. It wasn't safe to reach out. Not yet, anyway.

As if triggered by my meandering thoughts, I caught a glimpse of a man who was either Robert Bullard or his long-lost twin. I stretched and yawned, using the motion to cover a slight turn of my head, but the man was gone. The cold feeling he'd awakened in my chest remained.

My suitcase rolled down the belt. I grabbed it and made for the door. I needed to hurry if I didn't want to miss my bus.

One nice thing about jet lag: it can lend an air of re-signed unreality to everything, so situations that would normally seem time-consuming or pointless become dreamlike and fine. I picked up my prebooked ticket from the Greyhound window and climbed onto the bus that would take me to Madison, pausing only to get a Snickers bar and a bottle of Dr Pepper from the vending machines in the bus depot waiting room. My high-calorie snacks tasted like high-fructose corn syrup, cheap chocolate, and chemicals. In short, American. I was home.

I was one of the first people onto the bus. Moving quickly, I jammed myself into a window seat, unzipped my backpack enough to let the mice see out the window without revealing themselves, and put my head against the glass, closing my eyes. Sleep came almost instantly, hitting me with the hammer strength that only seems to follow travel. I never even felt the bus engine come to life. I was gone.

"Priestess."

The whisper was low, insistent, and next to my ear. I made a grumbling noise, and didn't open my eyes.

"Priestess, the Driver of Buses has announced our stop. If you do not wake, I fear we will journey onward to Parts Unknown." A sharp tug on my earlobe punctuated the words.

Aeslin mice have remarkably sharp little claws on their handlike paws. When an Aeslin mouse grabs something sensitive, like an earlobe, it's hard not to pay attention.

"Ow," I muttered, and opened my eyes. Rolling fields of wheat almost ready for the harvest greeted me.

"Hail," squeaked Mindy, still barely above a whisper. She could teach classes on stealth to the rest of the colony when she got home. "No one has troubled your slumber. No one has touched you, or attempted to claim that which is not meant for them. Have we Done Well, Priestess?"

"Mmm-hmm," I said, and yawned. I usually try to avoid talking to myself in public, but this was a Greyhound bus: no one would pay attention or care, as long as I kept it to a low roar.

Of course, that didn't mean Robert wasn't nearby. Maybe I was being paranoid, but the nice thing about paranoia is the way it can keep you alive.

"Have you seen Robert?" I asked, pitching my voice as low as I could.

"No, Priestess," said Mindy. "He did not board this vehicle. For now, we are In the Clear."

"Great. Get back in the bag." I felt her scuttle down my shirt. Yawning again, I sat up and pulled the second half of the Snickers bar out of my pocket. Midway through the motion, I realized there was someone sitting next to me: a wild-haired teenager with eyes as wide as saucers. Oh, joy and rapture. A civilian. I didn't even bother to smile as I looked at him and asked, flatly, "What?"

"Lady, I don't want to like, freak you out or anything, but a mouse just ran into your backpack."

I nodded. "I know. She's mine."

He blinked. "You don't keep her in a cage?"

"Why would I? She knows better than to chew on my books, and it's not nice to animals to keep them in little prisons. I believe in a fair and equal relationship between people and members of the animal kingdom." I scowled at him. "Why? Don't you?"

Confronted with what he was probably assuming was a member of PETA — and not having noticed my leather shoes — he shied away. "Totally, lady, whatever you say. I just wanted to help."

"Well, thanks, but I don't believe in 'help' that enslaves my fellow creatures."

He shook his head and turned away. Not before I heard his mutter of "Freak." I didn't contradict him. The last thing I wanted to do was strike up a conversation with someone I would never see again when I was jet-lagged and exhausted. I needed to save what strength I had.

Then the road bent, just a little, and the Madison skyline came into view.

It wasn't as tall as Chicago or as iconic as London or even as urban as Minneapolis, but there was something to be said for seeing a city appear and knowing I'd be staying there for a while: that I'd have time to unpack my things, wash my clothes, and maybe even re-henna my hair, depending on the facilities at the carnival. My first stop was a motel at the edge of the college district, bare bones and dirt cheap, with clerks who wouldn't ask too many questions and other residents who wouldn't notice if I lit myself on fire. I'd get a good night's sleep, shift myself a few hours back onto local time, and check in with Margaret before I went to find the carnival.

Everything was going to be fine. This time, for sure, everything was going to be fine.

Everything was not going to be fine. Nothing was ever going to be fine again.

The motel where I was staying looked like the sort of place that would feature heavily in a horror movie, something indie with "Camp" or "Blood" or "Night" in the title. Not a major release by any stretch of the imagination. They didn't ask to see ID when I showed up to check in, which was basically the biggest warning sign they could have flashed in my direction.

"Have a nice stay," said the desk clerk, handing over a key—an actual *key*, not a magnetic key-card—attached to a plastic fob.

"I'm going to get murdered here," I said genially, taking it and leaving the lobby before something in there could accidentally come into contact with my skin. The place didn't look like it had been cleaned since the 1970s, if ever. It was possible the depressing atmosphere had caused even the mold to shrivel up and die, leaving the motel preserved for all eternity.

Outside, the motel followed the classic Middle American theme, with doors pointing toward the parking lot and a metal railing stippled with rust surrounding both the stairs and the second floor. I hefted my suitcase against my hip to keep the concrete steps from destroying the wheels, walking past door after identical door until I reached the one assigned to me. The key stuck when I jammed it into the lock. I wiggled it hard, forcing it all the way in before opening the door to reveal a tiny room with a single queen bed, a floral bedspread, a television that was probably older than I was, and two members of the Covenant of St. George.

I did not scream. I did not slam the door. I *did* freeze, but I think that can be forgiven: six weeks of pretending to be an ally does not undo a lifetime of sensible fear. The Covenant were not my friends.

"Hey," I said, with forced joviality. "Did you pick the lock on my room?" *You sillies,* said my tone. *I would have let you in.* "Can you teach me to do that?"

"Shut the door," said Robert.

I stepped inside. I shut the door. I even put down my

suitcase, to make it look like I wasn't planning to bolt at the slightest sign of danger. I did not take off my backpack. My willingness to risk myself did not extend to letting them get my mice.

"I was against sending you on this jaunt from the beginning," said Robert. His tone was flat; his eyes were cold. It was like being lectured by a lizard that had decided to spend some time in human form. "You're American, and Americans are inherently untrustworthy. You don't understand tradition. Not really. Not down to your bones. You're also very new. No one should be in the field after only six weeks with us. It's inappropriate, and it's unfair to you. If you fail, it will be counted against you forever, when we were the ones who sent you into something you're not prepared for."

"I thought this was going to be me and Margaret," I said. I allowed a note of irritation to creep into my tone. I didn't like Margaret, but in a distant, terrible way, I recognized her as family. And no one treats my family badly but me. "Why are you here?"

Margaret, standing against the wall, didn't meet my eyes. That probably wasn't a good sign.

"I don't know how much you retained from your lessons, but our Maggie is the latest scion of a line known for throwing traitors. She's not allowed to leave the United Kingdom without a minder, lest she go the way of all Healys and defect. She and I have worked together before. She knows how to take orders from me. As to why you weren't told, it was a test. We wanted to know how you'd behave if you thought you weren't under supervision."

"Well?" I spread my arms wide before allowing them to slap back against my sides. "Do I pass, or is this where I try to see whether I can run faster scared than you can murderous? Because I can run really fast when I'm scared."

"Calm down, Miss Brown. You comported yourself admirably. You didn't draw excessive attention, you moved between your checkpoints without hesitation, and you didn't have unnecessary contact with civilians.

All in all, you did as well as could have been expected, and substantially better than I'd expected from you."

My first impulse was to get angry. Fortunately for me, my second impulse was to simper and look flattered, and that was the impulse that won. Baiting a member of the Covenant when I was exhausted and unarmed didn't seem like a good way to keep myself breathing.

"So what happens now?" I picked up my suitcase, walking over to sling it up onto the dresser next to the ancient television. "I *need* to get some sleep before I talk to the carnival. I'm so tired that my hair hurts."

"What happens now is we leave." Robert pulled a battered smartphone out of his pocket, holding it up for me to see. "There are two numbers programmed into this. 'Sue' will reach Margaret. 'Tom' will reach me. Only call if you have something to report, or if your life is in danger. Otherwise, you're expected to text us both at ten-seventeen every evening to tell us what's going on. References to food, cats, or having a good time will be taken as a sign that your mission is going well; references to alcohol, dogs, or frowny faces will be taken as a sign you need assistance."

I raised an eyebrow. "You're not the one who came up with this code, are you?"

"Whatever gave you that idea?" asked Robert, lobbing the phone at me. "And it doesn't matter who conceived the code, as long as you stick to it religiously. If you miss two check-ins in a row, we'll come for you, and we won't come gently. Either Margaret or I will call to inform you of any changes to the mission. Do you understand?"

"I do," I said. "Are you going to back off now, and let me convince these people that I'm on their side? Because I can do it, but only if you leave me the time I need to work."

Robert looked at me assessingly. I stayed where I was, trying not to squirm. I needed him to give me the freedom to act. I needed to be able to approach these people on my own terms, to get them to trust me, so I could figure out whether I'd be able to protect them.

And whether I should. If they were responsible for those disappearances—if they were kidnapping children, and especially if those children weren't alive—I would normally have notified my family, and we would have dealt with it. Dealing with it didn't always end bloodlessly. So if they were killers, and turning them over to the Covenant could strengthen my cover, why shouldn't I do exactly that? Why shouldn't I protect humanity and myself at the same time?

I swallowed the urge to shake the thought away. I was tired, and these people were getting to me. I needed to sleep. I needed to *rest*. Once I'd done that, I'd be able to think more clearly, and the idea of turning innocent cryptids over to the Covenant of St. George would stop seeming like something that could ever, ever be "all right."

(Yes, sometimes we killed, and sometimes we did it because cryptids were putting humans in danger. But there was a big difference between a clean kill on home ground and inviting the assassins over to play.)

"You've got your own reins," he said, and stood, walking over to clasp my shoulder firmly. "Don't fuck it up, Annie-girl. You're not going to get another shot."

Then he turned and walked out. The silent Margaret trailed after him, pausing only to shoot me a pained look. I felt almost bad for her. It was pretty clear how the hierarchy here worked, and she wasn't anywhere near the top.

The door slammed behind them. I was alone—only not quite. Shrugging off my backpack, I put it down next to the bed, yawned, and said blandly, "It's sure nice to have a little privacy again."

The sound of scurrying feet from under the bed told me Mindy had taken the hint, and was hauling Mork along with her while she searched the room for listening devices, hidden cameras, and other things that could ruin my night. Without Chloe there to snore and provide cover, I couldn't talk to the mice until we were sure that it was safe. So I sat down on the edge of the bed to wait.

It was a nice bed. So nice. So soft. So comfort . . . able . . .

The room was dark. When did that happen? I blinked several times, trying to make the light come back. The light did not come back. I sat up. Doing so revealed that I'd been lying down before, still fully clothed, atop the sheets of my cheap motel room bed. Well, that probably cut down on the bedbug risk. I glanced at the clock next to the bed. Three AM. I'd been asleep for eleven hours.

"Did someone get the number of that truck?" I asked, of no one in particular.

"There was no truck, Priestess," said Mindy solemnly. "You were Asleep. Exceedingly and utterly Asleep. We attempted, in the traditional manner, inserting pencils in your nose, but you did not wake. You merely threw the pencils across the room and muttered."

I would have been mad, but that particular tradition was my fault, triggered during Alex's "fall asleep doing his homework" phase in high school. I should have known the mice would be watching when I started jamming pencils in my brother's nose, and more, I should have known they would promptly make a holy ritual out of it, because that was what the mice *did*.

"Right," I said, muffling a yawn before I asked, "Did you find anything? I'm assuming no, because you're talking to me."

"We found one device for the listening," said Mindy. "We moved it to the room next door. The woman there is sleeping. We will move it back before she wakes. We have further examined the telephone you were given. It contains no devices for listening."

"Good thinking." There could still be spyware on the phone, but as I wasn't planning to use it for anything the Covenant didn't want me to, that wasn't going to be a problem for me. Bugs that could catch me talking to the mice were a much bigger concern.

Mindy preened. So did Mork, but more shyly. He was still trying to get accustomed to living in a world where his holy figures *talked* to him, rather than shouting "eek, a mouse" and throwing things in his direction.

I yawned again, stretching this time, and wrinkled my nose as I got a whiff of what all that travel had done.

"Okay, I'm disgusting, I'm going to go take a shower. Did you check my bags?"

"There are no unfamiliar devices in your personal possessions; they are not monitoring you in that manner," said Mindy.

"I would bet you my entire checking account that this," I held up the phone Robert had given me, "is equipped to track my every move, even if it doesn't have any listening devices in it. Luckily for me, I'm planning to go where they want me. Got anything else to report?"

"We have stolen half the cheese intended for the continental breakfast," said Mindy.

I shrugged. "Cool by me. Okay, go get their listening device so I can 'wake up' and take a shower. I smell like road kill."

"HAIL THE SHOWER!" proclaimed the two mice, as loudly as their tiny rodent lungs could manage. Then they scurried away, leaving me sitting in the bed and contemplating a future that contained too many variables.

At least it also contained a shower. The mice returned, and I got out of bed. Time to see what was going to happen next.

Eleven

"People can be awfully confusing sometimes. Knives are easier, but knives won't
ever love you."

—Alice Healy

*Walking across a field, because that's a great thing to
be doing at eight o'clock in the morning*

Checking out of the motel was as easy as checking
in: again, they didn't want to see ID, they just wanted
to know if they were gonna get their money. Since I was
using a card provided by the Covenant, I had no issues
with that. (The tip I'd left for the maid was my own
money, but I felt a little bad about how much cheese the
mice had stolen from the kitchen. I had to do something
to assuage my conscience. It turns out redemption costs
twenty dollars left on your pillow. Learn something new
every day.)

According to the briefing I'd received from Margaret
before we boarded our respective flights, I'd find the
Spenser and Smith Family Carnival in a local farmer's
field. They'd rented the place through to the end of the
month, either because business was good or because
they were enjoying the rare spectacle of Wisconsin
during its brief "humans can live here without suffering
overly much" season. My family lived in Michigan before we moved to Oregon, and I firmly believe there's a
reason we chose to leave. Anyplace that gets more than
three feet of snow during an average winter is not a
place where people should be. Unless they are Yeti, and

then they can live wherever they like, but I'm not coming over.

There was a bus from the motel back to the airport, and another from the airport to the middle of goddamn nowhere, which was naturally my stop. It roared away as soon as I stepped off onto the hard-packed shoulder of the road. I barely noticed. I was too busy staring at the tents across the field, as brightly colored as a promise, pennants fluttering in the wind like beckoning fingers trying to lure the indecisive. I started toward them, properly lured. Walking along the road to the front entrance would have been the simplest thing, but all it would get me was a locked gate and maybe some suspicious carnies wanting to know why I was sniffing around. Sure, my suitcase made me look like your classic case of "running away to join the circus," but this wasn't a circus. It was a carnival. The rules were a little different.

Fortunately, I didn't need a rulebook, because I already knew them. I've been running away to join the carnival over and over again since I was six years old and my parents dropped me at the Campbell Family Carnival to learn how to fall. (Nobody teaches you how to fall like a carnie.) It was the first place where I'd felt like I was *me*, Antimony, not just the annoying youngest Price kid. I was defined by more than my place in the family, and it was amazing. If I were ever going to do something other than live the life I have, I would probably go home to the carnival and never leave.

For example, what distinguishes a carnival from a circus? One word: rides. Carnivals have rides. Circuses do not. There's always the rogue rule breaker of a show that decides to have a pony ride or something to entertain the little ones while the clowns get their greasepaint on, but that's about it. Most carnivals don't have a big tent or a tradition of headline acts these days; that went away when people realized it was cheaper and easier to license a Ferris wheel than it was to license a lion. At the same time, everyone loves a good trapeze, and a carnival with a big tent is a carnival that's making extra cash.

(On the whole, smaller, family-owned carnivals will

have big tents, while larger, franchise carnivals that get State Fair gigs will not. But nothing's universal. That's something people learn fast when they start trying to put labels on the wide, weird, wonderful world of the traveling show. Nothing is *ever* universal.)

The field had been harvested recently. Stubble crunched under my feet, providing a constant, irregular accompaniment to my footsteps. The farmer would burn it after the carnival moved on, forcing the nutrients back into the soil to wait for another growing season. It was all very pastoral and organic, and it made me yearn for my customary world of smooth tracks and spinning wheels, where nothing was green but everything was suitable for bleeding on. Bleed here, you'd probably summon something.

Summon something. Now *there* was an idea. I was in North America: I might not have a safe way to phone home, but I could call for Aunt Mary, and if she heard me, she'd come. She always comes. Aunt Rose was also an option, although her limitations meant it might take her longer to get the message to my folks. Mary is a crossroads ghost; she doesn't have to follow the roads. Rose, on the other hand, is and will always be tied to the kindness of strangers, at least when it comes to getting where she wants to go.

The carnival's bone yard was coming into focus ahead of me, more details appearing with every step I took. As with most of the bone yards I'd known, the edges were defined by cars and pickup trucks, parked to block as much real estate as possible from prying townie eyes. After that came the honey buckets, placed to be convenient for the camp without reminding everyone that they were there. The only people who'd choose to lay camp right next to a honey bucket were the ones with small children who didn't yet understand the need to hold it; everyone else would be deeper in.

(Before the lingo gets too thick and turns confusing: the bone yard is the space behind the show where the carnies sleep. Some bone yards are sterile and orderly, indistinguishable from an RV lot. Others are a tangled welter of tents, and look a lot like a campground or a Renaissance Faire. Something that's true of one bone yard may not be true for any others. Most don't have running water, since they tend to be thrown up in vacant lots and farmer's fields, appearing in an hour and disappearing like smoke. Chemical showers and honey buckets — porta-potties — are common, and finding a spot with access to both while not needing to smell either is a common challenge. The older the show, the more tatterdemalion the bone yard. Here endeth the first of what will surely be many vocabulary lessons.)

It was early enough that I didn't see anyone moving around. Carnival folks tend to be nocturnal, and not just because a surprising number of them are bogeymen. Shows happen at night; the tents look best at night; the games seem the least rigged at night. If someone isn't a night person before they join the carnival, they are afterward, once they've learned to sleep when the rubes aren't present. I was getting close enough to pick out the bumper stickers on the cars, close enough to see the colors of the camp tents. This was a good-sized show. I could see six RVs, and at least three times as many tents and portable huts. They probably had a hundred people working for them, maybe more, depending on how many acts appeared nightly in that big tent of theirs.

The air held the delicate mixture of sweat and tears and diesel and hay that haunted my childhood, back when I spent my summers traveling with the Campbells, when I'd thought a life spent on the road was something to aspire to. Maybe it still was, on some level. When you never woke up in the same place for more than a few weeks at a time, you never had to worry about making friends or fitting in with anyone outside the show. You could just relax, and let people take you at face value.

I stepped past the bumper of the first truck. I was no longer in the open field: I was on carnival ground now, with all the responsibilities and rules that came with it.

And someone was watching me.

It was a subtle feeling, a prickling in the hairs on the back of my neck and a tightening in my skin as the part of my brain that was older than civilization and had never really come down from the trees tried to alert the rest of me to danger. My fingertips grew hot. I balled my hands into fists, muffling the incipient flames against my palms. I wasn't here to burn the place down. I was here to convince them to take me on as a member of their family, no more, no less. It was already a tall order without adding arson to the mix. I took a breath, damping down both panic and pyromania, and kept walking.

The air in the bone yard was silent and still, shielded from the wind by the way the vehicles were parked. A faint breeze still whispered through, but it was nothing near as strong as what was blowing outside. Someone was awake enough to be smoking an early morning joint, or else someone had smoked themselves recently to sleep; the sweet, almost medicinal smell of pot hung around a green nylon tent, thick enough to be noted, thin enough that it wasn't a surprise when the smoker failed to put in an appearance.

I passed the honey buckets. A flicker of motion caught my attention. I turned, and there was no one there: just the green vinyl side of a portable toilet, complete with helpful, obscene graffiti suggesting I do something anatomically impossible to start my day off right. I frowned and resumed walking.

I didn't know who I was looking for: my briefing from the Covenant hadn't come with anything as useful as a top-down org chart to tell me who was in charge of hiring and firing. I just knew that if I kept going, eventually someone would stop me to ask what I was doing.

"Stop."

Like that, for example. I stopped. I turned. I offered the speaker what I hoped would look like a timid smile — although given how tired and jet lagged I was, it could have looked like a baby-eating grin and I wouldn't have known. Travel really screws with the body.

"Hi," I said. "I, um, was hoping to find someone who's in charge?" Always make it a question. Questions are harmless. Questions say, "I don't know what I'm doing, ergo I cannot be planning to do you harm." Questions say, "No one would find my body for at least a week." Questions *rock*.

The man behind me frowned suspiciously. He was Asian, taller than me by at least three inches, and wearing a gray sweatshirt with holes in the hem, like it should have gone to the rag bag months ago. He might have been cute if he hadn't been looking at me like I was a new species of bug; as it stood, I sort of wanted to punch him until he stopped. His hair was cut in a short, practical style, a little floppy at the front, close-shaven where it tapered toward the nape of his neck, like he had better things to worry about than grooming. Really, the oddest thing about him was that he was barefoot. I've done my share of barefoot running around in bone yards, and it's generally pretty safe—carnies don't go in for breaking bottles where they sleep any more than the next person. But that was in summer. This was late September in Wisconsin, and there was definitely a nip in the air.

"Why?" he asked. "Who are you?"

"Um, why would be because I don't feel like explaining who I am eleven times while I work my way toward the boss conversation, and who would be Timpani Brown, late of the Black Family Carnival. I'm looking for work."

His face underwent a remarkable series of transformations, from suspicious to familiar to sympathetic and finally back to suspicious again. "Last I'd heard, the Blacks were camped in Vancouver," he said. "It's a long way from Vancouver to here."

"Then the last you heard is pretty damn out of date, because the Blacks are dead." The irritation in my tone was aimed more at myself than at him. Even if Timpani Brown had never existed, I was still claiming acquaintance with the dead—something long exposure to Aunt Mary and Aunt Rose told me wasn't to be done lightly. If I kept telling lies, I was going to wind up haunted. "They picked the wrong place to lay the bone yard, and they paid for it. I was away at school; I lived. Now I'm homeless and don't have a family to vouch for me. So if you could point me to someone who'd like to listen to a sob story, I'd really appreciate it, Mister . . . ?"

"It's not even noon yet," he said, ignoring my request for his name. "I'm sorry about the Blacks, but honestly, how many shows do you know that get up and running this early?"

"Pretty much none," I said. "Try telling that to the bus routes. I got here when I got here, and I figured worst case scenario, I'd crawl under a truck and sleep until somebody woke me up."

"That's a good way to get yourself run over."

"Better than sleeping in a townie shelter. People there don't have any respect for a girl's personal space."

He took a step closer, like that had been a dare. Jerk. "They're probably also less likely to throw you in the dunk tank for disturbing them."

"Probably," I agreed. I didn't give any ground. Going by his build, he was either a performer or a manual laborer; going by his hands, which were callused but clean, he was a performer. Weight lifter, maybe, or acrobat. Either way, I knew his type. Territorial, suspicious, endemic to carnival bone yards. He probably thought he was a lady-killer and wondered why I wasn't swooning. Double jerk. "Look, I walked a long way to get here. Can you either show me someplace I can crash for a few hours, or tell me who I should talk to about earning a bunk on a long-term basis?"

"How about you come back when we're open and buy a ticket like all the other rubes?"

"I don't have any money, and I don't have anywhere to go. I'll wait."

He frowned. Whatever script I was supposed to be following, I wasn't doing a very good job of it. "Come on, shoo," he said. "I have shit to do."

"Like what?" I asked, injecting a challenge into my tone. If he wanted to flex his belonging at me, I was going to refuse to back down. It was a little "no, *you* move" of me, but that attitude had served me well as the youngest child in my family, and I couldn't imagine it failing now.

"Like working out," he said. "It's easier in the morning, when there's no one around to need the ropes."

"Ropes? You do trapeze?"

He nodded, jaw tight.

Great: here was a chance to show I could be useful, even if it was in a small way. "I'm trapeze trained," I said. "I'll spot you."

"Why would I trust someone I just met to spot me?" he asked with a sneer. "That doesn't seem very smart."

"Since you were on your way to work out without a spotter, familiar or otherwise, I'm not expecting 'smart' from you," I said. "Come on. It'll let you decide whether I'm a scary stranger or not. And you'll have a spotter, which believe me, is better than the alternative."

He waffled for a moment, looking like he couldn't decide one way or the other. Finally, reluctantly, he said, "All right. But the moment you do something I don't like, you're not only done helping me, you're getting kicked off the grounds. I can't stop you from coming back tonight. I *can* make sure everyone with the authority to hire you knows you're a bad idea."

"I've been a bad idea for most of my life; I think I'll take the chance," I said, smiling. He frowned and started walking again, his shoulder bumping mine as he made his way out of the bone yard and toward the big tent. I didn't protest—it was a small gesture of territorial dominance, perfectly normal—just chased after him, leaving the slumbering carnival behind.

As with most shows, this one had taken steps to split the bone yard from the midway. We had to pass through three layers of heavy tarp tied shut with pieces of rope before we emerged into the shadow of the Scrambler, lights dim and control panel unattended. The stranger hurried past it, and I hurried after him, letting his sense of direction provide me with the time to check out the show.

You can tell a lot about a carnival by seeing it in daylight, without the motion of crowds and the sound of calliope music to serve as a beautiful distraction. Twilight makes even the shabbiest of shows seem magical and elegant, worthy of your trust and your time. Daylight strips that away, leaving reality behind. The reality of the Spenser and Smith Family Carnival was this: if they weren't running the red line of bankruptcy, they were close enough to see it on a cloudy day, and they didn't care, because every penny they got was going right back into the show, tucked into the mended skirting of the dark rides and welded into the shining struts of their kiddie-coaster. The midway games were rigged and the scares were artificial, but they were bought and paid for with good, honest toil, and nothing I saw set off any red flags worth mentioning.

The stranger reached a solid wall of canvas, painted in the red-and-white stripes that have been customary for such things since the 1800s. He gave me a dour look before pulling aside a flap that had been nicely camouflaged by the repeating pattern and slipping inside. I followed him, not willing to let him out of my sight for any longer than necessary.

The air inside smelled like sweat, popcorn, and horses; they had at least one animal act. I inhaled appreciatively before looking around at the collapsible bleachers and the two tall poles holding the artificial sky in place. As expected, they were kitted out for the flying trapeze, with a net stretched out beneath them to catch anyone who misjudged the distances and fell. Any carnival that cared this much about the condition of its equipment would also care about the condition of its people. Not too much, though. The sort of townie who pays to see a carnival trapeze act wants to think there's the potential for a fall, for blood on the sawdust and screams ringing through the air; that's why there was only one net, and no trampoline.

No trampoline . . . "Hey," I said, looking around for the stranger. "When's the last time you had a trampoline act?"

"No one pays to see somebody bounce up and down like a kid," he said. I followed his voice to the edge of the bleachers. He'd stripped off his sweater, revealing the top half of what could have been a wrestler's uniform. It also revealed his back and shoulders, which were muscled in that unique, incredibly appealing carnival-boy way.

"Um," I said intelligently, before swallowing the surge of hormones (and shaking away the sparks in my fingers) and saying, "A good trampoline act does a lot more than that. But whatever, it's your show. Where do you want me?"

"How about Minnesota? That would make a good start." He started wrapping his hands. "I don't know what you're hoping to accomplish. I don't do the hiring, and if I did, I wouldn't recommend some weird chick who wandered out of the fields and started harassing me."

"Maybe you would and maybe you wouldn't. Either way, I'm here now." I propped my suitcase against the nearest bit of bleacher and shrugged out of my backpack, looking thoughtfully at the trapeze rig. "You might as well get some use out of me."

"You can break my fall if I land on you." He untied his pants.

Under normal circumstances, a man I'd just met getting ready to remove his pants would be greeted with averted eyes, or possibly a kick to the junk. In this case, given what I'd already seen of his uniform, it wasn't a surprise. He saw me looking and froze. I raised an eyebrow.

"Problem?" I asked.

"Yeah," he said, retying the drawstring. "I don't know you well enough for you to see that much of my ass."

"Suit yourself," I said. My own clothes weren't the best for this sort of thing, but I had leggings under my jeans, and my bra was all-purpose enough that as long as I didn't do anything overly fancy, I'd be fine. I pulled my sweatshirt off, revealing the tank top beneath, and bent to untie my shoes.

When I looked up, the stranger was watching me again, frowning slightly. He looked confused, like he couldn't figure out why I was putting up with his crap. Honestly, if I hadn't known about the Covenant team waiting for me to report back, it wouldn't have made sense to me either.

"Can I help you?" I asked. I stepped out of my shoes before unbuttoning my jeans.

His eyes widened. "You don't think we're going to—I mean, I didn't bring you here so I could—"

"As good as it is for my self-esteem to have strangers freaking out at the idea that I might be about to attempt having sex with them, no, I don't think that," I said, and peeled off my jeans. The dinosaur bones printed on my leggings were startlingly white in the gloomy tent. "I just don't think denim is the best thing for workouts. How come you get to strip and I don't?"

"Because I *live* here," he said sourly. He turned and stalked toward the net. Lacking anything better to do, I followed him.

He went up the short rope ladder to the net proper. I followed him there, too. He stood, gripping the individual strands of the net with his toes, and glared at me.

"Seriously?"

"I'm your spotter," I said, spreading my arms for emphasis. I wasn't sure how he was staying upright; I needed the flats of my feet against the grain, or I would have fallen straight through. "Do something for me to spot."

He muttered something unintelligible and made for the post that would take him to the trapeze. I followed as far as the net, climbing up and positioning myself on the rope lattice, feet spread, toes gripping hard to give me extra purchase. That was as high as I was planning to go. This carnival didn't know me. Maybe more importantly, I didn't know this carnival. Every swing and piece of rope has its own personality, its own quirks and difficulties. I would no more go onto someone else's trapeze without a proper introduction than I would put on someone else's underwear. (Actually, the underwear thing is a lot more likely. Bleach can forgive many sins. Gravity forgives nothing.)

The man climbed to the midpoint of the post before unhooking a swing. Not one of the really high, really dangerous ones: the most he could fall would be fifteen feet. Still high enough to snap a neck like a piece of kindling, but a decent height for the first time working with a new spotter. I moved to the side of the net, bracing myself, and prepared for what came next.

What came next was flight. He launched himself into the air, arms ramrod straight, body pointed like an arrow. I've seen a lot of flying trapeze in my time, from all sides of the rope, and it was still enough to bring my heart into my throat with delight and *wanting*. There are so many tricks that can't be performed with only one person. I wanted to be up there so badly that it hurt.

I'm not Verity, with her singular passion for dance, putting it even above her duty to the family, and I'm not Alex, for whom physical exercise has always been something to support his research. I think she'd be happy if she never had to think about anything ever again, and I think he'd be perfectly content as a brain in a jar. I'm somewhere in the middle. I'm the greedy one. I want it all, right now, and all for me. I wanted to find a way to save my family. I wanted to know that I was doing the right thing by being here. And I wanted to be on that trapeze.

The stranger swung back and forth, flipping and twisting on the swing. His form was perfect, but there was something too tight about his shoulders, like he was holding back.

"Look alive!" I shouted.

He shot me a startled look and let go of the swing, twisting in the air before he grabbed it again and let it carry him back to the pole. He hooked the swing back into place, leaned forward, and shouted, "I'd look a lot more alive if you'd get out of here!"

"Not happening." I crossed my arms. "Impress me. Or at least show me why you're up there and I'm down here."

"I'll have you know, I—"

"Samuel Coleridge Taylor, what in the *hell* do you think you're doing?"

The stranger—Sam, apparently—blanched. I turned toward the source of the new voice. It belonged to a short, plump woman with pale brown hair, wearing a patchwork robe over blue jeans and an old yellow sweater. She wouldn't have looked out of place in the stands of a derby match, shouting for her granddaughter to throw a couple of elbows already, did she think this was a *game*. She was striding toward us with remarkable speed, given the length of her legs.

Someone landed beside me in the net. I glanced to the side, confirming that it was Sam, completing an unsafely swift dismount. I couldn't blame him. I would have dismounted in a hurry if this woman had been yelling at me. Speaking of which . . .

"Young lady, you'd best get down from there this instant. Our insurance doesn't have a line for stupid townies breaking legs on our equipment." She came to a halt next to the net, folding her arms and glowering at the two of us.

"Yes, ma'am," I said. "Sorry, ma'am." I've done my share of graceless dismounts, from my share of equipment. No dismount will ever be as graceless, or as swift, as my dismount from that net. I landed on my feet. That was about all that anyone had any right to ask of me, given the circumstances.

"And *you*!" Her wrath switched to Sam, who dropped down to stand next to me. "What were you *thinking*? Oh, no, wait, never mind, you weren't thinking. Really, Samuel, I expected better from you. This is . . . this is . . . I don't even have words for what this is!"

"Sorry, Grandma," said Sam.

Since her attention was on him, I took the opportunity to mouth "Coleridge?" at him, raising my eyebrows.

He glowered at me. 'Shut up,' he mouthed.

I grinned.

"As for you," she said, turning back to me in a motion swift enough to effectively smack the smile off my face, "I don't know where you're from, but you can go right back there, and tell your little friends that we don't need your kind here."

Wait. Crap. This wasn't what I'd been trying to accomplish. "No, ma'am, I think I've managed to give the wrong impression—"

"I don't," said Sam.

"—I'm not a townie. I mean, I'm not from this town. My name's Timpani. I used to be with the Black Family Carnival. I came here looking for a job."

The woman stopped for a moment, frowning as she looked at me. Finally, she said, "The Blacks, eh? You don't have that look to you."

"I'm a Brown, ma'am. I was a knife-thrower and trampoline artist with the show. I wasn't there when the accident happened, and it took a while for me to, well . . . there was a little money, and I didn't feel up to dealing with the road, so I didn't hurry."

"But now the money's running out, and you're getting tired of having the same roof overhead every night, is that it?" she asked. I nodded. She shook her head. "We can't help you. We're a full house, and we don't have room for wild cards."

"Please, I'm begging," I said. "I don't have anywhere else to go."

"And I'm telling you I'm sorry, but we can't help you," she said. "This isn't a show for dilettantes. I don't know what you've been doing since your show closed, but whatever it was, you can go back to it. Get out of the business, or wait until someone's hiring."

"But—"

"Go." She pointed an unshaking finger toward my things, waiting abandoned next to the bleachers.

I looked at her bleakly, then turned and started back toward where I'd left my shoes. This was dandy. I didn't know how the Covenant would react when I told them the carnival wouldn't have me; I couldn't imagine it was going to be good, for me *or* for the show. I could tell them why I was really here, blow my cover and explain the situation, but what if the Covenant was watching? More, what if these people were the reason those kids had disappeared? I could tip them off when they really deserved what was coming to them. Or I could refuse to tell them when they were innocent.

Fieldwork was too damn hard for me. I wanted to go home, put my skates back on, and put all this behind me.

My backpack was lying on its side. The top zipper was

open. Not a lot; just a few inches. More than wide enough for an adventurous mouse to have squeezed through. "Shit," I whispered, opening the zipper wider and sticking my head into the bag. I didn't see any mice. That didn't mean much. It was a pretty full backpack. Trying *not* to look like a crazy townie girl who was talking to her dirty underwear, I whispered, "Hey, are you still in the bag? I need you to show yourselves, because I'm getting kicked out."

No mice answered the call. There was a distinct lack of mouse-ness from the backpack.

"Excuse me, young lady? I need you to put your clothing on and get out of my carnival."

I pulled my head out of the backpack, shooting a panicked look at the woman, who was closer now than she'd been a few seconds before. "Er," I said.

She raised an eyebrow.

I could probably leave and trust the mice to find me: Aeslin mice are remarkably good at tracking down the things that matter to them, like cheese, cake, and members of the family. Or I could gamble on the fact that carnies are carnies the world over, and carnies who don't know about the cryptids they share the road with are rarer than hen's teeth. (Since female basilisks are also called "hens," and most definitely have teeth, that's pretty damn rare.) There was no way the Covenant had eyes in this tent. They wouldn't need me if they did. Hell, if I played my cards right, this might save me. I took a breath.

"Just one thing," I said. "Professor Xavier is a jerk."

"HAIL!" squeaked two tiny voices, running out of the dark beneath the bleachers. One of them—Mindy—clutched a piece of pink circus popcorn in her front paws. Mork was empty-handed, but had added a piece of bright green ribbon to his evolving ensemble, knotting it twice around his tail before tying it off in a festive bow. They ran straight to me, and then *up* me, scaling my body as easily as if I were a flat surface.

When they reached my shoulder I straightened. Sam was staring at me. So was the woman.

"You're a mouse-trainer?" asked Sam, after a momentary silence. "I didn't know mice could be trained."

"Hush, Sam," said the woman. She looked at me, taking a step closer. "Do you know what you have there, girl?"

"Yes, ma'am," I said. "I'm sorry they left the backpack. They must have felt safe here. They're used to carnival folk."

"Oh," said the woman, in a small voice.

The mice said nothing. Technically, Aeslin mice can't lie: that's part of what makes them valuable as a living record. Anything they see or hear, they repeat without modification. Mindy, however, had been training for years to be part of my priesthood, which involved a lot of sharing hotel rooms with the rest of my roller derby team, and thus a lot of keeping her little rodent mouth shut. Mork didn't share her training, but he'd been surviving in the walls of a Covenant residence without anyone knowing he or his family were there. Both of them knew when to stay quiet. If I was lucky, this woman would take their silence for shyness.

"What are they?" asked Sam.

"Aeslin mice," I said, meeting his eyes with what I hoped look like a cool lack of concern. "They're as smart as you or me. Well, as smart as me, anyway. The jury's out on you."

His cheeks reddened.

"Please don't bait my grandson," said the woman, eyes still on the mice. "He doesn't do well with being teased."

"Can we start over, ma'am?" I switched my attention to her. "I really didn't mean to make any trouble. I just need a place to be, one that's not out there. I need a carnival."

"So you do," she said, and smiled hesitantly. "My name is Emery Spenser. This is my show, as much as it's anyone's. You've met my grandson, Sam. I can't offer a place under the big tent without seeing what you can do, but anyone the mice trust is someone we can trust, at least on a trial basis. I ... I never thought to see their like again. Welcome to the carnival, Miss Brown."

I smiled as bright as I could. "Thank you for having me," I said, and the mice cheered while Sam scowled, and everything seemed right in the world.

Twelve

"A full stomach heals most ills. Except for the ills that leave you without internal organs. Those are harder to heal."

— Evelyn Baker

The Spenser and Smith Family Carnival mess tent, a little after ten

As with most shows, the mess tent was both part of the bone yard and apart from it, tucked to one side where the messy business of living wouldn't interfere with the equally messy business of feeding the whole shebang. Emery led the way across the deserted midway to the mess, chattering the whole time about where they'd acquired this game or when they'd last repaired that ride. She talked like a dotty aunt trying to introduce her entire swarm of semiferal cats, and I adored her for it. Sam trailed behind us, back in his sweatshirt but still barefoot, with a seemingly permanent scowl on his face. It appeared he didn't trust me.

It was almost a pity I couldn't tell him how good his instincts were. They'd serve him well, assuming the show survived my time with it—and its potential future encounter with the Covenant of St. George.

There were people up and moving around when we reached the mess. Two were peeling potatoes; a third was setting up a row of coffee urns that wouldn't have looked out of place at a Starbucks. From the smell of it, they were all dispensing the same brew: black, hot, and strong enough to strip paint. The urge to get a cup was strong.

Jet lag might have gotten me out of bed, but it couldn't keep me there, and a wave of exhaustion was teetering over me, threatening to bring me crashing to the ground.

"Have you eaten?" asked Emery. She took a seat at one of the long collapsible plastic picnic tables. Sensing that the interview was about to begin, I sat across from her. The mice ran down my arm and sat, primly, in front of me.

"No, ma'am," I said. "I got off the bus and came pretty much straight here."

"You allergic to anything? Gluten free, non-dairy, any of the usual restrictions?"

"No, ma'am."

"Glad to hear it. We respect dietary needs—we have to, if we don't want to kill people by mistake—but we're not set up for anything catastrophic. Sam, get the lady a plate and a cup of coffee."

"Okay, Grandma," said Sam, and skulked off, pausing only to shoot a glare at me.

"You'll have to forgive my grandson; he doesn't like strangers," said Emery.

"Huh," I said. "Well, I don't much like strangers either, so I guess I can't blame him. You're his grandmother?"

"Yes. His mother, my daughter, left us a long time ago. Don't look so distressed—she didn't die, she left. She couldn't deal with certain realities of her life as a mother, and she felt I was better equipped. Her loss, as I always tell Sam." Emery fixed me with a steely gaze. The pleasantries were over. "How about you, Miss . . . Timpani, wasn't it? Do you have any family?"

"None to speak of at the moment, ma'am," I said. "I've been on my own for a while now."

She glanced at the mice, clearly checking to see if they were upset by what I was saying. Using Aeslin mice as a living polygraph was clever. Unfortunately for her, nothing I was saying was technically a lie. The mice wouldn't have reacted even if they'd been less well-trained than mine were. That's the beauty of being the gray child. I knew how to color outside the lines.

"That's a pity and a blessing at the same time. Once you've lost everything you have to lose, transition gets easier." Emery leaned forward. "What can you do? Don't lie, and don't exaggerate. You have a pair of Aeslin mice with you. That alone buys you an audition, and possibly a berth, if you don't need to go terribly far. They're rare creatures in this day and age. They deserve to be protected."

"Yes, ma'am, and I'm doing my best to do right by them." Mindy looked up at me, bristling her whiskers into a fan, and I resisted the urge to cup my hands around the mice and protect them from prying eyes. Aeslin mice were pushed to the brink of extinction by a combination of monster hunters and overly-ambitious showmen who thought talking mice were the flea circus of the future. "I do trampoline work, some trapeze—give me a good partner and a solid net and I'm up for almost anything. No high wire or tightrope work. My balance is good, but it's not superhuman. I'm an excellent knife-thrower, hit what I'm aiming for nine times out of ten, even when I'm in motion. Um. I know how to make coffee, I can change the tires on a car, and I roller skate."

Emery raised an eyebrow. "You . . . roller skate."

"Yes, ma'am. Sometimes while throwing knives. It can be pretty impressive if I do it right, and it's definitely fun for the crowd. Um, I know how to rig most throwing games, and can play the plant if I'm not doing my own knife-throwing act." Playing the plant meant being the one to walk the midway, looking delighted by the chance to show my skills. It meant winning a lot of stuffed rabbits that would then go back into the general pool to be won again. And it meant not doing anything more public-facing, since the rubes tended to get pretty pissed off when they realized the girl who'd shilled them into plunking down five or ten or twenty dollars on an unwinnable game was also the carnival marksman.

"You realize I'm going to ask you to prove every skill you've just listed for me," said Emery. "Are you *sure* this is the resume you want to go with?"

I paused to do a quick review before offering, "I also

mend my own clothes, don't snore, don't smoke, and mostly don't bite people."

"The standards were very low at your original show, weren't they?"

"I work to my strengths," I said, and shrugged. "Not attacking people without cause is a strength."

"I see. And how did you come to acquire your traveling companions?"

"They've been with my family for generations. They need me." Still not a lie. Still not the entire truth. "I guess this is where I tell you that I know the mice aren't the only strange things in the world, and that it's not my business if not everyone with the show is entirely human. Ma'am."

Emery's eyebrows rose. "That's blunt."

"I try to be."

Sam's return cut off her reply. Emery flashed him a smile and relieved him of a plate, which she set in front of me. "I'll want a demonstration of the things you say you can do after lunch. Until then, eat, rest, and try not to make too much of a nuisance of yourself. Sam, show Timpani around, and take her to Umeko's old trailer, I think. Umeko hasn't used it in months, and Timpani will need a place to sleep for as long as she's with us."

"But, Grandma—" Sam began.

"No arguments. Breakfast and tour guide. That's a good boy." She stood, kissed him on the temple, and walked away, leaving me to blink after her.

"I guess my interview's over," I said.

Sam scowled as he sat in her vacated spot. "Did you fail it? Please tell me you failed it."

"I don't think so," I said, pulling my plate closer. The theme of the meal seemed to be "beige." Scrambled eggs, oatmeal—with brown sugar and butter, at least, which elevated it to the level of "actually food"—two pieces of cornbread, and a glass of orange juice. I gave one of the pieces of cornbread to the mice, who cheered enthusiastically before vanishing under the table with it. Like most mice, Aeslin do not enjoy having humans watch them eat.

"Damn," said Sam.

I raised both my eyebrows. "Are we going to have a problem?"

"It depends. Are you going to leave?"

"I told you, I'm looking for a permanent show."

"Then yes, we're going to have a problem." He scowled harder at me.

If there's one thing I'm good at, it's being scowled at. My siblings have been doing it for as long as I can remember. I picked up my fork and began mashing my scrambled eggs into the oatmeal. "Too bad. You're not totally unfortunate on the trapeze. Your form isn't great—"

"Hey!"

"—but that doesn't mean you don't have potential. We could have had a lot of fun."

"Oh, please," he scoffed. Actually *scoffed*. "Like you could keep up with me?"

I shrugged broadly. "You could try me and find out. Maybe I'll surprise you."

"Or maybe you'll drive me insane with your insistence that you belong here, and your voice will magically become the dulcet humming of the spheres."

I blinked. "Harsh."

To his credit, Sam looked faintly abashed. "Sorry."

"I mean, inventive, and points for the use of 'dulcet,' but . . . harsh. Do you talk to *all* the new girls like this, or did I get really lucky somehow?"

"We don't get that many new girls. Especially not ones who wander out of a field in the middle of the week and disrupt my workout."

"So I'm a novel experience. Goodie for me. It's always nice to have absolutely no expectations to fail to meet." I pointed my fork at Sam's plate. It was laden about three times as heavily as mine, but I couldn't blame him for that. He was eating like an athlete, and feeding me like, well, a stranger who could damn well get her own second helpings. "You want to call a ten-minute truce while we inhale sufficient calories to keep body and soul together?"

"Sure," he said, looking relieved that he wasn't going

to need to talk for a few minutes. We set to eating our respective breakfasts.

He was definitely a faster eater than I was: I wasn't sure he paused long enough to chew between bites. I mashed everything into one big beige pancake of oatmeal and eggs and bready bits, and began to eat, measuring the tent around me as I did. That's the nice thing about meals: people expect a little quiet, and that can create the perfect opportunity to get the lay of the land.

Not many folks were up yet—it was way too early for this kind of show to be really active—but the ones who were seemed pretty normal for the carnival setting. They wore jeans, sweatshirts, and the occasional long skirt; unlike Sam, most of them had shoes on, proving they were smarter than the average trapeze artist. A few cast curious glances in my direction. None seemed really unfriendly, not the way he did. Leave it to me to find the one person in the show who didn't like new people.

Despite his triple portions of, well, everything, Sam finished first. He pushed his plate away, eyeing what was left on mine dubiously. "Did you have to kill it before you could eat it?"

"It never hurts to be sure," I said, before taking another bite. "The oatmeal's good."

"Don't sound so surprised."

"Okay, this?" I pointed my fork at him. "Getting old. Dial it down if you don't want me to accidentally kick you at the first opportunity."

"You'd never catch me."

"The cocky always have the farthest to fall." My breakfast was basically over: there were only a few scraps remaining. I looked under the table. Mindy and Mork had annihilated their cornbread and disappeared, which probably meant they were back in my bag. A quick check confirmed that yup, I had two peacefully sleeping Aeslin mice curled up in my pencil bag. They must have been as exhausted by all the travel as I was.

I looked back up to find Sam watching me, an expression somewhere between wariness and hope on his face. It faded as soon as he realized I was looking at him.

"Come on," he said brusquely, snatching my plate. "I'll show you around."

"Great," I said, and followed.

There is no "normal" where the American carnival is concerned, especially not when dealing with a hybrid show like Spenser and Smith. But there are certain attributes that remain constant, if only because they represent the most effective way of doing things, and carnivals are all about maximizing effectiveness. The more streamlined the show, the faster it will be to set up and tear down—and when a town decides to change a local ordinance because they want those traveling weirdoes out of the field, it helps to be able to get out in less than six hours. Not as big of a concern these days, when carnivals are rarer and hence a more exciting spectacle, but still, it's good to know that a quick exit is possible.

With a tent show, the layout frequently goes something like this: the front gate and ticket booth, which will be as secure as needed, given the attractions on display; the midway and entrance to the big tent; the entrances to the smaller, sideshow tents, of which the Spenser and Smith Family Carnival had six; the rides at the back, both to lure townies through the entire show, and to minimize the distance any given component would have to travel. The only exception at this particular show was the Ferris wheel, which was set up right at the end of the midway, where its lights and slow, romantic turn would attract even more people than the greater thrills beyond.

It was a nice little operation. I would have enjoyed attending it, screwing with the people manning the games of chance, and coming away with a few new stuffed toys. As it was, I felt bad for coming in under false pretenses, and wary at the same time. Three teenagers were missing. That was more than enough to justify intervention by my family—and if the Covenant got involved, it was going to be seen as more than enough to justify a massacre. I needed to be on edge until I could either clear the carnival's name or condemn it once and for all.

Sam said as little as possible during my tour, which was no surprise. He kept looking up like he expected something to drop out of the sky and save him from the necessity of showing me around.

Finally, once we had exhausted the wonders of the closed midway and the powerless rides, he led me back through the tarp to the bone yard. It had woken up while we were walking around: there were people everywhere now, some with plates from the mess tent balanced on their knees, others firing up personal barbeques. A surprising number of people seemed to think hot dogs were an appropriate breakfast food. Oh, well. It was no skin off my nose.

Sam clearly knew the bone yard by heart, and led me between tents and vans without pausing. If he'd been marginally friendlier, he would have been the perfect guide. As it was, I sort of wanted to punch him in the throat, just to see if it would get something out of him other than a scowl.

He stopped at a small RV. "Here," he said brusquely.

I Spocked an eyebrow at him. "You might want to use a few more words. This sentence no verb. This sentence barely nouns."

"Oh, my God, could you be more annoying?"

"Yes. I assure you, I could be more annoying." I looked at the RV. "What is 'here'? Is this my temporary home?"

"Yes," he said. "Umeko moved in with her boyfriend, and since they seem pretty stable, you get her room for the time being."

I blinked. "I was sort of expecting to be sleeping on someone's floor. New girl, and all."

"We don't trust you enough to let you sleep on someone's floor." He smiled for the first time, showing me all his teeth. "See, quarantine is a useful principle that you should probably get used to."

"Social quarantine. Nice." I tried the door. It swung open to reveal a narrow room slightly bigger than my closet at home. It contained a bunk, a counter, two cabinets, and a microwave. I'd be able to change my clothes, if I wasn't too picky about needing to stand up straight. "Cozy."

"It's that or sleep in the field."

"Given that glorious range of options, cozy sounds good to me." I stepped up into the RV. Then I frowned. "This is about half the size I expected from the outside."

"Yeah, the other half is where we keep the pythons."

It took me a second to realize he wasn't kidding. "Lovely," I said. "I'm assuming since Emery told you to put me here, she'll be sending someone to get me when it's time for my audition?"

"Yeah," said Sam.

"Fantastic," I said, and took great pleasure slamming the door in his face.

Of course, this left me, my suitcase, and my backpack in a room barely large enough to deserve the name. I hoisted the suitcase onto the bed before wiggling out of my pack and putting it carefully on the counter. I didn't want to wake the mice if I could avoid it.

A cabinet door next to the microwave concealed a minuscule closet with a mirror on the inside. I squinted at my reflection: the frizzy braids, the deep circles under my eyes. I looked the part of someone who'd been beating the road for months, looking for a new place to belong. So why the hell was Sam so reluctant to believe me?

The bed, though narrow, looked comfortable. I decided to test it out by sitting down. Just for a minute. The mattress was thin. That didn't matter. I yawned, closing my eyes. I wasn't going to sleep, I was just going to take a second to center myself. I wasn't going to sleep, I was just—

Someone was hammering on the door of the RV. I opened my eyes. The light slanting through the tiny window over the bed had changed, becoming brighter and more direct than should have been possible, considering the early morning fog.

"Uh-oh," I said, and sat up.

My entire body ached. It felt like I'd been doing

Pilates in my sleep, working my core until it gave up completely. I stood on shaky legs and staggered to the door, opening it to reveal Sam. He was wearing jeans and a different sweatshirt, this one much less shapeless and sleepwear-esque. He still wasn't wearing shoes.

"Do you have some sort of religious issue with the idea of shoes?" I blurted.

He blinked. "If that's what passes for 'hello' on your world, it's no wonder you're an exile on ours."

"HAIL!" squeaked the mice. I looked behind me. Mindy and Mork were standing on the counter, under a little mouse lean-to they'd constructed from four plastic forks and a paper plate.

"Not going to ask where you got those," I said, and turned back to Sam. "Sorry. I guess I was more exhausted than I thought. I crashed like the Hindenburg. What time is it?"

"Almost three," he said. "Grandma wants you."

"Do I have time to change into something that smells less like I've been sleeping in it for the last six hours?"

Sam actually smiled, thin-lipped and chilly. "No," he said. "If you're going to work this show, you're going to come when my grandmother calls."

"Goodie," I said, and hopped down from the RV. I was still wearing my shoes. Hooray for the unexpected nap. "All right: take me to your leader."

If the bone yard had seemed populous before, it was nothing compared to now. There were people everywhere, from the thickly muscled men and women in overalls moving heavy equipment from one place to another to the tattooed, strikingly-dressed performers, ride monkeys, and pitch men. There were also children, a surprising number for a show this size. Several of them went racing past, too caught up in their game of tag to register the fact that I was a stranger. I watched them go, feeling oddly wistful.

"Hey."

I turned to Sam. He was looking at me, a surprising degree of understanding in his eyes.

"You okay?" he asked.

I nodded. "Just a little homesick," I said.

"Well, don't worry," he said, the moment of understanding passing as quickly as it had come. "Grandma's going to work you until you don't have the energy to be homesick."

"That's what I'm counting on," I said, and followed him through the tarp, onto the great sawdusted backbone of the carnival, which was lumbering to life around us. None of the rides were running yet, but they were swarming with carnies, checking the bulbs and the bolts, making sure that everything was good to go. About half the games were unshuttered, their pitch men going through their paces. The smell of hot dogs and popcorn drifted on the wind, sweet and close and demanding my attention. *You could belong here,* it said. *Just breathe in, and belong.*

I wasn't the first person to hear the siren song of the carnival. I won't be the last. I followed Sam into the big tent, where Emery Spenser stood with her hands on her hips, watching critically as two trapeze artists with half Sam's skill flew through the air. She turned as we approached, seeming to intuit our presence, and smiled thinly at the sight of me.

"You look better after a few hours of sleep; less 'resurrected corpse,' which is always a good thing. The rubes don't pay out for a sickly girl, remember that. Now. We don't have time to change the performance schedule for tonight, and I'm not going to ask anyone to give up their slot for you. Understand?"

Well. That was getting right to the point. "Yes, ma'am," I said. "Whatever you need me to do."

"I can't trust you as a pitch man, and I'm not going to use you as a lure until I know whether I want you somewhere else. So for tonight you're in here, on popcorn and candy duty. We've got a costume that should be about your size, and I'm sure your hair knows what a brush is; reintroduce the two and be here for curtain at six."

I resisted the urge to stare at her. "I'm going to be a candy girl?"

"For tonight, yes. Here." She produced a stack of

throwing knives from inside her jacket and offered them to me. "Impress me."

Impress her. Right. I took the knives, weighing them in my hands, trying to get a feel for them. This was the second time in a relatively short period that I'd been handed knives by a virtual stranger, and I was starting to miss my *own* knives, weighted for my personal use, more and more. Really, I missed all my weapons. I'd never been unarmed for this long, not since I was big enough to hold a fork.

"Am I allowed to throw knives at your grandson?"

Maybe not the most politic of questions. Her eyebrows climbed toward her hairline. So did Sam's. For a moment, the family resemblance between them was so visible it hurt. Then, looking amused, she smiled.

"Yes, you can throw knives at my grandson, but you're not going to hit him," she said. "He's faster than you think."

"Good to know," I said. "Is there a plank somewhere that I can use?"

"Sam, get the lady a plank."

Sam, who did not look happy about this plan, frowned before heading off across the tent. I began stretching out my shoulders while Emery watched.

"Sorry," I said. "I'm a little out of practice."

"And yet you want to throw knives at my grandson?"

"Well, like you said, he's fast. It'll be okay." That, and this was a trick I'd done before. The knives were decently weighted; they must have belonged to a professional knife-thrower. That was good. Sam was returning with a two-by-four. That was also good. "Okay, I'm going to say I've got fifty feet accuracy on these, forty if I'm throwing straight up. Sam? I'm going to close my eyes. Go somewhere — anywhere — within fifty feet of me, and call my name."

"And then you're going to throw a knife at me."

"Yes. And then I'm going to throw a knife at you. Hold the plank at chest-level, if you would."

"You meet the *best* people at the carnival," he grumbled, and turned to walk away. I closed my eyes. I didn't see him go.

"You're sure about this?" asked Emery. "You only get one chance to impress me."

"Yes, ma'am," I said.

"*Hey, rube!*" Sam shouted from behind me.

I whipped around, peeling a knife from the stack and flinging it in the direction of his voice. He was tall, but his voice was taller; he'd climbed the bleachers. That adjusted the angle of my throw, and I twisted my wrist to accommodate it. There was a thunk a second after I threw the knife, followed by Sam swearing.

"Keep moving!" I said. The next knife was already in my hand, ready to go.

The next "hey, rube" came from the side, at floor-level; the one after that came from about ten feet up, as he'd partially climbed one of the poles. Each time, the shout was followed by the sound of my knife hitting its target. Each time I heard a knife hit home, my shoulders unkinked a bit more. I was starting to enjoy this. The Incredible Cristopher had insisted we all learn blind fighting alongside the more standard, open-eyed knife-throwing tricks, since they're much more impressive for the average crowd. It's always nice to have the wisdom of my teachers confirmed.

"All right," I called. "Sam, can you get up on the edge of the net and then jump down?"

"Uh, no?" he replied. "You're going to skewer me and say it was an accident."

"Please. If you're as fast as you say, I couldn't skewer you if I wanted to."

"Do as the lady says, Samuel," said Emery.

He swore again. Then: "Do you want me to tell you when I'm jumping?"

"Please."

"I'm jumping!"

It wasn't much warning, but it was about what I'd been expecting. I threw the first knife as I was already dropping to my knees, threw the second knife before I hit the ground, and threw the third knife from a kneeling position. All three audibly struck home. I spread my arms and opened my eyes. "Ta-da!" I announced.

"Indeed," said Emery, looking thoughtfully at the board in Sam's hands. Seven knives bristled from its surface. Not all of them were well-seated—they'd fall out at the slightest pressure—but they'd gone into the wood and they'd stuck, which was more than enough for show purposes. "What else can you do?"

"I used to do a thing with roller skates and balloons and throwing knives at the balloons while I skated; I can throw knives from a trampoline without stabbing myself, much, and I'm good at moving targets. I'm better with my eyes open, but I figured that for a quick and dirty demo, this was the way to go."

"You certainly got my attention," said Emery. She took the plank from Sam. "You can do this reliably?"

"Yes, ma'am." I climbed back to my feet. "Twice a night, three times on the weekends."

"We'll see about finding a slot for you—*after* tonight. Tonight, you're a candy girl."

"Whatever you need from me, ma'am." I meant it, too. If she was putting me to work, she was trusting me—and more, she was making it possible for the rest of the show to trust me. It would be substantially easier to find out what had happened to those missing kids if I actually belonged here.

"Sam?"

"Yeah, yeah, get the girl who just tried to skewer me a costume." Sam shook his head. "I'm going to run away and become an accountant."

"Of course you are, dear." Emery patted his shoulder encouragingly. "Now chin up and get ready for tonight, both of you. It's going to be a marvelous show."

It was, in fact, a marvelous show. There were clowns, hula-hoop dancers, a few stilt walkers, and of course, the darlings of the flying trapeze. The two who'd been going through their paces while I was throwing knives at Sam were siblings from the Ukraine. They didn't speak any English—or they didn't admit to speaking any

English—but they flung themselves into the air with the giddy abandon of people who were sure that, in the unlikely event of an accident, their bodies would burst into birds and fly away before they could hit the ground.

Sam's solo act was good. Not the best I'd ever seen, thanks to that odd tension he carried in his shoulders; he was fast and clean, but he wasn't *fluid*. He never relaxed into the motion the way he should have. But he caught every swing the Ukrainian twins threw at him, and he moved between them with the speed and dexterity of a man who'd been born never to set foot on the ground.

"Candy girl."

The voice was unfamiliar. I turned, and found myself looking into the eyes of a strikingly beautiful Japanese-American woman with bright red streaks in her feathered black hair. Her face was made up like a firebird, all bright reds and yellows, blending into the sequins and feathers of her costume. I put on my best dealing-with-the-public smile. "Yes?"

"You're in my old room, candy girl. What hole did they dig you out of?"

"Oh! You must be Umeko. It's a very nice room. Thank you for letting me use it." Technically, she hadn't had anything to do with my being put in there—that was all Emery—but it's always better to play nice when possible. "You look amazing. What do you do?"

"You'll see in a second, candy girl." She pushed past me, her shoulder knocking against mine. Three more women in similar, if more subdued, costumes followed her, each carrying a bucket and a set of sticks with padded Q-tip ends. The audience quieted. Apparently, they'd seen this act before. That made sense: the carnival had been in town for at least a week, and they must have had a few things more impressive than a standard trapeze to still be drawing this sort of crowd.

The music stopped. The women put down their buckets, forming a loose circle. Umeko took up a position at the center, spreading her arms and bending backward, becoming a tightly drawn bow of a woman, ready to fire. One of the women dipped the ends of the giant Q-tip into the nearest bucket. Her left hand moved subtly as she did it, lighting an unseen match. To the audience, it must have looked like the Q-tip burst into flame with no mechanical assistance.

She threw the burning Q-tip to Umeko, who snatched it out of the air and began to spin it, a baton-twirler working in flame and sequins instead of the football field. The other girls lit their own Q-tips, and suddenly there were four women dancing in flame, the only music the crackling of the fire and the chiming of the tiny bells they had braided in their hair.

My left hand caught fire.

It didn't hurt; for a moment, I didn't even notice. When I did—largely because I'd just ignited a bag of M&Ms—I swore and ducked beneath the bleachers, beating the flames against my leg. They were a lovely shade of blue, which would have been a lot more aesthetically pleasing if I hadn't been *in public* and *on fire*, neither of which was a good thing at the moment.

The M&Ms burned with a much more standard orange flame. I stomped them out and slumped against the nearest support beam, trying to get my breath back.

"Shit." There didn't seem to be anything else to say under the circumstances, so I said it again: "*Shit*." I needed to go home. I needed Aunt Mary and Grandpa Thomas' diaries and time to deal with this where I wasn't going to get spotted by a Covenant operative and burned at the stake for the crime of . . . setting myself on fire. This was all complicated, and I didn't have the time for complicated anymore. Complicated was just too much for me.

I heard a thump. I turned. Sam was behind me, the frown on his face visible even through the gloom beneath the bleachers. "What are you doing under here?" he asked.

"Um," I said. Then: "One of my bags of M&Ms caught fire. I came under here to stomp it out." I pointed at the singed, crushed bag as evidence.

Sam blinked. "How did you get a bag of M&Ms to catch fire?"

Well, Sam, it turns out some kinds of magic run in families, even human families, and I'm becoming a walking Stephen King novel. No. Saying that would not get me anywhere good. It might get me thrown out of the carnival, which was the last thing I wanted right now. I forced a smile, shrugged, and said, "I don't know. It was about the same time as Umeko and her dancers went on, so maybe there was a stray spark? Or . . . something. It burned, I fixed it, I'm sorry."

"You are so weird," he said, and walked away, leaving me alone with the smell of burnt chocolate and the hammering of my heart.

Umeko and the fire-dancers were still in the ring when I emerged. That was good: I hadn't screwed anything up. They really knew what they were doing, too. They were wearing so many feathers that it was a miracle none of them went up like a candle, but they respected the fire and the fire seemed to respect them in turn. They dipped, wove, and pirouetted through the flames, and Verity couldn't have done better, not with all her years of training.

Someone signaled for me to come over. I hurried to oblige. Selling candy isn't the most useful thing in the world, but it was a distraction, and I needed a distraction. If I watched the fire for too long, I was afraid my traitorous fingertips would go up again. Becoming the Human Torch had never been on my extended list of things to do.

The fire dance finished. The clowns went on again. I kept selling candy, and minute by minute, we chipped away at the evening, until the tent show was over, and the audience began filing out. The performers had already vanished, to discourage loitering; it was just me, the other two candy girls, and the people with brooms who'd appeared to start resetting the ring almost the second it was empty.

"Timpani!" The voice was Emery's. I turned. She was striding toward me, streaks of greasepaint on her cheeks. The carnival didn't have a ringmaster as such—that was more the purview of the circus, which depended more on spectacle, and less on things like candy sales—but it had been clear from the start of the evening that if anyone was in charge here, it was her. She was wearing tight white spandex pants, and a black bustier which, combined with her makeup, made her look twenty years younger, and probably made Sam uncomfortable. It would have made me uncomfortable if she'd been my grandmother. Not fair, but there it was.

(Yes, my grandmother looks about the same age as my older sister. There's "my grandmother looks younger than she is," and there's "my grandmother is encouraging people to look at her breasts." One is normal. The other is disturbing.)

"Yes, ma'am?"

"Sam told me about your little accident. Apart from that, how was your evening?"

"Good, ma'am. Sold a lot of candy, didn't trip over my own feet, or accidentally stab a townie. I think I did okay."

"Excellent." She patted my cheek. "Drop what you have left back with the supplies for tomorrow night, and get out of that costume. Supper's on at the mess, and you don't want to miss out on that. You did very well. I think this is going to work out just fine."

I beamed. "Thank you, ma'am."

"Don't thank me. We're going to work you harder than you've ever been worked before, because you don't have the luxury of being family here. But we'll take care of you."

I nodded, swallowing the impulse to thank her again. "Can I check out the rides after I eat?"

"If you have the stomach for it, yes. Just tell the jocks you're Emery's new girl, and they'll let you ride." Her gaze darted to the side, as if she'd sensed some disturbance in the Force. "Hey! Be careful with that!" Then she was off, leaving me to my own devices.

It was almost nine-thirty. The Covenant expected me to check in at ten-seventeen. I ducked out the back of the tent, pausing at the supply closet to drop off my candy and earnings with the bored teenager doing inventory. She didn't even glance at me as she took the tray out of my hands. Either candy girls were interchangeable to her, or she was in a real hurry to get back to her game of Words with Friends. Or both. Whatever the reason for her ignoring me, I answered it with a wave and a smile, and took off for the bone yard.

Before, I'd been a stranger in street clothes, wandering where I had no business being. Now, I was still a stranger to most of the people I passed, but I was a stranger in sequins and fringe, and I clearly belonged. I was greeted with curious stares or friendly nods. No one glared. No one loomed. They just let me go by.

My temporary home was exactly as I'd left it, except for the mouse lean-to on the counter, which had doubled in size. There were walls now, made of scraps of wood. I eyed it. "Are you being careful when you scavenge? You know there are giant snakes in the other half of this RV, right?"

"Yes, Priestess," said Mindy. "We have avoided the Realm of Unreasonably Large Pythons."

"Good." I began stripping off my sequined leotard. The sequins scratched my skin. "Anything unusual happen while I was out?"

"A human woman with red in her hair came and looked inside; we hid," said Mork.

"That's Umeko. This was her place before Emery put me in it." I was going to have to look into locking my door. Aeslin mice are rare, which makes them valuable. We've had people try to steal portions of our traveling colonies before. I wasn't going to let that happen to Mindy and Mork.

(Paranoid? Sure. Not everyone is a bad guy. But since I was infiltrating the carnival on behalf of the people I was infiltrating on behalf of my family, it was reasonable for me to be a little twitchy. It's hard to know who you can trust when you can't even figure out whether you're allowed to trust yourself.)

"Should we let her see us, Priestess?" asked Mindy.

"Better not," I said. "For right now, try not to show

yourselves to anyone unless I'm here with you, and even if I am here, don't come out unless I say it's okay, or it's Emery. She's the boss. We're going to play nicely with her."

"Yes, Priestess," chorused both mice.

"Excellent." I changed back into more normal attire: jeans, a Helsinki Roller Girls tank top, and a hooded sweatshirt. As long as I didn't wear any derby attire pointing to the Portland area, I was okay, and it would explain my roller skate skills. It's always best to hide things in plain sight when possible.

And just to hide them, when plain sight wasn't an option. I looked ruefully at my hands. The more stress I was under, the more fires I was going to start, at least until I got it under control. It couldn't even be *useful* fires. That sort of thing takes years of practice, and according to Grandpa Thomas' diaries, the most he'd ever managed was a sort of small fireball that landed two feet away from him and set half the lawn aflame. Not really combat-efficient, especially not when I had knives. Sure, I could take out a field or something, but since I wasn't planning to go up against the Children of the Corn any time soon, I wasn't in the market for a field to fight.

My fingertips started heating up. I shook them until they stopped. The mice were rustling around in their little house, which was more . . . concrete . . . than temporary Aeslin mouse dwellings tended to be. I wondered whether Mindy's quest for the missing colony hadn't also been about bringing in some new blood. Our colony was stable, but they hadn't had any newcomers in generations, thanks to that whole "functionally extinct" thing. The Aeslin mice in England were distant cousins, emphasis on *distant*. If Mindy wanted to take advantage of that, I wasn't going to interrupt her. At least one of us had a love life to speak of.

It's not that I *don't* date. It's that *I* don't *date*. I am an essentially misanthropic person: I don't like people much, and they usually reward me by not liking me either. Which doesn't mean I hate everyone. I like the girls

I skate with. I love my cousins. I even like my siblings, when I'm not hating them. It's just that none of those people are good romantic prospects.

The clock on my phone ticked over to 10:17 PM. I opened a group chat to "Sue" and "Tom" and typed "LOL having best time, food great, wish you were here." I signed it with three smiley faces and a heart, supposedly for veracity, but really because I knew it would irritate Robert. Anything I could do to get on his nerves without putting myself in danger was a-okay by me.

A minute passed. The phone buzzed. "Tom" had messaged me back, saying, "Glad to hear it, talk tomorrow." No smiley face. No hearts.

"Because that doesn't look like a secret message at *all*," I muttered, dropping the phone on the bed and standing. The carnival was open until midnight. I wanted to see it. I wanted to see it all.

The air in the bone yard smelled like charcoal and burnt marshmallow, a camp-out bonfire scent that I remembered from the few autumns I'd been able to spend with the Campbell Family Carnival. I wasn't hungry enough to trade precious midway time for the mess tent, and besides, I had a few bucks in my pocket; if I needed food, I could always throw some cash at the show and pick up a hot dog. Sacrilege, really—if I was pretending to be a carnie, I needed to be a proper skinflint about giving money to the carnival—but this was my first night, and I figured I'd be forgiven, if it came to that.

I walked across the bone yard, taking note of the larger tents and where the conversational clusters had formed, before letting myself through the tarp and into the shadow of the rides. Screams greeted me as the roller coaster went whizzing by. Small as it was, it was still a novelty here, and people enjoy novelty. The history of the human race has been one long quest to find new, novel things, and then kill, eat, or enslave them. There's a reason the aliens haven't made an appearance yet, is what I'm saying.

The Scrambler was scrambling and the Bumper Cars were bumping, but I ignored them both, heading for the first and most important goal a girl can have at the carnival: the Ferris wheel. It was a tall, glowing monument to the show, and from the top, I'd be able to see absolutely everything, from the shape of the bone yard to the movements on the midway. I couldn't think of a better way to officially start my stay.

There was a short line at the ride. The townies who had to work the next day were drifting out, and many were stopping to blow their last few ride tickets on the big wheel. (Many, but by no means most. The majority would wind up taking a fistful of tickets home, to act as the most expensive useless souvenirs in the whole place. There are many ways to make a profit, if the people running the show know what they're doing.) I stepped into place, waiting patiently until it was my turn to step up to the ride jock and say, "Excuse me, I'm—"

"I know who you are," said Sam, turning and scowling at me. "If I let you on the ride, will you not talk to me anymore?"

"For at least ten minutes, sure," I said.

"Then get on." He jerked his chin brusquely toward the swinging seat that had just descended into place.

Staying and arguing with him about whether I was going to leave seemed counterproductive. I flashed him a sickly sweet smile and skipped over to the ride, climbing up and pulling the safety bar—such as it was—into place. The Ferris wheel began to spin. I relaxed into my seat and watched the carnival unfold before me like a beautiful picture.

The midway had been a ghost in the daylight, gray and waiting for the night. It was alive now, resurrected in lights and sound and the moving feet of carnies and townies alike. From up here, as the Ferris wheel took me higher, there was no difference between the two. Most of the people I'd known from both camps would take offense at that, but that didn't make it any less true. Seen from a great enough distance, all the little differences smooth away, and only the big picture remains.

The big tent was a striped shadow behind me, and the lights of the bone yard twinkled past the carnival bawn, turning the field into a spray of stars. It was beautiful, and it was fragile, and it was up to me whether this place would be protected or have the Covenant fall upon it like a ton of bricks. That was more responsibility than I'd ever wanted.

Speaking of responsibility ... "Betelgeuse, Betelgeuse, Betelgeuse," I muttered, as the Ferris wheel moved toward its highest point.

The seat rocked, hard, from the extra weight of Mary appearing next to me. "I wish you wouldn't call me that way," she said, words doing nothing to conceal her relief. Her arms were around my shoulders a second later, pulling me close. "I was so worried about you. When did you get back to North America? And what are you doing ..." She seemed to register her surroundings for the first time. "... on a Ferris wheel?"

"It's a long story, and we only have until we make it back to the ground; someone might notice that I've suddenly acquired a passenger," I said. "Can you let my parents know that I'm not in Europe anymore, but that it's not safe to look for me or try to make contact?" Asking Mary for things has to be done carefully, to avoid triggering her connection to the crossroads. Fortunately, she's been a babysitter longer than she's been a ghost, and checking in with the parents is almost always allowed.

Mary's eyes widened. "The Covenant still has eyes on you?"

"In a manner of speaking." I laughed mirthlessly. "They're the reason I'm here. They have me undercover with this carnival, to find out whether it's, quote, 'harboring monsters,' unquote. My life is a Shakespearean comedy."

"Wait." Mary leaned away, eyeing me. "You're telling me the Covenant is watching you *right now*?"

"Yes. Hence my calling you while I was at the top of a Ferris wheel. The lights will screw up anyone watching me with a telephoto lens, and if I was under that kind of scrutiny, I'd already be dead. They would have noticed the mice."

"Wasn't there someplace more private?"

"I have a room in an RV, but I don't know how secure it is, and I can't risk the carnival hearing me say the word 'Covenant' in mixed company. Not unless I want to find myself buried behind the bone yard."

Mary shook her head. "And here I used to think your grandmother was trouble."

"We get better at complicating things with every generation. Which, speaking of, I set myself on fire earlier tonight. Do you know a way to make this *stop*?"

"Honey, we've talked about this. If you're a magic user—"

"Yeah, the 'if' is off that sentence. Now it's more 'if I'm going to survive learning to control this crap.' Isn't there a way to put it on hold until I get home and can safely work on it?"

"I'm sorry. Not that I've ever heard of. Just try to stay calm, and it should be all right." The Ferris wheel was gliding into its downward arc. Mary pressed cool lips against my temple. "I'll tell your parents you're alive."

Then she was gone, and I was alone when the motion of the wheel carried me back to ground level. Sam was still manning the ride. I nodded to him, and he scowled to me, and I went around again, back up into the star-spangled carnival sky. All my troubles were on the ground. If it had been up to me, I would have stayed up there forever.

Thirteen

"They called me the Flower of Arizona. A name like that, it never dies. It just keeps moving forward, into legend. If you're lucky, it'll take you along."

— Frances Brown

The Spenser and Smith Family Carnival midway, the following afternoon

THE SUN WAS WARM on my shoulders as I carried boxes of stuffed animals down the midway, pausing at each open game to check their stock. There were subtle differences in the prizes offered by the various pitches, but most were variations on a theme: brightly colored plush toy, great for your girl, make a memory for your kids. Some rotation was necessary during the week, to make it look like things were being won. The pie-in-the-sky prizes could stay—the giant teddy bears, the crystal unicorns, the things virtually no one ever *expected* to win—but the little day-to-day things had to move around. Otherwise, someone who came to the show often enough might start to do the math and come up with an answer they didn't care for.

The pitch men and games operators were strangers. Most of them didn't take the time to introduce themselves, just rooted through my box of toys, snatched a few they thought might earn a dollar, and tossed in the requisite number of returns to keep the numbers up. About half the midway games were privately owned, rather than part of the carnival proper: their operators were parked on the far side of the bone yard, and while they mingled with the rest of us when necessary, they also kept to themselves a surprising amount, cooking in their own RVs and gossiping with each other, rather than the rest of the show. It made sense. Better not to get attached if you weren't planning on staying.

After I was done with the games, I made for the supply tent next to the reptile trailer. That was where the pythons that roomed next to me were displayed during the day, for the delight and edification of the masses. Alex would have been in heaven. I didn't really see the point—you can find a wide assortment of snakes at most pet stores, to say nothing of zoos—but there were kids dragging their parents into the tent whenever the show was open, so it must have held a certain appeal for some people.

A woman sat outside the reptile trailer, a small, spade-nosed snake twined around the fingers of her right hand and a cigarette clamped between the fingers of her left. She was wearing a pink-and-red sari over hot pants and what looked like a sports bra, and her long black hair was a tangled mess containing at least three more snakes, if the variously colored scales peeking through were any indication.

I let myself into the supply tent, dropping my box of plush toys next to the disinterested man whose job it was to check them back in. He grunted acknowledgment. That was all he did: he didn't even look up from his clipboard as I turned and walked back out again.

The woman with the snake took a long drag off her cigarette, blowing it out slowly before she turned to look at me. "Morning, new blood," she said.

"Morning," I said carefully. "I'm Timpani. You are . . . ?"

"Ananta," she said, returning her attention to the snake on her hand. "What are you running from, little drum girl?"

"I don't know," I said. "Life, I guess. I grew up with the carnival. Not having it anymore didn't make sense. So I'm running away from figuring out what I want to be when I grow up." All of that was technically true, even if it was mostly bullshit at the same time. I thought. I hoped.

When the hell did everything get so complicated?

"Well, this is a great place to run away to," she said, and took another drag off her cigarette. "Nobody's going to come looking for you here."

"I hope that's true."

"Has been so far for me." She held up her hand so I could see the snake she was holding. "This is a hognose. He's venomous but good-natured and short-toothed, which makes him unlikely to bite. He can't be out of his tank when we have townies here, for insurance reasons, so I wanted to let him get some air before we opened."

"He's beautiful."

"All my snakes are beautiful."

An awkward silence fell between us—awkward on my part, just silent on hers. I wanted to ask whether she was a wadjet, based on the scrambled cues she was putting off. I couldn't do it. The girl I was pretending to be wouldn't know what a wadjet *was*, much less that they could be identified by a laissez faire attitude about poisons, being immune to essentially all of them.

I'd never stopped before to consider how much of an advantage my family name was in the work we did. Back home, I could walk up to cryptids, or to people I suspected of being cryptids, and count on my family name— the weight of it, the *history* of it—to pull me through. Now, without the word "Price" to open doors for me, I was left standing on the outside, trying to figure out how I was supposed to get myself in. If Ananta was a wadjet, I had no way of making her trust me enough to say so.

Finally, I coughed, and asked, "How long have you been with the show?"

"Six years and counting," she said. "Emery has been good to me. I own the RV where you're sleeping, drum girl, did you know that? It's my storage space. When we're on the road, that's where I sleep."

"In the room where I'm currently staying?"

"No." She sounded amused. "On the other side,

among my snakes. I hope you don't snore. You'll be a poor bedfellow, if you do."

The image of sleeping completely surrounded by snakes was enough to make me shiver. I suppressed it and said, "I don't snore, but I do scream when something slithers under the covers unexpectedly."

Ananta's smile was swift and sharp. "Then we'll do fine. You might want to move along. I'm about to air out my rattlesnakes."

I moved along.

The midway was coming alive, but I didn't have a part in any of it. The stuffed animal job had been a sop, something Emery threw at me to keep me busy while Sam did his morning workout and she planned the night's show. This whole carnival was an odd hybrid of past and present, blending archaic traditions with modern ideas about layout and design. And, like any show, it had the capacity to keep its own counsel.

I tried to breathe normally, to relax into the moment as I walked through the shadow of the Ferris wheel and into the corridor of slumbering rides, their mechanical arms reaching for the sky like giants praying to some unknowable god. Please let us have another good night; please let us continue to operate smoothly, without needing repairs or replacement or anything else so expensive as to run the risk of pushing us into the red; please let the townies go home happy, telling their friends to come and see the wonders of the carnival.

Please let the townies go home at all.

I might have missed the hand, if I'd been walking with someone else; if I hadn't been looking at everything around me with quite so much focus, quite so much simple longing for answers. It was a small thing, pale and almost hidden by the base of the Scrambler, which was raised nearly three feet off the ground by the mechanisms that kept it spinning. The fingers were curled inward, like the legs of a dead or dying insect, and there was no way in the world for it to be anything other than what it was. All the tricks of light in the world couldn't have made it look any less like a hand.

My mouth went dry and a wave of dizziness washed over me as the blood drained from my head. I caught myself on the nearest railing, careful to touch it only with my palm, which would leave no fingerprints; if this was about to become a crime scene, the police wouldn't be able to place me here with any certainty. It wasn't much. It was, under the circumstances, the best that I could do.

"Hello?" My voice sounded weak, querulous; it broke at the end of the word.

The owner of the hand did not respond.

I took a step toward the Scrambler. When the hand didn't move, I took another, until I was next to the ride. I crouched. The hand was attached to a woman, and the woman was lying on the ground, eyes closed. She was wearing jeans and a sweatshirt, and she could have been a townie, and she could have been someone with the carnival who I hadn't had the opportunity to meet yet, and it didn't matter either way, because I couldn't see her breathing.

Antimony Price wouldn't scream. Antimony Price would assess the situation calmly, figure out her next steps, and begin putting her plan into action. It was sort of nice *not* to be Antimony Price for a change. My scream was loud enough to send the crows roosting atop the ride scattering into the sky, and the echoes of it lingered. Just me, the maybe-dead girl, and the scream.

The rides were almost the full length of the midway away from the big tent. I was closer to the bone yard, or to the games that were in the process of setting up. There was no way Sam should have been the first to reach me, but somehow he was, appearing as if by magic. He took one look at what I was looking at, and then he was pulling me back, putting his arms around me, shielding me from what I shouldn't have needed to see in the first place.

He smelled like hot sweat and chalk dust, the scent of a thousand cheer competitions and childhood gymnastics meets. I relaxed into the aroma more than I relaxed into him, realizing only after the fact that the two were currently indistinguishable, and I was allowing myself to be comforted by a man who didn't like me one bit.

It was still better than looking at what might be a dead body that I couldn't do anything about. I didn't pull away. If Sam thought better of holding me—since I liked him about as much as he liked me—he could be the one to let go.

Footsteps ran toward us, and Emery asked, alarmed, "Sam? What's going on?"

"Under the Scrambler, Grandma," said Sam. "Timpani found her."

There was a pause, broken by a soft gasp and Emery saying, "Oh, that poor girl. That poor, poor girl."

I pulled away from Sam, who didn't try to stop me; at the first sign of resistance, he just let go. "Who is she?"

"Savannah. She's one of the other candy girls. Didn't you meet her last—no, you wouldn't have. You came in so late. Damn." Emery scrubbed at her face with both hands. She was wearing jeans and a patchwork jacket that looked like something out of one of the crunchy granola hippie catalogs Aunt Jane sometimes received. The thought brought on another wave of missing the security of my family. "There's still makeup on her cheeks. She must have been out here all night."

"Is she ... ?"

Emery nodded, the bleak look on her face filling in the missing pieces. "We'll have to contact the local authorities. We're her only family. The poor thing."

"Did someone hurt her?"

Sam went still beside me, and Emery did much the same, both of them freezing in place. Then, with a sigh, Emery said, "There's no blood, and her clothing is intact. She may have just collapsed. Regardless, the police will want to know. Sam ... ?"

"On it," he said, and turned and walked away.

I watched him go before turning back to Emery, a silent question in my eyes. She sighed again. "I'm sure there were people with your original show who wouldn't have taken kindly to the police showing up without warning them. He's not going to help a murderer hide, if you're worried about that, but there are always those for whom involving the authorities will be a step too far. Do you understand?"

"I do," I said meekly. "I'm sort of one of them. Can I . . . ?"

Emery nodded. There was no surprise in her expression. If anything, she looked relieved that the new girl was running away when the police were on their way, rather than standing her ground and demanding to be a part of the investigation. "Go back to the bone yard. Be in the mess tent when I need you."

Which really meant "go to the mess tent and stay there, since there's no telling when I'll be done with the townie police." That was fine by me. It meant Emery was planning to discuss the event with me, not just push it to the side, and would put me in the perfect position to watch the other members of the carnival finding out about the death. Losing one of their own wasn't the same as townie kids disappearing—in some ways it was better, in a lot of ways it was worse—but that didn't mean the two things didn't have the same origin.

I didn't see Sam as I made my way through the canvas flap and across the bone yard to the mess tent. There were a few people there, nursing cups of coffee or getting into position early for the best shot at lunch. I grabbed a mug and a bunch of grapes and took a seat at one of the tables near the back, where I'd be able to see anyone who came in.

Almost anyone. I'd only been sitting there for a few minutes when Sam demanded, from behind me, "What did you see?"

I jumped enough to slosh hot coffee onto my hand. I stuck my scalded fingers into my mouth and turned to glare at him.

Sam looked briefly repentant, but only briefly. "The coffee's never hot enough to do any real damage; people get mad sometimes, things get thrown, and we don't provide free weapons. What did you *see*?"

I took my hand out of my mouth. "I saw a hand under

the Scrambler, and when I looked closer, I saw it was attached to a body. I screamed, you came, your grandmother told me to come here and wait for her."

"Why?"

"Why did I scream, or why did she tell me to wait here?"

"Both."

"I screamed because I saw a body." I kept my voice tightly measured, swallowing the urge to yell. It wasn't going to make things better. It might make things worse. "I came here because I don't want to talk to the police. I don't want to talk to the police because if you'll think way, way back to *yesterday*, the Black Family Carnival was wiped out in a freak accident, and if they ran a background check on me, they might decide 'freak accident' is another way of saying 'Annie did it.'"

Sam looked at me suspiciously. "Did you?"

"What? God, no. And if I had, would I really be like 'oh, yeah, I killed everyone, guess I couldn't resist the opportunity to do it again.'" I glared at him. "Fuck you for even asking."

To my surprise, Sam looked abashed. "Sorry," he said, running a hand through his hair and dropping into a seat. "I didn't think before I opened my mouth. That happens sometimes."

I forced myself to relax, giving him a sidelong look as I measured his reaction. He was wearing jeans and a sweatshirt again, and again, he had no shoes. "Don't your feet get cold?"

"Nah, I spend enough time sticking them in my mouth that they never get the chance."

I snorted. "Was that a joke? Did you actually make a joke?"

"I'm not *completely* humorless," he protested. "Just . . . Grandma says I'm mildly xenophobic. I like people fine when they're ours. I'm not too big on people from the outside."

"Meaning me," I said.

He nodded. "Meaning you. Outsiders are more trouble than they're worth."

"I guess you're not wrong," I said. "I mean, I've been here, what, twenty-four hours? And I'm already finding corpses on the midway."

Sam grimaced. "Something like that. I know you didn't hurt Savannah."

"How do you know that?"

"Because I would have seen you."

I blinked. "You realize that's basically an admission that you've been following me around." And I hadn't noticed. That was . . . worrisome.

"Yeah, but Grandma knew I was doing it, so it's okay." He shrugged. "You're new, I get nervous, she doesn't care if I watch you for a few days while I decide whether or not to demand you go. Those damn mice screwed everything up. Without them, I would've been able to ask her to get rid of you yesterday."

"You are taking talking mice remarkably well." I gave him a searching sidelong look, trying to find some sign that he wasn't human, that he'd been touched by the cryptozoological world. I didn't find one. He looked like an ordinary, if tall, Asian man in his mid-twenties. He wasn't exactly what I'd call break-the-bank handsome, but he wasn't unfortunate to look at either, and when he was on the trapeze, looks didn't matter nearly as much as the strength of his arms and the grace of his turns. "Have you seen Aeslin before?"

"No," he said. "I thought they were just, you know, a myth. But there they are. With you. Why are they with you?"

"They've been with my family for generations. We have a responsibility to them, to keep them safe. I can't do much, but I figure I can protect two mice that really and truly need me."

"I hope so," said Sam. "A lot of things need protecting." He sat up a little straighter.

I followed his gaze to the mouth of the mess tent, where Emery was entering, accompanied by several people I didn't recognize. None of them were wearing police blue. That was a relief. They looked like the sort of pitch men, ride jocks, and carnies that any good owner could collect during a walk along the midway, and not one of them looked happy.

Emery clapped her hands, bringing the conversations in the mess hall to a screeching halt. "Everyone, if I could have your attention for a moment? By now, there's a good chance you've heard about the police currently canvassing our rides. There's been an accident. Savannah is gone."

A few gasps, a few mutters, but on the whole, silence: people were listening. More were coming in through the open door, drawn by the sense of something important happening, and they were quiet also, letting Emery speak.

"Right now, it looks as if she died of natural causes. The police are going to look into the matter. As we were already confirmed in this location through the end of the weekend, they're not asking us to do anything out of the ordinary, just stay where we are, try not to impede their investigation, and not leave without clearing it with them. As long as nothing unusual comes to light during their examination of her body, we'll be able to leave as normal. The Scrambler will be closed tonight, for obvious reasons."

Mutters broke out around the room. No one asked their questions loudly enough to be answered, and that, too, was only to be expected.

Carnivals exist in a strange sort of twilight where the law is concerned. A lot of crimes get blamed on carnies—thefts, vandalism, the sort of thing that's likely to be bored teenagers letting off a little steam; by pinning it on someone from outside the community, people can avoid painting their own children as criminals. Sometimes it backfires spectacularly, allowing future killers to fly under the radar, never held responsible for their own actions. Other times, it ends with innocent people rotting in townie jails, pinned down under fixed roofs that they'd spent their lives avoiding. Because of that, a lot of carnies don't trust the townie law, and will do whatever they can to keep from getting outsiders involved.

A few people cast hostile glares in my direction, and

that, too, was only to be expected. I was the new thing here, and the night I'd come to the show, one of their own had died. Sam wasn't one of the ones glaring, which was new and also a little weird. Maybe finding a body had been the icebreaker we needed. In which case, wow, was I staying the hell away from him. Some ice is not meant to be broken.

"Thank you, all," said Emery, and started across the tent to where Sam and I sat. It took her a while to reach us—people kept stopping her to talk, and to her credit, she listened with her full attention every single time. When she did reach us, she looked at me, not her grandson, and said, "It looks like a heart attack. I thought you should know, since you found her."

"Thanks," I said. "That'll help me sleep tonight."

"No, it won't."

"No, it won't," I admitted. "But it does help. At least a heart attack probably means she went quickly." Although what had she been doing under the Scrambler? That part didn't make sense. Collapsing in the middle of the walkway would have increased her chances of getting found while there was still something that could be done to save her. Instead, she'd gone into the dark, alone, and she'd died there, alone. Something didn't add up.

"Probably," agreed Emery, and I saw shadows in her eyes that matched the one in my own. She had her own suspicions. But I was the new girl; it wasn't my place to ask her for them. And she was a relative stranger; even if she'd asked me, I wouldn't have told her.

We looked at each other across a bridge of all the things we couldn't safely say, and neither one of us said anything at all.

Fourteen

"Secrets are like bricks. Sometimes you
need them if you want to build a wall. Other
times, they'll only weigh you down."
—Enid Healy

The Spenser and Smith Family Carnival, that night

THE BIG TENT WAS PACKED WITH BODIES, so many that
even the standing room spaces at the top of the
bleachers were filled. There weren't many kids, either:
these were adults and teenagers, following the scent of
blood on the wind as they strained to catch a glimpse of
a murderer. Whether Savannah had died of natural
causes or not didn't matter to them: they were here looking for excitement, and they were—by God—going to
get it.

"One of ours dies, it's a miracle for business; one of
theirs dies, and they run us out of town on a rail," said
Ananta, pushing past me with a Burmese python the
length of a car draped around her shoulders. Around us,
the townies cheered as Sam took to the flying trapeze.
"Watch yourself tonight."

I nodded, acknowledging her warning before I went
back to chucking overpriced candy to bloodthirsty townies. We'd been instructed to take them for every cent
they had. With the police investigating Savannah's death,
most of the local parents were going to stay away, thus
showing that the desire to protect children sometimes
looked a lot like common sense. We'd have one night of
incredible crowds, maybe two, and then they'd be gone,

melting back into their lives without a second thought for the supposed "murder carnival." That was bad for long-term business, but meant we needed to make a week's profits in two nights. We could do that. If we were fast and ruthless, we could do that.

After the tent shows were done, I was supposed to scrub off my makeup, switch my sequins for street clothes, and wander the midway teasing townies into winning plush toys for their significant others. I was looking forward to learning the scam on some of those games. It seemed like a good way to kill an evening, and maybe if enough of the pitch men vouched for me, Emery would let me switch to throwing knives sooner than later.

One nice thing about being considered for a knife-throwing act: I wasn't unarmed anymore. I'd managed to talk Emery out of a set of throwing knives, which she expected me to chuck at a piece of plywood near my RV, keeping myself in practice. And I was going to do that, because no skill, ever, has been so perfectly developed that it doesn't need to be maintained. It was just that I was also going to conceal knives all through my clothing, tucking them into the seam folds and natural pockets of the hems. Every knife made me feel a little safer, and a little more like myself.

It was nice to feel like me again. I'd been starting to worry about forgetting who that was.

The fire dancers were taking the floor. Umeko was as bright and vibrant as she'd been the night before: if Savannah's death had impacted her in any way, she wasn't allowing it to show in her performance. I paused to admire the artistry of their movements, feeling the heat rise and sparkle in my fingertips. I forced it back down as best as I could, and it must have been pretty decent, because I didn't catch fire, and neither did any of the remaining candy in my tray. Of which there wasn't much. A townie boy with more money than sense flagged me down, buying my last two bricks of pink popcorn and my last pack of peanut butter cups, and I was out.

The walk under the bleachers was easier tonight: at

least now the way was familiar, and I knew what I was
and wasn't likely to trip over. It would have been even
easier in roller skates. If Emery was going to insist I keep
playing candy girl, maybe I could convince her to let me
do it on wheels. It would add a little flash and glamour to
the job, at least as far as the townies were concerned, and
impressing them was the whole point of the exercise,
right?

I made my way to the supply closet, trading profits
and empty space for a fresh load of candy. The bored-
looking teenager who counted me in and counted out
my restock didn't talk to me, except in quickly muttered
numbers that seemed to matter more to her than made
any sense. She didn't offer, and I didn't ask. People run
away to join the carnival for all sorts of reasons

The smell of sweet cedar smoke hung in the air outside the supply closet. I took a step toward the big tent,
and stopped when the tarp twitched. Someone else was
about to come out.

Pure instinct drove me into the shadows next to the
wall, melting back and pressing myself flat until I was
nothing but shape and potential. There was little light
back here, and my sequined top was barely an afterthought in a night filled with flashing rides and the gleaming halogens inside the tent. That's why, when the door
opened, I saw them, and they didn't see me.

Umeko was the first out, cheeks still bright with heat
and eyes sparkling with the joy of the performance. Next
out was not one of her dancers, but a townie boy, no
more than nineteen, staring at her with enormous moon-
calf eyes, like he'd never seen anything so beautiful in his
life. It was an understandable reaction—she was a gorgeous woman, and she was in the best of her element in
that moment—but something about him seemed *off*, like
a few essential functions had been disconnected before
he'd walked out of the tent and into the night with a
stranger.

I could have stepped out of my shadow and confronted them. I could have asked where she was going,
veiling my demand for information in concern, or in a

newbie's casual violation of personal space. I didn't. I held myself still until the two of them had passed me, and then I carefully removed my tray and set it flush to the wall, where no one was likely to see or steal it. My costume was glittery, but it didn't have anything on it that would jingle or chime to announce my presence. This was as good as it was going to get.

Umeko and her boy walked on. And I? I followed them.

She knew the carnival as only someone who'd lived here for years could. Utterly unconcerned, her hand resting on the boy's arm, she walked down the back of the midway, behind the games, where no one was likely to see or suspect her. She led him past the games, through the shadow of the motionless Scrambler. He didn't even look at it. That was when I knew something was truly *wrong*. No townie who'd come to a carnival the night after someone had died there would have been able to walk past the well-publicized site of the body discovery and not at least *look* at it. Human nature is many things. "Predictable" is first among them.

She led him through the tarp wall and into the bone yard. I hung back for a count of ten, and then went through after them.

The bone yard was dark, the lights turned down to keep from attracting too much townie attention. For a moment, I thought I'd lost them. Then a rectangle of light opened to my left — an RV door being unlatched — and I turned in that direction, trusting logic to win out over coincidence.

There was a sound. It wasn't a scream, more like a sigh of resignation; a giving up, a giving in, a deciding not to fight any longer. I broke into a run.

The RV where I assumed Umeko had taken her townie boy was dark, the windows covered by sheets of what looked like tin foil. It was large enough for two people, and I remembered belatedly that Umeko had moved out of the space where I was now living because she was sharing living space with her boyfriend. I hadn't met him yet. Still, if she had a live-in lover, it was even stranger for her to be wandering off with townie boys. I moved closer.

The material blocking the windows wasn't tin foil. It was some sort of thick, cottony material, like the novelty webbing that Halloween stores sell by the roll. It wasn't the oddest decorating choice I'd ever seen, especially not in a bone yard, but it still struck me as strange. I didn't know how many layers of webbing it would take to block a window so completely that even the light couldn't get through. A lot. I was sure of that much. It would require a *lot*.

My fingers were heating up again, the magic triggered by my anxiety and confusion. I shook my hands to cool them, taking a step back. If Umeko wanted to have a threesome with a townie boy—or wanted to cheat on her boyfriend—that was no business of mine. All I could do by interrupting them was make an enemy I couldn't afford, not while I was still in my trial period with the show. Umeko and her fire dancers were a main attraction. I was a scruffy knife-thrower from a dead carnival. There was no contest.

Someone inside the RV squeaked. It was a small, tight, *pained* sound that made the hair on the back of my neck stand on end. Maybe there was no contest, but sometimes, interrupting is the right thing to do. Emery would understand, especially when Umeko yelled for backup and everyone saw how *young* the townie boy was. Umeko was a grown woman. She should have known better.

Fingertips hot, I approached the RV and rapped my knuckles against the door. The sound was muffled somehow, like the room on the other side was swaddled in some sound-deadening substance. There was no answer. I counted to thirty before knocking again.

"Umeko? Hi, it's Annie," I called, in my brightest, perkiest cheerleader voice. "Are you in there?"

"What do you want, new girl?" There was something subtly wrong about Umeko's response. She sounded like the room, like she was speaking through some thick, absorbent material. "Go away. I'm busy."

"Oh, see, that's sort of what I want," I said, still bright, still perky, still trying to ignore the growing heat in my hands. "I was watching you dance tonight, and you dropped a couple of your big feathers. The flame-retardant ones? I know those are expensive, like, twenty bucks each, so I grabbed them for you." I was lying through my teeth, but that didn't matter. Once she opened the door, I would grab the townie boy, and we'd be out of here.

"Leave them with costuming."

"But these are yours. Didn't you pay for them with your own money?" I knocked again, dialing up the obnoxiousness. "Come on, just let me give them to you. I'll go as soon as I give them to you." Let her think I was a fawning sycophant, trying to curry favor with someone above me at the show. Let her think I was too stupid to take a hint. Let her think whatever she wanted, as long as she opened the damn door.

There was a pause. Then, sweet but still muffled, Umeko said, "I try so hard not to involve the carnival, but you're so new. You're so fresh. No one will miss you. No one will think it's strange that you've chosen to move on. You've made poor choices, little girl. Very poor choices indeed."

Something about that voice told me to get the fuck out of there. That wasn't an option, but I could at least back up a little. It was the right call. The door of the RV slammed open so fast that it must have been kicked, whistling through the space where I'd been standing before it hit the limits of its hinges and hit the side of the vehicle, hard enough to leave a dent. And Umeko emerged.

She wasn't the beautiful fire dancer anymore—or maybe she was, only more so. Her face was still lovely, if somewhat distorted by the cluster of additional eyes that had opened in a shallow arc across her forehead. The reason for her muffled voice was harder to ignore: huge, vicious-looking mandibles had pushed out from between her red-painted lips, pulling them into a perpetual grimace and baring her still-human teeth in what I could only see as a threat display. Her arms were gone. So was her clothing. Her torso was exposed, small-breasted and sinuous, forming a graceful line down to the pendulous bulb of her spider-self.

Spiders can be beautiful. The spider that was Umeko was beautiful. It was vast, elegant, and sleekly white, more like a black widow or an orb weaver than a tarantula, with long, thickly-jointed legs that tapered to blood-red points. She moved like a dancer. She *was* a dancer. She was just something more than merely that.

I am enough of a nerd that my first thought was "drider." My second thought was "oh, shit." And my third thought was "I am in range of those legs." I leaped backward a bare second before her front two legs slammed down on the place where I'd been standing, hard enough that they buried themselves easily six inches into the ground, piercing and penetrating it.

"You should have backed off," she hissed, and reached for me again.

I wasn't there anymore. I might not be wearing skates or waving pom-poms, but one of the few things roller derby and cheerleading have in common is the way they teach their participants to *dodge*. I've saved myself some expensive dental work and serious injuries by dodging the oncoming bodies of my teammates, and while I wasn't quite ready to suit up and cheer next to Umeko, that didn't mean I was going to stand still while she hit me.

"What are you doing with that kid?" I demanded, pulling one of the knives from inside my glittery candy girl's uniform.

Umeko sneered. "None of your concern," she said, and lashed out with two of her legs, forcing me to duck. Too late, I remembered that most spiders can balance on four legs when they need to; two more of her limbs were waiting for me, latching around my ankle and yanking me to the ground.

I'd been hoping to get through this without blood-shed, but that only worked when everyone was playing by the same rules. I flung the knife I'd been holding. It flew straight and clean, embedding itself in the central joint of one of the legs holding me in place. Umeko shrieked, a high-pitched, inhuman sound, and dropped me, even as she stabbed at my chest with two more of her legs. I rolled aside and scrambled to my feet, readying two more knives, mentally running down the lists of giant spider and spider-esque cryptids.

In the end, there was only one thing that she could be—one thing that matched both her behavior and her description.

"You're a Jorōgumo, aren't you?" I demanded, dancing back as I tried to get out of her range. "I didn't know there were any of you outside of Japan. What are you *doing* here?"

"Trying to eat," she snarled, and struck at me again. She was fast. She was also in pain, and not expecting me to be nearly this much trouble. For the moment, I was keeping ahead of her. That wasn't going to last. I needed to end this, or she was going to end *me*.

My family is not the Covenant. Our unwillingness to kill cryptids who haven't yet committed murder is part of the distinction. "Where's the boy?"

Umeko's smile was rendered terrible by the mandibles still forcing her lips apart. "He was delicious," she said. "I'm sure you'll taste even better."

She lunged for me, for the first time putting her entire body into the motion, and she was *fast*, even faster than I'd thought she was. So fast there was no way I was going to be able to roll out of the way this time. I braced myself for impact—

—only to have something slam into her from the side, knocking her body off course. She went down hard, legs akimbo, armless torso sliding across the uneven ground of the bone yard. She shrieked, another inhuman sound. It hurt my ears. I staggered to my feet, filling my hands with knives as I struggled for my balance.

The something that had slammed into Umeko seemed to realize I was there. It turned toward me, eyes wide and surprised. It was a tall, sinewy figure, with a tail almost as long as its body, and a face that was faintly simian, somewhere between the average man on the street and an extra from *Planet of the Apes*. Its feet were bare, which only made sense: they were more than halfway to being an extra pair of hands. It blinked. I blinked.

"Sam?" I asked, finding my voice.

"Annie?" he said, the word sounding more than halfway to "oh, shit." Unlike his face, his voice hadn't changed.

That wasn't the only reason to be concerned. I felt my own eyes widen, and shouted, "Get *down*!" a bare second before two of Umeko's limbs scythed through the air where Sam was standing. She was fast, and somehow he was faster: what should have been a killing blow turned into a wide miss as he dashed away, winding up standing next to me.

"What are you *doing* here?" he asked.

"She took a townie boy back to her trailer. Didn't seem right, so I followed," I said, keeping a careful eye on Umeko, who was tensing for another strike. Her slide across the bone yard had opened a wide, bloody scrape in her side and limbless shoulder; there was a chance the pain would distract her from killing us, but, really, I just expected it to make her angry. "What are *you* doing here?"

"It's my show!"

Umeko struck at us. Sam leaped straight up. I dove to the side, only to find myself lifted into the air as he wrapped his tail around my waist and jerked me into the air. I squeaked surprise before I got my wits back, and flung a knife at the off-balance form of Umeko, skewering another of her joints. She roared. I landed, hard, on the roof of a nearby RV.

"Warn a girl next time!" I snapped, readying another knife.

"*Me* warn *you*?! You're the one chucking knives at a giant spider!"

"Jorōgumo," I said primly. Umeko was back on her feet, beginning to clickety-clack her way around the RV where we were standing. "Japanese origin, also known as 'the binding bride.' They're a type of therianthrope. They feed on humans."

"Uh," said Sam. I glanced at him. He was watching me

with open concern. It was surprisingly easy to read his expression, despite the bone and muscle changes that accompanied his transformation. "How do you know all this? Shouldn't you be running and screaming right now?"

"Running and screaming comes later, after we don't die," I said. "It would be a little self-indulgent right now."

Sam shook his head. "Holy shit, you're weird. I didn't think—"

He stopped speaking as a loop of silk whipped up from beneath us and locked around his throat, cutting off his air supply. Alarmed, he clawed at the silk, only to topple off the edge of the roof as Umeko yanked and gravity kicked in.

Well, shit. I ran to the edge of the roof, trying to calculate the angles and the height and all that other fun shit that normally isn't my problem, because when I jump, I'm counting on the surface I land on to be yielding, if not actively rubbery.

Yielding. Rubbery. Umeko was reeling Sam in like a fisherman reels in their line, her legs occupied with the complicated business of twisting more and more webbing around him. Her attention was focused on her captive, and not on me. And her abdomen sure did make a tempting target.

Saying a quick prayer to whatever saints looked after the stupid and the suicidal, I leaped, my feet aimed straight for the widest point of the Jorōgumo's body.

Spiders are beautiful, dangerous, alien creatures. They can be tiny or enormous, venomous or harmless to humans. They have just as much diversity as anything else on the planet. But there's one thing all spiders have in common. They're surprisingly fragile. Drop a tarantula, and its exoskeleton will shatter like glass. The spider will die. They can survive without food, without air, without several of their limbs, but break that surface, and they're gone.

My feet slammed into Umeko's abdomen just above the filigree markings that slashed across the ivory like arachnid tattoos. There was a moment's resistance, like I was stepping on eggshells. Then it gave way with a terrible squelching, squishing sound, and my momentum carried me right through her, into the soup of her internal organs, which had never been meant to take this kind of damage. Umeko screamed again, high, shrill, and despairing. She twisted to look at me, and all of her eyes were wide, filled with terror, as she saw what I'd done to her.

There was no way she could have survived that sort of damage. At this point, the only thing I could give her was a quicker death. Most things with a human torso and an animal body have differently ordered organs, but all of them have this much in common: they still need to breathe.

My legs were bare, and beginning to tingle from their contact with the contents of Umeko's body, which had almost certainly contained at least one venom sac, if not more. Hoping Sam would be able to get loose and free me before I succumbed, I flung another knife, catching Umeko in the throat. She closed all her eyes but the most human pair, looking briefly, terribly grateful. Then she collapsed, falling in a heap of tangled legs and broken body, atop the still-webbed Sam.

I thought about going to him, about helping him. But the poison was already working at me, and it seemed like too much trouble. I fell in turn, and the world was dark, and nothing hurt. Nothing hurt at all.

Fifteen

"The world is weird. Never challenge it to get weirder. You'll lose."
— Jane Harrington-Price

The Spenser and Smith Family Carnival, inside a private room, some undefined amount of time later

SOMEONE HAD PUT A WET washcloth on my forehead and pulled a warm blanket up to my shoulders, a seemingly contradictory blend of temperatures that said "safety" on a deep, almost elementary level. If there were wet washcloths and warm blankets, the world was functioning the way it was supposed to; things were going to be all right. Somehow, things were going to be all right.

"Her breathing just changed." The voice was Sam's. The tone was new. He didn't sound wary or annoyed: he sounded exhausted, and a little confused, like reality had rearranged itself while I was sleeping, and had not yet had the courtesy to tell him exactly what the hell was going on. "I think she's awake."

"If she's awake, she'll let us know." The second voice belonged to Emery. It was kind, although it took on an edge as she continued, "And hopefully she'll let us know soon, since I'd like a few answers."

I know how to take a hint. I didn't open my eyes or push away the blankets as I said, "I'm here. Is it okay if I don't move? My hands feel all tingly."

"That would be the spider venom," said Emery. "You're lucky you didn't die. You're even luckier that you had no open wounds."

Open wounds: right. Lots of spiders have venom that does nastier things than just killing a person. Fortunately for me, most of those nastier things aren't topical. The venom needs to get *inside* the body to really start doing damage. "I should play the lottery," I said.

"Maybe you should," said Emery. "Or maybe you should just tell me who the hell you are, and why you're here. I don't suggest you lie to me a second time."

I recognized her tone. That was a dangerous tone. I didn't want to open my eyes. I did it anyway, choosing situational awareness over comfort.

The ceiling was draped in dark blue fabric. Crystals hung from it, suspended on fishing wire, alongside a plethora of stars and moons that looked like repurposed Christmas ornaments. I sat up, looking at the bed I was in at the same time. It was about as wide as mine, but half again as long, covered in quilts and heavy blankets. The sort of bed that would belong to someone who didn't like to be cold.

Sam and Emery were nearby, Sam sitting in an old easy chair, Emery leaning against the wall. There were shelves on every available surface, crammed full of books and small souvenirs. Some of them looked like they should belong to a child—building blocks, a toy train, a plush monkey with half its fuzz rubbed off. This was definitely Sam's room, which meant I was in their shared RV, which meant I was in a lot of trouble. Emery was still wearing her announcer's outfit, with pancake and rouge caked onto her face until she could have passed for a woman twenty years younger, under the right light. The stark fluorescents of the RV were not the right light. And Sam . . .

Sam was still a monkey who also happened to be a man. The blend of the two was so seamless that special effects companies would have swooned to see him. It was easier to take in the details here, when a giant spider-woman wasn't trying to kill us. His hair had been black in his all-human form, but it was a dark brown, ticked with pale blond, now that he'd transformed. His eyes were exactly the same.

"Well?" prompted Emery.

I panicked. It was the only explanation for why, when faced with the opportunity to tell the truth and be believed, what came out of my mouth was, "My name is Timpani Brown, ma'am. I just left out a few things about what happened to my home show. Like how it was Apraxis wasps that came out of the trees and left everyone dead. I'm as human as they come, but not all the people I traveled with were."

"How is it you were able to identify a dangerous therianthrope when it was in the process of trying to kill you?"

I allowed a little irritation to creep into my voice. "How is it you weren't, ma'am? Umeko was one of yours, but Sam looked as surprised as I felt when he showed up and she was a spider. Why is it a surprise I'd know about more things than just mice? I live with talking rodents that worship me as a living link to the divine. You've got to figure that opens a girl's mind."

"She's got a point, Grandma," said Sam. "We should have known."

I blinked. "You mean you really didn't?" It had been a shot in the dark, intended to deflect. I hadn't been expecting to hit anything.

Emery sighed. "Umeko was with the show for years. *Years*. She never seemed to get any older. I assumed, I suppose, that she was some sort of yōkai, something that aged slowly if at all, but it wasn't my place to ask. We respect the privacy of our performers, as long as they do no harm. There are worse things in the world than spider-women and talking wasps, Annie. You're young yet, and you've been lucky enough not to run afoul of anything truly terrible. If you had, you wouldn't be here."

"She means the Covenant of St. George," said Sam. He shivered, the fur on his head puffing out a bit, like the early stages of a threat display. "They're zealots and killers, and they're part of why my mom couldn't deal with the idea of getting too attached to me. They wouldn't care that your mice are adorable. They'd just care that they're too weird to exist, and they'd kill them dead. And you, too, for 'consorting with demons.'"

"What swell people," I deadpanned. The tingling in my feet was fading. I sat up in the bed, beginning to massage my right wrist with my left hand. It had been a while since I'd been hurling knives with quite that combination of speed and force. "I don't know much about Jorōgumo, but it's possible they have a sort of . . . larval stage where they can pass for ordinary humans. A lot of yōkai go through something like that. So maybe she looked human for so long because she sort of was."

Emery's eyes narrowed. "How do you know so much if you're just a girl from a carnival that got wiped out by wasps?"

"We had a family of kawauso with the carnival for a while. The kids were too young to hold human form very long, so everyone sort of knew, even if most people pretended it was just a really weird otter show. I like to talk to people. I learned some stuff about yōkai. Inasmuch as you *can* learn stuff about yōkai that applies to more than one type. I mean, the word is sort of Japanese for 'cryptid,' but with a lot of other cultural stuff appended."

Sam and Emery were both staring at me. Well. In for a penny, in for a pound.

"Umeko was pretty nasty to me, and I remembered she had a boyfriend, so when I saw her leaving with a townie boy who didn't even look like he'd graduated from high school, I figured I'd follow and make sure she understood that the night after a death on the grounds was not the time to go messing around." I paused, and my next question was laden with genuine concern: "Is he okay? Were we fast enough?"

"He is," said Emery. "We think she had some sort of paralytic in her saliva. She put him to sleep. He was about half-webbed when we opened the RV." She looked away at the end, eyes darting to the side. Not toward Sam, either: she was avoiding us both.

I took a deep breath and asked, in as gentle a tone as I could manage, "He wasn't the only one, was he?"

"No," said Emery, looking back to me. "There were five others, including her boyfriend, Pablo. I didn't even notice that he was gone. He'd been webbed up in there for so long that he'd become a mummy; we had to identify him by his tattoos. I don't know what we're going to do with the bodies. We can't dump them, or someone will connect them to the carnival. But that boy you saw her take . . . all the others were about the same age. She took teenagers. Their parents must be worried sick."

"The carnival is still the common factor if you find a way to dump them." I hated those words. I hated them as they were leaving my mouth, and I hated them even more when I saw them strike home. Emery's lips turned down in a pained frown that had nothing to do with disapproval, and everything to do with understanding what I was about to say. "Maybe the local police departments will put together that the carnival was in town when the kids disappeared and maybe not, but Umeko is dead, and she's not going to be taking any more kids. But if they're all found in the same place . . ."

"Then people are going to ask questions, and we're not going to have any good answers for them," said Emery grimly. "They have to be runaways. If they're found, we're painting a target on our backs, and we won't survive whatever comes after."

"Yeah," I agreed. I could spin this. I could tell the Covenant Umeko had acted alone, and that the rest of the carnival hadn't known they were harboring a monster; I could tell them I'd killed her myself. Although . . . "What did you do with Umeko's body?"

"Shoved her in the RV with her victims, so she wouldn't scare the shit out of people when they came to see what all the screaming was about," said Sam.

"Language," said Emery.

"Sorry, Grandma." He ducked his head, tail twisting around his ankle in a gesture that I immediately translated as shuffling his toes in embarrassment.

"What *are* you?" I blurted.

"Um," he said. "Human, on my mother's side. Fūri, on my father's." He looked at Emery for support.

"Didn't anyone ever tell you it's rude to ask such blunt questions?" she asked.

"He's a monkey, and a giant spider-woman just tried to kill us both," I said. "I think the trauma excuses a little rudeness."

"I don't mind, Grandma," said Sam. "She didn't scream or freak out or anything when I showed up. That's pretty cool. I'm okay if she wants to ask questions."

Oh, I wanted to ask questions. I wanted to ask about a hundred questions, and then a couple hundred more follow-ups. Yōkai are plentiful in Japan and China, but not many have made the move to North America, which has its own cryptids, not all of whom are friendly to newcomers. The name fūri was familiar in that "I probably saw this once in a book" sense, but it didn't come with any details.

"Maybe later," I said, and pushed back the blankets, swinging my feet around to the floor. I was wearing someone else's flannel pajamas, easily three sizes too big for me. They had a drawstring waist, pulled tight to keep them from falling down. That was a nice touch. I leaned down to roll up the cuffs, running my fingers along the skin of my ankles in the process. It was red and slightly inflamed, like I'd managed to acquire a bad sunburn in the middle of the night.

"You're going to peel," said Emery.

"Probably," I agreed, and stood. My legs supported me. Since that was their job, I was pleased. "Did you throw away my shoes?"

"They were sort of ruined," said Sam. "You got giant spider-lady guts *everywhere*."

"Yeah, well, I was out of knives and options," I said. "You're welcome, by the way."

"Are you going somewhere?" asked Emery.

I nodded grimly. "Jorōgumo don't eat much in their spider forms, which is how any of them have managed to survive. I don't know if they're cross-fertile with humans, but some therianthropes are—"

"Like Dad," said Sam.

"—and since her boyfriend was her first victim, there might be an egg sac in there." I shook my head. "You said Umeko was with you for years, seeming totally human the entire time. So maybe Jorōgumo have babies the human way. But they could just as easily hatch, and I'd rather we found that out now, instead of hearing the babies start to scream when we set the RV on fire."

"Who said anything about setting the RV on fire?" asked Emery.

"Do you have a better way to get rid of a dead spider-woman? We can't bury her. Not after Savannah. Digging a big hole would be deeply suspicious. A small burn, on the other hand, if we wait to do it until we've moved on, and we control it properly, looks like an accident. Spread out the trauma. Save some for the next town."

"I really wish that didn't make sense," said Emery.

"Believe me, so do I," I said. "Do you have a pair of shoes I can borrow?"

"My shoes wouldn't fit you," she said. "Sam, can you please take Annie back to her own room so that she can get some clothes?"

"Sure, Grandma," said Sam, and crossed the room to where I was standing, and picked me up. My size didn't seem to be a problem for him: he just hooked an arm under my knees and hoisted me high.

"I can walk!" I protested.

"But you won't," he said, and walked out of the room.

Sam and Emery lived in a large enough RV to give them each a private bedroom, which meant it also had a living room larger than the entire available living space in my RV. Sam carried me past the couch and dining table before using his tail to open the door, stepping through and into the bone yard. The sun was up. People were moving around. If any of them were surprised by the appearance of a six-foot-tall monkey man with an armful of pajama-clad human female, they didn't show it; a few of them even waved. Sam was apparently a common sight around here.

Which meant . . . "Were you so snappy with me when

I showed up because I meant you had to stay human-looking?"

"Uh, yeah," said Sam. He hopped down from the steps, absorbing the three-foot drop easily. He crouched. "Hold on tight."

"Hold on tight for—ahhh!"

Being a monkey person didn't just make Sam faster and a little bit taller: it apparently also converted his legs to some sort of piston system, granting him the ability to leap tall buildings in a single bound. In one jump, we were on top of the RV. In another, we were on the next RV over, moving fast enough that it took my breath away—at least at first.

By the third jump, I was starting to enjoy myself.

By the fourth jump I was thinking about what he could do in a more urban setting, or a proper jungle, or really *anywhere* that would have things for him to grab and swing from, rather than leapfrogging across a relatively horizontal plane. He was getting some serious air on his jumps. He could have done a lot more with mechanical assistance.

"You okay?" he asked, after I'd been silent for a few seconds.

"Whee!" I replied.

Sam blinked. "Okay, holy shit, you're weird."

"Never said I wasn't," I said blithely.

Sam hit the roof of a large RV before hopping down to ground level and gesturing grandly with his tail to the door of my room. "You are delivered. Mostly. I'll carry you in. I don't want you telling my grandmother I didn't get you all the way home."

"That's very sporting of you."

"You haven't seen my grandmother mad yet." Sam walked up the steps to my RV, again opening the door with his tail. It was a neat trick, and neatly enough performed that I didn't think to warn him about what he was walking into.

The mice were well-trained. Mindy and I had spoken at length about why it was important for her to stay concealed from the Covenant, and Mork came from a colony that wasn't as accustomed to being seen as the home colony. But that didn't mean they'd be able to resist one of the Priestesses being carried in by a man who clearly wasn't human. There was no reason for stealth in *that* situation. And in fact . . .

"HAIL!" shouted the mice, as soon as the door was open. What they lacked in numbers, they made up for with enthusiasm. "HAIL THE RETURN OF THE PRECISE PRIESTESS! HAIL THE COMING OF THE VERY LARGE MONKEY!"

Sam stopped. Sam blinked. Sam said the only thing that made any sense under the circumstances: "What the fuck?"

Mork and Mindy had continued to refine their little house, decking it out with pennants made from ride tickets and bits of text torn from carnival posters. It was a tiny work of art, and more than suitable for two Aeslin mice. They had also, it was clear, gone scavenging when I didn't make it home the night before. The counter around their house was covered with popcorn, wads of cotton candy, and half-eaten hot dogs. By any rodent standards, they were going to be eating like kings.

"Aeslin mice. They're pathologically religious," I explained. "Put me down."

Sam put me down. "I knew they talked. I didn't know they, uh, did *that*."

"You get used to it," I said. "Mork, Mindy, this is Sam. You don't need to hail him, but he's safe enough that you don't need to worry if it just slips out."

"HAIL!" cheered the mice.

Mindy stepped forward, fanning her whiskers out before she said, "Priestess, your telephone rang many times during the night. Many, many times. We did not answer it, for lo, did you not say 'Keep Your Paws Off'? But perhaps it was important."

My stomach flipped over. I only had one phone, and only two people had the number.

And I had missed a check-in.

Turning to Sam, I smiled as brightly as I could while

also feeling like I was about to throw up, and asked, "Meet me at Umeko's RV? I need to change out of your pajamas and into something a little more actually mine. I'll need about fifteen minutes."

"And to make a private phone call," he said, with a sour expression that was much more like the Sam I knew than his friendliness of the morning so far had been.

I nodded. "And to make a private phone call," I agreed. "I don't know who called, but if it mattered enough to keep trying, I should probably let them know that I'm okay, I was just caught up in the carnival. Don't worry about me telling tales out of school, if that's why you look so worried. I'm pretty good at keeping secrets." Sometimes *too* good.

Sam continued to look dubious as he nodded and said, "All right. But if you're not there in fifteen minutes, I'm coming back here to get you."

"Deal," I said.

I followed him to the RV door and watched as he walked away into the bone yard. Then I stuck my head outside and looked up, making sure that he hadn't somehow doubled back and returned via one of the neighboring roofs. There was no one up there.

Locking the RV door didn't make it much more secure. It was still a thin-walled tin can, bordered on all sides by people I didn't know and couldn't trust yet with the secrets that defined my presence here. It was enough to make me feel a little bit better. I sat down on the bed, retrieving my phone from beneath the pillow, and checked the call log. Eleven missed calls, six from "Sue" and five from "Tom." Since Margaret was my official contact, I selected "Sue" and hit the button to call her back.

The phone rang. I closed my eyes. The phone stopped ringing.

"What the *hell* are you playing at?" demanded Margaret.

"The disappearances were connected to the carnival, but they didn't know," I replied. "One of their performers turned out to be a giant spider-woman who'd been kidnapping locals to use as a larder."

Margaret didn't say anything.

"I saw her leaving with a local boy last night, and I followed, because I thought something seemed wrong with the situation. When she saw me, she transformed." Not quite true, but true enough: it looked like the truth, from a distance. "I managed to get a knife in her throat before I fell on her carapace and shattered it. She died, and I passed out from the venom, hence my not being able to take your calls. I only just woke up."

"We'll be there inside the hour." Her voice was steel and sharpness, and in it I heard the end of everything.

"No," I said, as quickly as I could. "Don't."

This time, her silence was dangerous, the silence of a snake deciding whether or not to bite me.

I hurried to fill it. "The rest of the carnival didn't know about her, I'm sure of it. I've spoken to their leader, and she was genuinely stunned. If you come in now, a lot of innocent people are going to get hurt. *Human* people. If you give me more time, I can find out whether anyone here isn't quite as innocent as they seem. I can flush them out for you."

The Covenant understood the meaning of "acceptable losses" better than I liked, especially when they were talking about humans who willingly associated with monsters: they thought the species as a whole was better off without harboring traitors. At the same time, they tried to keep a low profile when they could, and they didn't go in for wholesale slaughter. It was messy and tended to attract attention.

Margaret's voice was cold as she asked, "Are your loyalties wavering, Miss Brown?"

My loyalties had never changed. They just weren't where any of these people expected them to be. "No," I said. "I want to prove myself. Having the two of you come in and take over the situation doesn't let me do that. It proves I can yell for help when I don't actually need it. Please. Give me more time."

"If you miss another check-in, we're done," she cautioned. "We won't allow you to risk yourself for the sake of impressing us."

"I won't," I said. "I promise, I won't. I just feel like I can learn more if I stay here than if I leave now." And I *would* be leaving if the Covenant came. Not for the reasons they thought, either. If they were coming to clean up the mess Umeko had made, that was going to mean killing everyone else here. I'd be warning the carnival and running for the hills as hard and as fast as my legs would carry me. There was no way I could go back after doing something so blatantly contrary to the Covenant's interests.

But I also knew I couldn't live with myself if I allowed innocent people to suffer because I'd run away too soon. Maybe if I stayed long enough, I could find a way to get all the cryptids to leave with me, so the Covenant would find nothing to destroy when they arrived. I wasn't going to be a party to deaths. I just needed time. If I had that, I could figure everything else out.

"I'll explain things to Robert. He may still try to overrule me—this is technically my mission, but he outranks me." The bitterness in her voice mirrored the bitterness I'd heard so often in my own, when circumstances forced me to work with my older siblings against my will. It was weird, feeling sorry for a member of the Covenant. I didn't like it. Life was so much simpler when it was black and white. Unfortunately for me, the deeper I got, the more things seemed to depend on shades of gray.

"Thank you."

"Don't fuck this up, Brown." The line went dead. Margaret had hung up on me. I lowered the phone, looking at it for a count of ten. Then I stood. Time to get dressed. I had a dead spider-woman to see.

Sixteen

"I don't care what else you do. Just come
home to me."

— Alice Healy

**The Spenser and Smith Family Carnival, outside the
RV that used to belong to Pablo and Umeko**

SAM WAS STILL A MONKEY when I trotted up to Umeko's
RV. The ground around it was shredded and torn,
commemorating our battle, and a large patch was stained
with grayish sludge. That must have been where I'd
smashed through her body. The grass there was dead.
The grass immediately around it was dying. Just the sight
was enough to turn my stomach.

"Who was calling?" demanded Sam. Apparently, my
brief time in the safe harbor of his good graces was
coming to an end, and we were once again sailing the
choppy seas of him being a total asshole all the goddamn time. That was almost comforting. I'd only been
with the carnival for a little while, but I had a lot more
experience with Sam being a dick than I did with him
being nice to me.

"Insurance," I said. "I'm the sole survivor of the family carnival, which doesn't come with all that much in the
way of money, but does come with a lot of 'hey, we want
to make sure you're not secretly a serial killer.'"

"Are you?"

"No."

"Good to know." Sam looked at the closed RV door.
The weird cottony stuff still covered the windows. In the

daylight, it was much easier to tell that it was webbing, piled thick and tight against the glass. "How did we miss this?"

"You knew her. Them. They were friends of yours. I mean, I don't know about you, but I don't spend a lot of time waiting for my friends to turn into killers."

"You said 'killers.'" He turned to look at me. "Don't you mean 'monsters'?"

Ah. So this was what had taken us back to Assholeville, where Sam was mayor and I was a threat to his way of life. "No," I said. "I meant 'killers.' Umeko wasn't a monster. If she's been with you for years and seemed human all that time . . . maybe she didn't know how to be a Jorōgumo without hurting people. I'd probably freak out pretty hard if I woke up one morning with four extra limbs and no hands. There was no one here to tell her it was normal and teach her what to do."

Sam stared at me. "You're serious."

"I am. I mean, I'm sorry Pablo died, I don't know if he was like your BFF or something, although I guess probably not if it's been this long without you noticing. But it wasn't Umeko's fault that she didn't have a guidebook for being what she was. She was killing people. That's a choice she made, and I'm not sorry she paid for it. I am sorry she wound up in that situation in the first place." I shook my head. "If *I* were an actual spider-centaur, I'd go to Comic-Con as the Stalk from *Saga* and get my picture taken with every famous person I could find."

Sam was still staring at me, looking increasingly dubious. "Were those actual words, or did you get nervous and vomit up a bunch of random syllables?"

"It's good to know that even when you're uncomfortable, you can still be a dick," I said. "I get why you're uncomfortable. I'd be uncomfortable, too, if our positions were reversed. And I sort of get why your grandmother is letting me look into this with you."

"Why?"

"Because I don't think you like humans much, and that's sort of dangerous, given how outnumbered you are." I left Sam gaping at me as I walked up the steps to

Umeko's RV. The door wasn't locked. It probably should have been. I took one last breath of fresh air, pushed the door open, and stepped inside.

Being a two-person unit, this RV was substantially larger than mine, although it followed most of the same structural notes: there's only so much that can be done with a house on wheels. The door was connected to the main living space, the front room and kitchen, while a short hall at the back led to the bedroom and chemical toilet. At least, I assumed that was where it went: it was sort of hard to tell, on account of all the webbing.

It wasn't just the windows Umeko had covered in thick, cottony strands. It was the walls, and the ceiling, and the furniture, creating a silken tunnel leading where the hall had been. It looked like a tarantula's burrow. It looked like the sort of thing that would make a Jorōgumo feel safe when everything was falling apart around her.

The floor was relatively free of webbing. I picked my way carefully across the room to what looked like a bookshelf, based on the shape it made through the thread, pulling a knife from inside my shirt and beginning to slice my way inside. The webs here had been exposed to the air long enough that they'd lost most of their stickiness; this wasn't a hunting burrow. It was home.

Cutting through the silk was unsurprisingly difficult. The stuff was thick and sturdy, intended to form a permanent barrier. I kept working until I reached the bookshelf, peeling sheets of webbing aside as I looked at the titles. There were several books on Japan, and a bestiary I recognized from our library at home. I worked it free, flipping through until I found the entry on the Jorōgumo. Umeko had scribbled notes in the margins all around the description of the yōkai, culminating in an inky scrawl.

"'My skin is not my own,'" I read aloud. "'Things are moving inside me. How do I make this stop? Help. Help.' Sam?"

"Yeah?" His voice came from right behind me, gruff and heavy with suspicion.

I hadn't heard him enter: calling his name had been an

educated guess. It's always nice to know that I can still predict the movements of my enemies. "Did Umeko know?" I turned to face him. "About you?"

He raised an eyebrow. It was impressive, given how low his hairline currently was; the expression caused the eyebrow to effectively disappear, turning his entire face into a quizzical look. "I don't think she could have missed it," he said. "People who don't like the fact that the boss's kid is a monkey don't last long around here."

"She still thought she was totally alone." I handed him the book, and watched as he read Umeko's notes. His eyebrow dropped back into its original position. His whole face fell a moment later, leaving him looking despondent and ashamed. "I guess monkeys still being mammals meant she didn't feel like she could come to you when she started to change."

"I had a crush on her when I was a kid," he admitted. "She was pretty, and she laughed a lot, and I thought maybe she'd be my girlfriend. She told me she was too old for me and too different from me, and one day I'd meet a nice fūri girl and settle down. So she knew the name for what I am. I don't know why she wouldn't ask for help."

I did. My family is accepting of all the differences in the world. No one batted an eye when my grandparents adopted Sarah, and Johrlac are commonly accepted as the most dangerous cryptids in the world. We have two dead aunts, my cousin is half-incubus, my other cousin is half-succubus, and our walls are full of talking mice. And I *still* hadn't told them when my fingers started getting hot, or when I'd accidentally set fire to my sheets in the night. Some things are a step too far. They're terrifying and personal, and telling people about them would make them real. Worse, telling people about them might make those people look at you differently. It might make them change the way they treat you. I wanted to be Antimony Price, little sister, roller derby girl, and journeyman cryptozoologist, not Antimony Price, living fire hazard. So I'd kept my mouth shut in the beginning, and the more time that passed, the more impossible it had felt to tell.

"Maybe she was scared," I said quietly. "Don't you ever get scared?"

"All the time," said Sam.

I looked at him, and he looked at me, and the silence between us stretched out into something sharp and new, something I couldn't put a name on. Which was, naturally, when the webbing next to my left hand burst into flames.

"Shit!" I yelped, and began swatting at the fire, trying to beat it out. If the whole web went up, we were both in a lot of trouble.

The bestiary hit the floor with a thump as Sam dove out of the RV. I took a breath to start cursing at him, and stopped as he dashed back inside, now holding a bucket.

"Get out of the way!" he shouted.

I dove to the side. He doused the flame with water. The smell of char and damp spider web filled the RV. I coughed. Sam dropped the bucket.

"What the fuck, Annie?" he demanded. "Are you some sort of pyro?"

"No," I said. "I . . . I don't . . . I don't know anything about Jorōgumo webbing. Maybe it's really flammable." There it was: the proof that sometimes, telling the truth was too much to ask. Sam wasn't a friend, but he was potentially an ally, and I didn't want him looking at me like I was a freak. It says something about my idea of "normal" that I thought the man who walked like a monkey was going to judge me for setting a few fires with my mind.

"So be more careful," he said. "I don't feel like hauling your ass out of the fire."

"Yes, sir," I said. The bookshelf was soaked: if there were any more clues to be found there, they'd need to wait until it dried. Maybe the bodies—

I stopped. Keeping my voice very level and calm, I asked, "Sam? Where are the bodies?"

"We put Umeko in the bedroom. That's where . . ." He stopped. Swallowing hard, he continued, "That's where we found the cocoons."

I followed his gaze to the webbed tunnel. "I always liked haunted houses," I said, and began walking in that direction.

It must have been hard for Umeko to move around the RV when transformed. The tunnel was narrower than her body had been, and while she could squeeze, the positioning of her legs meant she'd probably preferred to walk with them spread out at her sides, giving her greater control. I didn't know how long she'd been able to assume her full spider form, but it looked like she'd never been able to let herself live openly as what she really was. Maybe it was wrong of me to feel bad for someone who'd been responsible for so many deaths. I couldn't help myself. Umeko had been a victim of circumstance, just like the people she'd killed.

The bedroom door, like the floor, was unwebbed. I opened it, and there was Umeko, still in spider form, sprawled across the bed with her limbs all akimbo and her mouth hanging open, mandibles limp between human lips. Her abdomen was a deflated sack, leaking unspeakable fluids onto the duvet. The smell of decay was in the air, faint enough that it seemed to be coming entirely from Umeko herself.

And then there were the cocoons.

As Emery had said, there were five of them, large enough and with a distinctive enough shape that there was no question they were human. The one nearest the bed was oddly incomplete; a man's head protruded from the top, skin drawn tight across the skull, a rose tattoo on the side of his neck. I frowned before climbing up onto the bed, careful to avoid the fluids leaking from Umeko, and beginning to slice the cocoon open.

"Uh, you didn't say anything about playing with the corpses," said Sam. "I am not here for corpse-bothering. Honestly, I'd rather not be here at all."

"I'm not corpse-bothering," I said. "I'm checking something." I continued to slice at the webs covering the hapless Pablo until I exposed his neck and shoulders. There it was, as I'd more than half-expected: a vicious

puncture wound in the flesh above his collarbone. It
looked like the sort of thing that would have been left
behind if Umeko had bitten someone. If there was any
mercy to the placement of the thing, it was that he'd
probably bled out before her venom could kill him.

And she had loved him. She'd left her own space to
share his—no small thing, in a world where privacy was
so precious and so hard to come by. There were no signs
of predation on his flesh; I didn't want to completely un-
wrap him, but every part of him I could see was still intact, if withered and wasted away.

"I don't think she meant to do it," I said, looking at
the wound. "I think she moved in with Pablo because she
was scared and thought she could control it, and then he
walked in on her, or she shifted in her sleep, and when
he screamed, she bit him. Instinct took over. She loved
him, and she killed him, and after that, there was no way
she could tell anyone what was happening to her. They
would have looked at her like she was a monster." I
hadn't known her, but I could absolutely understand
why she hadn't wanted that to happen.

And then she'd become a monster, because that was
how she'd been thinking of herself. Sometimes we
change in terrible ways without even realizing it.

Sam's tail nervously twisted around his waist, twining
and knotting in a way that seemed to soothe him, at least
a little. "We should have realized something was wrong.
I should have noticed when I stopped seeing Pablo
around."

"Can't change the past. Can just try to do better in the
future." I climbed off the bed, leaving the ill-fated Pablo
webbed to the wall. I hoped he'd been happy with
Umeko, before the changes she was undergoing had
killed him. I hoped he'd known she didn't mean to do it.

"What are you doing now?"

"Just looking." The other four cocoons were the victims that had attracted the attention of the Covenant in
the first place. Somehow, their intelligence teams had
missed one. I wasn't going to report that part. Anything

that encouraged the Covenant to improve their surveillance wasn't a good thing as far as I was concerned. "Has Umeko been eating normally? I mean, have you seen her in the mess tent with the rest of the show?"

"Yeah," he said. "She's mostly been drinking protein shakes and stuff, but she's been eating. Why?"

"Because some spiders will web up prey for later. For lean times. They eat what they can and save what they can't." *Please, let me have this,* I thought, bringing the knife toward the first of the cocoons. *Please, give me one good thing, to make up for Umeko, and the instincts she didn't get to choose. Please.*

"I don't understand."

"Just cross your fingers, okay?" Corpses would be difficult to dispose of without endangering the carnival. Living victims would be even harder. Somehow, I thought everyone involved would be cool with the complication.

Gingerly, I cut the webbing away, peeling it back from the pale face of the boy Umeko had stolen. He was young, maybe seventeen, with a strong jaw and those annoyingly long eyelashes that always seem to go to the boys. I pressed the first two fingers of my left hand against his neck, counting slowly as I waited.

I had just reached ten when his heart thumped, once.

"He's alive," I said, and started cutting again, faster this time. "Sam, help me. We need to get them out of here."

"What?"

"They're alive!"

Sam rushed to help me, and together, we lowered the first survivor to the floor.

They weren't all alive: only two, the first and the last, had survived what Umeko had done. The other two had partially liquefied inside their cocoons, and a substantial amount of what should have been there was missing.

Umeko had been doing her best to stay away from human flesh, but without someone to help her balance her diet, the protein shakes hadn't been able to cut it.

There was no egg sac.

It was odd. I was furious at the loss of life, but I still felt terrible for Umeko. What she'd been through, what she'd been forced to do by her own body. None of this was her fault. She'd done it, and she'd paid for it, but it hadn't been her choice, and it hadn't had to happen.

If the Covenant hadn't wiped out so many of the Jorōgumo, maybe Umeko would have had a supportive community around her, one that could tell her how to handle the changes she was going through. If humans hadn't reacted so badly to the idea of sharing the world with people who weren't like us, maybe she wouldn't have become a killer. Sometimes monsters are made, not born.

Neither of the survivors had any memory of what had happened to them, or any idea of how much time had passed. Emery let them call their parents, hovering nearby while they explained that the carnival had saved them, not stolen them. Maybe it was the fact that any memories they *did* have would center on a giant spider, but both boys sounded utterly sincere as they spun a tale of being knocked out cold until the heroic carnies—me and Sam, who had been conspicuously absent since the teens woke up—rescued them. Emery agreed to hold the show where it was until their parents could come and pick them up.

The teens who hadn't made it were still in Umeko's RV. Unless the police did a door-to-door search, the bodies wouldn't be found—and the police weren't going to do a door-to-door search. They didn't have any reason, and the only person they knew had died had been a carnie, not one of their own.

Emery was pressing mugs of tea on the boys. I slipped out.

Sam wasn't in the mess tent. I hadn't expected him to be. I hadn't known him long. I'd still known him long enough to know that when he was stressed, he went for the trapeze.

The bone yard was buzzing and the midway was deserted: classic early morning. Our posted hours would have the show opening for business at four. I wondered whether Emery would delay that, given the circumstances, but I rather suspected the thought would never cross her mind. The show must go on, after all. I made my way to the big tent and slipped inside, pausing by the bleachers to let my eyes adjust.

Sam was on the trapeze, swinging back and forth with a ferocious, fluid grace. The odd stiffness I'd seen in his shoulders before was gone, replaced by utter relaxation and a spine that seemed to be made of wire or live ferrets or something other than rigid bone. No wonder he'd been tense before: he'd been fighting to keep looking human when he should have been letting himself go and relaxing into the moment.

I watched him for almost a minute. He was graceful in motion, spinning and flipping and leaping farther than a human acrobat could pray to achieve. He used his hands, feet, and tail almost interchangeably; he was more likely to break a fall with his foot than his tail, but I assumed that was because of the way shock was distributed through the body. Having his tail pulled couldn't feel awesome. Yelling didn't seem like the thing to do. He was lost in his own world, letting gravity speak for him.

Slowly, I bent and removed my shoes.

There's something exhilarating about the long climb toward a trapeze swing. Every step means there's farther to fall, and plenty of opportunities to consider just how bad an idea this is. My toes gripped the rope, holding me fast as I ascended. The muscles in my shoulders had already started to ache by the time I reached the platform. I'd been throwing knives and working on the trampoline, doing laps and push-ups and sit-ups and all that fun bullshit, but those all work different muscle groups. They didn't suspend my body weight from my arms the way climbing or the flying trapeze did. I was out of practice, and I was probably going to pay for this tomorrow. That was okay. I've made a long habit of writing checks against my future, and so far, I've always been good for them.

There was a small ball next to the hook holding the swing for this side of the trapeze: cheesecloth filled with powdered chalk. I picked it up, beating it against my palms until they were white and dry. Sweat is the enemy of the flying trapeze. Lose your grip once you're out there, and you could very easily become an interesting smear on the tent floor—not a fate I've ever aspired to.

Sometimes I think my parents encouraged me to take trapeze classes because they thought it would bring me closer to my sister. Verity's all about flirting with gravity and plummeting to her doom. It backfired. The more I learn about proper form and safety on the trapeze, the more I hate the way Verity risks herself for nothing more important than a temporary thrill and the joy of looking like Batgirl. It's careless, it's selfish, and it's going to get her killed one day, which will probably result in my parents deciding I'm not allowed to climb anymore, since gravity is only allowed to claim one of their children.

Verity never learned to appreciate how her actions could affect the rest of us. And now here I was, infiltrating a carnival under a false name for the benefit of the Covenant of St. George, all because Verity Price didn't understand consequences. I loved my sister. I was never going to learn to like her.

I took a deep breath, pushing thoughts of Verity and my family aside. Then I unhooked the waiting swing, locked my wrists into position, and jumped.

Trapeze is never safe. All the bells and whistles in the world won't save you if you screw up. That doesn't mean it has to be dangerous, if it's done correctly. There was a moment of beautiful, stomach-dropping freefall before the swing snapped tight beneath me, and then I was sailing in a hard, glorious arc toward the middle of the tent, where Sam, wide-eyed, was swinging my way.

"What are you doing?" he demanded, before his swing carried him past me. He let go, flipped around, and swung back in the opposite direction.

I laughed and did the same, hitting my remount as hard as I could to build up more momentum. The trapeze is sort of like a combination of the dreaded chin-up and the beloved swing set. It's all about the shoulders and the core, but the legs can be used to make things faster or slower, depending on what you do with them. I wanted to synchronize with Sam, enough that I could talk to him.

My swing carried me in his direction. Trying to sound casual despite the burn in my shoulders, I said, "You weren't going to come down, so I came up. You okay?"

"Not really." There was another pause as our swings separated us. When they brought us together again, he continued: "One of my friends was a yōkai and I didn't know it, so I didn't help her." Break, resume. "Now three people are dead, and she's dead, and it sucks."

Break, resume. "I'm sorry. There was no way you could have known."

"There should have been!" Break, resume. Sam scowled at me. "How good do you think you are?"

Break, resume. "I'm not bad."

"Then come over here. This is confusing."

I blinked, momentarily grateful for the momentum that was already taking me away again. Did I really want to do this? I'd known him less than a week, and he'd been an absolute jerk to me for more than half that time. He might drop me just for fun.

And if he did, there was a net. I know how to fall. There was nothing to lose by trying, and quite a bit to gain. When my momentum carried me back to him, I let go of the swing, hands outstretched to grab hold. He caught them with his feet, which was a little odd, and proceeded to jackknife on the swing, bringing me up so that I could grab hold of it. We wound up face-to-face, our noses only inches apart, with my hands to either side of his. We were still swinging.

"You weren't kidding about having some trapeze training," said Sam.

"Nope."

"Your form's shit, though."

His tone was goading—he was trying to pick a fight in whatever way he could—but that didn't matter, because he was right. I shrugged as much as my current position allowed and said, "I haven't been practicing much lately. Hopefully now that I'm working with the show, your grandmother will let me on the swings."

"Oh, yeah. The insurance thing." Sam smiled a little. "I promise if you fall, I'll totally lie and say you tripped over something on the ground."

"I'm going to hold you to that." It was almost soothing, swinging back and forth like this, letting Sam be the one to compensate for our combined weight on a single trapeze swing. "I really want Emery to let me perform. Knives or trapeze or whatever."

"Why? What makes it so important to you?"

Because it was something I couldn't do at home; because it was something that would make me feel like I was a part of this show, and not a liar skating across the surface. Because it would let me burn off some of the nervous energy that writhed and twisted underneath my skin, turning every move I made into the rough action of flint against stone. The more restless I became, the more fires I set. I'd never even felt my hands heat up on the derby track. There had to be a correlation.

Because I wanted to fly.

"I want to be useful. I'm not a very good candy girl. I don't like people enough for them to feel like buying things from me."

Sam snorted. "Okay, wow, 'I'm a jerk' is the best reason I've ever heard for letting somebody throw knives at people."

"I know my own strengths." My shoulders were beginning to shake in a way that spoke of muscle fatigue. I grimaced. "Can you get us to the platform?"

"Sure thing." Sam pulled back, setting up the momentum for a harder swing. All the amusement was gone, replaced by a serene professionalism. No one screws around on the flying trapeze. That sort of thing gets people killed.

Maybe it was the shift in our speed, or maybe it was

just my arms finally giving up on my listening to them. Whatever the reason, my left hand slipped, dropping me into a one-handed grip. I barely had time to widen my eyes before my right hand slipped as well, and I was falling.

Sam's tail wrapped tight around my left ankle, jerking me to an abrupt stop.

"Hey!" I yelped. "Watch it, Spider-Man!"

"Calm down, I'm not going to Gwen Stacy you," he said.

I blinked. "You know Spider-Man?"

"Uh, hello, not culturally illiterate here; also, a monkey." Sam stopped working the swing. It lost momentum until we were hanging in the middle of the trapeze, his tail still around my ankle, keeping me from falling into the net below. Not that *far* below; the tent was thirty feet high, giving us a twenty-foot trapeze. Sam was six feet tall, and his tail extended about three feet past his toes, giving me an eleven-, maybe twelve-foot drop from where I dangled. Not too bad.

"I think the only thing I read more than Spider-Man comics when I was a kid was this beat-up old version of *Journey to the West* that Grandma got for me," he continued, before saying, "Brace yourself."

He let go of the swing.

I yelped. Sam laughed. We weren't plummeting; we'd stopped almost as soon as we'd started. I looked up. He had hold of the swing again, with his left hand only. The resulting slant in his body had dropped me easily another foot toward the net.

As I was currently angled, I was going to land on my head. Well. That, at least, was something I could fix, and while my shoulders may have suffered during my Covenant-directed training, my core strength was still excellent. I sat up in the air, folding myself as close to double as I could manage in my current position.

"All right," I said. "Drop me."

Sam looked surprised, but did as he'd been told. I continued bending forward, wrapping my arms around my legs to make it more likely that I would land on my ass.

Trampoline is *great* for teaching a person which parts of their unique body are best for landing on. In my case, all glory to the butt.

Said butt slammed into the net with remarkable force, given my short fall, and I bounced a few feet into the air. I released my legs, twisting around, and on my second impact, grabbed the net with both hands, preventing a third. Then I rolled to the side, making space for Sam.

He didn't fall so much as drop, landing with both feet and one hand gripping the net. His tail lifted, curling behind him in classic simian style, and if they'd wanted a poster image for him, that could have been it. See! The Amazing Monkey Man as he falls from great heights like it's no big deal!

"You okay?" he asked, and there was genuine concern in his voice. I wondered how young he'd been when he learned humans were breakable, that they couldn't catch themselves the way he could. He'd probably given his grandmother dozens of panic attacks before she'd learned that the rules for him were different.

"Yeah," I said. "Thanks for the save."

"No problem," he said, and took his hand off the net, offering it to me.

I only hesitated for a moment before I took it. He pulled me easily back to my feet and smiled at me, a little shyly, like this was a point he didn't reach with many people. I smiled back. We stood there on the net for several seconds, smiling at each other, me holding onto his hand.

Then he let go, and took a step backward. "This is usually where new people start asking me awful questions. If you're going to ask me awful questions, go ahead and do it."

"You've already revealed yourself as a Spider-Man fan, and I'm more of an X-girl, so I don't think I have anything further to discuss with you," I said, and walked toward the edge of the net. "Unless you're about to reveal a secret passion for, like, peanut butter and bacon sandwiches. Which I can at least understand, even if I don't share it."

Sam raised an eyebrow. "You don't have *any* questions about the whole monkey thing?"

"Well, last I checked, being a yōkai was genetic, and Emery's your grandmother, and you've already told me your dad was a fūri, and since therianthrope genes are usually dominant, you take after his side of the family." I shrugged. "There aren't that many questions to ask." That was a lie. There were *dozens* of questions to ask. It was just that most of them were intrusive things about his biology, and I didn't have a good explanation for why I'd want to know. "It's for the family records" wasn't going to cut it when I wasn't using my family name.

Sam raised the other eyebrow. "You are ... really chill. Are you on drugs?"

"Not enough of them," I said, grabbing the side of the net and lowering myself down. "Nothing stronger than caffeine. Life is weird enough without needing to decide on the fly whether or not it's really happening. Why? What do you think I should be asking?"

"This is usually where people look all sympathetic and ask if my mom ran away because of the tail."

"Did you have the tail as a baby?"

Sam nodded.

I grinned. "I hope your grandma has pictures, because holy shit, that must have been adorable."

"Okay, there's a script, and you're refusing to follow it in any meaningful way," said Sam. He scowled. "Mom didn't leave because I was a yōkai, she left because she wasn't ready to have a baby and my father had already fucked off to wherever it is monkey-men go when their tourist girlfriends get pregnant. She knew I was probably going to have a tail before I was born. And then Grandma told her about the Covenant, and she couldn't deal, so she ran."

"Cool," I said. "Got anything else you want to crankily clear up before I can not ask about it?"

"I hate bananas."

"What, even banana splits?"

Sam nodded grimly. "All bananas."

"Then you're missing out, but I can't say I blame you.

People have probably been waving those things in your face since you were a kid."

"God, yes." Sam hopped down from the net. "I don't blame Grandma so much, because bananas are great for babies. Soft and easy to chew and shit. But then she saw me peel one with my feet and just lost it. For like the next three years, every time we had company, she was handing me a banana and waiting for me to do the cute thing. These days, even the smell is enough to make me gag."

"Legit," I said. "I'm the youngest of three. My older siblings used to pick on me, because hey, that's what baby sisters are for. So I got really, really good at fighting back, and then they went and told our parents *I* was picking on *them*. My mom tried her best to stay neutral, but my dad always sided with my big sister, even when he thought he wasn't. My reactions to her are almost Pavlovian at this point."

Sam frowned. "I thought your whole family died with the carnival."

Crap. "They did," I said. "I haven't fully adjusted to that, I guess. Things you don't talk about don't seem real."

"Tell me about it." He took a deep breath and *rippled*, simian features folding back into his body like someone had come along and revoked the rest of our CGI budget. In only a few seconds, he was the boy I'd met in the bone yard, with nothing to set him apart from anyone else except for his bare feet.

Well. Maybe that was all. "Is there a hole in the butt of your leotard?"

"And most of my pants," he said. "It's easier for me to get dressed like this and then relax, because my tail will go where it needs to be. Working jeans on *over* a tail is a special kind of torture."

"Relax . . ." I cocked my head. "This takes effort."

"Oh, yeah. Being human is . . . it's not hard, because I've been practicing all my life, but it's like trying to maintain good posture, you know? Part of you is always focusing on standing up straight, instead of on doing something important, like breathing or remembering where you left your phone."

"Huh." Most therianthropes seemed to default to a human shape—or that was what we'd always assumed. All the therianthropes I'd ever had the opportunity to talk to had grown up among their own kind. Maybe staying human was an effort for them, too, and they'd never thought it was anyone's business but their own. "If this is hard, why are you all human again?"

"Because you got squirrely about talking about your family, which probably means you're about to bolt, and I figured I'd walk you to the bone yard." He shrugged. "Either the police have already come and gone, and I can relax, or there will be strangers there, and I hate trying to explain how I got my makeup to look so good."

"Heh," I said. "Humans don't like to believe what they see with their own eyes sometimes."

"If they did, I'd probably be in a government lab being taken apart right now."

"True." I started for the bleachers, where I'd abandoned my shoes. "And you know they never warm the scalpels. It's always 'hello, nice to meet you, let me have your spleen.'"

"Why the spleen?"

"Because it's fun to say." I pulled my shoes on. "Thanks for catching me when I fell."

"Thanks for coming up to get me." Sam smiled a little. That hint of shyness was back, coloring the edges of the expression, making them seem almost sweet. "I don't get to fly with other people all that often."

"What, you've never worked with a partner?"

"Sure. But most of them only stick around long enough to get really good, and then they move on to a circus or something else where they can make more money. The trapeze acts we get here are always closed units. They want to fly together, not with the owner's weird kid." Sam shrugged. "It is what it is, you know?"

"Well, I'll fly with you any time."

He smirked at me. "You just want to fly."

"Your point? We could have a lot of fun up there. Don't Gwen Stacy me, and we'll be fine."

"I wasn't anywhere *close* to snapping your neck."

"Says you," I said.

We were still laughing as we walked out of the big tent, into the afternoon air. The smell of popcorn was starting to drift from the midway as the show geared up for opening, and everything was perfect.

Seventeen

"Sometimes what matters isn't the grand adventure, it's the small adventures that happen when no one's really looking."
—Evelyn Baker

The Spenser and Smith Family Carnival, ten days later, camped outside St. Cloud, Minnesota

THE SKY WAS A FASCINATING SHADE of slate gray, promising rain sometime in the next twenty-four hours. Because this was Minnesota, that rain could happen at any time. And because this was Minnesota, none of the locals gave a fuck. The midway had been packed with bodies since the gates opened. The lines for some of the more popular rides actually snaked all the way around the walkway, creating navigational hazards and keeping the ride jocks hopping. I looked yearningly at the spinning frame of the Ferris wheel. I hadn't been able to take the time for a ride in three days, not since we'd finished setup and invited the crowds inside.

Emery was thrilled, as well she should have been. We'd left Wisconsin terrified the authorities were going to shut the whole place down. But Savannah had been one of our own, and the teenagers we'd recovered from Umeko's trailer had fallen over themselves swearing that they hadn't been abducted by anyone associated with the carnival. Personally, I thought that was mostly because they didn't want to think too hard about what had *actually* happened to them, but the outcome was the same: we were in the clear, and able to move on.

(Savannah's death had been ruled natural causes. Her heart had just stopped. It's possible to die of fear if something is far enough outside what the mind can accept. As ways to go, it wasn't among the worst.)

Margaret and Robert were still following the show, now holed up in a rental apartment nearby, keeping an eye on the locals and replying to my nightly updates. Neither of them had set foot on the grounds, thankfully. There were some secrets I knew I wouldn't be able to keep if they saw the people I was spending all my time with. Like Ananta, the wadjet, or the giggling bogeyman twins who ran the Haunted House dark ride. Most of the carnival was made up of humans, but there were exceptions, and those exceptions were, near as I could tell, harmless. They just wanted to make people happy. They weren't doing any harm.

I had no idea how I was going to get the Covenant to leave them alone.

Drawing the knot on my gown a little tighter, I walked down the narrow alley separating the rides from the back of the big tent. We were doing three shows today, answering local demand with a gleeful expansion of our offerings. The main trapeze act, the Amazing Johnsons, had already flown at the morning show and would be flying again in the evening, taking to the swings for the delight and edification of what was estimated to be our largest crowd yet. They were good, and they were flashy, and most importantly, they looked like what people expected to see on the flying trapeze, two perfectly matched bodies launching themselves into the air without giving a damn about whether or not they hit the ground.

Sam and I were a bit less standard. He was stiff when he flew in human form—and he always flew in human form for an audience—while I was tall for a trapeze girl, with boobs that required a lot more scaffolding than the norm. We were still death-defying and high off the ground, but we weren't as fast, ironically.

We were, however, one of the only trapeze acts I knew of to incorporate knives into the process. So there was that.

I slipped into the tent, walking under the bleachers to where Sam was waiting for the cue to go on. He took in my fluffy pink dressing gown with a smirk. "Are you a pretty princess?"

"I am the prettiest fucking princess you are ever going to see," I replied. "You think I'm going to walk through a crowd of townies in sequins and fishnets? You're high."

"I did it."

"You do not have double-D breasts."

"I'd look sort of silly if I did," he said. "With my shoulders, I'd definitely want a G-cup."

I snorted and elbowed him in the side. Sam grinned.

Much of his earlier asshole routine had been exactly that: a routine. Now that he knew I wasn't going to freak out on him for the crime of having a tail, he was actually pretty decent company. Snotty and snide and prone to making terrible jokes when we were practicing, which had dropped me into the net more than once, but still, decent company. It helped that even when he was cracking wise, he caught me every time. I can forgive a lot of sins for a trapeze partner who never misses their grip on my ankle.

The fire dancers, minus Umeko, were leaving the ring. Emery strutted out to the center, and began winding up the crowd with her next spiel. I wasn't sure I'd call Sam's and my routine "a daring glimpse of athleticism and grace," but whatever got butts into seats was okay by me.

She stopped talking. The crowd applauded. I untied my dressing gown and let it slide to the floor before following Sam out into the bright lights of the ring, both of us smiling and waving to the people in the bleachers. I couldn't make out individual faces from where we were, but I didn't need to. If you'd seen one crowd, you'd seen them all. They would be watching us with wide eyes and clasped hands, some because they wanted to see us fly, others because they wanted to see us fall. There will always be people who watch the flying trapeze the way they'd watch a train wreck, and as long as they aren't jinks or mara, that's fine by me.

(Jinks are human-looking cryptids that feed on luck—either good or bad. I wouldn't mind losing a little bad luck in midair, but when there's nothing between me and a messy end but a thin net, I don't want to risk losing so much as a crumb of good luck. A jink who wanted to screw with a trapeze act could wind up killing a lot of people. Mara are also human-looking cryptids, but they feed on life energy, putting their victims into a dreamlike stupor. A mara who wanted to screw with a trapeze act *would* wind up killing a lot of people. Sleepwalking is one thing. No one does sleep trapeze.)

I reached my platform and spread my arms, back straight as an Olympic diver. On the other side of the wire, Sam stood on his own platform, posture mirroring mine. If we'd been part of a larger show, something like Cirque du Soleil, we would have been fifty feet off the ground and protected by filament-thin harnesses designed to give us a few more seconds to react if we slipped and fell. Since we were in a small, family-owned show, with the smell of sawdust clinging to our nostrils, we had a net, and we had each other. We had to trust that what we had would be enough.

Sam unhooked his swing. I unhooked my swing. Together, without saying a word, we flew.

Sam was always going to be a little stiff and over-precise in his human form. I thought he still performed astonishingly well, given that he was essentially performing on the flying trapeze while clenching every muscle in his body. It put us on roughly the same level, his stiffness counterbalancing the fact that I was still getting back into practice. It was only Sam vouching for me, and the fact that my time on the trampoline made me an essentially professional faller, that had convinced Emery to let me into the ring at all.

We spent a few minutes doing the standard tricks, swinging back and forth, trading positions, flipping in midair—the things that are incredibly hard but still look easy enough for people who've seen a trapeze act before to take them for granted. Then we returned to our platforms, and I picked up a heavy bandolier, holding it up to show the audience. Most of them wouldn't be able to see exactly what it was, just that it was some sort of shoulder sash that glittered when the light hit it. Getting it on took almost thirty seconds, because it had about a dozen Velcro straps, all of which had to be fastened tight. When it was done, I took down my swing and turned to the middle of the tent, nodding to Sam. He nodded back.

We jumped.

There was nothing ornamented or fancy about this jump: it was pure business. When we reached the center, we released our swings and exchanged them, me letting his swing carry me higher, him landing upside down, feet now hooked over my swing, so that his locked knees held him in place. We passed each other, crossed back, and when we were approaching the center for the second time, I let go of my swing, going into a tight corkscrew fall. Sam grabbed my feet before I could drop too far. The audience dutifully applauded, thinking this stunt had been the point of our setup. It was impressive, after all, and not something I would have attempted with someone shorter, or without a net.

"Ladies and gentlemen, I'm afraid you've been somewhat deceived about the nature of tonight's routine," purred Emery over the loudspeakers. "Boys?"

A group of bare-chested carnies in tight satin pants began strutting out from between the bleachers, to the delight of some, the discomfort of others, and the confusion of even more. Each of them was carrying a bullseye on a stick. The shortest was four feet tall; the tallest, ten.

The men took up positions around the outside of the ring, in front of the watching bleachers of townies, and hoisted their bullseyes into the air. I reached into my bandolier and pulled the first two knives, holding them so they glittered in the light, making sure people had a chance to see the sparkle. They might not understand it at first, but I had every faith they'd appreciate it once they realized what was going on. I moved the first knife into a flinging position. Letting it go would signal Sam to begin the next part of our routine.

Then I froze.

The lights were only blinding from the platform. With Sam holding my feet, while I still looked dazzlingly high, my head was really only about twelve feet up. That was part of why Emery had agreed to this act: I wasn't firing blind.

Margaret Healy was in the fourth row of the bleachers, a box of popcorn in her hand and a sardonic expression on her face. At least she was eating the popcorn, one kernel at a time, utterly relaxed. She knew there was no one in this room she couldn't take.

She shouldn't have been here. I'd been checking in every day, I'd been making my excuses and telling my lies, and she shouldn't have *been* here. There was no *reason* for her to be here. Not unless they'd decided to doubt me for some reason. I felt my fingertips heat up, until the knives I was holding were so hot that I could barely keep my grip. My fire couldn't hurt me when it was *on* me, but the heat I created was a killer once it had transferred to something else.

"Annie, come on," hissed Sam through gritted teeth. "We're going to run out of momentum."

I was supposed to be Timpani Brown. The sight of Margaret Healy shouldn't have terrified me: it should have reassured me that everything was okay, my allies had my back. The combination of the pain from my heated knives, his voice, and who I was supposed to be brought me back. I shook off my paralysis, slapped a smile across my face, and flung the first knife. It flew straight and true, impacting with the tallest of the bulls-eyes before most of the audience realized what had happened. The carnie holding the pole gave it a spin, showing off what I'd done, and the room erupted into applause. Throwing knives from the flying trapeze? Now *that* was something new!

None of them seemed to notice that the knife was smoking where it had slammed into the wood. Hopefully, no one was going to ask me about the scorch marks.

Sam tightened his grip on my ankles and threw himself to the left, starting us spinning wildly. Only it wasn't really that wild, because we had practiced this move until we could do it blindfolded (not that Emery was going to let me add "can't see" to the list of things making this particular knife-throwing act so dangerous). We spun, and I threw, drawing knife after knife and flinging them at the waiting targets. It was a variation on the routine I'd done to impress Leo on my first day of Covenant training, and it worked exactly as it was intended to. The audience roared louder with every knife I threw, until my hands were empty and I spread my arms in the signal for Sam to let me go.

He released my legs, and I fell to the waiting net, landing on my back and rolling for the side to finish my dismount. Once my feet were on the ground, I bowed to the crowd which roared appreciatively, and trotted for the bleachers, vanishing beneath them.

On the trapeze, Sam was pulling himself out of his spin. He'd go into another series of flips and tricks after this, keeping the audience entertained while the clowns finished setting up their act. Normally, I would have waited for him, letting him walk me back to the bone yard. Not today. The sight of Margaret sitting in the bleachers had chilled me to the core, and I didn't want to stay out in the open a moment longer than I had to. Maybe more importantly, I didn't want her paying too much attention to Sam. Let her see him as the guy I was doing a random trapeze act with and nothing more. Please. Let her overlook him.

The corridor we used to get between the bone yard and the big tent without passing through all the rides was clear, and I broke into a run when I was halfway down it, realizing only as I hit the tarp "door" to the bone yard that I'd left my dressing gown behind. It was too late to go back for it now. I kept running, hoping the worst that would come out of this day was a lecture from Emery about being careful with my things.

I hit the door to the RV so hard and fast that the mice didn't have time to cheer before I was inside. The phone was on my bed, the screen telling me I had four missed messages. The door slammed. The mice began to cheer. I whipped around, stabbing my index finger at where they stood on the counter. They stopped, going still as only prey animals truly can.

"Disappear," I said, in a harsh whisper that still felt like it was far too loud. "Margaret Healy is here, at the carnival. You know what will happen if she finds you. Don't be found."

The mice didn't say a word. They just vanished, scampering behind the microwave and out of view. Their little mouse-house was still there, but that was okay: I could claim it was some kind of weird hobby, a handicraft to let me pass the time. Aeslin mice are scrupulous about hygiene. There would be no droppings or food scraps inside the building for her to find.

My hand shook as I picked up the phone and swiped my thumb across the screen. As I had expected, all four messages were from Margaret:

SUE (11:35): Planning to come see you today.

SUE (11:37): I understand you're putting on quite the little performance there at the noontime shows. Can't wait to see for myself.

SUE (11:40): Come find me when you're finished. I'll be waiting where you found the dead girl.

SUE (11:42): Don't make me wait for long.

That was where the messages ended. I would have been happier if they'd never started in the first place. My hands were still shaking as I dropped the phone on the bed and stripped off my costume, trying to find some comfort in the essential ritual of folding it and hanging it over the back of my one folding chair. It would need to be washed, of course, but I wasn't set up for that, and so the responsibility fell to the costume mistress, who really just wanted to see that I was making an effort.

By the time I was standing naked and alone in the RV, I'd stopped shaking and started tapping into something much cleaner and more familiar: anger. How *dare* she come here, when I had done nothing to make her suspect that I was lying to her? How *dare* she follow up on me like I was some sort of liar?

But I was a liar, and even if she didn't think of me as one, she would think of me as a raw recruit, someone whose indoctrination had been stopped too soon in order to send me on the sort of assignment that could easily become a loyalty-breaker. As far as she knew, this was the world I came from, and I was showing every sign of assimilating back into it. What would the Covenant do if I told her I wanted to stay here, that being a warrior for the secret survival of the human race had been a whim, but this was what I loved?

I had a feeling Robert would make sure I went back, while Margaret would take the punishment for my wanting to stay in the first place. That was the real trouble with him being here. He made her subservient, because of her family—because of *my* family—and the desire to prove herself to him made her dangerous. Goodie.

Getting dressed only took a minute, in part because I was still running around unarmed most of the time. I wouldn't have been able to explain my customary number of weapons to Sam when I stripped for practice, or to Emery if she stopped me and noticed that I clanked. It was almost ironic. My siblings used to make fun of me for being a brawler, but these days, the fact that I was good at punching people was the only reason I didn't feel defenseless all the damn time.

My hands were heating up again as I left the RV. I shook them briskly, trying to chase the heat away. It was just starting to fade when a shape landed in front of me with a soft thud. There was no warning.

"Ahhh!" I shouted, and swung for the figure's head before I had time to realize who it was. Blame it on the tension: with the Covenant this close, coherent thought wasn't high on my list of skills.

"Whoa!" Sam danced backward, dodging my fist so easily that it was almost insulting. Nothing human could have gotten out of my way that fast. Then he paused and sniffed the air, tail curling into a question mark. "Dude, Annie, did you have a match in your hand or something?"

"Um." The fur on his cheeks wasn't burning. That was good. Nothing else about this was good, but at least I hadn't managed to set him *actually on fire*. "No. It just smells really smoky for some reason. I think they're burning a bonfire somewhere near here? Anyway, I have to go, sorry." I tried to step around him.

True to form, Sam was immediately in my way again. Sometimes his speed was awesome, like when I slipped during practice and he kept me from eating net. Other times, it was a pain in my ass. "Why didn't you wait for me today? Are you okay?"

"I had to be somewhere, and sort of, but I still have to be there, so please, can I explain later?" I looked at him plaintively. "This is one of those things I absolutely have to do."

Sam's expression turned suspicious. "Did you see someone you knew in the stands? Is that why you got all weird before you started throwing knives? Because we have bouncers."

The thought of the carnival's bouncers going up against a trained member of the Covenant would have been laughable if it hadn't been so chilling. "*Please* don't do that," I said fervently. "Yes, I saw someone I know. I need to talk to them alone. If you have them thrown out, it's going to cause all kinds of problems that I don't want to deal with."

"Are you in trouble?" He took a step closer, face grave. I'd never seen him look so serious about anything, not even when he seriously wanted me to go away. "If you are, I want to help. You know that, right?"

"Reel it in, Parker," I said, in my best Gwen Stacy voice. He laughed, some of the seriousness going out of his posture. That was good. I didn't need a knight in shining armor saving me from the . . . knights in shining armor. Okay, that metaphor sort of got away from me even as I was putting it together. "I'm okay. I'm not going to be in trouble if I go see this person."

"And after, you'll tell me what's going on?"

I paused. Finally, I said, "I'll tell you what I can. But a girl's got to have some secrets, or no one's going to show up for the next issue."

"I'll trust you this time, Annie, but you scared me. Please don't let yourself get hurt because you don't think we'll stand with you. We'll stand with you." He paused before amending, "*I'll* stand with you."

"I believe you," I said, and smiled. This time, when I stepped to the side to get around him, he didn't move to block me. I hoofed it for the edge of the bone yard, only pausing when I reached the tarp. I looked back. Sam was still there, backlit by the afternoon sun, watching me go.

I raised one hand in a wave. He waved back, and I slipped through the tarp, back into the carnival proper.

Where I found the dead girl: that was pretty clearly the Scrambler, where Umeko had left poor Savannah's body after frightening her to death. I walked down the corridor of rides, flinching from shadows, waiting for Robert to jump out at me. He didn't. Ride jocks and carnies nodded in my direction as I passed them, acknowledging me as a part of the family without making a big deal of it; there was always the chance, after all, that I didn't want to put up with townie attention right now, and they respected that.

Not everyone who works for a carnival is a *good* person, any more than any group of people defined by a common shared trait will consist entirely of good people. But the sort of folks who wind up finding their homes under the big tent and in the bone yard understand the importance of privacy, even when that privacy is found in the middle of a crowd. They'd let me be. They'd gossip about whatever they happened to see, which made it important for me to keep things with Margaret as uninteresting as possible, but they wouldn't interrupt.

Margaret was next to the Scrambler with a stick of cotton candy in her hand, munching pink fluff as she watched the ride whip around and around. I stopped next to her and waited.

"Did you know they call this stuff 'cotton candy' here?" she asked.

"Um, yes, because that's what it's called," I said. "Why, what do you call it?"

"Candy floss. Makes more sense, if you ask me. Cotton's not a food."

"Neither is floss."

"Fair enough." She took another bite, still watching the Scrambler. "Is this ride safe?"

"All the rides are safe." The kids and teens who traveled with the carnival—all children of older carnies, who were *very* careful to keep copies of the paperwork that proved there hadn't been a kidnapping close to hand—went under the rides every morning, hunting for pieces that had fallen off during the previous operating day. Then would come any necessary repairs and safety checks, which Emery took even more seriously than some of the shows I'd known. A little effort was better than a wounded townie. A wounded townie could spell the end of everything.

"It doesn't look safe."

"It's not supposed to look safe." Rides that looked *too* safe weren't interesting to thrill-seekers. The Scrambler wouldn't hurt anyone who didn't have a preexisting medical condition, but it had that air of giddy danger that would attract local teens who wanted to know what it felt like to be shaken by a giant.

"Huh." Margaret took another bite of her cotton candy before she turned to me and asked, "Want to show me where you're sleeping? I'm ever so curious about what our little Annie gets up to when we're not around."

"I can't," I said. "My room's in the bone yard—er, that's carnival lingo for the camping area out back—and I can't bring a townie there without getting in trouble. I'm still too new to have visitors over." And no amount of people giving me space would extend to cover Margaret. If I walked back there with a stranger, we'd be swarmed, with Sam at the head of the pack.

I hadn't recognized him as yōkai when we first met. I also hadn't had that much experience with yōkai in general, or with fūri in specific. Margaret . . . I had no idea what kind of fieldwork she'd done, or where, or what sort of cryptids had been involved. For all I knew, she'd spend five seconds in his presence and know exactly what he was. He'd been a jerk when we first met, but that didn't mean he deserved to be stabbed to death by my Covenant handler. Being an asshole is not supposed to be fatal.

"Fine, then," she said, tone cooling. "Take me someplace we can have some privacy."

I hesitated, reviewing my options as quickly as I could. Then, in a resigned voice, I said, "Follow me," and started across the avenue.

Carnival rides come in four flavors. The thrill rides, like the Scramblers and the coaster, are designed to provide as much bang as possible for the townie buck, encouraging people to come running back. The kiddie rides, the bumper cars and the spinning cartoon animals, those are for the townies too young to ride anything else, and are usually set up near concessions selling brightly colored candy (for them) and even brighter booze (for their beleaguered parents). You've got the old standards, the Ferris wheels and the carousels and the bumper cars, the things everyone expects to see at the carnival, the things that are almost more noticeable when they're absent. And then you have the dark rides.

Dark rides are simple cars on fixed tracks, moving in infinitely repeating loops through meticulously designed environments intended to titillate, frighten, or delight. Or at least, that's the idea. Most dark rides are just good places for teenagers to make out, drunk townies to pee over the sides of their cars, and people to get good and high. The average carnival haunted house contains as much free-floating marijuana as a Grateful Dead concert. But they're pretty private, and unless it's one of the rare rides with living carnies incorporated into the circuit, no one will hear a word that's said inside.

The Spenser and Smith Family Carnival's Haunted House was run by a pair of bogeymen, and there was no way Margaret wouldn't see through their thin layers of Cover Girl foundation to the grayish skin beneath. So I steered her in a different direction, until we stood in front of the Tunnel of Love: a carefully assembled artificial canal system in which boats floated, separated by giant rubber duckies, to make sure every couple could feel confident about their privacy. Someone must have realized the duckies weren't exactly *romantic*, because they had big red hearts for eyes, adding that little touch of absolute ridiculousness that really made the ride a tourist destination.

But this was the middle of the day. Even the darkest parts of the Tunnel were filled with grainy gray light, destroying the fragile illusions created by the Christmas lights and tulle-filled dioramas. Once the sun went down, the place would be hopping. Until then, the ride jocks were lounging, trying to look like they expected people to ride when they actually didn't.

One of them was doing her nails when we approached. Her eyebrows rose at the sight of me, and rose farther at the sight of Margaret, who had finished her cotton candy and was now licking the residue off of her fingers.

"Okay, gotta say, not what I was expecting, Annie," said the ride jock, and put her nail polish aside. "You want to ride?"

"Please," I said. "What do you mean, not what you were expecting?"

"Sweetcheeks, if you have to ask, there's a disappointed string of boys behind you stretching from here to Canada." She nimbly unhooked the rope intended to keep drunk townies from falling into the canal—it had happened, and more than once, during my short time with the show—and beckoned toward the nearest swan-shaped boat. Maybe that was part of what made the ducks seem so ridiculous. With their heart eyes and open mouths, they looked like they were eternally lusting over the oblivious swans. Waterfowl romance isn't the sort of thing that turns most people on.

"Your chariot to the balmy fields of Cupid's regard awaits," said the ride jock.

I wrinkled my nose at her as I walked past and got myself seated in the slightly sticky chlorine-scented swan. Margaret followed. The ride jock flipped a switch and the ride's gears engaged, pulling us forward, into the heart-shaped maw of love.

Margaret waited until we'd traveled about fifteen feet before she asked, in a low voice, "Are we being watched?"

"Security cameras cost money; waterproof security cameras cost more," I said. "No one's watching. Or listening. Most of the things that happen inside a Tunnel of Love aren't things anybody wants to hear."

"There's a whole industry built on proving you wrong about that one, but we'll let it pass for now," said Margaret. She turned to face me. The dimness of the tunnel's interior kept me from seeing her expression, but her posture was enough to tell me I needed to take her seriously. "Robbie's worried you might be going native. To tell you the truth, after today, so am I. Have you been compromised, Annie? There's no shame in it. I told them you weren't ready for fieldwork."

"I don't know what you mean by 'compromised,'" I said. "Are you asking whether I'm happy? Yeah. I am. This is . . . this is what I *know*. This is sequins and rope burns and uncomplicated choices, and I'm good at it. It doesn't make me work harder than I want to. It doesn't make me think about what happened to my family. But if you're asking whether I'm a traitor, the answer's no. I haven't broken any promises, to anyone. I'm here because we need to know how many of these people are innocent, and how many of them knew about the monster they were harboring."

The words were like an oil slick on my tongue, bitter and poisonous. I sounded like a Covenant member. And sure, I could tell myself I was just playing a part, saying the things she expected to hear, but how many times could I say them before some sliver of me started to believe them? We are our words as much as we are our actions.

"I find it difficult to believe that these carnie folk of yours could have been traveling with a giant spider and not noticed."

"She changed," I said earnestly. "I saw it myself. She looked like an ordinary woman, until she didn't. If she'd never changed in front of them, they would have had no reason to know."

"She changed in front of you."

"She was trying to kill me, because she didn't think anybody would care. I was new. They'd just assume I'd gotten bored when the carnival life wasn't all glitter and glamour, and she'd have a full belly without risking anything."

Margaret kept looking at me. I kept my face as composed as possible. I didn't *think* she could see me, but lighting was unpredictable in the Tunnel of Love; maybe I was better lit than she was. Finally, she asked, "How much longer do you think you'll need? We came here for a purge, not to twiddle our thumbs in motels."

"I thought you came here to observe and determine what needed to be done," I said. "What do you mean, you came here for a purge?"

Margaret was silent.

"They didn't *know*, Margaret. They didn't do anything wrong. They thought she was human like them."

"Like them?" Margaret chuckled darkly. "Oh, this was a mistake. Annie, there are at least three monsters hidden in this freak show. Maybe you can't see them, but we can. The fact that they're pulling the wool over your eyes about what they are means they're probably fooling you about other things. Like whether they knew."

"Three monsters?" I squeaked, heart racing. "I didn't . . . I mean, I haven't seen . . . I don't think they're lying to me, Margaret. I just need a little more time to be sure."

"I'm not happy that you haven't spotted them," she said.

There was something in her tone that made me think I might have a chance. "So let me try," I said. "I can keep investigating, and I can look harder. Please, I just don't want anyone innocent to get hurt."

"You mean you don't want your trapeze boy to get hurt."

I went very still.

"Don't worry, Annie. He's as human as they come, and if you're sure he's innocent, I'm willing to defend him to Robbie." Margaret patted me on the shoulder. It was strangely comforting. She was family, after all, even if she didn't know it. "All right. I'll tell him you're still working with us, and that you'll have the answers we need soon. But, Annie, when this carnival moves on, you're not going with it. Wherever it's going."

It was hard not to hear that as the threat it was. I forced my voice to stay light as I said, "Thank you. I won't let you down."

"No. You won't."

The mouth of the Tunnel was ahead of us, dazzlingly bright after the dimness inside. We drifted out into the afternoon, bumping our way down the narrow canal to the exit, where we stopped. The ride jock appeared, opening the rope, and Margaret hopped out, walking away without looking back.

The ride jock—I suddenly wished I knew her name, so I could think of her as something other than a title— looked at me quizzically. "You okay? You look like you've just seen a ghost."

"Ghosts aren't nearly as scary," I said, and stood, stepping out of the swan, back onto stable ground.

The ride jock rolled her eyes. "Tough girl. Right." She snapped the rope back into place. "I hope you got what you wanted."

"That was never an option," I said, and walked away, vanishing into the carnival.

Eighteen

"Don't wait. Waiting is for people with time
to spare, and baby, that's never going to be
us."

—Frances Brown

*The Spenser and Smith Family Carnival, heading for
the bone yard, between a rock and a hard place*

THE SKY NO LONGER LOOKED like a promise of rain as I
made my way back to the bone yard: it looked like a
promise of apocalypse. The world was going to burn. The
only question was how much of it I could save.

There was no way I could let the Covenant take the
carnival. These people had done nothing but welcome me
since I'd walked into their bone yard. What Umeko had
done was unforgivable, but Umeko was no longer here to
be forgiven. She had paid for what she'd done, and two of
her victims had gone safely back to their families. It was
cold comfort for the ones we'd buried with her, whose
parents would never have the closure they needed, but at
least she wouldn't hurt anyone else. All the others, Emery,
Ananta, the bogeymen at the Haunted House, Sam . . .
they were innocent. Species didn't matter.

There was no way I could *stop* the Covenant from taking the carnival. They knew it existed; I was here because
it was on their radar. I could kill both Robert and Margaret in cold blood, walk away from them with family blood
drying on my hands, and it would just convince the rest
of the Covenant that these people were a threat, because
they'd assume the carnival had done it. No way a trainee

could take down two of their operatives without help, right? I'd turn myself into a murderer for nothing more than a stay of execution. That wasn't right either. None of this was right. And I didn't have a solution.

I stopped about ten feet from my trailer. The door was closed; it didn't look like anyone had been there since I'd left. I just couldn't shake the feeling that I was being watched.

Experience has taught me that when I feel like I'm being watched, I almost certainly am. "I know you're there," I said. "You can either come out or go away. I'm not in the mood."

There was a soft thump behind me, and Sam said, "Annie? You okay?" He sounded oddly anxious, like he'd been waiting and worrying since I'd walked away from him before.

I turned. He was only a few feet away, and he looked as human as I did. That alone was enough to be unusual. He didn't like maintaining human form when he didn't have to: it was tiring, and it was necessary enough of the time that he shed it quickly when he got the chance. But here, now, he was just a barefoot boy standing in a bone yard, looking at me with worried eyes.

It was funny. I'd thought he was average-looking when I'd come to the carnival. Ordinary, even. But now, I looked at him and saw one of the handsomest men I'd ever known.

"Yeah," I said.

"Who was that woman?"

The thought of coming up with another lie was suddenly exhausting. I was so tired of lying to everyone. "I can't tell you," I said. "I wish I could, I really do, and I hope you'll let me have this. Please don't push."

Sam blinked slowly. "Are you in some sort of trouble?"

My laughter was bitter. From the look on his face, it surprised him as much as it had surprised me. "I guess you could say that. I've been in trouble for a long time." My fingertips were heating up. I shook my hands, hard, trying to chase the heat away.

Sam reached out and grabbed my wrists. I froze.

"I won't push," he said gently. "I don't want to push. I just want to be sure you're okay. You'd tell me, right? If there was anything I could do, you'd tell me about it?"

"If there was anything you could do, you'd be the first person I told," I said solemnly. His fingers were familiar by this point, and having him hold onto me like that was more comforting than I would have expected. He was the one who caught me when we flew, who made sure I wouldn't fall. Why shouldn't he be the one to catch me now?

"Good," said Sam. "Um. Annie?"

"Yeah?"

"I — you — I was a real jerk to you when you showed up, and I'm sorry."

"I was making you stay human when you didn't want to," I said, making no effort to take my wrists back. Security was something I very much needed at the moment. "I'm not mad anymore. It made perfect sense."

"Yeah, but it didn't make sense then, because I couldn't tell you — I didn't want to tell you, you were this weird human girl shoving yourself into places where you didn't belong, I just wanted you to leave — and so I was a jerk for nothing. I'm sorry."

It seemed oddly important to him that I accept his apology, so I nodded and said, "It's okay, Sam, it really is. If I was mad at you then, I'm not mad now. I forgive you. I forgave you the first time you saved my life, if I'm being completely honest. We're good."

"We're good?"

"We're good."

"Good," said Sam, and smiled lopsidedly for a moment before the expression faded back into solemnity. "Because, you know, it's been a while since I had a partner, and you're smart and funny and you read comic books, even if you have terrible taste —"

"Hey," I protested. "The X-Men are a viable franchise that will rise again."

" — and you're pretty good on the trapeze, for a human, and you know things about yōkai, and would it be okay if I kissed you, maybe?"

I stopped. "Wait, what?"

Sam blanched. "Okay, that was a lot less smooth than I thought it was going to be. I'm sorry. I'm going to go."

"No, seriously, what?" He was still holding my wrists. I stepped closer, pulling my arms toward my body, not to break away, but to force him to mirror the movement. "You want to kiss me?"

"Um, yes? If that's not the right answer, I'm willing to try another one."

"You know there's things about me that you don't know, right? Things you might not like so much when you find them out."

Sam shrugged. "There's things about everyone that I don't know. I like you. That's enough for right now, y'know?"

I did know, funnily enough. My life was a series of moments labeled "right now," and while this version of now might be coming to an end soon, that didn't mean I couldn't enjoy it while it lasted. Sam was a beautiful man. The trapeze had given him the sort of upper body that most people could only dream about, while genetics had given him even, symmetrical features, dark eyes, and the sort of lips I could absolutely see kissing.

So I leaned in, and I kissed him.

Sam only hesitated for a moment before he was kissing me back, letting go of my wrists in order to put his arms around me. We were standing in the middle of the bone yard, and the air smelled like a mix of popcorn, diesel fumes, and bonfire, and that was exactly right; that was what every first kiss should smell like. He wasn't so tall that I was going to get a crook in my neck, and he wasn't so short that I felt like an Amazon; instead, I got to tilt my chin back just *so*, and lean up just *so*, and kiss him like the girls in the movies always kissed their boys. I got to kiss him like I meant it.

When we broke apart, his cheeks were flushed, and I was sure mine were even brighter. I could feel the burn prickling in my skin, different from the fire that sometimes flashed through my fingertips. Sam's hands were pressed against the small of my back, holding me up in a different way, keeping me stable and locked in place.

"Um," I said. "Hi."

"Hi," said Sam. He looked as dazed as I felt, like he'd played out this moment in his head, but had never taken it any further: this was as far as he knew the story. "That was nice."

"Only nice?" I shook my head. "Nice isn't good enough. We should try again."

"Good point," he said, and leaned down, and kissed me harder.

This time, I wasn't so swept up in "I am kissing this person for the first time" that I couldn't pay attention to the details, like the way his hands tightened against my back, or the fact that his skin smelled like chalk dust and, distantly, clean, sun-warmed fur, like he was always carrying the memory of his alternate form with him. He was kissing me human, and I wasn't sure whether that was because he was tense about the idea of kissing me at all or because he wasn't sure I'd want to kiss him fūri, and in the moment, I didn't care. He was kissing me. That was all that mattered.

Again, we pulled apart. Again, his cheeks were bright, and mine were burning, and while we still seemed to be alone, I couldn't shake the feeling that we were being watched from every possible direction.

"Okay," I said. "Who told you they'd seen me going into the Tunnel of Love?"

"Babs," he said. "She was the ride jock on duty. She wanted me to know that you were going to break my heart."

She would have had plenty of time to run and tell him while Margaret and I were floating through the dark, and to be honest, it was almost a relief to hear that she'd left the ride unattended. Eavesdropping on someone inside the Tunnel wasn't easy, but that didn't make it impossible — not by any stretch of the imagination. The things Margaret and I had discussed had been vague enough to be unclear. They could still have gotten me in a lot of trouble.

"I might still break your heart," I said. "You never know."

"Yeah, but there's a big difference between 'I had a crush and she turned out to be into townie girls' and 'I got to spend time with a great girl and then we broke up,'" he said, before blanching. "Uh, not that I'm saying we're a couple just because you kissed me, like, I get that it doesn't work that way, but if you wanted to like, go on a date or something, I would be cool with that. Really cool with that, even."

"Where could we go?" I asked. "We're in the middle of Minnesota."

"Well, I don't know if you were aware, but . . ." Sam leaned conspiratorially close, and whispered, "There's a *carnival* in town."

I blinked. And then I grinned.

"Just let me get changed."

Okay, so yeah, maybe it was irresponsible for me to decide to go on a date when the Covenant of St. George was breathing down my neck, waiting for me to provide them with evidence that they were allowed to kill everything in sight. But the key word there was "waiting." The Covenant was waiting for me to find them something they could use to justify what they already knew they wanted to do. They might get tired of waiting and move eventually. They weren't going to move today. And oh, God, I needed a break.

I also needed a shower. I'd gone straight from the trapeze to meeting with Margaret, and while it was possible to have fun hanging out and stinking of sweat, it usually required the other people to be sweaty, too. By the end of the average roller derby match, the entire team stank like road kill, and we were fine with that, because it was everyone. Sam, on the other hand, had clearly showered before coming to ask for smooches, and I was *not* going to meet him for our first date smelling like something had died.

My tiny slice of RV did not include a shower. I stripped and grabbed the bucket with my soap, shampoo, and loofah before pulling on a bathrobe and stepping into a pair of flip-flops. There were camp showers set up in secluded areas all around the bone yard, with changing tents right outside. It wasn't the same as a real shower—oh, I missed real showers—but it would get me clean, and the nearest one wasn't very far away.

The bone yard was still relatively empty when I stepped out of my RV and made a beeline for the shower. I could get in, scrub myself down, and then—

Emery was sitting outside the changing tent, smoking a clove cigarette, utterly relaxed. She looked like she'd been there for a while. I stopped. She lowered her cigarette and smiled, the slow, deadly smile of a viper that's spotted its prey.

"Ah, Miss Brown," she said. "I was hoping you'd stop by."

Meaning someone had told her about me kissing Sam, and she'd known that if it was going to go any further, I'd be coming for a shower. Yippee. I love people who think like horror movie monsters when approaching social interactions. Oh, no, wait. That other thing. I *hate* people who treat social interactions as an opportunity to scare the crap out of some innocent young ingénue, namely, me.

"Well, this is where the shower is, so I guess it was sort of inevitable," I said, trying not to sound querulous, and failing utterly. "Is the hot water broken?"

"No, the shower is fine. It's even unoccupied. What are your intentions toward my grandson?"

Sweet and to the point. "Right now, to meet him for some carnival rides while not smelling like I just came off the flying trapeze. I'm pretty sure my pits could kill flies at twenty paces."

"That's not what I meant, and you know it." She leaned forward. "Sam is a special boy. He deserves better than someone who's going to flirt and then run off on him."

"I'm going to do my best not to hear that as you ordering me to put out for your grandson, but if you ever decide to have this conversation again, maybe you should watch your wording," I said, tone going chilly. "Right now, my intentions are exactly what I just said. He asked if he could kiss me. I said yes. I enjoyed kissing him, so when he suggested a date, I said yes to that, too. He's smart and funny and good looking, and yeah, I'd like to get to know him a little better, but I'm not planning to marry him, and I'm not planning to break his heart for fun. Anything between those extremes is not actually your business, ma'am. We're both adults."

"He's only twenty-three."

"And I'm only twenty-two. If we break each other's hearts, it's a learning experience. At least we're doing it in an age-appropriate manner." I wanted to cross my arms and glare. My basket of bathing supplies made that impossible, even as my bathrobe was robbing me of the gravitas I desired. "I get that you want to protect him. He's your family. Family matters more than anything in the world. I even get that you're probably pretty wary of me. I'm the new girl, I'm the one who killed Umeko, I'm an unknown quantity. But, ma'am, he's the one who kissed me. He's the one who decided I was a risk worth taking. You should respect that."

"Delilah was my only child," said Emery. "Sam's mother, you understand. I did as well as I could with her, but I was trying to raise a little girl and a carnival at the same time, and sometimes she didn't get as much of my attention as she needed. I was a Spenser before I married Michael Taylor, and this show is mine by right. People didn't always see it that way. They were used to listening to my father and his partner, and with both of them gone, the carnival needed me more than my own daughter did."

I didn't say anything. This smacked of confession, and more, of justification; like she had to say this before she could lean one way or the other. She was either going to endorse my date with Sam or forbid it, and if I wanted any hope of the former, I needed to let her talk.

"Delilah would have been a little wild anyway—Spenser blood—but she rebelled by rejecting everything I was. Went off to school, got a business degree, went to

China to work for an electronics company as their liaison to the American business world, and met a man who swept her off her feet, literally. She knew what he was when she got involved with him. She didn't think they could have babies together. When she found out she was pregnant, she was on the next plane home. First time she ever asked me for anything. She asked me to take care of her son, because she couldn't. There was no place in her world for a baby, much less a baby with such unique needs. I'm all he's ever had."

There was a quiet finality in her words: she had said her piece. I looked her squarely in the eye and said, "You've done an amazing job. He's a great guy. A little prickly with new people, but so am I, so I don't have a problem with that. Now let him do an amazing job. Let him try something new."

" 'Something new' being you?"

"For now." I shrugged. "I won't be with this show forever. But I'm a great gateway to the wonderful world of dating. He's twenty-three. Let him get started."

"How do you know I haven't?"

"Because this is the first girl speech. I'm assuming he's messed around with some of the carnie girls—he didn't kiss like it was his first time—but he's never really dated, or you wouldn't be talking to me like this."

Emery was silent for a long moment before she said, "He's all I have. Delilah taught me my lesson. This carnival, this show, it doesn't matter nearly as much as my family."

"I know," I said. "I'll respect that. I'm not playing with him. But how's he going to feel if I say I can't go for a ride on the bumper cars because his grandmother said no? He gets to make his own choices. He chose to ask me."

"Be gentle with him." Emery stood. "I won't forgive you if you're not."

"That's all right, ma'am," I said. "I won't forgive myself."

Emery looked at me thoughtfully. Then she nodded, as much to herself as to me, and walked away, leaving me alone in front of the changing tent.

"Well, that was bracing," I muttered, and ducked inside.

It took less than fifteen minutes to scrub my body, wash my hair, towel-dry my hair to a point where I felt comfortable braiding it, and bolt back to my RV. The mice cheered at my appearance, cheered at the sight of me putting on a nice dress and sturdy black Doc Martens, and cheered one more time as I was rocketing out the door, letting it slam behind me. I kept running as I hit the bone yard, navigating it faster than I ever had. Fifteen minutes to shower, another five to change, plus however long I'd been talking to Emery. That was enough to make me worry that Sam thought I'd ditched him, or—

He was standing next to the canvas flap separating us from the rest of the show, and he grinned at the sight of me. He'd changed, too, trading his usual bulky sweater and sweatpants for jeans, a tight white shirt, and a denim jacket. He was even wearing shoes. I blinked, slowing as I approached, until I stopped in front of him.

"Who are you, and what have you done with Sam?" I asked.

"Arm," he replied. Obligingly, I stuck out my right arm. He fastened a rainbow wristband around my wrist before holding up his left hand to show me that he was wearing the same. "All-ride pass. Sure, we can ride for free anyway, but this way, we look like locals."

"Most people want to run away to join the circus, not the townies," I said.

Sam's grin widened. "Most people aren't us. See? I'm even in costume for the occasion."

"Very striking," I said. "The shoes are a nice touch. Why do you own shoes?"

"Sometimes Grandma sends me to the grocery store." I must have made a face at the mention of Emery because Sam paused, looking at me carefully, before he sighed and asked, "Did she corner you already?"

I chuckled weakly. "Before I could even make it to the shower."

"She always worries about me getting my heart broken,

but she's the reason most of the girls my age won't even look at me twice." Sam leaned in to kiss my forehead. "I've managed to date more than she thinks I have, and I'm not as breakable as she makes me out to be."

"I know," I said. "I'm here, aren't I? If you were the frail little flower she thinks you are, I'd be in my RV, writing you a nice 'it's not you, it's me, I'm afraid of breaking you' note."

"Cool. Just so we're clear." Sam offered me his arm. "Would you like to go to the carnival?"

I slipped my arm into his, locking them together and holding on tight. "I would love to."

For most of my life, if I've been at a carnival, I've been there because I belonged. Either I was summering with the Campbells or pretending with Spenser and Smith, but I was never a townie girl, never just an attendee; I saw the nuts and bolts, not the beautiful facades. The illusion wasn't for me. But as I held Sam's arm and he led me through the narrow canvas tunnel running behind the attractions to the front gate, I started to wonder what it would be like if they *were* for me. If they were designed to titillate and delight the townie girl I'd never been, but sometimes dreamed of being, when I was tired of being banged around by every preternatural creature this side of the prime meridian.

We emerged at the front of the show, popping out of the canvas a few feet to the left of the admissions booth. The man on duty was familiar in the vague "I've seen you around" sense, and he smirked as Sam and I walked past, Sam holding up his arm to show his glittering wristband.

"Your date's a cheap-ass, honey," called the man.

"I'm okay with that," I called back.

Sam looked theatrically hurt. "I am not a cheap-ass," he said. "This is good for every ride we have. Oh, and here." He dug into his pocket before handing me two more wristbands, one red, the other candy-striped in red and white. "Concessions and games. See? I'm not a cheap-ass. Only the best shit I can get for free by asking my grandmother to give it to me."

I snorted. "I think you just gave the *definition* of cheap-ass, dude." But I fastened the wristbands to either side of the glittery unlimited rides band. It was an oddly touching gesture. Sam could have gotten any of those things by being Emery's grandson; even the things that wouldn't be available to all carnies, like open access to the games, were there for the boss's kid. All he had to do was hold his hand out and it would be filled. The fact that he'd actually acquired the wristbands meant he wanted this to be just the two of us, without the specter of who he was hanging over our heads.

It was nice. Neither one of us was bringing our family on this date—although in my case, it was because he thought my entire family was dead.

We strolled arm in arm onto the carnival grounds, which began with a large circular area ringed in side-show attractions and booths selling concessions and souvenirs of all sorts. The Ferris wheel rose majestically in the middle of it all, stretching toward the sky. We both looked at it with our own flavor of longing before agreeing, through a silent glance and a mutual nod, to come back later, when the crowds had thinned. Ferris wheels are always magical, but there's something about riding on one that's mostly empty that changes the experience. We walked on.

Ananta was outside her snake tent, an albino python wrapped around her shoulders, several nearby children watching with wide, fascinated eyes. She grinned when she saw the wristbands we were wearing, and called, "You've proven your sincerity by offering access to our entire show. Now prove your bravery by leading your girl into my den, where serpents slither and sincerity is tested!"

Sam laughed before looking at me and asking, "You wanna see some snakes?"

"Just glad I know it's not a metaphor," I said, and laughed at the look on his face. "Let's go."

The inside of Ananta's attraction was dark and cool and smelled faintly rich, that deep reptile smell I will always associate, on some level, with my brother Alex.

But the reptiles were thriving; even I knew enough to know that. Two-headed corn snakes, great, lazy pythons, and quick, scampering lizards lined the walls. There was a tank filled with waxy-looking tree frogs the size of my fist.

There was also a tank filled with adolescent cobras that looked at us with interest but without alarm. Two of them exchanged a look before lifting the first third of their bodies off the ground and flaring their hoods, some-how managing to seem bored even in the midst of what should have been a threat display. I leaned a little closer.

"Sons or brothers?" I asked.

The cobras looked surprised, which was a neat trick, since they didn't have eyelids. Their hoods retracted be-fore they twined around each other. I nodded.

"Makes sense. Nice to meet you."

I straightened up and turned to find Sam looking at me quizzically.

"What was that about?" he asked.

"Just meeting the locals. Do you know their names?"

"Ananta never told me."

"I'll ask her later." Wadjet women look human; wad-jet men and boys look like cobras. Wadjet males nor-mally can't stand one another's company, although related males too young to mate can sometimes cohabi-tate when in the presence of an older female relative. Ananta was keeping these two calm just by being nearby.

Sam shook his head. "You're weird."

"Is that a problem?"

"You kidding? It's half of why I wanted to kiss you."

I raised an eyebrow. "What's the other half?"

"I don't know if anyone's told you this before, but you have *amazing* breasts."

I laughed. I was still laughing when we left the reptile show, and after that, it seemed like I just didn't stop. We rode every ride, some of them twice, flashing our wrist-bands at the ride jocks with wide grins on our faces. At least a few townies went off to buy wristbands of their own once they saw how much fun we were having (and after we'd skipped to the front of the line, which again, we could have done anyway, but you can't buy "works for the show," and you can buy "priority unlimited ride access"). Sam ate six hot dogs with the sort of focused intensity that he normally reserved for trapeze practice. I ate two in the same amount of time.

He kissed me in the Tunnel of Love, with giggling townies in the boats to either side of us, separated only by the heart-eyed ducks.

He kissed me in the haunted house, while white-sheeted ghosts popped out of the walls and made moaning noises that occasionally verged on pornographic, and caused me to start laughing mid-kiss. Sam joined in and laughed with me. What else were we supposed to do?

He kissed me in front of a basketball-toss game, after winning me a little stuffed bear, and I kissed him in front of a dart game, after winning him a giant stuffed alligator. The game operators in both cases shook their heads and rolled their eyes and raked in the profits as people queued up for another shot at a task that suddenly seemed achievable.

We traded in the night for kisses, one entertainment at a time, and if the people operating those entertainments smirked and grinned at the sight of us, it didn't matter. We walked, hand in hand, down the midway as the show was closing around us, watching the townies pouring toward the exit, our stuffed toys in our free hands. All the rides had stopped running, encouraging people to head out a little faster. Sam grinned when he realized that, pulling me toward the Ferris wheel.

"Come on," he said. "Last stop."

The ride jock on duty started to wave us off when he saw us coming, but stopped when he realized who we were. "I heard you two were playing townie," he said, friendly enough, if amused. "Am I supposed to be your last stop?"

"I can handle the wheel," said Sam. "Why don't you go get a cup of coffee?"

"Cool by me," said the ride jock. "She's all yours." Then he leered at me, just to make sure we got his point, before he laughed and wandered off.

I leaned against the fence while Sam stood next to the controls and scowled at anyone who seemed too interested. "How is this supposed to work? Riding alone is fun and all, but it's not really a good end to our date."

"You'll see. Just trust me for a minute."

"Hmm. Trust you." I tilted my head, pretending to think about it. "I suppose you've earned a little trust. I shall trust you for one minute."

"Thank you." He leaned against the ride console, continuing to glare at townies as they walked past. He had an excellent glare. He'd clearly spent a lot of time perfecting it.

I took advantage of the pause to look at him. I'd been looking at him all night, but this was really *looking*, the sort of sappy, concentrated stare that only ever seemed to be okay on a night like this one, under the cloudy Minnesota sky. Before he'd kissed me, he'd been Sam, a boy I liked okay, but didn't really have any illusions about. He'd been nice, he'd been funny, I'd had a few dirty thoughts about the strength of his hands and the seemingly effortless way he lifted me on the trapeze, but that had been about as far as it had gone. I had long since learned not to expect anything more than that, because it never happened. When it came to guys, I was too loud, too aggressive, too sarcastic—too *me*. Boys wanted delicate and dainty and flirty and fun. They wanted my sister. I was an afterthought at best.

Except for Sam, who was apparently not interested in what boys wanted. He wanted what he wanted, and what he wanted was me. So I looked at him, standing there with his shoulders stiff and his face fixed into a scowl, obviously weary from the effort of staying human for so long. I would have felt bad about that, except for the part where everyone makes an effort on a first date. I had smiled, and ridden things I normally would have passed on, and not punched anyone who made comments about my skirt riding up when I was leaning forward to throw darts. We were both putting our best face forward.

I just hoped he didn't think this was the face I needed.

"Okay," said Sam, snapping me out of my contemplation. "Get on."

I looked around. The townies were gone. There might still be a few lingering on the grounds, but they no longer had the numbers to compel anything from the staff. "Get on?"

"The Ferris wheel."

I gave him a dubious look. "Again, I don't want to ride alone."

"Just get on."

The Ferris wheel was a tempting circle cut out of the night. I shook my head to remind him of my doubts, and I got on, settling myself into the waiting basket seat and clipping my safety bar across my lap. The wheel began to turn. When it reached the top, it stopped, and I was suspended against the night, with the darkening carnival spread out in front of me, the bone yard twinkling beyond it like a field of stars. I relaxed against the seat, enjoying the way it rocked, and the feeling of the wind blowing through my hair.

At least, until the seat rocked violently from the impact of something larger than I was. I whipped around, tensing. Sam grinned at me. He was hanging off the side of the basket seat, his tail curled around the safety bar and his bare feet gripping next to his hands. For the first time all night, he actually looked relaxed.

"Took you long enough," I said, forcing my own shoulders to unlock. "Give me one good reason I shouldn't tell you to scram now that I've remembered how nice it is up here."

"I'm super cute," he said earnestly. "Science says you should let me stay."

"Oh, well, if it's science, come on in."

He slipped into the seat, getting the safety bar across his lap, and started to inhale—the first step to tensing enough to be human again. I didn't stop to think, just reached over and grabbed his hand, breaking his concentration.

"Don't," I said. "You're fine exactly as you are."

Sam blinked. "Are you sure? I mean, I've never . . ."

"You mean the girls who've kissed you before have only ever wanted to kiss you when you looked human?"

He nodded. I wondered whether it was a sign of becoming a jealous girlfriend that I suddenly wanted to punch all his exes. I decided probably not. I was not Scott Pilgrim, and this was not a video game. They were just all jerks.

"Then they were jerks," I said, word mirroring thought. "Come here."

He scooted over, looking almost shy. I leaned over, and I kissed him.

His skin was warmer this way, but his lips were the same, and his hair felt like fur when I slid my fingers through it. He wrapped his tail around my waist, pulling me closer still, and we sat there at the top of the Ferris wheel, kissing each other and pretending that the rest of the world didn't matter, because in that moment, in that embrace, it didn't.

Nineteen

"We can run from our past, but the past follows. One step at a time, forever, the past follows."

—Enid Healy

The Spenser and Smith Family Carnival, the next day

THE PROMISE OF RAIN the sky had been making for days was finally being fulfilled. The clouds had ripped open shortly after midnight, forcing an all-hands rush for the midway to close down games, cover concessions, and tent the rides, which now lurked, plastic-covered monstrosities presiding over a sea of mud.

Most of the carnies were either in the mess tent, playing cards and yelling at each other, or hiding in their RVs to avoid playing cards and yelling at each other. I fell into the latter category. I'd spent most of the morning helping the Aeslin mice remodel and expand their little house, enjoying the opportunity to sit around in my pajamas without worrying about someone asking me to do something.

There was a knock on the RV door.

I turned to look at it, unable to stop myself from considering how flammable the person on the other side was likely to be. This was supposed to be a day off to think about how I was going to keep the Covenant from screwing everything up. The rain *said* so.

The person knocked again. I sighed, stood, and walked the three steps necessary to open the door.

Sam, standing barefoot in the rain with a large

umbrella in his hands and his tail wrapped around his own waist, presumably to keep it from getting wet, smiled cautiously up at me. The faint smell of damp fur accompanied him. It wasn't unpleasant, but it was oddly unexpected. "Hey," he said. "You're up."

"Yeah, but not dressed," I said. "Did you want to come in? The mice are singing hymns about home repair."

"Hail!" squeaked Mindy.

"No, I'm good," said Sam. "I'm going to be heading into town around noon to get supplies and stuff. I figured you might want to come along."

"What made you think that?"

"The part where I've known these people for my entire life, and being rained in with them still makes me want to scream and claw my eyes out."

"Fair." I glanced over to where Mork and Mindy were carrying stacks of Popsicle sticks gleaned from the midway around their house. "Can we stop at a craft store? I need to pick up some wood glue."

"Sure. See you at my place at noon?"

"Sure," I said, and matched his smile with one of my own. He went squelching off into the mud. I closed the door, took a step backward, and sat down heavily on the bed.

"Priestess?" I looked up. Mindy had moved to the edge of the counter and was looking at me with concern. "Are you well?"

"Everything is very confusing right now, Mindy, that's all."

Mindy bristled her whiskers at me. Behind her, Mork was continuing to check the length of the Popsicle sticks against the walls of their house. He wasn't as comfortable addressing me directly as she was. He probably never would be. The branch of the family we'd left in England had a lot to answer for. "Because of the Work You Do, or because of the Work You Want?"

Aeslin mice are always truthful, but not always perfectly literal. I smiled at her, sadly. "A little of both, with a side order of I think I really like a guy, and I can't possibly have him, because he's part of the work I want, and the work I'm doing is just going to put him in danger."

"Is it not tradition to travel to carnivals and fall in love under false pretenses? Did not the Violent Priestess ride a white horse and love the God of Unexpected Situations in a place very much like this one?"

"Yeah, but Great-Grandpa Jonathan didn't tell Great-Grandma Fran nearly this many lies." Living with the Aeslin mice means being more in touch with our ancestors than the people we went to school with. It's necessary, to understand the twists and bends of their oral tradition. "Sam isn't going to forgive me when he finds out who I really am. I can't even be mad at him for that. I wouldn't forgive me either. So I can't have him, and that means I shouldn't like him more than I already do."

"But you can save him."

"Yes," I said, with a firm nod. "I can save him, and that's going to have to be enough. No matter what I want, no matter how much I wish I could do this differently, that's going to have to be enough."

Mindy looked at me solemnly. "We will have so many sad songs to sing when we go home."

"Yeah, I guess we will." I stood. "Figure out what you want from the craft store while I get dressed. I'll even bring you rhinestones, if you want them."

If there's one thing in this world that I know I can rely on, it's the joyous cheering of the Aeslin mice.

An hour later, I walked up to the RV shared by Sam and Emery, feeling oddly like I was wearing some sort of costume by going out in jeans, a plain black hoodie over a roller derby tank top, and hiking boots. They were the kind of clothes I wore every day when I was home, when I was Antimony, but here, I was a girl who wandered around in sequins and fishnets, and this seemed too plain. The rain had stopped at some point, although the sky was still dark with clouds, and the mud sucked at my feet with every step I took.

Then the door opened, and Sam was grinning at me, and my outfit didn't feel like such a big deal. Especially since he was wearing jeans and a Spider-Man shirt under the denim jacket he'd had on the night before. He was in his human form, probably because of the shoes on his feet: toes took more kindly to being squashed than the semi-fingers he normally sported. Also, it was a lot easier to go shopping with a man than with a monkey.

"Ready to go?" he asked.

"Born ready," I said. "Sometimes at night, I weep because I'm not lost in a Target at that very moment."

"In that case, we're going to have an awesome day." He looked over his shoulder. "I'm heading out, Grandma!"

"Obey the speed limit and don't get pulled over," Emery shouted back.

"I will and I won't!" he said, and bounced out of the RV, pausing only to reach into the bucket next to the door and snag his umbrella. He closed the door with surprising gentleness, flashing me another smile before he started toward the edge of the bone yard where the trucks were parked. "We need to go to the grocery, Costco, Target, and you said you needed a craft store, right?"

"Yeah, for the mice," I said. "If we pass a beauty supply shop, I'd like to stop there, too."

"Why?"

"Henna." I held up a hank of my hair, showing how faded it had become. "I'm a natural brunette, and I like the red highlights I get from a good henna treatment. Also, it means I don't have to condition as often. I'm not low-maintenance, I'm just lazy."

"Lazy." Sam snorted. "If you're lazy, I'm a lemur."

"That explains the stripes on your tail."

He snorted again before walking to the nearest pickup truck, a big, muddy white thing, and unlocking the doors. "Do lemurs eat bananas? Because if they don't, I might be willing to consider a reclassification."

"You know, I honestly don't know." He unlocked the passenger side door. I got into the truck, fastening my seat belt before I said, "We could go to the zoo sometime and ask the lemur keeper, but that could have unintended consequences."

"You mean like me refusing to stop yelling at kids in the petting zoo?"

"And me getting into a fight with anyone who let their kid tease the bears, yeah."

"So probably a bad plan." Sam started the truck and pulled out, into the muddy field. The tires jerked and shuddered through the ruts. I added "decent driver" to the list of things I knew about him. "I guess I'll stay a fūri, and we'll just go to Target."

"Sounds like a good plan to me," I said. We drove in comfortable silence for a few minutes before I said, "I had a nice time last night. Thank you."

"You weren't the only one." His smile was sidelong and shy. "I've never kissed a girl when I wasn't trying to look like this." He waved a hand at himself, indicating his generally human appearance. "It was really nice."

"Any girl that doesn't want to kiss you when you're being yourself isn't worth kissing," I said firmly. "That sort of thing has no place in a relationship."

"Are we in a relationship?"

The question sounded sincere. I paused, calming my initial terrified reaction, and rubbed my suddenly hot fingertips against my jeans before I said, "Not yet. We might be. I mean. I could see that happening. Maybe. Couldn't you?"

"Right now, I think I'd run away with you if you asked me to." The admission was shy but sincere.

And I considered it, I really did. Not for long, but . . . I'd have to go back for the mice. That was the only thing I couldn't leave behind. We could run for the hills, and the Covenant would never find us. I could even warn Ananta and the bogeymen before we went, give them time to get out of there. The Covenant wouldn't kill innocent humans, I was almost sure of that. They'd raid the carnival, find nothing there to cleanse, and go home.

Even as I thought about it, I knew I was lying to myself. The Covenant would kill everyone they thought had been collaborating with the "monsters," and then they'd come looking for me. If we ran, I could never go home, and Sam's home would be destroyed. We'd be alone together forever, and while I liked him a lot, I didn't know if I could learn to love him under those circumstances. We'd make ourselves into exiles, not even knowing if we'd still like each other in a year. It wouldn't be right. It wouldn't be fair.

"That might be a bit much, but I'd agree to another date, if you wanted one," I said. "I really did have a great time."

"Another date it is," he said. "I'd punch the air, but I'm driving."

"I appreciate your restraint," I said gravely.

Sam laughed and drove us into town.

St. Cloud, Minnesota, was a town like any other: probably super boring to the inhabitants, who had already discovered all its mysteries, but fascinating to the pair of us, strangers who'd been camped outside its boundaries for days. Sam slowed as we hit the city limits, backing off the gas until we were moving at exactly the speed limit, and we goggled at everything around us like the tourists that we were.

"When I was a kid, I thought McDonalds was the best thing in the world, because there was one everywhere we went," said Sam. "It was like ... maybe we'd be in a town that thought video games were evil or where I was the only Chinese person people had ever seen, but there was always a McDonalds. Happy Meals made everything better."

"I can't decide whether that's sweet or sad," I said. "I have a thing for diners. There are seven million different ways to bake a pumpkin pie, and I am going to taste every single one of them before I die."

"So you're saying I should take you to a diner."

"No toys with the hamburgers, but the odds are good the meat is cow, not rat or squirrel or whatever else the folks back at McDonalds HQ have been able to shove into a grinder."

"You make an excellent point." Sam turned into the Target parking lot. "Our mission awaits."

"Let's do this."

Sam shopped like a man who'd been going on supply runs since the day he was old enough to get his license: quickly, efficiently, and with a refreshing lack of screwing around. It probably helped that Targets only have, like, five floor plans, which means that even if you've never been to a specific store before, familiarity with the chain will make it easy to navigate. He picked up detergent, shampoo, conditioner, and enough ramen to constitute a health hazard anywhere else in the world. I looked at him quizzically at the last. He shrugged.

"Everybody eats it, so it makes a good filler food between meals. Haven't you wound up in the mess tent when it wasn't officially lunch?"

"New girl," I reminded him. "I try to avoid the mess tent unless you or Emery will be there, because I still don't have much to talk about with anyone else. I'm getting there. It's going to take me a little while."

"We've got time," he said, and smiled, and everything was fine. Except for the worm of guilt twisting in my gut, and the heat in my fingertips, because we *didn't* have time. The Covenant was coming. I'd allowed myself a night to play and just be a girl, out with a boy, enjoying the world, but that didn't change the fact that time was running out for me—and if I didn't find a way to stop what was coming, it was running out for Sam, too.

After Target came Costco, where we bought tubs of condiments and canned meat and so much toilet paper that the clerk looked at us like we were planning some sort of nefarious tissue escapade. Sam showed all his teeth when he smiled, which didn't seem to calm her any, and I barely managed to keep my laughter in check. The back of the truck was starting to look like a target for local thieves, and Sam took more and more time securing everything with rope and tarp and bungee cords. A van would have made more sense for this sort of outing but less sense for the carnival. There are always compromises in the real world.

At the craft store, he parked where he could see the truck from the store windows and helped me wander the aisles, picking up wood glue and Popsicle sticks and nontoxic paint and a few little pieces of "fairy furniture" from the floral department, which were intended for flower arrangements, but would be perfect for Aeslin mice.

(The sort of people who build "fairy gardens" would be unhappy if they managed to attract real fairies. There are lots of different creatures humans have called "fairies" across the years, and the only thing they all have in common is the way they'll hurt people if given half a chance.)

The clerk at the craft store didn't bat an eye at my assortment of things. She probably saw stranger on a daily basis, which is part of why I like craft stores so much. There's always someone there who outweirds you. It really takes the pressure off.

We were almost to the door when I stopped, eyes fixed on the bulletin board where local crafters peddled their wares. It wasn't *just* crafters: there was also a section for local events, farmer's markets and yard sales and pet adoptions. And one big, largely black flyer advertising a no-holds-barred match between two teams I'd never heard of before. That didn't matter. What mattered were the words "flat track roller derby" and "hell on wheels" and "one night only." The words that read like home. The words that should have been above *my* name, encouraging people to come and watch my friends throwing themselves into the wind, knowing they would never hit the ground.

For the most part, I'd been keeping myself too busy to really stop and think about my situation. In that moment, looking at that flyer, I ran out of momentum, and the homesickness flooded in, washing everything else away.

"Roller derby, huh?" said Sam. "You a fan?"

"Huh?" I tore my eyes away from the poster, turning to face him. I managed to nod. "Yeah. I like roller derby."

"You know, I've never actually been to a match? Is that what they're called, matches?"

"Games."

"Okay. Still never been." He glanced at the flyer. "It's tonight. The show's closed because of the rain. We could go."

The words echoed in my ears. We could go. Or I could stay home and keep trying to find a solution to the situation I found myself in. But that wasn't going to help, was it? I'd just be sitting alone, not coming up with anything. I've always thought better when I thought at the track. The sound of heads bouncing off the track is remarkably good at shaking things out of my own skull.

It couldn't hurt anything. There was nothing left to hurt.

"Please?" I asked, the word coming out meek and eager and hungry, like a child on Christmas morning, asking to open just one present.

Sam beamed. "It's a date."

It took an hour to get back to the carnival and unload the truck. The rain resumed twice during that time, but that was what umbrellas and extra hands were for: as soon as we pulled into the bone yard, all the people who knew we'd been on a supply run were there to rush us, helping us get everything out and distributing it where it belonged. Ramen was apparently serious business with these people.

Sam kissed me before he went to tell his grandmother we were back, and he didn't seem to care who saw him do it: the carnies who saw the quick, glancing gesture grinned at me, some approvingly, others leering, but all apparently unbothered. Gossip spreads fast in a show like this. When everyone lives in everyone else's back pocket, that sort of thing is a form of currency. Without it, how would anyone know who it was safe to tease?

Mindy and Mork accepted my offerings of paint, glue, and tiny chairs as their due, scurrying off with them after shouting "HAIL" an appropriate number of times. The Aeslin model of religion involves a lot of gifts from the gods. This created the temporary privacy I required to get ready.

When I'd packed to run away to the Covenant, I hadn't been allowed to take anything that might indicate a geographical tie to Portland. Confusing the issue, however, had been considered perfectly fine. I had derby shirts with logos ranging from Helsinki, Finland, to Cardiff, Wales, with a few smaller American and Canadian leagues in the mix to keep things as unclear as possible. I picked out a bright orange-and-black Buenos Aires Tarantellatulas tank top, pairing it with a black pleated skirt and a pair of fishnet tights. Sure, it was a team no one would have ever heard of, but the illustration was of a girl on skates with a tarantula tattoo; I was pretty sure this crowd would get the idea.

My hair was too faded for my tastes—it would have been better freshly hennaed, bright and blazing and perfect. I compensated with orange-and-black makeup to match my shirt, blew my reflection a kiss, and grabbed my umbrella before ploughing back into the bone yard, heading for the truck as fast as my legs would carry me.

Sam was already there. His eyes widened at the sight of my outfit, and when I was close enough he said in a strangled voice, "Wow. Staying tense enough to look human all night is *not* going to be a problem."

"Is that supposed to be flattering?"

"Yes," he said, with a firm nod. "It is *extremely* flattering. Nothing more flattering has ever been said in the history of mankind."

"In that case, thank you." I leaned up to kiss his cheek.

My lipstick was heavy-duty enough to leave no marks behind. "Let's get our derby on."

"It's going to be a great night," said Sam, and opened the truck door, waving me inside. I got in, beaming at him, and didn't say a word, because I was pretty sure he was right. Everything was going to be perfect.

Twenty

> "When someone judges you for something you can't help, try to forgive them. They don't understand. And if they keep doing it, knock their fucking teeth in."
>
> — Jane Harrington-Price

A warehouse in downtown St. Cloud, Minnesota, heading for the collapsible bleacher seats, ready for the game to begin

Tickets were twenty dollars at the door, thirty for the remaining VIP seats—which meant, among other things, *having* seats, since there were only enough spaces in the bleachers for about half the crowd. The rest would be standing at a barely safe distance as the derby girls blazed by. I'd willingly forked over the extra cash for a pair of black wristbands and a place in the front. If I couldn't skate, I was going to sit.

"Is our entire dating life going to be defined by wristbands?" asked Sam, fastening his around his wrist.

"They make great cheap souvenirs," I said amiably. "I'd roll with it if I were you."

"Is that a derby pun, or are you telling me to relax?"

"A bit of both." I took a deep breath, inhaling the mix of sweat, stale beer, and competitive fury that filled the air. It was almost intoxicating. If I closed my eyes, letting the clack of wheels on the track and the buzz of the crowd fill my ears, I could pretend I was home. This was an away game, something where I didn't need to skate, and I was attending with my new boyfriend, who had somehow gotten serious enough that I was willing to take the risk and show him to the league.

"Ow!" Sam let go of my hand. I opened my eyes to find him blowing on his fingers, looking bemused. "Did you feel that? It was like everything got super-hot all of a sudden."

"Um." I shook my own hand, not to soothe a burn, but to chase the heat out of my fingertips. If I was going to start setting fires when I was content, too, I was about to have a serious problem. "Probably one of the lights throwing down sparks. Come on, let's get a drink before we find our seats."

"I don't do beer when I'm in public," said Sam, almost sheepishly. "It makes me relax."

And when he relaxed, he wound up with a tail. "Good decision," I said. "I don't do beer, period. I'm not happy with the idea of losing control. But the nice thing about apple cider is the way it *looks* like beer, thus dodging the judgment of the masses, without actually *being* beer. You, too, can drink the fruits of the orchard and not worry about intoxication."

"Teach me more of the strange ways of your people," said Sam.

"Sort of inevitable." I passed a five to the girl at the window, who had purple-streaked hair and an almost feral grin, and received two cups of hot apple cider in return. Sam took one of them with a nod of thanks. I toasted the girl, stuffed a dollar into the tip jar, and began the familiar process of wending my way through a warehouse, looking for a seat.

Unlike the home games, where we owned the warehouse and could control the way it was set up, every away game was an adventure in figuring out exactly where we were supposed to be, and what we were supposed to be doing while we were there. But the elements were always the same, lending an air of comforting reliability to the layout, even though I'd never seen it before. The ticket window was at the front, at the start of a narrow corridor that herded us past the concession stand and one final opportunity to upgrade our tickets. Then it widened, with the skate mall—a little room packed with vendor tables and booths, half flea market, half dealer's hall—to our left, and the louder, more raucous arena to our right. We bore right, and the loudness opened up, becoming a ringing bell of noise. The track was in the center, being circled by derby girls in the process of warming up, surrounded by bleachers and standing-room space, with the announcer's table on a raised platform to one side, and I had never been happier to be somewhere, and I had never felt half so far from home.

Sam and I made our way to the roped-off VIP seats, flashing our wristbands at the man guarding the rope. He nodded brusquely as he let us through, and I felt a pang at his lack of recognition, even though he'd never seen me before. This was my world, same as the carnival was Sam's. Somehow, I'd become a stranger in my own world. All the logic I possessed—this wasn't my home territory, I'd never skated against these people, anonymity was key to my survival right now—couldn't take the sting out of realizing how easily I could fade away.

Normally, if I'd been at a game in a territory that wasn't my own, I would have been wearing my team shirt, the words FINAL GIRL blazoned across the shoulders, marking me as part of the clan. This situation was anything but normal.

"These names are *nuts*," said Sam, snapping me back into the present. I turned to him. He was reading from the program for the evening, looking faintly awed. "It's the St. Cloud Storm Chasers vs. the Rockville Rollers. The captains are Tornado-si-do and Sedimentary My Dear. It's like . . . I don't know, race horses gone weird."

"Not a bad description," I said, watching the circling roller girls with a practiced eye. One group was in white tank tops and red hot pants, with twisters painted on their helmets. The other wore khaki shirts tied over yellow tank tops and khaki shorts, and had rock hammers on their helmets. "Okay, so the ones sort of themed like weathergirls who've survived a hurricane, those are the Storm Chasers. The ones in khaki are the Rollers." I'd never seen a geology-themed team before. Truly the world of roller derby is vast and complicated.

"Okay," said Sam. He lowered his program and looked at me expectantly.

I raised an eyebrow. "What?"

"How does this work?"

"Oh. Uh ... rules of roller derby are simple. You have two primary positions on the track: the jammer, whose job it is to skate fast and score points, and the blockers, whose job it is to keep her from doing her job. Each team will field four blockers and one jammer per jam—which is roller derby for 'inning.' You can tell the jammer by the star on her helmet. When the whistle blows, she'll start trying to break through the pack of blockers. Whichever jammer breaks out first is the lead jammer, she controls the play. If she calls it off, it ends. So your team's jammer has two goals—to score a lot of points, and to stop the jam before the other team's jammer scores any points at all. Make sense?"

"Nope," said Sam. "Whoever invented this game was really into breakfast foods."

"Just jam," I said. The lights flickered. The girls skated off the track. The game was about to get underway. I scooted closer to Sam, leaning my head against his shoulder and forcing myself to relax. This was my world. This was my favorite sport. Sam didn't know how big a deal it was for me to take a guy to a derby game, and he was never going to, because my time with the carnival was drawing to an end: soon I was going to disappear, and become just another person who'd let him down.

Until then, we had this. The announcer began naming the girls as they poured back out onto the track. The Storm Chasers were wearing their team shirts now, which were white and tight and more TV news than the norm, keeping with the "weathergirl" theme. The Rollers looked about the same as they had during practice, although several had added smears of glittery "dirt" to their makeup, like they'd just come from the world's sparkliest quarry.

The whistle blew. Play began. I kept my head against Sam's shoulder, except when something happened that was exciting enough to make me cheer—which meant I was almost constantly in motion, popping out of my seat and thrusting my arms into the air, shouting at a bad call from the refs, cheering for a good jam. I had fallen easily into cheering for the Rollers, who seemed to be the underdogs in this particular pairing. It's always good to scream for people who need it.

The bell sounded halftime with the Storm Chasers leading 115 to 75. I sat down and took a long pull from my lukewarm cider, only to find Sam looking at me with admiration.

"I've never heard somebody scream so much when they weren't on a roller coaster," he said. "Run away with me."

"Tempting, but your grandmother would kill us." Assuming she found us before the Covenant did. Assuming they found us before Sam heard what they'd done to his family, and didn't kill me himself. "Want to go check the shopping? There's usually someone selling cupcakes."

"Oh, see, that's not fair. Turning my head with baked goods? You're a foul temptress or something."

"Or something," I agreed. We left our programs on our seats. It didn't guarantee they'd still be there when we got back—if whoever stumbled across them was drunk enough, we'd have to find another spot—but it was something, and it wasn't like we couldn't find replacements.

Sam slipped his hand into mine as we walked toward the shopping area. If I closed my eyes, I could pretend I was back in Portland, safe among my own people, with a boy I liked beside me. That was about as close as things got to perfect.

The shopping area lived up to my first impressions of it: a square in the middle, formed by shoving tables together, and longer rows of tables around the outside, mixing derby gear and the souvenir booths for the respective teams with local nonprofits, bakers, and advertisements for the junior derby league. Their advertising featured a lot of screenshots from the Ellen Page movie that came out a few years ago, and while it was hard not to see that as dated, it was also a nice try at attracting the attention of any teenagers who happened to wander through.

I bought a snickerdoodle cupcake with bacon sprinkled on top, and was nibbling at it as Sam thumbed through a stack of discount derby T-shirts.

"What the fuck are *you* doing here?"

The voice was familiar enough to be an icepick in my heart. I almost dropped my cupcake before I turned to face the woman standing behind me. She wasn't one of the skaters, but she was wearing a Rockville tank top, this one for the Clockpunchers. She was part of the same league. Her hair was snowy white, cut in a harsh bob that framed her face like she was a character out of *Tron*, programmed to be perfect, never a thing out of place. Even her eyeliner was flawless, blending seamlessly into the gold corona of her eyeshadow.

She looked like something from a movie about the American derby scene, and her name was Adrienne, and I was in a lot of trouble.

"Just shopping," I said, as lightly as I could, trying to force back the heat rising in my fingertips and slow down my heartbeat at the same time. Neither worked. My body was betraying me, too caught up in its panic to listen. "Nice to see you found a new league to skate with. I won't keep you."

"Why not, *Final Girl*?" She stressed my derby name as she stepped closer to me, a smile curving up the edges of her perfectly painted mouth. "You don't have any aconite on you tonight. We could have a rematch, on *my* home ground. Want to try me? You could find out once and for all why cheaters never prosper."

My fingertips got even hotter. My throat was dry; I couldn't speak.

Once, Adrienne had been a skater for the Wilsonville Rose Petals, and once, I had helped to drive her out of town and out of our league, because she was a mara, a sort of energy vampire, and she had gotten some good skaters injured with her careless feeding. She knew where I was from. She knew I had no business here.

She could ruin everything.

"Annie?" Sam stepped away from the T-shirts, putting a hand on my shoulder and doing his best to loom as he glared at Adrienne. "Is this girl bothering you?"

Adrienne's eyes widened. She looked from Sam to me, eyes lingering on the logo on the front of my shirt — the logo that said nothing about where I was from, who I skated with, who I was. Slowly, delightedly, she looked up to my face, and asked, "He doesn't know, does he?"

"Don't," I said, through gritted teeth.

"Oh, because you listened to me when I asked you to stop? When I asked what gave you the right? You decided I was a monster, and you were the Final Girl, and you chased me away from my life without even answering me." Adrienne took another step toward me, but her eyes were on Sam. "Better watch yourself, before she decides you're a monster, too."

"You were hurting people," I said.

Adrienne didn't take her eyes off of Sam. "I was hungry," she said. "When you're hungry, you got to eat. I bet the pigs think you're a monster. I bet the cows tell their children stories about you. Nobody died."

"That isn't the only measuring stick."

"It is for me." Adrienne shifted positions, angling her body toward Sam. "Do you know who your girlfriend really is? I didn't. She said her name was Annie Thompson. Said she was a skater, just like me. The Final Girl. The one who doesn't drink or smoke or swear, and makes it out of the movie alive. But she's not a damn thing like me — or like you." She dropped her voice so she wouldn't be overheard by the people moving around us, shopping, trying to mind their own business in the face of what looked like a personal dispute. "I know you're not human. I can taste it when I inhale. Better be careful with her, because all she's ever done is lie to you."

Sam didn't say anything. But his eyes darted toward me, a quick, confused gesture, and I knew that he was listening to her, and I knew that I was screwed.

"Let's get out of here," I said, grabbing for his hand. "She's just fucking with you."

"I'm warning him," she snapped, looking back to me. "I *asked* about you, after you drove me out of Portland. I asked everyone I knew if they had any idea who you were, because normal people don't have aconite and unicorn water lying around, waiting to be used on an innocent mara who just wants to eat. Normal people wouldn't know where to begin. And you know what I found out? 'Thompson' isn't even your last name."

"Please don't," I whispered. It was a small, futile thing: it did nothing. But once she'd approached us, there'd been nothing I could do. Once she'd spotted us, targeted us, I'd been trapped. Sure, I could have decked her, started a scene and run, but that wouldn't have changed the fact that Sam would have questions now, and once he had questions, it was all over but the answering. And the crying. That was going to be a factor, too.

"Why? Don't you like paying for what you've done? Funny, that, given who you are." She turned to Sam. "Meet Annie Price. As in, *those* Prices. As in, I'd watch myself, if I were you. She's probably out to screw you the way she screwed me."

I closed my eyes. When I opened them again, Adrienne was beaming at me, smiling bright and vivid as the morning.

"Nice seeing you again, Final Girl," she said. "I guess this time, the monsters won." Then she turned, and walked away, leaving me staring after her.

My shock only lasted a moment. "Sam, I'm sorry—" I began, turning to face him.

He was already gone.

The rain was bucketing down outside, and Sam had our only umbrella. I caught up with him halfway across the parking lot, my hair already plastered to my head and my clothes sticking to my body. "Sam, wait," I cried.

"Why? So you can tell me more lies?" He stopped walking, shoulders rigid, and didn't look at me. I started to reach for him. The rain struck my fingertips and sizzled, turning to steam. I pulled my hand back.

"It's not what you think," I whispered.

"Oh, it's not?" He finally turned around. The way he looked at me . . . it was like he was seeing a stranger, someone he didn't know and didn't want to. "Because I watched you when she was talking, Annie. You looked scared. You looked like the jig was up. And now I'm pretty sure that's because it was. Or are you going to tell me she's the liar here?"

I didn't say anything. He wouldn't have believed me. I've always been good at setting things up so that people will believe what I need them to believe, but I've never been a very good liar. The two skills are not the same.

"That's what I thought." He gave a small shake of his head. "I trusted you. We all trusted you. I *kissed* you. And you were lying the whole time. You were sneaking around, *lying* to us, for what?"

"I had to."

"You had to."

"Yes. Sam, please, this isn't what you think. This isn't—"

"It's not what I think? It's not what I *think*? Because I think it's someone from a known Covenant family sneaking around and telling lies about who she is. I think you killed Umeko. Did that have to happen? Or did you just tell us more lies to make it okay?" He took a step toward me, seeming suddenly much larger than I was. "I think you make me sick."

"Sam—"

"Don't talk to me. Don't look at me. Find your own damn way back to the show, and you better pray my grandmother isn't waiting outside with a shotgun."

He turned on his heel and stalked away across the parking lot, leaving me standing alone in the rain, while cheers erupted from the warehouse behind me. I had never felt more alone, or farther away from home. And I had no idea what I was going to do.

Twenty-one

" 'I'm sorry' is not a magic spell that makes everything better. I wish to God it were."

—Alice Healy

The edge of the field where the Spenser and Smith Family Carnival is camped, waiting for a miracle

I FORKED OVER THE COST OF MY RIDE, and the cab drove off. It vanished in the rain, leaving soaked, sobbing girls and the question of the carnival behind, and for a moment, I envied the driver like anything. He was going home to a life that probably made a lot more sense than mine did, and he was never going to need to look back. It felt like these days, looking back was all I ever did. That, and looking over my shoulder for the disaster I knew was coming.

My time with the Spenser and Smith Family Carnival began with me walking across a field toward the bone yard. There was a certain beautiful symmetry to ending it the same way. The rain poured down, drenching every inch of me, and the mud sucked at my boots so badly that I got bogged down several times, winding up with my arms pinwheeling and my feet anchored to the ground. If the Covenant realized my deception and came for me, there'd be nothing I could do to stop them. But maybe that was true anyway. I'd been so focused on working with them that I hadn't been focusing on finding a way to make them go away. No matter how I looked at this, I'd failed someone, even while I was doing the best that I could.

My real mistake had been in thinking, even for a second, that I could get through this unscathed; that I was having my first big adventure, not interacting with real people in the real world, where there were real stakes. People who weren't going to behave like the NPCs in my video games and just disappear when their part in the story was over. People who *wanted* things.

For a little while, Sam had wanted me, and I'd wanted him right back. Maybe that was the worst thing, out of all the terrible things I'd done, because if I'd told the truth—if we'd met when I was Antimony, not Timpani or Annie or any of the other people I'd been pretending to be—we might have had a chance. I was going to have to live with that. For the rest of my life, I was going to have to live with that.

The bone yard looked exactly the same as it had when we left, even down to the truck, parked back where it always was. Something shifted underfoot as I passed it. I looked down. One of the roller derby programs had fallen in the mud, soaking up the rain. I hadn't even realized he'd taken one with him. I stopped there, rain dripping from my hair, blinking back the tears that were threatening to rise and overwhelm me. Then, leaving the ruined reminder of a ruined evening behind, I walked on.

The lights were on in the RV Sam shared with Emery. I stepped up to the door and knocked, as firmly as I dared. My fingertips were hot, but my body felt weak, wrapped in a cocoon of sorrow and regret. I didn't like feeling this way. Probably no one did.

The door opened. Emery was standing there, expression icy. There was no welcome there, no indication that forgiveness was even possible, much less going to be offered.

"Well," she said. "I suppose you'd better come inside."

"Thank you," I said. It was small, and silly, the response of habit and all the good manners my parents had been able to beat into me, but under the circumstances, there was nothing else I could have said. If not for the rain, I would have expected to come back and find the bone yard gone, following the carnival into parts unknown. Can't safely dismantle a roller coaster in a rainstorm.

Sam was already there, back in his natural form, sitting at the small folding table in the kitchen. The fur on his cheeks was slicked flat, and his tail was wrapped so tightly around one of the table's legs that I wasn't sure whether he was going to hurt himself or rip the table apart. Maybe both. He had the strength for it, and he certainly had the anger.

Emery closed the door before turning to face me, folding her arms, and asking, in an almost reasonable tone, "Why should we let you leave here alive?"

"Because if you don't, everyone in this carnival is going to die."

The words fell between us, heavy and unwelcome, almost seeming to have a physical presence in the room. Then Sam moved.

I'd seen him before, when he was on the trapeze alone, or when he was running to get somewhere and didn't need to worry about being spotted by townies: he was one of the fastest living things I'd ever encountered. I'd been assuming I knew *how* fast. But I'd never seen him angry. One second he was at the table. The next, he was grabbing me by the throat and slamming me against the wall of the RV. It was like he'd flickered through the intervening space, ignoring it as inconvenient. I had the time to go limp, letting as much of the impact flow through me as possible, before I was hitting metal hard enough to make the whole RV rock.

"You're *threatening* us?!" he snarled. I'd never noticed how sharp his canine teeth were in this form. They didn't distort his speech at all; they had seemed somehow unimportant. But monkeys bite, and if he bit me, I was going to be in a world of hurt. "You come here, you *lie*, and you're *threatening* us?!"

"Can't . . . breathe," I wheezed. I didn't struggle or grab for his hand. That was just going to make him angrier, and under the circumstances, I didn't want to make him angrier. It was starting to really sink in that I was unarmed and he was faster than I was. I should have come up with an excuse to find out how *strong* he was. Too bad I'd missed my window.

"Samuel, put her down," said Emery.

"She lied to us," said Sam. He didn't take his eyes off my face. "She lied to us, and she snuck into our home, and she made us *trust* her. I'm not going to put her down."

And I'd kissed him. That was a second layer of anger and betrayal: I could see it in his eyes. Maybe if I'd just kissed him when he was human, but no, I'd had to go and be the first girl who didn't care what species he was, because either way, he was *Sam*. My parents had done too good a job of teaching me that people were always people. The fact that he sometimes had a tail didn't make him any less a person than the fact that, say, Sarah was essentially a wasp with boobs.

The fire was building in my fingertips again, strong enough that I expected to start setting things ablaze any second. Which gave me an idea. Maybe it was a bad one, but it was better than nothing: I grabbed Sam's wrist with both hands. The smell of burnt fur filled the air as he swore and dropped me. I landed hard on my ass, and scrambled backward as fast as I could, away from the wall and the enraged yōkai.

Emery put a hand on Sam's shoulder, stopping him from coming after me. "Samuel. Be calm."

"She *burned* me!" he exclaimed, holding up his arm.

"I'm sorry, I'm so sorry, I didn't mean to hurt you, but I couldn't breathe," I said, virtually babbling. I pushed myself off the floor, climbing to my feet. "It just happens sometimes, when I'm upset."

"A nascent magic user," said Emery. She sniffed. "No wonder they're willing to risk you. By the standards of the Covenant, you're little better than the innocent people you destroy. How does it feel to know that they're going to turn on you any day now? Is that why you lingered here so long?"

I rubbed my face. "I'm not Covenant," I said. "I mean, my family isn't Covenant. We quit over a hundred years ago. We've been independent cryptozoologists for four generations, and people won't stop thinking that because we were Covenant once, we're Covenant forever."

"So why are you here?" demanded Sam.

I lowered my hand. "The Covenant sent me."

Silence fell, thick and dangerous. Finally, in a low voice, Emery said, "You can't have it both ways, girl. Either you're Covenant, or you're not. Either you're a monster, here to kill us for the crime of being different, or you're not. Pick a side."

"See, we like to say that sort of thing like it means something, but it doesn't, because the real world is complex and contradictory and it doesn't do 'pick a side' like it's easy," I said. "Do you remember what happened on *Dance or Die* last season?"

Sam blinked, his anger fading into confusion. "Are you seriously asking for a reality TV recap in the middle of a fight?"

"There *was* a fight," said Emery slowly. "I don't watch the show, but I heard about it. A group of snake cultists summoned their god live on network television. A bunch of people died. Including most of the snake cultists. And a girl who claimed to be a member of the Price family declared war on the Covenant of St. George." She gave me a critical look. "Supposedly the girl was blonde. And petite."

"Whereas I am a tall brunette. Yes, the world is very confusing, and I don't look like the rest of my family," I said. "That was my sister Verity. She blew our cover. The Covenant was supposed to think we were dead and gone forever, not claiming to own an entire continent. Now they know we're back. We needed to know what they knew. We needed to know what they were *planning*. And I, as you so graciously noted, don't look like a Price." Or rather, I did, and no one remembered what a Price was supposed to look like, because the Healy genes are so dominant.

Dealing with people who treat heritage as a sign of virtue was exhausting. Punching them all would have been a lot more fun.

"I saw that," said Sam. "It was a trick. The Covenant trying to lure us out. Why else wouldn't they have cut the camera feed?"

"No, it was my sister, and she's not smart enough to come up with a plan that elaborate," I snapped. "She's a ballroom dancing cryptozoologist who wound up in the wrong place at the wrong time, and now I get to clean up her mess. And they didn't cut the feed because I'm pretty sure no one knew what to do until it was too late."

"I am not following this *at all*," said Sam. "Can I hit her now?"

"They sent me undercover," I said, before Emery could give him permission. I didn't know who would win in a knockdown fight between me and Sam now that I knew he was coming, but one or both of us would be severely hurt in the process, and I . . . I didn't want to hurt him.

God. Having feelings for people who aren't part of my family sucks.

"Who sent you undercover?" asked Emery.

"My family. They gave me a new name — technically a name I already owned, so if the Covenant had any psychics or routewitches working for them, they couldn't catch me in a lie — and an identity that matched my skills, and they sent me to the Covenant to find out what I could about their plans for North America. We're afraid there's going to be a war, and there aren't that many of us. Even if we managed to save ourselves, a lot of people would be hurt." We could disappear — we'd done it before — but the cryptids of North America hadn't been subjected to a full Covenant purge in over a hundred years. They wouldn't be ready. We wouldn't be able to save them.

"Your name is really Timpani?" asked Sam.

"No," I said. "It's Antimony. But my middle name is Timpani. Antimony Timpani Price. Sort of a palindrome, only not quite, see?"

Sam didn't look like he saw. He was looking at me like I was something he needed to scrape off his shoe. "You lied about everything, didn't you?"

"Not everything," I said softly, and looked away. In a more normal voice, I continued, "The Black Family Carnival really did get wiped out by Apraxis wasps, and I have the skills to pass as a carnie girl—my family's been associated with the Campbell Carnival for generations. I trained there. Knife-throwing with the Amazing Christopher, trapeze and trampoline with Grayson Campbell. I can back up what I say I am. There was no way for the Covenant to confirm I was who I said I was, so they just worked me hard until they believed me."

"Very much like we did," said Emery.

"Yeah, well." I turned back to her. "The Covenant noticed you because of what Umeko was doing. They'd seen the reports of the disappearances after your show came through town, and they put two and two together and decided, hey, we have a girl in training who has the perfect background to infiltrate and find out what's really going on."

"So wait," said Sam. "You were sent undercover with us by the people you'd been sent undercover to spy on?"

I nodded, unable to keep from smiling grimly. "It's a goddamn Shakespearean comedy, being me. The Covenant knew about the disappearances, and wanted to know whether they needed to do a purge, and I'm not their only American, but I'm their only carnie-trained operative. I couldn't stop them from finding out about Umeko—not after some of her victims survived—but I could tell them that no one else here knew a damn thing. I've been trying my hardest to convince them that the rest of you are human and should just be left alone."

"Has it worked?" asked Emery.

"No." I fought the urge to look away again. "They know about at least three of the cryptids with the show, although they still think Sam's human. I'm just a trainee to them. This is a test, meant to determine how trustworthy I am, and honestly, I'm pretty sure I'm failing it. They're going to come for a purge."

"And why should we start believing you now, when all you've done is lie?" asked Sam. "The Covenant wouldn't send someone they'd just met out into the field."

"Normally, your grandmother wouldn't let someone she'd just met go out on the trapeze. There's always extenuating circumstances. This time, my family is the extenuating circumstance. The Covenant wants someone who can help with situations like this one, who can move in a traveling show without standing out like a sore thumb. That's me. But that means accelerating their normal timetable for training, and shoving me into the field before I'm technically ready." To be honest, I was relieved. I didn't know how much Covenant indoctrination I could have taken before I'd either snapped, or started to listen. "I never wanted to lie to you. I've been trying to minimize it since the day I got here, and to make the Covenant see that they'd be better off leaving you alone. I'm not the reason they noticed your existence. Umeko did that. If anything, I'm the reason they've spared you for as long as they have."

"What do you want, a medal?" Sam glared at me. "I don't care why you lied. You're still a liar. I can't believe I fell for it."

"Yeah, well, you're not the only one," I said. I looked toward Emery. "My handler gave me an ultimatum earlier this week: she said when the carnival moved on, I wouldn't be moving with it. She probably thinks I expect that to mean she'll let you all go. She doesn't know how much experience my family has with her people. They're going to burn it to the ground. They don't like killing innocent humans, but they consider voluntary association with cryptids to be a crime. None of you are innocent in their eyes."

Emery stared at me. "You're not serious. None of this . . . you can't be serious."

Sam didn't say a word. He just kept looking at me like I was lower than dirt, an expression that made me want to crawl into my waterlogged tank top and hide. It's too bad cartoon physics aren't a real thing. I could have disappeared completely, if they were.

"I'm sorry, but I'm serious," I said. "You can ask the mice, if you like. You know Aeslin mice don't lie."

"I've heard rumors of a surviving colony living with

the Price family," said Emery, in a thoughtful tone. Then she shook her head, glaring at me. "You can't just waltz in here and tell me the Covenant of St. George is coming like it's nothing big. This is my home. These people are my family."

"Yes, I know," I said. "I want to help you save them."

"How are you proposing to do that?"

The time for lying was over. Maybe it had been over for a while, and I just hadn't noticed. Things might have been better if I had. "I don't know," I said honestly. "But I'm a Price, and I can find a way, if you'll let me."

"I'll be honest with you, even though it seems you've never extended me the same courtesy," said Emery. "I don't see where we have a choice."

For once, I didn't have anything to say.

"Now, if you don't mind, I'd like some time with my grandson, and I'd like you to begin packing your things." Emery made both these statements seem perfectly normal and reasonable, like they were the sort of things she said all the time. "You've upset him quite a bit, and you promised me you wouldn't do that. He's a sensitive boy. I'm afraid I won't be able to forgive you for what you've done, and I simply can't have people I don't trust traveling with the show. It's bad for morale. You're going to find a solution to this little problem you've brought to our door, and then you're going to leave."

"Yes, ma'am," I said, and took a step toward the RV door. "I'll get started now."

"Do that," she said. Sam wouldn't even look at me. I pushed the door open, and fled back out into the rain. I had to fix this. I didn't think I could.

The rain was coming down harder than ever as I ran through the bone yard. That was something of a relief. I didn't know how fast news traveled during a storm, but I knew how fast it traveled when the sun was out, and I didn't want the entire carnival to hate me. Not yet. It was inevitable at this point—maybe it always had been—and I wanted to put it off as long as I possibly could.

I reached my RV without seeing another living soul, unlocking the door and stepping inside, into the dry and warm. The mice, who were standing on the counter out-side their elaborate little house, greeted my return with cheers. Aeslin mice are good like that. As long as their gods and priestesses are around, they figure the rest of the world will sort itself out. Sometimes I really wish I could share their outlook on the world.

"Hi, guys," I said, easing the door closed behind me. "Mork, I need to talk to you."

The newer of my mice looked faintly alarmed, slick-ing his ears against his head and pulling his body down toward the counter. "Priestess?" he squeaked.

"You lived with the English branch of the family for a long time, even if they didn't know that you were there. If Margaret were going to launch an attack, how would she do it?"

"The Impassioned Priestess is not a bad person," he said, tone going anxious. "She has been Misled. It is Not Her Fault."

"I'm not trying to point fingers or assign blame; I'm trying to save lives." My clothes were sticking to my skin. I began stripping them off and dropping them into the sink, where they could dry without ruining anything else. "She told me that when this carnival moved on, I wouldn't be moving with it. I don't think she meant I'd be leaving quietly. She knows about at least three cryp-tids within the show. What is she going to do?"

"She travels in the company of the Quiet Man," said Mork slowly. It was the first time I'd heard a title as-signed to someone who wasn't a part of the Aeslin reli-gious structure, but it fit. Robert was often quiet, listening and planning until he felt the need to act. He was very much in charge. Margaret knew it, and so did I. "He will come in from the back, with sharpened knives and si-lence. He prefers the unlit hall. The Impassioned Priest-ess would fight the world face-to-face, if she thought she could. She likes her enemies to see their deaths ap-proaching."

"Okay." I pulled my bathrobe on. The RV felt like it was shifting around me, going from a temporary home to a waiting room, a place to pause before action resumed.

It hurt. "Are they going to call for reinforcements, or are the two of them going to try to take on this carnival all by themselves?"

Mork lowered his head, whiskers drooping. "I am sorry, Priestess. I have failed you."

"What? What do you mean?"

Mindy put a paw on his shoulder. "You must speak. If you do not speak, she cannot know, for did not the Thoughtful Priestess say We Are Not All Mind-Readers Here, We Leave That To Sarah?"

Mork sighed. It was a small, pained sound, and I've spent enough of my life around Aeslin mice that it nearly broke my heart. Raising his head, he met my eyes and said, "If she has given you the Indication that the End is Nigh, then she is no longer alone with the Quiet Man. That is not how Things Are Done. Two is a reconnaissance team. More are required, for a Cleansing. More are required, for a Purge."

"How many more?" I asked.

"I Cannot Say. At least two. Perhaps more. This is a Small Target, poorly armed, unprepared. They may think four is enough."

I stared at the mouse in horror. Mork ducked his head again, shame radiating from every line of his tiny body.

"I have failed you," he moaned. "I am unworthy of the hallowed space of the Family Attic."

"You have done no such thing," I said. "You haven't failed me; you're still getting used to the idea of what it means to serve your gods. You'll get used to it. And if anyone failed here, it was me. I didn't tell you when Margaret came to speak to me. That was my fault."

"I must Redeem Myself," said Mork stubbornly. "I will return to England, and face my punishment."

"No," I said. "You will not." There was no way I was sending this mouse back to the Covenant to be killed—and they *would* kill him, once guilt drove him to reveal himself. Even if he hadn't been an Aeslin mouse from my family's colony, and hence my responsibility, Mindy had been putting on an awful lot of weight in the past few weeks, and while I wasn't going to ask her for details, I was pretty sure my colony was going to expand if I didn't get home soon.

(Aeslin mice have a longer gestation time than normal mice, and tend to only have one or two babies at a time. They also don't eat them. Aeslin mice are much better than normal mice.)

Mork made a small wailing noise and began supplicating himself to me. Mindy interposed her body between the two of us, whiskers slanted in embarrassment. "I will talk to him," she squeaked. "I am sorry."

"Don't be," I said. "He helped."

More were coming than just Margaret and Robert. I should have guessed as much. Unless they were planning some sort of airstrike, there were too many people here for them to take out on their own.

I didn't have an umbrella, but I had the classic sheets of newspaper, intended as bedding for the mice. I grabbed a thick stack, stepped into my flip-flops, and said, "I'll be right back," before stepping into the rain once more. I wasn't going far this time: just around the side of the RV to the other door, which I had never seen open.

I knocked. I waited. Ananta opened the door, eyes widening when she saw me. Like me, she was dressed for staying where it was dry, not going out in the rain, in a knee-length black T-shirt over soft gray leggings. Unlike me, she didn't have makeup melting down her face or glitter tangled in her hair.

"Did you lock yourself out?" she asked. "I have a spare key."

"No," I said. "May I come in?"

Ananta went still. "That may not be the best idea."

In for a penny . . . "I know you're a wadjet," I said. "I know at least some of the cobras in your exhibit are your brothers. I don't know why you're with the carnival, and I don't much care. I need your help."

Ananta had seemed still before. Now she was frozen, reduced to a perfect, reptilian motionlessness that made me wonder how I could ever have thought, even for a second, that she was a mammal. Finally, softly, she asked, "How do you . . . ?"

"Please."

Ananta nodded, leaning out the door to take a quick look to either side before she stepped back and let me into her half of the RV.

The smell of snake struck me the second I stepped inside, ten times as strong as it had been in the wider, airier reptile show tent. The lights were low, and the heat was high, enough that I wished I had something on under the bathrobe and could take it off, at least for a little while. There was a bed, long and narrow and currently occupied by two adolescent cobras. And an iPad. The sight of a cobra clutching a stylus in the last few inches of its tail was definitely a new one. I blinked. The cobra, lacking eyelids, did not blink back, but did flare its hood out a few extra millimeters, making sure I remembered that it was a dangerous snake, and should not have its Netflix time interfered with.

Most of the space in the RV was taken up with rack upon rack of reptile enclosures. There were tanks on the counter, and a large, open tank taking up most of the small dining table. Ananta had structured her life around her charges as well as her brothers, and was probably perfectly content to do so. Family, after all, comes first.

"All right," she said, shutting the door. "Talk."

"I know you're a wadjet because I'm a trained cryptozoologist, and I know they're your brothers because they're not your sons, and there's no way you could have two unrelated male wadjet in the same tank without one of them killing the other," I said quickly. Even if I hadn't been surrounded by snakes, female wadjet have their own venom, and are perfectly capable of doing a lot of damage when they feel threatened. "My real name is Antimony Price."

"Price? Really?" Ananta took a step toward the bed, putting herself between me and her brothers. "Like Alex Price?"

"He's my brother," I said, suddenly serene. Alex

mostly worked with reptiles, and there was a male wadjet living at the zoo where he'd been working for the past few years. The wadjet community knew him as a friend and ally. Thank God. "Look. My sister accidentally declared war on the Covenant, so the family sent me to England to infiltrate the Covenant and find out how much they knew about us. Only they didn't count on Umeko killing those people and attracting attention."

"The Covenant sent you to infiltrate the carnival and find out what was going on," said Ananta. I nodded. She groaned. "Humans are the *worst*. You're always scurrying around and kicking over other people's anthills. Why didn't you say something sooner?"

"Because I was trying to do as little damage as possible. Before we found out about Umeko, I didn't know for sure whether the carnival was aware of the disappearances and just covering them up, or whether you were all innocent. After we found out about Umeko, I was trying to convince the Covenant that everyone here was human and deserved to be left alone."

"That's a human thing, too. That weird savior complex."

"You can't honestly tell me the Covenant has a savior complex."

"Can't I?" Ananta raised an eyebrow. "When they got started, humans were at the bottom of the pecking order. The only thing you had going for you was the speed with which you bred. Even at our greatest, the wadjet could never compete, because we have too much trouble mating. The Covenant began as an attempt to save your species from extinction. It got out of hand when they learned to love killing. Now we get people like you and your family, trying to rebuild what your own species destroyed. It's all about savior complexes. It always has been. Not that I mind, since it means I get to live in a world where some people don't want to kill me on sight, but seriously. You think you can fix everything. You can't."

"I need to fix this."

Ananta nodded. "Yeah, it'd be nice, since you fucked

it up. But you didn't make Umeko do what she did, and you didn't attract the attention of the Covenant. You're a pawn for once, just like all the rest of us. What did you think I could do to help you?"

"You own this RV, right? And the tent where you do your reptile show?"

Ananta nodded again, slowly this time, like she wasn't comfortable with where this conversation was going. "I do."

"Great." I smiled sunnily. "Tell me about the way the carnival's insurance is set up."

Twenty-two

"You won't get everything you want in this world. That's a good thing. What you do get will matter more, because you've earned it."
— Evelyn Baker

The big tent at the Spenser and Smith Family Carnival, sitting on the edge of the net, waiting for the sky to fall

THE RAIN WAS STILL COMING DOWN in buckets, turning the ground into a swampy mess and keeping the townies at bay. It was a blessing in disguise. No one was there to see the carnies sneaking away in ones and twos, packing themselves into carefully-selected RVs and rolling off down the road. Ostensibly, if anyone stopped them to ask, they were heading for our next site, checking to see whether it had better protections against the weather than this one. In reality, they were getting as far as they could from what was going to be one hell of a fight.

Emery hadn't wanted me there when she addressed the show; said my presence would be a confusing distraction, would keep people from focusing on what was important about the situation. I was pretty sure she just couldn't stand the sight of me, but didn't have a good way of getting rid of me, not without endangering the people we were both struggling to protect. So she'd gathered the rest of the carnival in the mess while I'd wandered down the deserted, muddy midway to the big tent. That had been more than an hour ago. The only person

I'd seen since then was Ananta, who had stopped in on her way to get the rest of the snakes from her tent.

"Did you get your things out of the RV?" she'd asked, and I had nodded. My suitcase was packed and hidden in the field; the tiny house where Mork and Mindy had spent their rodent honeymoon was in a box. Mork and Mindy were with me, curled in my backpack, talking about whatever it was Aeslin mice discussed when there were no humans around to hear them. It might have been safer to leave them in the field. It might not. If my suitcase got stolen, so what? If my backpack got stolen . . .

Any additional risk was worth it for the security of knowing where they were.

Ananta had paused, sizing me up. Finally, she'd said, "A lot of people around here are going to hate you. I'm not going to tell them they're wrong. But I'm not going to join in, either. Maybe we'll see each other again someday. You could introduce me to your brother."

"Sounds only fair," I'd replied. "I've met two of yours."

She'd smiled, and I'd smiled, and we'd only looked a little pained. Then she'd vanished back into the rain, to finish packing her snakes into great plastic tubs and carting them to the RV. She was gone by now, I knew, joining the quiet exodus. I hoped she could drive far enough to escape the Covenant's attention. I hoped she could be safe.

I hoped that for all of them.

At least I was armed now. Timpani Brown was buried, and with her went the need to seem like an ordinary trapeze artist. The throwing knives I'd borrowed for my act were tucked into my clothes, providing a comforting layer of metal against my skin. I'd also swiped a handful of darts from one of the midway games, reasoning that their absence would never be noticed, but it's always good to have a few more things to throw.

A shovel would have been better. A shovel, and time to dig about a hundred pit traps, and maybe some C-4. It was nice to be armed again, but dynamite would have been even nicer.

There was a flicker of motion from the bleachers. I turned wearily toward it. "You may as well come out, whoever you are," I said. "I'm not going to get any less cranky."

The motion resolved itself into Sam as he stepped out of the shadows and walked to the edge of the ring with deliberate slowness. My heart jumped into my throat and hung there, perfectly suspended, while I forgot how to breathe.

Finally, in a choked voice, I asked, "Did Emery send you?"

"No," he said. "She'd probably have told me not to come, if she'd known. She thinks I'm at the RV, packing my things. She wants me to ride out of here with the Knowles twins."

"The Knowles twins ... ?"

"They run the Haunted House, usually. They own half of it. Well, right now they do. After the insurance pays for us to get a new one, they're going to own the whole thing. That was their price for going, instead of staying to fight. Not that they *wanted* to stay and fight. They just wanted to own the Haunted House."

"They're probably not related," I said automatically.

Sam paused, confusion rippling across his face and chasing away any anger lurking there. For a moment, he looked at me like I was just Annie, the girl he flew with, the girl he kissed, the girl who sometimes said things that made no sense at all. "What do you mean?"

"Bogeymen stay home until they get married, so they can pay into the family; odds are good they're either a young married couple or engaged and trying to earn enough to pay for each other. Owning their own carnival attraction, and all its profits, would go a long way toward securing them a wedding." Bogeymen never like to feel like they owe anyone anything. There's a lot of reciprocity in their culture, and a lot of very detailed accounting.

"Okay, that's weird," said Sam. The confusion faded, replaced by stony coldness. I ached to see it go. "I wanted to talk to you."

"So talk. Unless 'talk' is your way of saying 'beat the shit out of you.' You'll need to get in line for that."

He grimaced. "I guess I deserved that."

"You think?"

"I overreacted before. I shouldn't have hit you. But you shouldn't have burned me."

"I burned you *because* you hit me."

"I guess that's fair," said Sam, looking down at his feet. "I'm better at holding a grudge than I am at apologizing. Can we be done with this part? Please?"

"I'm a pretty good grudge-holder myself," I said, thinking of Verity, thinking of slammed doors and icy silences. "Sure. Let's say just this once, the two grudges cancel each other out."

"Cool. Thanks." He looked up. "Do you think this plan of yours will work?"

I closed my eyes. "As long as we're careful. I think the Covenant will come looking for me when I don't call, because they consider me one of their own. We'll fight them. We'll lose. And we'll burn the whole place down around our ears." The inevitable arson investigation would find no accelerants; just the aftermath of an electrical fire that had started in the big tent and managed to spread despite the rain, destroying everything. Emery had shown me the carnival's insurance paperwork. They were covered thoroughly enough that they'd be closed for six months, tops, while they found and repainted their replacement rides. They might even wind up better off. Buying new would allow them to get equipment that needed less repair than their current worn-down rides and attractions.

Yes, they'd lose the memories and history associated with what they already had. But they'd be alive to make new ones. That had to be good enough.

"Grandma thinks I'm leaving."

"So you've said."

"I'm not leaving."

I opened my eyes. It was somehow unsurprising to see that Sam had crossed half the space between us. He was standing there, tail twining and untwining around his left ankle, watching me with that same cold flatness. I thought back on all the times he'd glared at me, or looked at me like I didn't matter, and realized, with a small flare of hope, that he was nervous.

"Why not?" I asked.

"Because I'm not my mom," he said. "I don't run out on people just because things get hard and I might get hurt if I stick around."

"Sometimes staying is a lot harder than running away," I agreed quietly.

"Annie . . ." He paused. "Is it still okay to call you that?"

"Yeah," I said. "It's 'Antimony,' remember? My Great-Aunt Laura was an ambulomancer. She made a prediction that could have applied to either me or my cousin Elsie, about needing to disappear under a name that was ours but wasn't at the same time. My parents named me 'Antimony Timpani,' and Elsie's parents named her 'Elsinore Norelle,' to make sure we'd be able to do what we had to, when the time came." I laughed bitterly. "When we were kids, we used to bet each other on who it would be. I never thought I'd win."

"Your parents named you to fulfill a prophecy?" Sam sounded dubious. I didn't blame him in the least. "Who are you, Anakin Skywalker?"

"I have not brought balance to the Force." I looked at him. I didn't feel like I had the right anymore, but that didn't change the wanting. That's the real problem with me. I always *want* something. I want my parents to be proud of me. I want to do things my siblings have never done, things that would make me something more than just the troublesome baby of the family. I want to skate. I want to be right.

I wanted Sam. Life would have been so much easier if I hadn't. But he'd kissed me, and I'd kissed him, and for a few crystalline moments, everything had seemed like it made sense. Everything had seemed *right*.

"No, I guess you haven't." He stayed where he was, looking at me. "I knew something was wrong with your story. Some of the things you'd said to me didn't track."

"I'm not the best liar."

"I know. All the good parts of what you said ... those were the true parts. I should have known something was up when you didn't freak out at the idea of kissing a guy with a tail." His lips twisted into something dark and wry. "Even the carnie girls don't like to kiss a monkey. They say it's kinky in the bad way."

"Then they're short-sighted. You're a much better kisser when you're not tense."

Sam's bark of laughter was so abrupt that it startled us both, creating a sort of stunned silence. He recovered first. "I shouldn't have left you in that parking lot. I was pissed, and I had the car keys."

"I deserved it. I shouldn't have lied." I shook my head. "Or maybe I shouldn't have taken you anywhere near a roller derby game. But I don't feel like that's a strong enough moral. 'To keep lying to your boyfriend, avoid beloved locations and pastimes.'"

"You really thought I was your boyfriend?"

I froze. The word had been an accident—but there are no accidents, as Elsie has always been so happy to remind me. The subconscious always makes itself known. I shrugged a little, looking down. "I thought you might be. Guess we'll never know now, huh?"

"Guess not." Sam looked around the tent. "Grandma's always been a stickler for fire safety. She says this place would go up like a candle."

"That's the hope."

"How long ... ?"

"We have about an hour before I'm supposed to check in. I won't. They'll come looking for me, and when they do, I guess they'll find me." I shrugged again. "After that, we'll see what happens. Either I win and the carnival burns and you all get away, or I lose and the carnival burns and I go back to England to answer for my family's sins."

"I'm not leaving."

"You keep saying that, but you're wrong. You have to go."

"No, I don't. Grandma says I do, but I'm an adult, and this is my home. I get to stay and defend it if I want to."

I slid off the net, holding my hands beseechingly toward him. "There's nothing to defend. We're letting it burn, remember? The Covenant thinks you're human. Margaret said so explicitly. We can't kill them all, even if we wanted to try, so we need this to work. We need them to think everyone died or scattered, and is no longer a problem either way."

"So what, you think I'm just going to run off and let you do this by yourself?"

"That was the idea."

The corner of Sam's mouth twitched. "That would make me a pretty shitty boyfriend."

"Since everything I've said to you was a lie, I think you're allowed."

"Not everything." He moved toward me with that unnerving speed, taking my still-outstretched hands and twining his tail around my waist, pulling me close to him. "Pretty sure you think I'm cute."

"Sam—"

"You lied to us. I'm not thrilled about that. I was pretty pissed, actually, and if we had more time, I still would be. We don't have more time. I've lied to everyone who's ever thought I was human. I've told stories to protect myself. And you never hurt anyone here who didn't try to hurt you first. I'd be sort of stupid to let this screw things up for us."

"Sam . . ."

He leaned in and kissed me, tail tightening around my waist as his hands tightened on mine. The heat was back in my fingertips, but it wasn't burning this time, more warming them to a slow boil. Together, we wrapped ourselves around each other under the big tent, and we let everything else go for a few minutes. There was no future for us. The girl he'd been kissing before didn't exist: this was the first time he'd kissed me and known my name, who my family was, where I came from. When this place burned, he'd disappear in one direction and I'd disappear in another, and we'd never see each other again. But oh, sometimes the future is a very long way away, and sometimes the present matters more than anything that might be coming down the line.

There was no hesitation in him now. The way he kissed me told me his thoughts were mirroring mine, at least on some level. He knew this was the last time, and while he might not have forgiven me fully for my lies, he was smart enough to know he'd regret it if he didn't give me a proper farewell. I let go of his hands, using mine to pull him closer, threading my fingers into the furlike hair atop his head. He responded by sliding his hands under my shirt . . . and stopped, pulling away, and bursting into laughter.

I blinked. My breasts had garnered a lot of responses since they'd started making an appearance back in middle school. Some of those responses had been more welcome than others. But I'd never had a guy get his hands on them and start laughing before.

"Excuse me?" I said, bemused.

"How many knives do you *have* under there?" asked Sam.

The mystery was solved. I grinned and said, "About thirty."

"How do you not cut yourself?"

"Practice." I leaned back, trusting the tether of his tail to keep me upright. "What are we doing?"

"Making out."

"I thought you were mad at me."

"I am, and I'm not, and it's confusing, and maybe if we had more time I'd be all sulking and broody and trying to work through my feelings about the situation, but we don't," said Sam. "You're going to burn down the world and then you're going to disappear and I'm never going to see you again. I'm not ready to never see you again."

"Hey, I have to be punished for my hubris somehow," I said, and leaned in, and kissed him.

We only had a little time left, he and I and the shadow of the big tent, where we'd learned to fly with each other, instead of only always flying alone. What we did there, in that quiet, shadowy space, would have to be enough to balance out everything that we weren't going to have. And by God, we tried. No matter what else we may have done, we tried.

When we rolled away from each other, straw and sawdust stuck to our backs and—in Sam's case—to the thin line of fur that ran from the base of his tail up to the nape of his neck, outlining his spine in bristling brown. I rolled further, reaching for my phone, abandoned in the welter of knives and clothing that I had shed.

According to the readout, it was 10:25 PM.

"I missed my check-in," I said, putting down the phone and reaching for my bra. "You need to go. You need to make sure everyone else is already gone. They're coming."

"You can't be sure—"

"My handler as much as told me they were getting ready to move. They're coming. They'll either think it's a rescue mission—that I screwed up and got myself caught—or that I've gone over to the wrong side and think I can save you all. Either way, it's to my advantage, because they don't know how much training I actually have. Now go. Make sure everyone else is out of the line of fire. *Please*."

Sam looked at me gravely. "I want to stay."

"I know. Doesn't change things."

"It never does." He kissed me, so quickly that I didn't have time to react, and then he was gone. He took his clothes with him. I hoped he had some practice at dressing while he ran, or else the members of the carnival who hadn't managed to evacuate yet were going to get one hell of a surprise. I know a naked monkey man would catch *my* attention.

I dressed slowly, taking the time to secure every knife and dart in its proper position. Margaret and Robert were staying in town. If they'd left the second I failed to check in, they'd be here within the next ten minutes.

Assuming their backup was already here, they'd need to rally the troops; I probably had until eleven or so before things got really ugly.

"Stay quiet," I said to my backpack as I slipped it on. It didn't respond, but I knew the mice would hear me, and obey. Obedience in the face of dire danger is an Aeslin survival trait.

Calmly, forcing my steps to remain even and my shoulders to remain loose, I walked to the tent door and stepped out onto the moonlit midway. The rain had stopped. The sky was clear, dominated by a vast, gleaming Minnesota moon. I looked up at it and kept walking.

The highest point in the carnival was the Ferris wheel. With no one to tell me it was dangerous or ask me to get down, it was an easy thing to climb the outside of the structure, using the struts and counterbalances to give me the traction I needed. I kept climbing until I reached the topmost swing, and stopped there, removing my backpack and tucking it under the seat. The mice would be safe. No one would find them unless they turned on the ride, and the Ferris wheel itself was basically fireproof. The controls might melt. The wheel would remain.

Gripping the safety bar, I straightened and turned in a slow circle, getting an idea of the landscape. The bone yard was dark. There were still a few RVs, trucks and vehicles deserted by their owners to create the impression that the show was normal, but the lights were off for the first time I could remember. The carnival sat in a field of nothingness, moonlight flooding the wide boulevards formed by rides and games and concessions. This was where I would stand. This was where I would fight. For the carnival, for the people who'd never asked to be a part of this, and yes, for my family, because every fight against the Covenant on American soil is a fight for my family. We chose freedom when we walked away. It was up to me to show that the choice had been the right one.

Nothing moved. I stood there, waiting for something to change, and when the change came, I nearly fell off the Ferris wheel—which would have been a swift, ignominious end to my adventure. I caught myself at the last moment, watching as the midway lights finished coming on, casting everything in a hundred candy-colored shades. The wheel began to turn, my swing descending toward the ground. There was no one at the controls. Whoever threw the switch must have shorted something out, because the Ferris wheel wasn't the only ride running under its own steam.

A dozen conflicting songs drifted from various rides, ranging from the spooky soundtrack of the haunted house to the tinkling fairy chimes of the carousel. I watched for people, but didn't see any, until the Ferris wheel was close enough to the ground for me to hop off. Drawing a knife from inside my shirt, I began walking, slowly and carefully, toward the front gate.

I was almost there when someone grabbed me from behind.

Twenty-three

"When the time comes, shoot to kill. Anything less is beneath you."

—Frances Brown

The midway of the Spenser and Smith Family Carnival, about to break somebody's nose

I WHIPPED AROUND, hand already raised, knife primed to release, and froze as I found myself looking at Leo Cunningham. Seeing him here was a shock. Seeing the relief in his eyes was somehow an even greater shock, like he'd been dropped in from an entirely different story.

"Leo?" I managed to squeak, voice cracking.

"Annie, thank God," he said, ignoring the knife as he threw his arms around me and squeezed me tight. "When you didn't check in, well. I won't pretend I wasn't concerned."

"Seriously, *Leo*?!" I pushed him away. I didn't have to feign my shock or dismay as I demanded, "What are you *doing* here? You don't do fieldwork!"

His expression softened, melting into a sort of sympathetic understanding. I fought the urge to slap that look clean off of his face. "Ah, of course. Annie, I know this must be all very confusing for you. Robert called the rest of the team in three days ago. We're going to help wipe this demon-infested traveling carnival off the face of the planet."

"But . . . but I thought we were going to let them go

once we knew that they weren't hurting anyone," I stammered. "Margaret said . . ."

"Margaret didn't want to upset you. It was only natural for you to sympathize with these people. They're much like the ones you lost, aren't they? But the ones you lost were human."

"So are the people here."

"No," said Leonard, and his voice was poisonously gentle, filled with a conviction I could hear but never share. It was the sort of voice people use with children who don't understand how the world works, and I hated him for it, even as I was obscurely grateful. If he was talking to me like this—if he was talking *down* to me like this—it was going to be a lot easier to kick his ass. "They're traitors to their own kind. They've harbored monsters. People have died. It's time for all of this to end."

I had one more card to play. It wasn't a good one. It was better than murder. "I thought you had to keep a low profile in North America, to keep those Price people from coming for you. Wiping out a whole carnival isn't keeping a low profile."

"They'll never know it was us," said Leo reassuringly. "I promise you that. We're quite good at covering our tracks. We've done this before. A little resistance was never enough to make us turn our backs on the people who needed us."

I stared at him. He smiled, clearly mistaking my dismay for surprise.

"Your job is done, Annie. We're not going to make you help with the cleansing, not as a trainee—not unless you wanted to." He held out his hand, beckoning me. "I'd be happy to show you what to do."

"What to do?" I asked. "I'm pretty sure I know what an invitation from the Dark Side looks like, thanks."

"What?" His smile melted into dismay. "What are you talking about?"

"And you didn't even offer me cookies," I spat, and punched him in the nose.

Leonard Cunningham was an experienced operative of the Covenant of St. George, trained in all the ways to fight and evade the "monsters" he'd dedicated his life to destroying. He had not, apparently, been trained in the way to fight or evade being punched in the nose by a woman he regarded as a harmless trainee. He went down like a sack of potatoes. I turned and ran like hell for the other end of the midway.

There was no way Reginald Cunningham would have allowed his grandson and heir to come to the States without backup: three people might be enough to cleanse a carnival, but not when one of those people was going to inherit the whole shebang. I had to assume there were at least four agents active and on the ground in the carnival now—maybe more, depending on how seriously they'd taken this incursion, and whether or not they'd really been expecting me to help them take out the carnival.

There were over a hundred people working here. What could they possibly have been planning that would take out that many noncombatants with less than an army?

The lights had come on without warning, and the rides all activated at the same time. That was more than a glitch; that was sabotage, pure and simple, the sort of thing that would normally have brought half the show running. The engineers would have been at the front of the pack, followed by the lookie-loos who wanted to be the first to see what was broken and carry the gossip back to the rest of the carnival.

Pop quiz: what do you call a distraction that draws people *in*, rather than pushing them *away*? Answer: a trap. You call it a trap.

Wishing for Sam's speed or my roller skates or at least dry ground—anything to increase my speed just that tiny fraction—I ran, head down, arms pumping. If I'd encountered another member of the Covenant field team during that run, I wouldn't have hesitated to kill them. Maybe it was murder and maybe it was a form of

existential self-defense, or maybe they had actually managed that tiny sliver of indoctrination, and made me stop
thinking of the people who opposed me as human beings. Whatever the reason for my change of heart, I was
still grateful when no one appeared to make me prove it.

This was a field when it didn't have a carnival in it: it
didn't have the infrastructure to run the midway, much
less a bunch of power-sucking beasts like the Scrambler
and the little coaster. The solution was simple enough,
and was universal to carnivals the world over now that
even the smallest traveling show boasted electric lights
and moving machines—a generator array had been es-
tablished in the ride alley inside a shed disguised as a
supply booth, tucked between the Scrambler and the
Centrifuge, a giant spinning bowl that plastered people
to its sides with the power of physics. Any power tamper-
ing would start there.

The door was open when I came skidding down the
aisle, feet slipping in the mud and breath catching in my
throat. I barreled onward, catching the edge of the door
and swinging myself into the darkened shed.

The blinking digital display on the bomb was more
than bright enough to catch my attention.

"*Shit*." Flipping the light switch struck me as a singu-
larly bad idea. If I'd been trying to get a bunch of carnies
to blow themselves up, wiring the light switch into the
trigger mechanism would have been the best way to go
about it. I didn't have a flashlight, but I had the fire in my
fingers, and I had the bright banners hanging from the
outside of the shed, camouflaging it as just another part
of the scenery. I leaned out and yanked a strip of fabric
down, wadding it into a ball and focusing on it as hard as
I can.

Come on, I thought. *Come on, come on, this is a stupid, pointless skill, and I'm going to get some use out of it
now, so come on.*

The wadded-up fabric burst into flame. I managed not
to drop it, which might have put out the fire, and instead
set it on the muddy ground, trusting the dampness to

keep the fire from starting too soon. The light it cast wasn't much, but it was enough to let me see what they'd done. The shed was wired to blow, with the timer mechanism and blasting caps both connected to a massive block of what looked like bright yellow modeling clay. That color and that shape could only mean one thing: Semtex. Because *that* was exactly what I needed tonight.

I've played with Semtex before, under controlled circumstances. It's pretty stable, as plastic explosives go, and it packs one hell of a kick. That block would be enough to vaporize anyone within twenty feet of the blast, and to damage a hell of a lot more than just that. I was right. This was a trap.

Only three wires connected the Semtex to the rest of the device. They weren't colored—that would have been too easy—and at least one of them was going to be a dummy. Cutting it wouldn't do anything, but could lead me to think I'd defused the bomb when I really hadn't. That left me two "live" wires. Cut one and save the day; cut the other and blow myself to smithereens. It would almost have been better if the bomb had been more sophisticated. The more moving pieces a bomb has, the easier it is to get an idea of how the manufacturer thought, and how to break what they spent so much time on making.

(Sure, it's also easier to blow yourself up, but there's a reason most police departments have access to a dedicated bomb squad. It's *always* easy to blow yourself up. I'm an amateur who mostly plays around with black powder and dynamite—the Looney Toons of explosive weaponry. Anything more elaborate than that is trending toward "out of my league.")

I stared at the bomb, all too aware of the open flame behind me and the fact that time was passing. They might have put the blasting caps on a timer, in case the carnies were too slow getting here. Or someone might have refused to evacuate when Emery told them to go, and be on their way to find out why the rides were on. I needed to do something.

There were three wires. Cutting any of them could

mean either salvation or a death sentence. There was one block of Semtex.

There was a loophole.

Leaning forward, I gingerly grasped the block of plastic explosives, aware that if it was old and unstable, or if the Covenant bomber had done a halfway-competent job, I was about to die. But a big explosion would bring the local authorities and destroy the carnival in a way insurance wouldn't pay for, and I couldn't do that to them. They deserved the chance to get away clean and start over, without me or the Covenant breathing down their necks. I had promised Emery I'd try. I was trying.

"Okay," I said, with a deep breath. "Here goes nothing . . . Mary! I need you! *Betelgeuse, Betelgeuse, Betelgeuse!*"

"You *know* I hate it when you call me like that," snapped Mary, materializing air next to me. "Also, sometimes, I'm going to be busy. Like, you get that, right? I have a life aside from babysitting y—"

If I asked, she'd have to involve the crossroads, and so I didn't ask as I yanked the Semtex away from the wall and hurled it at her, blasting caps and all. She had time to make a horrified face before she disappeared, taking the explosives with her. The bomb's digital control beeped once and sparked fruitlessly. There was nothing left for it to trigger.

"She's going to *kill* me for blowing up the ghost world," I muttered, and looked around the shed, settling on the repair kit next to the door. My makeshift torch was going out, but it still provided me with just enough light to see the flare gun when I opened the toolbox. I grinned ferally, grabbed the gun, and ran.

The dark rides were mixed in with the bigger power sucks, making it easier to control crowd flow. I ran until I found the ride I wanted. Then I stopped, turned to face the rest of the show, and pulled the trigger on my borrowed flare gun. A red flower blossomed in the sky above me. I stood my ground, waiting.

It wasn't a long wait. Three figures ran around the

Scrambler, two female, one male. I recognized the man as Robert and one of the women as Margaret. The third was a mystery to me, but as she was running in step with the other two, it wasn't a stretch to guess that she was Covenant. I aimed my flare gun at them and pulled the trigger again, forcing them to leap to the side to avoid being hit by a burning projectile. Now that they were well and truly pissed, I gave them a jaunty little wave, turned, and ran straight into the Haunted House.

As a dark ride, the Haunted House depended on a fixed track system that pulled the individual carriages through the scenes that had been constructed inside. The carriages were slow, ostensibly to give people time to take in the horrors around them, but really to make sure the townies felt like they were getting their money's worth from what was honestly one of the less thrilling attractions. There were no live performers—usually— and plastic skeletons just aren't enough to send the youth of today into an ecstasy of terror. As one of the youth of today, I know it takes a lot more than a few stuffed bats on strings to scare me.

Like, say, being pursued into a dark ride by three members of the Covenant of St. George. That was something I found plenty scary.

The carriages rolled by as I ran into the ride, following the track until I came to the Mad Scientist's Lab. Ducking behind the stereotypically green monster on his slab, I drew two knives from inside my shirt and crouched down, every muscle tense, every nerve on fire. At least my fingertips weren't heating up this time. Apparently, I had managed to let off enough of a spark in dealing with the bomb that I was going to need a little time to build it up again.

"Annie, darling, where are you?" The voice was Robert's, pitched low and sweet, virtually a purr. I stayed where I was, crouching down farther. "Come out, dearest, and we'll have a little chat about your behavior. This doesn't have to hurt, you know. Not unless you want it to."

I said nothing.

"I'll admit, I saw this coming. I told Reginald, I said 'she's too new, she's too green, they'll turn her head.' But I didn't think you'd be this willing to betray us. We're your family now, Annie. Come home to your family. Let us take *care* of you."

The way he said "care" made it clear I wouldn't enjoy whatever they were going to do to me. A lot of it depended on how much value the Covenant placed on me as a North American agent. They'd been kind up until this point, trying to woo me to their way of thinking. I had absolutely no doubt that they could be cruel, if they thought it would get them what they wanted.

I crouched lower, knives at the ready, wishing I'd thought to keep a little bit of that plastic explosive for my own use. Blowing him up wouldn't have been practical, but oh, it would have felt good.

"Annie, Annie, there's no need to be like this. These carnival folk, they've been kind to you, but they're never going to love you the way we will. At least in part because they're all going to be dead before morning. Leonard's out there right now, slitting throats and making sure there are no survivors."

Leo was doing no such thing. Leo was unconscious in the mud outside the sideshow attractions, and when he woke up, he was going to have one hell of a headache. There'd been no blood on his hands when he'd come looking for me. I'd been more of a priority for him than his orders. Poor fool.

"Oh, Annie." Robert's voice came from right behind me. Slowly, I turned, and there he was, bending to look under the slab where I was hiding. He smiled at the sight of me, expression grim in the black light illumination of the artificial lab. "I really thought better of you than this."

His hand lashed toward my face. I moved without thinking, bringing up the first of my knives and slashing hard across his fingers. My knives were designed for throwing, not cutting, but they had an edge on them; without it, they wouldn't have been able to pierce my targets the way they needed to. Robert bellowed. I rolled backward, flinging my bloodied knife at him as soon as I came upright again. It embedded itself in his shoulder. He bellowed again, louder this time, the sound filled with pure anger.

I turned and ran.

My theory of combat is simple: keep it as far away from myself as I can. I am a soft, squishy creature, with lots of moving pieces, and I want to keep all those moving pieces safely contained inside my skin. I'd been working with Robert for months, but we'd never sparred, and I didn't know his preferred weapons. He could be carrying anything. In lieu of more information, my best approach was a swift retreat.

I ran through the abandoned Transylvanian village and the hall of funhouse mirrors, dodging slow-moving carriages all the way. Next up was the swamp, where I could take cover behind the plastic banyan trees. I could—

Someone grabbed my arm, yanking me behind a mirror. I balled my hand into a fist and swung, hitting only empty air. Sam let go of me, giving me an offended look. He was back in human form, which meant that he was either tense, making an effort, or both.

"Punching?" he asked, in a low voice. "Really?"

"What are you *doing* here?" I hissed. "You're supposed to be evacuating the bone yard."

"It's done. They're gone. Everyone's gone." He continued to look at me admonishingly. "Did you honestly think you could *punch* me? I'm so much faster than you that's almost insulting."

"Sam." I grabbed the front of his shirt, pulling him toward me. This time, he didn't dodge. "The Covenant is here. In this building. They set a bomb in the generator shed. They're not fucking around. You need to get *out* of here."

Sam opened his mouth to answer. Then he stopped, and grimaced, and said, "Too late." There was a pained note in his voice, like he was doing his best to hold himself together. I took a half step backward and leaned to the side.

Margaret was behind him, a pistol in her hands. The barrel was digging into Sam's spine. He was fast—maybe the fastest living thing I'd ever encountered—but he wasn't fast enough to dodge a point-blank shot.

"Evacuation?" she asked, meeting my eyes and shaking her head. Unlike Sam, she made no effort to keep her voice down. She *wanted* the other people in this haunted house to come and find her. Everyone here was her backup, and my ending. "Oh, *Annie*. Robert said he was afraid you'd turn against us, but I never expected anything like this."

If she pulled that trigger, Sam was either dead or crippled for life. Neither option was acceptable. But if I could surprise her enough . . .

"You should have been expecting it," I said sweetly. "I was worried when I met you at Penton. I thought, 'Oh, shit, my sister said she was a smart one, she's going to see right through me.' But you never did. You kept thinking I was on your side. It's no wonder we always win when we go up against the Covenant. You're too stupid to beat us."

Margaret frowned, looking perplexed. "What are you talking about?"

Sarah brain-blasted Margaret back in New York, wiping the memory of her encounter with Verity from her mind. We were never sure how complete that wipe was, or whether Verity's appearance on television would open cracks in Margaret and Robert's memories. Everything I'd seen so far told me that it had been pretty damn complete . . . but nothing is perfect.

"Verity Price," I said. "Pretty, blonde, showed up on live television with a gun in her hand and blood on her cheeks. Remember her now?"

"You're talking nonsense," said Margaret.

"No, I'm not," I said. "I'm talking about my sister. But then, we've never been properly introduced, have we? Hello, *cousin*. I'm Antimony Price, and you deserve everything that's coming to you."

Margaret's eyes widened, searching my face, cataloging all the little points of similarity that could be family resemblance or could be genetic coincidence. She lingered on my hair, where my henna-free roots were growing in the same chestnut color as her own. With a shout of rage, she pulled the gun away from Sam and aimed it at my face. Sam's tail wrapped around her wrists before she could pull the trigger, yanking her arms toward the sky. I punched her in the throat. She went limp, and he dropped her.

"Now what?" he hissed.

I looked at Margaret's motionless body. She was family. She was the enemy. I needed to kill her. I'd never killed a human being before, much less one who was unconscious and unable to defend herself. For all that I had spent most of my childhood tormenting my siblings out of a twisted desire to make them love me, I had never wanted family blood on my hands.

But if we left her here, when the plan moved into its next stage, she was going to burn to death. How was that any better than a quick, clean pull of the trigger? I bent, retrieving her gun from the floor. It fit easily into my hand. I took aim on her head, thumbing off the safety as the world seemed to slow and narrow to that single point. Sam didn't say anything. I think he knew how difficult this was, and how much either answer would hurt me.

A gunshot rang out, the bullet whizzing past my head, close enough that I felt the wind of its passing. What felt like a rope was suddenly wrapped around my waist, yanking me out of the line of fire. I realized what it was a split-second later: Sam's tail. I took aim on the shooter, trusting Sam not to drag me into anything that would get me hurt. The gun jumped in my hand when I pulled the trigger. There was a shout from the shadows ahead. I'd managed to hit *something*. It was so much easier when the person I was shooting at was actually trying to kill me.

"Not a good place!" said Sam, and pulled me farther back, out of the mirrored chamber, into the artificial swamp. I looked over my shoulder at him. He nodded and unwrapped his tail from my waist.

"Come on," he said, offering me his hand. "We need to get out of here."

Robert would find Margaret. He would get her out of the Haunted House before it burned. I nodded, taking Sam's hand, and didn't fight as he swept me off my feet and jumped for the ceiling. It wasn't that high — maybe ten feet — and he was able to hook his free hand on one of the retaining bars holding up the scenery. He dangled as I shoved on the panels above his head, opening a "door" into the drop-ceiling where the mechanisms that ran the special effects and lighting were stored. Sam hoisted himself up, taking me with him into the dark.

The drop-ceiling was only a few feet high. He let me go, and together we crawled for the nearest exit. This had clearly been designed by the two bogeymen who owned the attraction: it assumed a level of skinny flexibility that most humans couldn't come anywhere near. Sam had to go human again, just to fit through some of the tighter spaces. By the time we reached the panel that would lead us to the roof, I was giving serious thought to becoming claustrophobic.

"When we get out of here, you need to run," I whispered.

Sam cocked his head, seeming to consider it. "Nope," he said finally.

"Asshole," I grumbled, and pushed the panel open.

It was a relief to be back in the fresh air after being squashed inside the Haunted House for so long. It was less of a relief when the bullets started whizzing by our heads. It wasn't that Robert was a lousy shot; we were at a bad angle, and he had Margaret slung over one shoulder in a fireman's carry, which had to be throwing off his aim. I yelped and ducked. Sam grabbed me around the waist — with his arm this time — and flung himself off the roof, back in full monkey-mode, leaping from the Haunted House toward the Scrambler. Which was still moving.

I screamed. I'm not ashamed of that fact. We were diving straight into the arms of a carnival ride that looked a lot like Lovecraft's idea of a blender, and we were probably going to die.

Only we didn't. Sam landed solidly on one of the rotating cars, grabbing hold with feet, tail, and free hand, and grinned at me. "Still want me to leave?" he asked.

"I am going to murder you myself," I snarled.

"Thought so!" he said, and jumped again, landing on the ground on the other side of the Scrambler. He put me down. I took his hand, and together, we ran deeper into the carnival, heading, whether by instinct or by design, for the big tent.

All around us, lights twinkled, music played, and the ghost town that was the carnival went through its paces, not seeming to notice the absence of the people who should have been there, filling it with light and life. The carnival didn't know that it was about to burn. A figure stepped around a corner up ahead of us. I had time to register who it was; then I was diving for the ground, yanking Sam out of the path of Chloe's crossbow bolt just before it scythed through the air where his head had been.

"Another friend of yours?" he demanded.

"Old roommate," I replied, rolling to my feet and pulling a dart from inside my shirt. The shaft was wood. The tip was metal. I tried to focus on the feeling of fire in my fingers, like I'd done in the shed, like I'd been doing unintentionally for months, and I threw.

The dart burst into flames in midair. It was still burning when it hit Chloe's shoulder. She yelped and dropped her crossbow, trying to beat out the fire with her hand.

"I want it!" I told Sam, and started running again, trusting him to catch up.

He did, easily, the crossbow in his hands. "First the gun, now whatever the hell this is—is this how you normally rearm yourself?" he asked. "You punch people and take whatever they drop?"

"It works in video games!" Chloe was now behind us, presumably no longer on fire, and definitely pissed off. I'd be pissed off, too, if someone I thought was an ally set me on fire and stole my stuff. I kept running.

There were four Covenant operatives at the carnival—at least. The bomb had clearly been their big plan, the thing that was supposed to turn the tide in their favor. They hadn't been expecting it to be defused, and they definitely hadn't been expecting me to evacuate the place before they could get down to the business of killing people. That was good. The element of surprise was no longer on my side. After knocking two of them on their asses and throwing a flaming dart at a third, any chance I might have been able to sneak up on them was well and truly spent. That was fine. "Subtle" has never been my specialty.

We ran until we reached the big tent and ducked inside. "Crossbow," I said, holding out my hand to Sam. He dropped Chloe's crossbow into it. There was already a bolt in the channel, waiting to be notched. Convenient.

"You said there was a bomb."

"Not the time."

"It's *always* the time when there's a bomb involved."

"They're going to catch up with us any second. Chloe's furious. Robert's . . . well, he's probably more furious. Mega-furious. You need to get out of here and let me work."

"You need to tell me where the bomb is."

I lowered the crossbow and frowned at Sam. "Have you ever worked with explosives? Do you know how to defuse a bomb? Can you recognize Semtex when you see it?"

He scowled. "No. I still want to know where the bomb is."

"I got rid of it."

"How?"

"I gave it to my Aunt Mary."

"Yes, you did, and we are going to talk about that *right now*, young lady," said a stern voice. I winced. Sam stared.

"Hi, Aunt Mary. This isn't a good time," I said, turning around and trying to see her the way Sam did. White hair and highway eyes that never seemed to settle on a color, but always gave the impression of looking at pictures of a road trip. She had somehow managed to get stuck in the 1970s where fashion was concerned, which probably felt very modern to her, since she'd died in the 1950s: she was wearing bellbottoms and a white peasant blouse with stalks of wheat embroidered around the neckline. And then there was the whole "suddenly materialized out of thin air" thing to consider, which probably made the rest of her appearance creepier.

"Annie, I do not mean to alarm you, but I think your aunt is dead," said Sam in a strangled voice.

"Anyone can have a dead aunt," said Mary cheerfully, before laughing at her own joke. The merriment only lasted for a second; then she was back to glaring at me. "You threw a *bomb* at me."

"You caught it. I needed it to go away."

"You could have given me a little warning!"

"No, I really couldn't have. Not unless I wanted to wind up in debt to the crossroads or exploded and haunting this field for the rest of eternity." I gestured between Mary and Sam. "Sam Taylor, meet Mary Dunlavy, one of my two dead-but-still-here aunts. Aunt Mary, meet Sam. He's the carnival owner's grandson. Now, if we're done with the niceties, the Covenant is outside, they're coming here, and I need to get back to work." I paused before giving Mary a hopeful look. "My mice . . ."

"Sweetie, you know it doesn't work that way," said Mary. She looked genuinely regretful. She's been with the family since my grandmother was born, and if anyone loves the Aeslin mice, it's her. "Nothing living can go into the twilight with me and come back out again. If I took them out of here, they'd die. At least with you, they've got a chance."

"Great." I shook my head. "Can you at least scout the Covenant for me?"

"You know better than to ask me for useful things."

Her calm declaration hung between us, bitterly cold and absolutely true. It was the difference between my two dead aunts. I would never have chucked a bomb at Aunt Rose without asking first. With Aunt Mary, I would never be able to ask.

"All right," I said. "Then I'm asking you to be useless. You can't fight and you can't help and I don't have any more bombs to throw at you. You need to go. The Covenant is coming. This isn't your fight, but it's mine, and I need to finish it."

"Okay, baby." Aunt Mary disappeared. She reappeared next to me, planting a kiss on my cheek and whispering, "You have no idea how much you remind me of your grandfather." Then she was gone entirely, leaving only the distant scent of baked asphalt in her wake.

"How normal is she for your family?" asked Sam. "On a scale of like, one to fucking weird?"

"She's about a three." I resumed aiming my stolen crossbow at the entrance to the tent. "You should go. Your grandmother will kill me if I let you get hurt."

"I should stay. I'll never forgive myself if I run. Or we could both go."

"I can't," I said apologetically. "The bomb didn't go off. They know something's up. I need to distract them, and if necessary, I need them to think they saw me die."

"So I'm making sure you don't *actually* die," he said stubbornly. Sam didn't have any obvious weapons. He braced his feet in the sawdust, balling his hands into fists.

I stopped arguing. We waited.

The tent flap rustled just before a small object rolled into the room. My eyes widened. So did Sam's, both of us realizing at the same time what it had to be. He was the first to react, naturally, his yōkai biology giving him the edge where reflexes were concerned. Almost too fast for the eye to see, he dove for the grenade, grabbed it, and chucked it back outside the tent. There was a shriek, followed by a boom that I felt all the way down to my bones.

"Okay, I take it back," I said numbly. "You can stay."

Sam raced back to my side, falling into a graceful, if uneasy, stance. Neither of us spoke.

This time when the tent flap opened, there was no grenade. Just the impression of a body racing for cover, followed by a gunshot. Hot pain blossomed on my arm.

I glanced down long enough to be sure that I'd only been grazed—bleeding out would have ruined my plans for the day—and hit the ground on my knees, pulling the trigger on the crossbow and willing fire onto the bolt the same way I'd willed fire onto the dart.

Nothing happened. Naturally.

"This is not a good time to roll a fucking one," I moaned, dropping the now-useless crossbow. It had seemed like such a *good* way to get fire onto the tent walls, and so much safer than my original plan. "Cover me."

"Cover you while you do what? Annie—"

I was already on my feet, running for the ladder that would take me up to the trapeze. The rope array was connected to the entire tent, anchored in half a dozen places. If it went up without an accelerant, it would be a lot harder for the insurance investigators to claim arson.

If someone had asked me a year ago whether I'd wind up trying to fight the Covenant of St. George while arranging insurance fraud, I would have looked at them like they'd hit their head. Good thing no one ever asked me that. I ran. Behind me, Sam was taunting Robert, working his way into a string of monkey-related puns that were just plain bad. He had a real gift for being a dick in the middle of a serious situation. It was probably the fault of all those Spider-Man comics.

"God bless Spider-Man," I muttered, and started up the ladder.

I had climbed a lot of ladders, under a lot of circumstances. I'd never attempted to climb all the way to a trapeze while my half-monkey maybe-boyfriend kept a Covenant operative distracted below me. It was a new, and bracing experience that I was in no hurry to have again.

But either Robert was the last Covenant operative in action or the other three were regrouping, planning their next attack. None of them were going to expect me to burn the carnival down around my own ears. I kept climbing until I reached the launching platform.

My hands weren't chalked and my clothes weren't right for this. I grabbed my swing from its hook anyway, taking a deep breath before I launched myself into the air. It was a smooth, easy arc from the platform to the center of the tent, where I let go of the swing. I had told Emery I didn't do tightrope work, and I wasn't lying about that, but that didn't mean I couldn't use the tightrope for other purposes. I grabbed it as I fell, hissing when the fibers bit into my palms, and hung there like a piece of washing drying in the wind. Closing my eyes, I tried to focus on calling fire into my fingers.

It didn't come. My hands remained as cool as any human's, perfectly ordinary, perfectly reasonable. I wasn't going to set anything on fire with a touch—oh, no—not me. I kept my eyes closed, trying to chase my frustration down and make it do something useful for me.

On the ground below me, Sam bellowed in shock and pain. My eyes snapped open as the rope burst into flame, burning blue-white and far too fast to be natural. I was my own accelerant, when I was frightened enough.

I let go of the rope and I fell, straight down, into the familiar embrace of the net. I twisted at the last moment, landing on my side, and rolled to the edge as the rope array above me was being consumed by the fire. I only got glimpses of the scene I was about to enter: Sam on the ground, still in his natural form, face covered in blood. Robert standing over him, gun raised, preparing to pull the trigger again.

I pulled a knife from inside my shirt as I rolled. I didn't think, I barely aimed; I just threw.

Before, in the Haunted House, I'd been asking myself whether I could kill another human. I'd managed to reach my twenties without killing a thinking being, and the idea of killing a member of my own species was horrifying and upsetting on a deep, visceral level, even when they belonged to the Covenant of St. George. I talked a good game, and I had the skills on paper, but could I do it in the real world?

My knife flew straight and true, embedding itself in

Robert's throat just below his Adam's apple. His eyes widened, the gun falling from his suddenly nerveless fingers as he clutched at the hilt with both hands, trying to pull it loose. He couldn't. He didn't have the manual dexterity left to accomplish what he needed to do. Looking at me with silent accusation in his eyes, he folded forward, landing on his face in the sawdust.

The tent above us was taking its cue from the ropes, and beginning to burn. If we didn't get out of here soon, we weren't going to be getting out of here at all. I ran to Sam, praying silently that I wasn't too late.

He'd landed on his back when he fell. The blood was coming from a shallow gash down the side of his head. Robert was too good of a shot to have miscalculated that badly, and at such a short range; there had to be something else going on. I dropped to my knees, fumbling for a pulse, and paused when I found it, not in the expected spot, but lower and off to the side. Sam's anatomy wasn't exactly human-normal. I knew from the way he jumped and swung me around that he had to have incredibly robust musculature. Incredibly robust musculature, in nature, often meant a denser skeleton, giving those muscles something to anchor against.

The tent was burning and Robert was dead and I still laughed through my tears as I leaned forward and pressed my forehead against Sam's, not caring if I got blood on myself. "You big dumb ape," I said. "You are literally too thick-headed to kill." The bullet must have ricocheted when Robert pulled the trigger. It would have been a shock to both of them—in Sam's case, a shock big enough to put him on the floor.

Sam groaned. I sat up, grabbing his arm and trying to tug him along with me.

"Come on, wake up," I said. "This place is about to go up like a birthday cake."

He groaned again, opening his eyes. He smiled at the sight of me. Something in my chest got tight and soft at the same time, like I was trying to sneeze with a mouthful of ice cream.

"Hey," he said, in a dazed voice. "So I just got shot."

"Yeah," I agreed, laughing a little. It was better than crying. Those felt like my only options at the moment.

"Am I dead?"

"Not yet. Can you walk?"

"Not yet."

"Okay. I'm going to get you to your feet. Can you focus enough to go human? You weigh less without all the extra muscle mass." Sam's speed had saved my life, and his fūri bone density had saved his. That didn't mean I could carry a six-foot-tall monkey-man who wasn't in a position to help me. There are limits.

"I can try." Sam closed his eyes again, grimacing. Slowly, his simian features melted away, replaced by the frowning man who'd met me on my first day in the bone yard. Without the fur to blunt the edges of the wound, the trench the bullet had dug into his forehead was substantially more brutal-looking. If he'd been human when Robert had pulled the trigger ...

Five minutes ago I'd been asking myself whether I could kill another human being. Now I found myself wishing I could bring him back to life so I could kill him again for what he'd almost done.

Gingerly, I worked my arm under Sam's shoulders and half-helped, half-pulled him to his feet. The heat from the burning ceiling was becoming increasingly apparent, although chunks of canvas had not yet started falling on us. That was coming. Once the fire traveled down the tent walls and began really getting to work, everything was going to collapse in on itself.

Sam held on as best as he could, head lolling and eyes still closed as I steered him toward the door. I only looked back once, in time to see the burning web of the trapeze break apart and fall onto the net. The heart of the carnival was dying. The rest would follow. I'd done this; it was on me. I turned away. I needed to focus on getting myself out, and on keeping Sam alive. If I could do those things, someday I might be able to forgive myself.

We stepped through the tent flap, into the cool, clean air of the Minnesota night. I froze, bringing Sam stumbling to a stop.

"What?" he mumbled, not opening his eyes.

"Problem," I said.

Margaret Healy, who was holding a pistol in her hands and had a vicious bruise stretching across her throat, sneered.

Twenty-four

> "Happy endings are for fairy tales. Try to focus on the ending that comes with the chance to start again."
>
> —Enid Baker

The midway of the Spenser and Smith Family Carnival, in the midst of an unwanted family reunion

"LOOK," I SAID. "Can't we talk about this?"

Margaret's sneer grew. "I should have known," she said. "You were too bloody perfect, and you were so *eager*. You wanted to *help*. I trusted you. I thought you were going to be one of us. Should have known you were a liar and a thief and a traitor born. Did they send you to punish me?"

I blinked. "Okay, you lost me." Sam was a heavy weight on my shoulder, eyes still closed, not moving. He hadn't spoken since he'd asked why we'd stopped. I knew he was conscious—he hadn't reverted to his fūri form—but he wasn't up for doing much beyond keeping himself awake. If I dropped him, that might distract Margaret for a moment. Not long enough. In a fight between gun and knife, the person with the gun already out and ready to fire is always, always going to win.

"Your bastard branch of the family," snarled Margaret. "Did they send you to punish me for not being one of them? For being *loyal* and *committed* and willing to do what's required to serve my species? You're the ones who lost your way, not me, but I'm the one who has to live with the consequences of your actions. So answer me. Did they send you as a test?"

I gaped at her, preparing to say something about how none of this had been personal. I stopped myself. The things she was saying, the way she was saying them . . . I'd heard them before. It was just that they'd always come from my own lips, and been directed at my sister. Verity, who did whatever the hell she wanted and left the rest of us to clean up her mess. Verity, the golden child.

Verity, who'd never been trying to hurt me, any more than I'd been trying to hurt Margaret. Choices had consequences, and yes, sometimes those consequences could get other people hurt, but that didn't make them personal. That didn't make them intentional. It just made them something else that had to be resolved.

"I'm sorry," I said.

Margaret flinched. "What did you say to me?"

"I said, I'm sorry. I'm sorry my great-great-grandparents had to leave their children when they left the Covenant; I'm sorry you grew up thinking you came from a family of traitors when really, you come from a family of impassioned, intelligent people trying to do the best they can. I'm sorry we abandoned you. I'm sorry we're never going to be a family in anything more than blood." The gulf between us was too great. I wasn't going to come around to her way of thinking, and she certainly wasn't going to come around to mine.

"You're trying to trick me," snarled Margaret, and steadied her aim. I realized, with a sick, sinking feeling that she wasn't aiming at me anymore. If she pulled the trigger, the bullet was going to go right through Sam's heart. Even shifting back to his natural form wouldn't save him from that. "I'll make you a deal, *cousin*. Come with me willingly, so we can learn everything you know, and I won't shoot your boyfriend dead in front of you."

"But you'll shoot him later," I said wearily.

"He's not human. He's a threat. He has to die."

"I'm not going to surrender."

"Then you're going to hold him while he dies, and I'm

going to take you anyway." Her lips drew back from her teeth in a noiseless snarl. "You pretended to be my friend. Well, you're going to be my redemption. You're going to—"

She stopped mid-sentence, an odd look spreading across her face. Then she fell forward, hitting the ground hard, revealing the man who was standing behind her with a hypodermic needle in his hand.

"Dilute manticore venom has a remarkable sedative effect when injected by someone who knows what they're doing," Leo said. There was a brittle sort of serenity in his voice. He was holding his composure by a thread.

"What are you doing?" I asked, sliding my free hand behind my back and beginning to slowly draw a knife from my waistband. "Where's Chloe?"

"I sent her to the car to bandage her wounds. I convinced her we could handle things without her." He looked down at Margaret, lying face down in the mud. "My sister is a little credulous sometimes. It comes of being excessively sheltered."

"Why . . ." I paused. "Why are you helping me?"

"Did you kill Robert?"

The knife was in my hand. I nodded mutely.

"But you didn't kill Chloe, and I could tell you didn't want to kill Margaret." Leo looked at Sam and frowned. "Did Robert shoot your friend?"

Another nod. It would be so *easy* to throw the knife, to catch him unawares. I hesitated. My time with the Covenant might not have changed my loyalties, but it had humanized them in a way I hadn't been counting on. They weren't a faceless enemy anymore. They were *people*. They had done to me exactly what my sister had worked so hard to do to Dominic: they had made themselves harder to kill.

"Then it's no wonder." Leo dropped the needle into the mud, crunching it under his foot. Behind me, the tent began to blaze more fiercely, the flames crackling as they devoured the canvas. He looked at me calmly. "It's too bad one of your friends managed to catch Margaret by surprise. You ducked back into the tent to regroup. You burned to death."

"What?" I stared at him. "Why would you do that?"

"Because you could have killed my sister, and you didn't. Because I've been reading the reports on your progress. You killed the Jorōgumo that had been hunting people. You didn't hesitate once you knew she was dangerous. You're going to come back into the fold, and when you do, you're going to be remarkable. I can wait for you. For a little while, I can wait." Leo's smile was quick and cold. "You'll find I can be surprisingly patient."

I stared at him. Finally, I said, "You knew. From the start, you knew."

"Oh, come now. You don't think the heir to the Covenant would be able to identify any member of an approved bloodline? I'll admit, you threw me at first. No one's seen a Price—a true Price—in so long. Who would have thought the Carew blood would be such a beast? Half the Healys look like Carews since we let Enid marry into the line. It was the cheekbones. I knew I'd seen them before. I went to Penton to check the portrait gallery, and once I realized what we had . . ." He shook his head. "It was too delicious. I had to get to know you. And truly, you've exceeded my expectations. I can't wait for you to choose us over the errors of your upbringing."

"So you'll let me walk away?"

"Why wouldn't I?" He seemed genuinely puzzled. "Any damage you do now happens under my grandfather's watch. When my time comes, I'll be the one who brings the Price family back where they belong. My predecessors could never accomplish that. So go, Timpani, or Antimony, or whatever you want your name to be. Go now, and go knowing that one day, you'll come back to me. I'll find you. When I want you, I'll find you."

I stared at him for a moment, all too aware of the burning tent at my back and the weight of Sam on my arm. That was what made up my mind. Sam couldn't handle another fight, and if I lost—if Leo killed me—he would be defenseless. He wasn't even supposed to be here. I was not going to burn down Emery's carnival and get her grandson killed in the same night.

Adjusting my grip on Sam, I offered Leo one last, silent nod and turned to walk, slowly, away from the burning tent, into the waiting darkness. Putting my back to a member of the Covenant was a calculated risk. I was trusting him not to pull a gun and shoot me as soon as I was defenseless.

He didn't. Sam hanging heavy off my arm, I left the fire, and the blood, and the carnival behind.

The bone yard was a ghost town. About half the RVs were there, but all their occupants were gone. I stopped at the Ferris wheel to retrieve my backpack before helping Sam to the first safe place I found—a flatbed truck old enough to be hotwired if the fire reached this far—and lowering him onto the tailgate. He was still human, which meant he was still awake.

"Hey," I said softly. "If you can stay like this while I clean your forehead, that would be great. If you can't, I'll work around it."

"Sure, Grandma," he mumbled.

I smiled to conceal my worry. "Wow, I'm your grandmother now? What's the word for an Oedipus complex that skips the mother and goes straight back up the line?" I slipped out of my backpack and unzipped it, rummaging until I found my first aid kit.

"Ask Zeus," he said.

"Now you're making jokes about the King of fucking everything that moves," I said, pulling out a gauze pad and soaking it with antiseptic. "This is going to sting." I pressed the pad against Sam's forehead.

His eyes snapped open. "Holy *shit*."

"I told you it was going to sting." I kept dabbing at the wound. It was deep enough to worry me. The bullet must have bounced straight off the bone. "Also, hi. Congrats on not being dead, you dick."

"Hey. You'd have been in real trouble without me and you know it."

"I do." I kept dabbing at the wound. "I'm in real trouble now. I need you to do something for me."

"Anything."

He didn't mean that—people never mean it when they say "anything"—but it was still nice to hear. "I need you to get my mice to an airport."

Sam blinked. "Come again?"

"If you get them to an airport, they can catch a flight to where the rest of my family is. They're good at sneaking onto airplanes. They'll be fine." The mice were also good at finding unattended phones. They'd fly to Portland, phone the house, and get picked up. They could tell my family what had happened. They could help them prepare.

"Why aren't you taking them yourself?"

I began applying butterfly closures to the wound on his forehead. "Because I need to go somewhere else. Someplace where no one can find me."

"What? Annie—"

"The Covenant knows my name and my face and where to look for me. Killing everyone who came here wouldn't have changed that; it would just have made me more of a target. I was careful, but they have things I've touched. I sweated in their training room. I bled—fuck, they did blood tests on me. They could have *vials* of the stuff, and they have witches. There's a chance they're going to track me, and if they do, I'm not leading them to my family." If I'd been able to slip away, I might have been okay, but I hadn't done that. I'd stayed, and I'd fought, and now they knew I wasn't just a trainee who'd chosen to run. It didn't matter if my reasons had been good and my choices had made sense at the time. They knew too much.

I had to disappear.

"I'll come with you."

I put the final butterfly closure in place before pressing my hand against his cheek and smiling at him. He smiled back, tentatively. I leaned in and kissed him, trying to put everything I had—every explanation, every apology, every scrap of affection I had—into the contact. His lips tasted like blood. Mine tasted like ashes. Together, we were a world on fire, and we never stood a chance.

Finally, I pulled back and said, "No, you won't. You'll find your grandmother. Help her start a new show. And get my mice to that airport."

"Annie . . ." He stopped. Looked at me. And finally said, "I don't love you yet. But I could have."

"Same here," I said, and kissed him again, and reached into my backpack. When I pulled my hand out again, Mork and Mindy were on my palm. I set them down beside him. Neither of them said a word. No cheering, no psalms, nothing. I nodded to them. They nodded back. Then I turned and walked away.

I didn't look back. Sometimes not looking back is the only mercy the world has left to show.

Epilogue

"Family is family, no matter how far away
you run. Their ghosts will always find you."
—Jane Harrington-Price

A small frontage road near Gainesville, Florida
Three weeks later

IT WAS THE MIDDLE OF THE DAY, and no one wanted to
pick up a hitchhiker. I kept my thumb out anyway as I
walked, trying not to look like the humidity was killing
me. It was a lie. I felt like I was going to melt. (Portland
is not a high-humidity city. Humidity takes too much
commitment, and Portland virtually *never* commits to
severe weather.)

Another car went zooming by. I did not flip them off.
I thought I deserved some sort of reward for that—like
maybe, I don't know, a ride?

It had been three weeks since I'd walked away from
the carnival, and bit by bit, the road was killing me. The
Covenant didn't know all my IDs, but my cousin Artie did,
which meant I didn't dare use any of my credit cards. I'd
hit the first ATM I'd seen, pulled out the maximum, and
thrown the card away. That cash had seen me across seven
states, onto several buses, and through a delightful assortment of diners, each a little more questionable than the
last. But the money was running out, and hitchhiking was
my best option, if I wanted to stretch it as far as possible.

"I'd kill for a new pair of shoes right now," I muttered.

"Be careful where you say that sort of thing."

I turned. Mary was behind me, her hair loose and blowing in the slight afternoon breeze, so that it formed a cottony corona around her head. I looked down, and winced. We were standing at a crossroad.

"I didn't mean it," I said quickly, looking up again.

Her smile was thin and sad, a skeleton of an expression, painted on the face of a ghost. "I know," she said. "You didn't do all the flowery bullshit that makes it a real request. You should still be careful. The crossroads know your name."

"Because of what my grandfather did."

"Among other things." She crossed the distance between us in four long steps, wrapping her arms around me before I could react. "We've all been scared witless, Annie—"

"You can't tell anyone you've seen me."

She let go and stepped back. "What?"

"I'm hiding, remember? Did the mice make it home?"

"Last week."

"Then you know why I ran."

"There has to be another way."

I shrugged. "Not that I've found yet."

"Fine, then." She took my hands. "You will call me weekly. You will let me see that you're all right. And in exchange, I'll keep your parents from tearing the world down looking for you. Deal?"

"Deal."

"Good. And remember, you just made a promise to a crossroads ghost. It's binding." She let go of my hands. "Why are you in Florida?"

"Because no one will look for me in Florida," I said. "I figure I can find work at or near one of the big amusement parks."

"Disney World?"

"Lowryland. It's smaller, which means less attention, and they're a lot less strict in their background checks."

Mary nodded. "Good thinking. You're being careful?"

"I am."

"Thank you for that. I'll see if I can scare up one of the local routewitches to give you a ride."

"That'd be nice. In the meantime, I guess I'll keep on walking." I offered her a wan smile. "No rest for the wicked."

"Never has been," she said, and disappeared.

I looked at the place where she'd been for a few long seconds before I turned and resumed walking down the road, into the hot Florida sun, leaving the past behind me.

Price Family Field Guide to the Cryptids of North America
Updated and Expanded Edition

Aeslin mice (Apodemus sapiens). Sapient, rodentlike cryptids which present as near-identical to non-cryptid field mice. Aeslin mice crave religion, and will attach themselves to "divine figures" selected virtually at random when a new colony is created. They possess perfect recall; each colony maintains a detailed oral history going back to its inception. Origins unknown.

Basilisk (Procompsognathus basilisk). Venomous, feathered saurians approximately the size of a large chicken. This would be bad enough, but thanks to a quirk of evolution, the gaze of a basilisk causes petrification, turning living flesh to stone. Basilisks are not native to North America, but were imported as game animals. By idiots.

Bogeyman (Vestiarium sapiens). The thing in your closet is probably a very pleasant individual who simply has issues with direct sunlight. Probably. Bogeymen are close relatives of the human race; they just happen to be almost purely nocturnal, with excellent night vision, and a fondness for enclosed spaces. They rarely grab the ankles of small children, unless it's funny.

Chupacabra (Chupacabra sapiens). True to folklore, chupacabra are blood-suckers, with stomachs that do not handle solids well. They are also therianthrope shape-shifters, capable of transforming themselves into human form, which explains why they have never been captured. When cornered, most chupacabra will assume their bipedal shape in self-defense. A surprising number of chupacabra are involved in ballroom dance.

Dragon (Draconem sapiens). Dragons are essentially winged, fire-breathing dinosaurs the size of Greyhound buses. At least, the males are. The females are attractive humanoids who can blend seamlessly in a crowd of supermodels, and outnumber the males twenty to one. Females are capable of parthenogenic reproduction and can sustain their population for centuries without outside help. All dragons, male and female, require gold to live, and collect it constantly.

Fūri (Homo therianthrope). Often proposed as the bridge between humans and therianthropes, the fūri is a monkey—specifically, a human—that takes on the attributes of another monkey—specifically, some form of spider monkey. Fūri transform instinctively, choosing their human forms for camouflage and their more simian forms for virtually everything else. A transformed fūri is faster, stronger, and sturdier than a human being. Offering bananas is not recommended.

Ghoul (Herophilus sapiens). The ghoul is an obligate carnivore, incapable of digesting any but the simplest vegetable solids, and prefers humans because of their wide selection of dietary nutrients. Most ghouls are carrion eaters. Ghouls can be easily identified by their teeth, which will be shed and replaced repeatedly over the course of a lifetime.

Hidebehind (Aphanes apokryphos). We don't really know much about the hidebehinds: no one's ever seen them. They're excellent illusionists, and we think they're bipeds, which means they're probably mammals. Probably.

Jackalope (Parcervus antelope). Essentially large jack-rabbits with antelope antlers, the jackalope is a staple of the American West, and stuffed examples can be found in junk shops and kitschy restaurants all across the country. Most of the taxidermy is fake. Some, however, is not. The jackalope was once extremely common, and has been shot, stuffed, and harried to near-extinction. They're relatively harmless, and they taste great.

Johrlac (Johrlac psychidolos). Colloquially known as "cuckoos," the Johrlac are telepathic ambush predators. They appear human, but are internally very different, being cold-blooded and possessing a decentralized circulatory system. This quirk of biology means they can be shot repeatedly in the chest without being killed. Extremely dangerous. All Johrlac are interested in mathematics, sometimes to the point of obsession. Origins unknown; possibly insect in nature.

Jorōgumo (Nephilia sapiens). Originally native to Japan, these therianthropes belong to the larger family of cryptids classified as "yōkai." Jorōgumo appear to be attractive women of Japanese descent until they transform, at which point they become massive spider-centaurs whose neurotoxic venom can kill in seconds. No males of the species have ever been seen. It is possible that the species possesses a degree of sexual dimorphism so great that male Jorōgumo are simply not recognized for what they are.

Laidly worm (Draconem laidly). Very little is known about these close relatives of the dragons. They present similar but presumably not identical sexual dimorphism; no currently living males have been located.

Lamia (Python lamia). Semi-hominid cryptids with the upper bodies of humans and the lower bodies of snakes. Lamia are members of order synapsedia, the mammal-like reptiles, and are considered responsible for many of the "great snake" sightings of legend. The sightings not attributed to actual great snakes, that is.

Lesser gorgon (Gorgos euryale). One of three known subspecies of gorgon, the lesser gorgon's gaze causes short-term paralysis followed by death in anything under five pounds. The bite of the snakes atop their heads will cause paralysis followed by death in anything smaller than an elephant if not treated with the appropriate antivenin. Lesser gorgons tend to be very polite, especially to people who like snakes.

Lilu (Lilu sapiens). Due to the striking dissimilarity of their abilities, male and female Lilu are often treated as two individual species: incubi and succubi. Incubi are empathic; succubi are persuasive telepaths. Both exude strong pheromones inspiring feelings of attraction and lust in the opposite sex. This can be a problem for incubi like our cousin Artie, who mostly wants to be left alone, or succubi like our cousin Elsie, who gets very tired of men hitting on her while she's trying to flirt with their girlfriends.

Madhura (Homo madhurata). Humanoid cryptids with an affinity for sugar in all forms. Vegetarian. Their presence slows the decay of organic matter, and is usually viewed as lucky by everyone except the local dentist. Madhura are very family-oriented, and are rarely found living on their own. Originally from the Indian subcontinent.

Manananggal (Tanggal geminus). If the manananggal is proof of anything, it is that Nature abhors a logical classification system. We're reasonably sure the mananaggal are mammals; everything else is anyone's guess. They're hermaphroditic and capable of splitting their upper and lower bodies, although they are a single entity, and killing the lower half kills the upper half as well. They prefer fetal tissue, or the flesh of newborn infants. They are also venomous, as we have recently discovered. Do not engage if you can help it.

Oread (Nymphae silica). Humanoid cryptids with the approximate skin density of granite. Their actual biological composition is unknown, as no one has ever been able to successfully dissect one. Oreads are extremely strong, and can be dangerous when angered. They seem to have evolved independently across the globe; their common name is from the Greek.

Sasquatch (Gigantopithecus sesquac). These massive native denizens of North America have learned to embrace depilatories and mail-order shoe catalogs. A surprising number make their living as Bigfoot hunters (Bigfeet and Sasquatches are close relatives, and enjoy tormenting each other). They are predominantly vegetarian, and enjoy Canadian television.

Tanuki (Nyctereutes sapiens). Therianthrope shapeshifters from Japan, the Tanuki are critically endangered due to the efforts of the Covenant. Despite this, they remain friendly, helpful people, with a naturally gregarious nature which makes it virtually impossible for them to avoid human settlements. Tanuki possess three primary forms—human, raccoon dog, and big-ass scary monster. Pray you never see the third form of the Tanuki.

Ukupani (Ukupani sapiens). Aquatic therianthropes native to the warm waters of the Pacific Islands, the Ukupani were believed for centuries to be an all-male species, until Thomas Price sat down with several local fishermen and determined that the abnormally large Great White sharks that were often found near Ukupani males were, in actuality, Ukupani females. Female Ukupani can't shapeshift, but can eat people. Happily. They are as intelligent as their shapeshifting mates, because smart sharks are exactly what the ocean needed.

Wadjet (Naja wadjet). Once worshipped as gods, the male wadjet resembles an enormous cobra, capable of reaching seventeen feet in length when fully mature, while the female wadjet resembles an attractive human female. Wadjet pair-bond young, and must spend extended amounts of time together before puberty in order to become immune to one another's venom and be able to successfully mate as adults.

Waheela (Waheela sapiens). Therianthrope shapeshifters from the upper portion of North America, the waheela are a solitary race, usually claiming large swaths of territory and defending it to the death from others of their species. Waheela mating season is best described with the term "bloodbath." Waheela transform into something that looks like a dire bear on steroids. They're usually not hostile, but it's best not to push it.

PLAYLIST:

Everybody needs a soundtrack, and Antimony is no different. Here are some songs to rock you through her adventures.

"Burn".............................. Mad at Gravity
"Dollhouse" .... Melanie Martinez
"Little Talks" .... Of Monsters and Men
"Lucky Me" .... Sarah Slean
"Hollywood's Not America" .... Ferras
"London Calling"................... The Clash
"Funhouse"............................Pink
"Trapeze" ....Patty Griffin
"How Do I Look?" ....Muzzled: The Musical
"Good Little Dictation
    Machines" ....Alleluia! The Devil's Carnival
"Out of the Woods"................... Taylor Swift
"Emperor's New Clothes" ....Panic! At the Disco
"Ferris Wheel" ....Rachael Sage
"Skeletons on Parade"..................Ludo
"No Spill Blood" .... Oingo Boingo
"Bleeding Out" .... Imagine Dragons
"Fly" ....Moxy Fruvous
"Hallelujah" .... Panic! at the Disco
"The Boy Could Fly"................... Rubylux
"Rock and Roll Queen" .... The Subways
"Bad Romance"......................Halestorm
"Sin for a Sin".................... Miranda Lambert

"Ship to Wreck" . . . . Florence and the Machine
"Mistakes We Knew We
    Were Making" . . . . Straylight Run
"Boats and Birds" . . . . Gregory and the Hawk
"Chasing the Sun" . . . . Sara Bareilles

ACKNOWLEDGMENTS:

Welcome to Antimony's adventures! Are you ready for ROLLER DERBY?! (Well. Some roller derby. More carnivals and theme parks and identity crisis.) I am so delighted to be here, six books in and still going strong as we head into a new phase of the Price family's history. Antimony has been waiting for a while for her star turn, and I know some of you have been waiting for her. Well, wait no longer—and best of all, she'll be back soon for book seven, *Tricks for Free*.

Enormous thanks go out to my carnival family, especially Lars, Davo, and my best-beloved Daniel, who said he wouldn't put scorpions in my bed again if I thanked him in a book; to my roller derby experts, Michael and Deborah Kwan, and to every derby girl who's had me excitedly asking her questions about the fine points of the game; and to Patty, who keeps me from accidentally wandering into traffic. As always, Phil is the man to blame for so much of what I do, and he shoulders that burden with good grace and terrible puns. Terrible, terrible puns. Thanks to Priscilla Spencer, for everything, and to Rob and Rachel, for everything else.

The machete squad gets thanked in almost everything I write, because they're worth it, and without them, I would have a lot more continuity glitches. Kory Bing illustrates the amazing Field Guide to the Cryptids of North America, which you can visit at my website—bring a net—while Tara O'Shea's dingbat and website design remains top-notch. I am the luckiest author in the world. Big thanks to the team at DAW, my publicity team at Penguin Random House, and to Aly Fell, whose cover illustrations are everything I could possibly have asked for.

While this book was being finished, I finally made the move I've been talking about for the last decade, relocating from California to Washington. Much of this process happened while I was in New York on business or traveling along the West Coast on book tour. Thanks to my mother, Micki McGuire, for supervising the California end; to Jennifer Brozek, for keeping an eye on the new house until we could move in; and to Michelle Dockrey, my best beloved fox girl, for organizing the moving party on the Washington end. As Wesley so often says, it takes a village to keep a blonde from disappearing into the swamp and never being seen again.

Thanks to my Magical Girl Urban Fantasy Tour buddies, Amber Benson and Sarah Kuhn; to all the bookstores that have hosted me in the last year; to Nikki and Mike (and Mina) for their hospitality, and to Cylia, for the cupcakes. Thanks to Borderlands Books, for putting up with me. And to you: thank you, so much, for reading.

Any errors in this book are my own. The errors that aren't here are the ones that all these people helped me fix. I appreciate it so much.

Seanan McGuire
The InCryptid Novels

"McGuire's imagination is utterly boundless. The world of her *InCryptid* series is full of unexpected creatures, constant surprises and appealing characters, all crafted with the measured ease of a skilled professional, making the fantastic seem like a wonderful reality."
—*RT Reviews*

"The only thing more fun than an October Daye book is an InCryptid book. Swift narrative, charm, great world-building . . . all the McGuire trademarks."
—Charlaine Harris

To Order Call: 1-800-788-6262
www.dawbooks.com

DAW 143

Seanan McGuire
The October Daye Novels

"...will surely appeal to readers who enjoy my books, or those of Patrica Briggs." —*Charlaine Harris*

"I am so invested in the world building and the characters now.... Of all the 'Faerie' urban fantasy series out there, I enjoy this one the most."—*Felicia Day*

To Order Call: 1-800-788-6262
www.dawbooks.com

DAW 142

Michelle Sagara
The Queen of the Dead

"Brilliant storyteller Sagara heads in a new direction with her *Queen of the Dead* series. She does an excellent job of breathing life into not only her reluctant heroine, but also the supporting players in this dramatic and spellbinding series starter. There is a haunting beauty to this story of love, loss and a teenager's determination to do the right thing. Do not miss out!"

—*RT Book Reviews*

"It's rare to find a book as smart and sweet as this one."

—Sarah Rees Brennan

SILENCE
978-0-7564-0799-5

TOUCH
978-0-7564-0844-2

GRAVE
978-0-7564-0907-4

To Order Call: 1-800-788-6262
www.dawbooks.com

Tanya Huff

"The Gales are an amazing family, the aunts will strike fear into your heart, and the characters Allie meets are both charming and terrifying."
—#1 *New York Times* bestselling author
Charlaine Harris

"Thoughtful and leisurely, this fresh urban fantasy from Canadian author Huff features an ensemble cast of nuanced characters in Calgary, Alberta.... Fantasy buffs will find plenty of humor, thrills and original mythology to chew on, along with refreshingly three-dimensional women in an original, fully realized world." —*Publishers Weekly*

The Enchantment Emporium
978-0-7564-0605-9

The Wild Ways
978-0-7564-0763-6

and now...
The Future Falls
978-0-7564-0754-4

To Order Call: 1-800-788-6262
www.dawbooks.com

Once upon a time...

Cinderella, whose real name is Danielle
Whiteshore, did marry Prince Armand.
And their wedding was a dream come true.

But not long after the "happily ever after,"
Danielle is attacked by her stepsister Charlotte,
who suddenly has all sorts of magic to call upon.
And though Talia the martial arts master—
otherwise known as Sleeping Beauty—
comes to the rescue, Charlotte gets away.

That's when Danielle discovers a number of disturbing facts: Armand has been kidnapped; Danielle is
pregnant; and the Queen has her own Secret Service
that consists of Talia and Snow (White, of course).
Snow is an expert at mirror magic and heavy-duty
flirting. Can the princesses track down Armand and
rescue him from the clutches of some of
Fantasyland's most nefarious villains?

The Stepsister Scheme
by Jim C. Hines
978-0-7564-0532-8

"Do we look like we need to be rescued?"

Gini Koch
The Alien *Novels*

"Told with clever wit and non-stop pacing, this series follows the exploits of the country's top alien exterminators in the American Centaurion Diplomatic Corps. It blends diplomacy, action, and sense of humor into a memorable reading experience."
—*Kirkus*

"Amusing and interesting...a hilarious romp in the vein of *Men in Black* or *Ghostbusters*."
—*VOYA*

To Order Call: 1-800-788-6262
www.dawbooks.com